"It's time I proved to you what you thought you imagined this morning." Before Emerald could protest, Apache drew her against him and wrapped an arm about her waist to prevent her from moving as his lips descended on hers. His mouth ravaged her tender flesh, his tongue forcing her lips open to explore the sweet cavern that had never known a man's touch.

Emerald gasped as a streak of lightning seared through her veins, melting all in its path. She trembled under the onslaught and unconsciously molded her body against his lean form as the kiss deepened.

At the taste of her lips, desire welled within Apache. Savoring the sweetness of her mouth, he gentled the kiss, then lifted her in his arms and carried her to the narrow bed.

RYAN'S GOLD

Cordia Byers

FAWCETT GOLD MEDAL • NEW YORK

A Fawcett Gold Medal Book
Published by Ballantine Books
Copyright © 1988 by Cordia Byers

ISBN 0-449-13144-0

Manufactured in the United States of America

First Edition: May 1988

To Pat and Marge—good friends.

Chapter 1

The roar of the icy white water rushing over the boulder-strewn creek bed filled Clear Creek Canyon as Emerald Banyon paused on the rocky bank and drew in a deep breath of the cold mountain air. The scent of snow filled her nostrils and made her shiver. It was only mid-September, but the weather here, in the foothills of the Rockies, was far different from that in the softly rolling mountains of north Georgia where she had lived for eighteen years with her grandmother.

Emerald shivered again and buried her chilled hands into the pockets of her woolen red-plaid coat. She was in high spirits and didn't mind the cold weather or any of the other discomforts she'd experienced recently. After so many years of missing her father, she had finally gained her heart's desire. Jim Banyon had decided to let her come with him to the newly formed Jefferson Territory. They were there to find the El Dorado that newspapers across the country claimed existed in that part of the Kansas Territory that had become known to all as Pikes Peak.

A bark drew Emerald's attention to the blue-tick hound that sniffed happily amid the boulders, pressing his damp nose into the crevices to search out any small quarry that might be hiding among the rocks. His long, speckled ears dragged on the ground, and he wagged his long tail enthusiastically, eager for a game with anything he might discover.

"Come on, Joe. We have to get back to camp with the water for Pa's breakfast. You know he can be a bear when he doesn't get his coffee in the morning."

At her command, Joe gave up his futile quest and loped down to the water's edge. He looked up to satisfy himself that Emerald was nearby before he turned his attention to quenching his thirst in the icy stream. He lapped up the crystal-clear liquid with his pink tongue and then happily licked his whiskers free of the excess moisture.

Emerald smiled at him. She loved the old hound. She'd raised him from a pup and he'd been her constant companion while growing up. Together they had explored the hills that surrounded Granny Banyon's farm, and during the lonely years of her adolescence, Joe's long ears had heard all of her confidences as they traipsed through the woods. Only to him had she revealed all the heartache and loneliness she had felt because of her father. She'd poured out her soul to the hound, telling him of her need to gain her father's love, of the loneliness she felt with only her aged, crippled grandmother for a companion. She'd told him of her dream that someday her father would remember that he had a daughter and want her with him. The hound had listened to all of her misery, and though she knew he couldn't understand what she was saying, just being able to express her feelings aloud had helped her to live with the pain.

"What would I have done without you, Joe?" came Emerald's soft question as she patted the hound's graying head. "You've been the one friend in my life that I could always count on to be there when I needed him."

Emerald's smile deepened as Joe nuzzled her hand and licked it affectionately. Kneeling at his side, she wrapped her arms around his lean neck and rested her head against his as she stared up at the tall peaks that towered over the foothills. They were so different from the blue mountains of home. She'd never forget her first sight of them as they rose up from the flat Kansas plains.

Even from a distance, they had been breathtaking in their grandeur. And after crossing six hundred miles of plains, with nothing but stunted scrub pine and grass to break the barren landscape, the peaks had been a welcome reprieve in addition to signaling the end of the journey that had brought father and daughter together after so many years.

The journey west had not been easy. Day after day of walking alongside the pack mules that carried all of their worldly possessions had tested Emerald's strength to the limit. There had been days when she'd had to focus her mind on just putting one foot in front of the other in order to maintain the pace her father had set for them. After the newspaper reports and the news the Russell party had brought with them when they returned to Auraria, Jim Banyon's eagerness to reach the gold-fields had made him heedless of all else except the gold fever that fired his blood.

Emerald had endured the hardships of the trail without complaint. Her joy in being with her father and her fear that he might regret bringing her with him had overcome the aching muscles and tired feet and the pain of her sunburned and insect-bitten skin.

Emerald glanced down at her red, chapped hands. They resembled a workman's hands far more than they did a young woman's, but she cared little that her palms were now calloused and her nails were chipped and broken. She had managed to hold her own beside her father and her hard work had finally paid off. The bond that she had craved all her life had begun to form between herself and Jim Banyon. She had earned his respect, and in time she hoped that it would turn into love.

Drawing her thoughts away from her relationship with the man who had sired her, Emerald glanced once more up at the foreboding sky. ''Joe, I hope Pa decides soon that it's time for us to head for Denver for the winter. I'm afraid if we wait too long we'll get snowed in. That ramshackle shack we threw together when we arrived won't be of much protection if that happens. Winter was bad enough back home in Granny's cabin, but I suspect it'll be far worse here.''

Joe wagged his tail in agreement.

''Come on, boy. Let's get back to camp.'' Emerald gave the hound a loving pat and then stood. She picked up the wooden bucket she'd brought with her and dipped it into a pool that had formed amid the boulders at the edge of the creek. When it was filled, she turned to the pine-needle-strewn path that led back to the camp through a stand of piñon pines.

Eager to get back to camp and settle down by the fire to await the breakfast scraps that Emerald would give him, Joe loped ahead. He paused intermittently to sniff the ground and to wag his tail as he waited for her to catch up with him before bounding on ahead. The routine was the same each day. He always kept her protectively in sight until they reached the camp clearing, where he turned the duty over to her father and stretched his old body out by the campfire's warmth.

Emerald topped the small rise that overlooked the clearing and found Joe standing, frozen, at the edge of the path. The bristles along his spine stood on end as he sniffed the air and let out a low growl.

''What is it, boy?'' she asked. Puzzled by his actions but knowing instinctively that he sensed danger, she scanned the area to see what had disturbed him. Joe let out another growl at the same instant she saw three masked men ride out of a stand of golden-leafed quaking aspen. A chill of apprehension raced up her spine at the sight. Even without the dog's primitive instincts to warn her, she knew that they meant no good to anyone in the Banyon camp.

Joe growled and raced down the path into the clearing before she could form the words to stop him. He barked and snapped at the horses' legs, making them shy and dance nervously under their sinister riders. The horses snorted and stamped as he nipped at their hooves with his sharp teeth. Before Emerald could call the dog away, one rider calmly took out his revolver and aimed it at Joe. The gunshot echoed through the canyon as the old hound tumbled into the dirt beneath the giddy horses.

As the sound died away, Emerald was already running toward the man. With a cry of rage and pain at the senseless killing of her lifelong friend, she bolted into the camp, determined to avenge Joe's death. Her flight was abruptly cut short by her father. He grabbed her roughly by the arm and shoved her behind him.

"Calm down before they blow your head off, too, girl," Jim ordered, keeping a wary eye on the three riders.

"You're not going to let them ride in here and kill Joe without a fight, are you?" she demanded, her fury blinding her to the threat that she and her father faced.

"Damn it, Emerald, use your head and keep your trap shut. There's more at stake here than that damn hound's life, if you'd take time to notice. These men didn't just come out here to shoot Joe," Jim growled as he looked up at the masked riders, who sat watching them quietly.

"I'd take his advice if I were you, little lady," the gunman said. "If your pa ain't smart, you'll both end up like that dog."

"What do you want?" Jim asked, eyeing the revolver that was aimed directly at his chest.

"All we want from you, Banyon, is for you to sign this here paper and then clear out. Now, that ain't too much to ask, is it?" the gunman said as he reached into his pocket and withdrew a piece of paper. He tossed it at Jim's feet.

A muscle twitched in Jim's cheek as he bent and picked it up. He gave a snort of disgust when he finished reading it and threw it back onto the ground. "Like hell I will. This land is mine. It's registered with the claims club in Denver, and I ain't got no intention of signing it over to you or anyone. If you think you can come in here and jump my claim without me doing anything about it, then you're mistaken, mister."

The gunman glanced over his shoulder at the man dressed in a black saddle coat and hat. Like his evil cohorts, he wore a mask; however, his was made of black silk.

"Boss, see how it is when you try to do a man a favor? I told you there was only one way to deal with the likes of him."

The man in the black nodded.

The gunman looked back at Jim. "I knew you'd be a fool, but don't let anyone say I didn't give you a chance." Before the words were completely out of his mouth, he raised the revolver and squeezed the trigger.

Jim jerked convulsively as the bullet hit him in the middle of his chest. The impact sent him tumbling backward into the dirt at his daughter's feet.

Emerald's scream of horror filled the air as she fell to her knees by her father's side. She clutched at his chest, where a widening scarlet circle spread across the front of his coat.

"Pa," she cried. "Don't die! Oh, God, please don't let him die." But even as she spoke, she knew her pleas were useless. The glazed look in her father's green eyes told her that Jim Banyon was dead.

"Little lady, your old man is done for and if you're smart you'll do as we say," the gunman said as he dismounted. The spurs on his boots jingled as he came forward. He stood towering over Emerald, his eyes regarding her cynically over the red bandanna that covered the lower half of his face.

Emerald's face was gray with shock as she drew her gaze away from her father's lifeless form and looked up at the gunman. Fear clogged her throat, but with an effort she swallowed it back. "What do you want of me?"

The gunman chuckled as he reholstered his gun and calmly folded his arms across his chest. A fire seemed to glow in his eyes as he looked at her speculatively for a long moment before glancing over his shoulder at the two mounted men behind him.

"The little lady wants to know what we want of her. This could turn out to be more interesting than we had planned."

"What do you reckon she'd be willing to swap for her life, Red?" came the whiny voice of the third horseman as he slid to the ground and moved to stand at the gunman's side. His beady eyes swept over Emerald as he chuckled.

"Keep your damn mouth shut," growled the man in black. The mask muffled his already deep voice and made it sound even more ominous.

"I didn't mean no harm, boss," Whiny apologized nervously. "I just got a little carried away at the sight of all that gold hair. The girl's a real looker for around these parts, or any parts for that matter. And I ain't never seen eyes like them before. They remind me of a mountain lion that I once kilt."

"We didn't come here for you to assess the girl's looks. I want that claim deed signed or you'll not get paid. After that is done, I don't give a damn what you do with her. Is that understood?" the boss said, his voice icy with contempt. He clenched his leather-gloved hands on the horse's reins to keep himself from venting his irritation at the man's stupidity.

"Yeah, boss," Whiny said, bobbing his head up and down.

Emerald shivered with dread as she stared past the gunman and up at the man he'd called boss. Attired completely in black, the boss was a sinister figure. But Emerald's apprehension was not caused by the clothes he wore. It was the man's eyes that chilled her to the bone. The cold expression in their dark depths made the freezing weather feel warm in comparison. She had only seen such unemotional eyes twice before in her life: once when Granny Banyon died and only moments before when she'd looked at her dead father. An icy hand squeezed her heart. In the frigid depths of those eyes she read her fate. These men intended to kill her, but before she died they planned to use her for their depraved amusement.

Emerald felt a scream building at the back of her throat, but she fought to control it. It would do her little good to succumb to the hysteria that was threatening to overtake her. Her only hope was the rifle resting on the wall in the cabin, and she had to stall for time until she could reach it. She had to keep her wits about her, and when the moment came, she must reach the cabin before they had a chance to stop her. It would still be three against one, but at least she would die fighting. That was more than her father had been able to do.

In an effort to keep her panic at bay, she tried to direct her thoughts away from the men's plan for her. Her gaze fell on the black-gloved hands of the leader of the trio. The leather was smooth and tight across his knuckles, emphasizing the intricate design that had been worked into the soft cowhide. It looked like initials, but she could not make them out.

"Bring me the deed when it's signed," he ordered. Emerald looked up and was captured once more by his cold, dark gaze. Their eyes clashed briefly before he jerked his horse about and kicked it in the side, and without a backward glance at her, he rode out of camp.

"Well, I guess that just leaves you and me to have a little fun, don't it, Red?" Whiny chuckled when the boss had ridden out of sight.

"You've been told once already to keep your damned mouth shut. One more slip and I'll leave you here to rot with Banyon," the gunman growled.

"Hell, let's quit arguing and get on to more interesting things. I shore could stand a piece of that before we go back to town."

Emerald scrambled to her feet and backed away from the two men. "I'll never sign your paper if you lay one hand on me," she threatened, regarding them warily.

"Now, girlie, why don't you just calm down. Ain't no use in trying to run. It'll go easier on you if you just let us have a little fun for all our trouble,'' Whiny said, taking a step toward her.

''Yeah, you sign the paper and give us some loving and we might just ride out of here and forget we ever laid eyes on you,'' the gunman added as he bent and picked up the paper that lay beside her father.

''Like hell I will,'' she spat, taking them by surprise with her sudden burst of spirit. Before they had time to react, she bolted toward the cabin. She ran inside, knowing that this time the devil was on her heels. She managed to reach the rifle and hoist it to her shoulder by the time the two men crowded into the narrow doorway. Thinking only of her survival, she aimed it at the gunman's chest and pulled the trigger. The hammer snapped, but nothing happened.

Emerald's last hope sank into oblivion as she realized her father had forgotten to reload the rifle after cleaning it that morning. In that split second, she knew her own death was imminent. The deadly glint in the gunman's eyes as he strode toward her told Emerald that there was nothing she could say or do to save herself. But even with the realization that she did not have a chance against him, she resisted him with every ounce of strength she possessed when he grabbed the rifle from her hands. Undeterred, she clawed at him, flailing at his head and shoulders in an effort to do as much damage as possible before she died. She raked at his eyes, tearing the bandanna from his face. And in a fraction of a moment, his features were branded onto her brain. His pale face was marked on the right cheek by a jagged red birthmark.

His face contorted with rage, and a low growl emerged from his throat as he gripped the rifle's barrel and stock with both hands and swung it upward so fast that she had no time to avoid the sharp blow to her chin. Stars exploded in Emerald's brain as she staggered backward and then sank, unconscious, to the dirt floor.

''Why in hell did you do that, Red? She ain't no good to us in that shape. And I was wanting a taste of something young, too. You can't find anything that looks that good in Denver. There's few enough women as it is, let alone any good-looking ones,'' Whiny said.

The gunman swung about, the birthmark on his cheek turning bright scarlet. "I'm tired of playing games. If you want a little ass, then you can get it like the rest of us down on Indian Row. Now go and get that bastard out there and drag him in here. I'm going to burn this place to the ground. We've wasted enough time as it is.''

"Ain't you a-goin' to see if she's dead?''

"If she ain't, she will be soon enough. Now get to it. I've a date with Lusty Sal tonight.'' The gunman strode from the cabin and watched with an air of disinterest as Whiny, huffing and puffing from the effort, carried out his orders. When Whiny was finished, Red closed the door of the cabin and stuck a dry pine knot into the campfire. When the rosin burst into flames, he tossed the torch onto the roof of the cabin and turned to his horse. Mounting, he watched until the wood blazed, and then he rode out of the camp, satisfied with a job well done.

Whiny followed close behind. The crime they had committed mattered little to him. He was a drifter and had done far worse in the past and would probably do so again in the future if it paid well enough. However, this would be his last job in the Kansas Territory. It was time for him to move on before he ended up dangling from the end of a rope.

With a low moan, Emerald roused from the black void of unconsciousness. Her eyes slowly fluttered open to see the flames licking ravenously overhead. Her mind still clouded, she stared groggily up at the orange tentacles that were devouring the timbers of the roof. Slowly, bits and pieces of the previous events managed to pierce the hazy realm of her consciousness, yet she was unable to grasp their meaning completely until she drew in a shaky breath and found her lungs burning from the heavy smoke that filled them.

The searing agony in her chest roused her from her torpor and made her fully aware of the danger that popped and crackled about her. Coughing and gasping for air, she forced herself to her hands and knees and began to crawl toward the door through the blinding haze that filled the cabin. Horror coursed through her as she found her path to safety blocked by her father's body. Futilely, she sought to drag his heavy form from the inferno that was consuming the cabin around them.

"Oh, Pa," she whimpered in despair when she realized that her only chance to save herself was to leave him. Sooty tears fell softly upon his still features as she pressed her lips to his brow and murmured her farewell. "I love you."

Heartsick with grief and numb with shock, she stumbled out into the cold gray morning as the roof of the cabin trembled and then collapsed behind her. Gasping for fresh air, she fell to her knees and watched the flames incinerate the timbers of the cabin and everything within it.

Hours later, Emerald still sat unmoving. Her face was gray and her eyes were haunted as she stared at the blackened ashes of Jim Banyon's funeral pyre. All that remained of the fire were lazy curls of blue smoke that rose toward the steely sky. Her eyes burned with the need to let out all of the pent-up emotions within her, but no tears would come to relieve the hollow ache in her heart. Her father was gone and now she would never have a chance to gain the love she had desperately needed from him.

Her keening cry pierced the deepening twilight as she wrapped her arms about her knees and began to rock to and fro. Her grief consumed her, making her oblivious to the night that was growing black and cold around her.

She sat wrapped in her cloak of misery, mourning the man who had sired her but who had never truly been a father to her. She grieved for the time they had lost and for the future that would never take place because of the vicious act of three evil men.

It was not until her teeth began to chatter from the cold that she slowly became aware of the danger she still faced from the icy-cold night. She realized that it would claim her as its victim if she remained immersed in her grief and self-pity.

Emerald gave herself a sharp mental shake. She would not let the night defeat her. She had to live to avenge her father's death. She would not die here in this lonely place and let the men who had killed her father escape without paying for their crime. She would brave the night and anything else she encountered in the future to see them brought to justice.

Drawing from the inner strength she had developed during the long years of hiding her pain, Emerald locked away her emotions and focused her efforts on enduring the night. She managed to find enough wood to build a fire, but it took all of her willpower to kindle the flames. After the horror of watching the cabin burn, she recoiled inwardly at the thought of fire. No matter how long she lived, she knew she would never be able to look into flames again without remembering the horror of that morning.

Through the long hours of the night, Emerald sat huddled by the campfire, reliving all that had transpired the previous day. By dawn, her resolve had firmed into an obsession. The gunmen had wanted this rocky piece of ground, but as long as there was a breath in her body, they would never get their hands on it. Nor would she rest until she saw them at the end of a hangman's rope. The thought warmed her chilled body.

Emerald knew the task she had set for herself would not be easy, but she also knew she could not rest until she had avenged her father as well as the dreams that had been lost with his death. She had time on her side, as well as the knowledge of the gunman's name and face. Also, she would never forget the ringleader. He was the one who had ordered her father killed. When she found the man with the birthmark, he would lead her to the man with the cold, dark eyes.

The icy winds howled mournfully down the slopes of the Rockies and into the foothills as the weather turned bitter. A few flakes of snow had already fallen, and the golden-leafed quaking aspens seemed to rattle a warning to Emerald as she worked to fashion a crude cross from two broken pick handles, lashed together with a strip of leather. She would not set out for Denver until she marked her father's pyre and buried the hound that had been her lifelong friend. This rough cross would have to do in place of the huge, carved headstone that she had often heard her father boast would mark his last resting place once he struck his bonanza and became a wealthy man. Ruefully, she realized the simple marker reflected the truth of his situation, rather than the dreams that had driven him to come west to the Jefferson Territory.

Sadly, Emerald shook her head at the irony of life. Her father had been only one out of thousands who had rushed into that part of the country. After the news of the Russell brothers' strike became known, men from all walks of life had hurried west. The country's depression had made the Georgians' find even more enticing. So they had come; some on foot, pushing their few possessions in wheelbarrows, or in laden wagons with "Pikes Peak or Bust" painted on the white canvas that protected their worldly goods from the rain and the wind. They left everything else behind and used any means they could to gain the money to reach the goldfields. However, few had been as lucky as the red-bearded Georgian, John Gregory, to whom her father had introduced her when they arrived in Denver. He had found color, and now everyone was claiming that Gregory Gulch was the richest square mile on earth. Most were like her father. They had found little for their efforts and had returned to their homes with their spirits and dreams broken.

Emerald released a long breath. By selling the farm in Georgia, her father had made sure that there would be no turning back for them. He had not considered the fact that he might not find any gold, and now, because of his illusive dream, she was left without a place to call home beyond this piece of rocky earth. Jim Banyon's dreams had always come first in his life. All else, including his daughter's welfare, was secondary and dispensable when it came into conflict with his greed for wealth.

Against her will, a burst of resentment flared within Emerald. She didn't want to feel the old, familiar antipathy toward her father building inside. She had thought those feelings dead since he'd brought her with him to the goldfields. Yet, in truth, she knew she'd never be able to rid herself of them entirely. No matter how her father's feelings might have changed toward her near the end of his life, her deep-seated anger at being abandoned to her grandmother's care after her mother's death still existed. She had loved her father, yet she didn't know if she would ever be able to forgive him for the years of loneliness she'd endured while he wandered, looking for easy riches. Nor did she know if she could ever fully trust any man again. Jim Banyon had made her wary of believing in men in general.

Emerald kicked at a stone in her path as she turned away from the charred remains of the cabin. She had to think of her future and not of the past. Thanks to her father's empty dream, all she had was her will to survive and the few nuggets they had found the day before his death.

Fortunately for her, the claim jumpers had not noticed the small leather pouch that had fallen out of her father's pocket when they dragged him inside the cabin. The few nuggets in that pouch were all that would stand between her and starvation once she reached Denver. She had nothing else to show for the months she and her father had worked panning gold. She didn't even have the old mare they had bought after selling the mules to get enough money to grubstake them. The poor, decrepit animal had died soon after they reached Clear Creek.

"Denver," Emerald murmured aloud. The thought of the boomtown was intimidating. After living on her grandmother's farm in the mountains of north Georgia, Denver was as foreign to her as another country. When she and her father had stopped there before traveling on to the goldfields, she had seen enough of it to know that it would not be easy for a woman alone to survive in such a place. The population was predominantly male. The streets were filled with miners who jostled for space amongst the mountain men and trappers dressed in greasy buckskins. For a young woman on her own, there would be more than starvation to worry about in Denver. A shiver of trepidation crept up her spine at the thought. By going there she would be placing herself into a dangerous situation, but she had no other choice. She would die if she remained at the campsite.

"I will survive," she muttered to reassure herself. Resolutely, she turned onto the winding trail. With only the few nuggets in her pocket and her resolve to see the men responsible for her father's death hanged to see her through, she headed toward Denver.

Chapter 2

As Emerald had feared, the snow began in earnest within an hour after she left the campsite. Large flakes fell from the leaden sky, blanketing the landscape in a thick, white carpet. The golden aspen and the blue-green spruce added splashes of color to winter's immaculate mantle, while gusts of wind formed drifts that soon made walking nearly impossible. Yet Emerald kept moving forward, trudging through the deepening snow, knowing that her only chance of survival was to try to reach Denver.

The morning had passed into afternoon when she began to fear that she had taken the wrong trail. Though she didn't know the area well, she remembered having seen several campsites along the way when she had first come to Clear Creek with her father. However, she had seen no sign of them since she'd veered away from the stream in order to stay in the pines that provided her some protection against the biting wind.

Emerald could see only a short distance in front of her because of the white haze that encompassed everything. It made it impossible for her to get her bearings, but she doggedly kept going. She suspected the worst but knew she could not turn back. There was nothing that awaited her there but death.

Her hands and feet grew numb from the cold and her thoughts of reaching Denver faded under the battering force of the snowstorm that was quickly turning into a blizzard. Her strength ebbing away with each step she took, Emerald realized that her only hope lay in finding some kind of shelter before it was too late.

The weather did not break, but worsened. The wind grew in force, buffeting her body relentlessly as she fought against it to stay on her feet. She staggered haphazardly through the snow, her breath coming in ragged gasps from the effort she expended just trying to put one foot in front of the other. Cresting a small hill, she felt her strength faltering and stopped to catch her breath.

The muscles in her legs felt as if they were on fire from the strain they had endured. She could no longer feel her fingers or toes, and her throat was raw from breathing the freezing air. Snowflakes clung to her lashes and to the strands of golden hair that were exposed below the brim of her hat as she stared at the valley below, willing herself to make the effort to descend from the hillside.

She had managed to dredge up enough strength to take only a few steps before she stumbled into a drift and collapsed at the base of a tall pine. Clutching the rough-barked bole, she made an effort to regain her footing, but she could not make her legs obey her command.

Emerald sagged with exhaustion. She knew she could go no farther. Resignation washed over her as she laid her cold-reddened cheek against the tree trunk and peered through icy lashes at the valley below. She saw the dim outline of what looked like a cabin through the white shroud of falling snow, but its vague image meant little to her in her benumbed state. Her mind was too dulled with fatigue to realize that safety lay only a short distance away.

The cold crept deeper into her body, making her drift into the shadowy land where illusions reigned. She dreamed of a great woolly bear that came toward her, walking on its hind legs, from the stand of piñon pines. In Emerald's imagination, its growl, combined with the

howl of the wind, resembled a man's deep voice as it
bent over her and shook her roughly by the shoulder
with a wide, furry paw.

Numbed emotionally as well as physically by the
frigid weather, she felt no fear as she stared up into the
animal's piercing black eyes and felt herself being lifted
into its powerful arms. Her mind and body succumbed
to the illusion, and she snuggled closer to the warmth
that she imagined emanated from the animal's furry
pelt.

The harsh white world of her dream changed suddenly into dim shadows, and the wind abruptly lost its
keening pitch, quieting to little more than a low moan
of despair. Vague images swirled through her mind as
she felt herself being lowered onto a soft bed. She gave
a weak cry of protest as the great beast attempted to
take its warmth from her and clung to him, instinctively
sensing that he was all that lay between her and death.

"You're safe now, but we'll both freeze if you don't
let me build a fire."

Groggily, Emerald shook her head and tried to draw
herself out of the strange fantasy in which a bear spoke
like a man. The effort was too much for her and she
gave in to the darkness that engulfed her.

Apache Ryan caught her as she fainted. He eased her
limp body back onto the bed and drew the rat-chewed
guilts up over her before turning to the task of building
a fire. Removing his furry mitts, he tucked them into
the pocket of his beaverskin coat and crossed to the
fireplace that the owner of the cabin had built from creek
rock and mud. Apache was relieved to see that Jeb had
left a pile of dry wood by the hearth and he was grateful
for the old mountain man's forethought. That small
stack of wood could very well save the girl's life as well
as his own if the blizzard did not let up soon.

Hunkering down in front of the cold firepit, he
glanced back at the still figure on the bed. He knew
from the bluish pallor of the girl's skin that heat was
the only thing that could save her. Had she remained a

few minutes longer in the storm, she would have frozen to death huddled at the base of that tree.

Turning his thoughts back to the task at hand, he placed several sticks of kindling on the grate, struck a match, and lit them. He held his breath until a fire blazed and then added the heavier logs to it. He smiled at his success when the flames began to devour the wood.

Crystal droplets of water dripped and splattered on the hearth as the heat began to melt the snow that clung to the dark beard covering the lower half of his face. Absently, he ran a hand over the fuzzy growth to rid it of the excess moisture before he shrugged out of his coat. He held the coat up to the fire to warm it thoroughly and then moved back to the bed to lay it over the girl. At the moment she needed it far more than he did.

After tucking the coat snugly about her, Apache stood gazing down at her for a moment, wondering what madness had possessed a girl her age to wander around in a blizzard.

It had only been by chance that he had seen her as he sought to reach the cabin and safety from the blizzard. Had he not glimpsed a bit of red plaid through the snow that was quickly obscuring her small form, he would have passed her by and would have never known that she lay buried less than a hundred feet from the door of the log cabin.

The girl had not been the only one who had been fortunate that afternoon, Apache reflected. He had begun to believe that he himself would end up an icicle until he sighted Jeb Taylor's cabin. He had been on his way to Denver when the storm broke and would have made it safely out of the foothills had his horse not stepped into a hole and broken its leg. That had left him to battle the inclement weather on foot. Just when he had begun to believe that he would not make it out of the mountains alive, he had remembered the old mountain man's cabin.

''I hope our luck holds and the storm breaks soon,

little one,'' he said to the unconscious girl as he perused her still features with the eye of a man who appreciated natural beauty in all of its forms. His gaze dwelt on her delicately sculpted face, with its arched brows and dark, feathery lashes that cast sooty shadows upon the pale skin of her cheeks. Her nose was narrow and straight above the full lips that were slightly parted as she breathed. The only flaw he could find in her appearance was the small, squared chin that seemed to proclaim a stubborn disposition.

''After the beating you took from the storm, you'll have to be stubborn to survive,'' Apache mused aloud as he bent to remove her hat in an effort to make her more comfortable. As the battered piece of felt came away in his hand, Emerald's long, burnished-gold hair spilled in a silken mass across the lumpy pillow.

Apache's breath caught in his throat at the sight, and he reacted without thinking. Totally unaware of the effect it would have upon him, he lifted a golden curl and felt its rich texture between his fingers. He realized his mistake too late. The touch of the soft hair aroused all of the memories that he had tried to erase from his mind during the past ten years.

Bitterness rose in his throat like bile as the images resurfaced with painful clarity. A muscle worked in his cheek as he clamped his teeth together and fought to bury them once more in the dark recesses of his mind where he kept the emotions that had been a part of him until the day he had returned to his home to find his life destroyed.

In one reckless card game, his father had forfeited everything he'd owned to a riverboat gambler. But the tragedy of that game of chance did not end for the Ryan family after the turn of the last card. Charles Ryan, devastated by the loss of his family's plantation and too cowardly to confront his son with the news, had taken his dueling pistol from its case in the study and used it on himself.

Apache closed his eyes as the vision of red arose in

his mind. His memory of that fatal day was always drenched in scarlet, from the red velvet drapes over the windows to the pool of blood in which he had found his father's body. To this day, he hated the color. It not only reminded him of Charles Ryan's death; it also represented the young heart that had been torn into shreds when it became known that Apache was destitute and the woman he loved had turned her back on him because he could not give her the place in society that she felt she deserved. When he had asked her to go west with him to start a new life, he quickly learned that love meant little to her. Rachel's refusal had been polite, but the courtesy was overshadowed by an icy façade that he had never suspected existed in the woman he had considered all sunshine and goodness.

Crushed by her betrayal and vowing never to become emotionally involved again, Apache had turned his back on his past and headed west. Rachel's cruel lesson had been the first stone in the wall he had erected about his heart, and through the years, he had built it higher. He had kept his resolve never again to love a woman so deeply that he would leave himself vulnerable to the agony he had endured because of the fair-haired Louisiana beauty who had wreaked such havoc upon his heart.

Apache had wandered from place to place trying to outdistance the memories that haunted him, but had never completely succeeded. His life on the frontier had not been easy or free of danger. He'd driven stages along the Santa Fe Trail, herded cattle from Texas to Kansas, and panned for gold in California. For a time he had lived among the Apaches, learning from them the skills that had earned him his name. He had found a small measure of peace among the stoic natives of the Southwest, but that, too, had come to an end when the chief had offered his daughter as a wife to Apache. His refusal to accept the chief's gift had severed the friendship between the two men and Apache had resumed his wandering.

To the world, Apache Ryan was a taciturn, guarded man who kept his own counsel until he was angered. Then he was unmerciful. He dealt swiftly with his enemies, his accuracy with a gun and a bowie knife making him as dangerous a foe as the Indians for whom he was named. Few men who encountered the dark-eyed, reclusive man were foolish or brave enough to incite his wrath.

Apache dropped the strand of hair as if it had turned into fire in his hand. His eyes glittered like cold onyx as he forced the memories back into their sealed compartment in his mind. The past was dead and buried, and he had no need for useless reflections on things that could not be changed.

Beau Alexander Ryan, the handsome, debonair son of Charles Ryan, no longer existed. In his place now stood a man known as Apache Ryan. He had been honed to a hard edge by the rough life he had lived during the past ten years. He was a man who could be deadly when challenged; a man who ignored his genteel heritage; a man who thought he no longer possessed a heart that could feel. He was also a man who was driven by a hatred that he could not relinquish. It festered in his soul, and he often wondered if it was the only thing that kept him alive.

Apache grated his teeth at the thought of Cash Dalton, the man who had been the cause of his father's suicide. The gambler now owned the Gold Dust Saloon in Denver, where he was growing richer by the day from the miners who drank the cheap Taos Lightning he served and gambled at his crooked gaming tables. The man seemed to have an uncanny ability to land on his feet when it came to his devious enterprises. No matter what foul means he used, Dalton invariably had the devil's luck in escaping from any retribution for the crimes he committed.

"But his luck is going to change," Apache mused aloud. "Because I'm determined to see that it does." It had taken him years to track Dalton down and nearly six months of patronizing the Gold Dust Saloon to find the tiny chink that would break the gambler's run of luck, but the time he had spent in Denver had been worthwhile. Unaware of who Apache was and thinking that he had passed out from too much Taos Lightning, Cash Dalton had discussed his plans with his hired gun, Red Beaudine, right in front of Apache. That information was what Apache had been seeking, and now that he had it, he planned to see that the gambler was ruined financially. However, Apache didn't plan to use the same means Dalton had used with his father. The gambler was too smart to chance all he owned on the turn of a card.

Apache smiled. He had devised a trap that would cause Dalton to lose all he possessed, and now he was returning to Denver to see it played out. He had set it in motion back East when he'd returned home to visit some old friends a few weeks ago. His family had lost everything financially, but he still had connections in the financial circles that dealt in stocks and bonds. They had agreed to help him achieve his revenge against the gambler who had ruined the dreams of the young man he had been so many years ago.

Dalton would never know that the investors who had agreed to back his venture to build a railroad through the mountains were friends of Apache's. Or that the stipulation in the contract that Dalton guarantee the right-of-way by investing his own money heavily in the project had been Apache's idea. If Dalton could not obtain the right-of-way, then he would be forced to forfeit his holdings in the railroad company and the capital that he had tied up in it. Dalton had foolishly agreed to their terms because he was confident of his success in gaining the parcels of land he needed to fulfill his part of the contract. Luck had never failed the gambler in the past, and he did not expect it to turn its back on him in this venture. However, he was completely unaware that Apache Ryan was determined to see that it abandoned him completely now.

Drawing his thoughts away from his reason for returning to Denver, Apache gazed down at the girl he had rescued from the storm. He knew from his earlier observations that when she recovered and the fresh bloom of health returned to her pale features she would be a beauty to rival any he had ever encountered. Oddly, the thought made something within him recoil in the dark cave where he hid his deeper emotions.

Since Rachel had left him, the very thing that had drawn him to her had made him wary of any woman who was equally endowed. He admitted that, in fact, the unconscious girl before him, with her dramatic coloring and features, made Rachel's memory pale; this girl was far lovelier than the woman who had broken his heart. Like Rachel, she possessed fair hair, but that was where the resemblance ended between the two. And even when he recalled Rachel's pale blond hair, it now seemed insipid next to the burnished gold locks of the girl lying on the bed. She reminded him of fire, while Rachel was ice. Recalling how much misery Rachel's beauty had caused him, he realized this girl's could devastate a man beyond redemption. With the thought, Apache felt his insides cringe and he gave an involuntary shudder. He wanted nothing to do with that type of trouble again.

Apache knew his feelings toward beautiful women were less than objective, but he could not change them any more than he could stop himself from breathing. He doubted if he could ever learn to trust one again. As a man, he still enjoyed female flesh, but his preference now ran toward those who were less endowed with nature's gifts.

Turning away from the lovely girl on the bed, he crossed the few feet to the fireplace and tossed another log onto the flames before settling his lean frame into one of the rickety chairs that graced the one-room cabin. Several of the worn hemp strings of the woven seat snapped under his weight, but he ignored them as he stretched his long legs out to the warmth of the fire and leaned back. Clasping his hands over his rock-hard belly, he glanced once more into the shadows beyond the realm of the firelight.

Beautiful women were not for him, he reiterated silently before turning his gaze back to the jumping flames. Through narrowed lids, he stared at the orange and blue tentacles that curled about the wood and his thoughts turned to the woman who awaited his return to Denver.

Hannah Becker, with her plain face and plump body, suited his needs well. He felt emotionally safe with her. When he took her to his bed, he was not haunted by the memory of another's slender arms about his neck or of a lithe young body pressed enticingly against him. Nor did she make demands upon him beyond the few moments of pleasure they shared when he visited the small boardinghouse she owned.

A widow who had lost her husband soon after they had arrived in Denver, Hannah enjoyed her relationship with Apache as much as he did. He liked her openness and her willingness to accept him as he was without expecting promises of undying love. He also admired her independent nature. She had often told him that she had no desire to remarry; she was satisfied with the life she had made for herself. She treasured her freedom after having been married to Herman Becker; a domineering and sometimes brutal man. Apache respected her decision and her strength of character. She was the only woman that he had ever met whom he could honestly say that about. Few females possessed the courage to run their own lives as the Widow Becker was doing.

Apache yawned and rolled his head to ease the tired ache in his neck and shoulders. The miles of walking through the storm had wearied him more than he had realized. The soothing warmth of the fire relaxed his tired muscles, and he let his chin drop to his chest. Soon his sooty lashes drifted down over his ebony eyes and he slipped into a light doze.

* * *

The wind's high-pitched shriek through the eaves of the sod-roofed cabin made Emerald sit bolt upright with an involuntary cry upon her lips. With twilight deepening into night, the howling of the wind aroused all of the childhood fears that Granny Banyon's ghost stories had ingrained in the depths of her subconscious mind through the years. She had sought to conquer them, telling herself that it was ridiculous for a grown woman to let herself be disturbed by the ghoulish specters her grandmother's tales conjured into life in her imagination. However, in her weakened condition, she could not seem to keep them at bay.

She trembled violently and clutched the tattered quilts to her breast as she became more aware of her strange surroundings. Staring wide-eyed about the cabin, she desperately tried to orient herself and to organize the wild thoughts that tumbled through her mind.

When her gaze fell on the lean figure sitting relaxed in the fire's glow, she blinked several times to be sure that her eyes were not playing tricks on her. When the image of the bearded giant did not fade, her heart began to thump erratically against her ribs. Cold fingers of alarm raced up her spine when his dark lashes fluttered open and a pair of speculative black eyes came to rest upon her. As he continued to regard her curiously without speaking, her knuckles grew white from the grip she held upon the frayed edge of the quilts.

Emerald made an effort to break the silence between them, but only a hoarse croak emerged from her sore throat when she tried to speak. After swallowing several times and moistening her wind-chapped lips, she whispered, "Where am I?"

"I'd say somewhere west of Denver." Apache yawned widely as he stretched his arms over his head to ease the tightness that had begun to make his muscles sore.

"How did I get here?" she asked, bewildered.

"I found you in the storm."

"The storm," Emerald breathed as the memory of

her last harrowing moments in the blizzard came abruptly to the surface. She had been vaguely aware of the cabin in the distance, but she had been unable to make her legs carry her toward it. Beyond that, she could remember little. All, except her strange dream of the bear, was a blur in her mind. Seeking to recall the moment of her rescue, she absently drew Apache's coat closer about her to ward off the chill that the fire had not chased from corners of the room. The moment her hand touched the fur, she realized with a start that she hadn't been dreaming. She had thought this man a bear because of the coat he wore. It had been this stranger who had lifted her into his powerful arms and carried her to the cabin. She owed him her life.

"Thank you for helping me. I would have died had you not found me when you did," Emerald said, trying to express a small measure of her gratitude.

Apache shifted uneasily in his chair. Strangely, the sincerity in the girl's simple statement made him uncomfortable. It roused a response within him that he did not want to acknowledge.

"You're not out of the woods yet," he answered gruffly, ignoring her thanks. "If the storm doesn't let up soon, we'll both end up freezing to death. Old Jeb only left enough wood to last through the night."

Emerald shivered. The man's curt tone and grim predictions effectively silenced her. She pulled the quilts up about her shoulders and sat listening to the angry howl of the wind that sought entry into their momentary haven. The cabin trembled and seemed to groan under the force of the storm as if to impress upon its inhabitants the danger that awaited them outside its walls.

Emerald glanced uneasily at her silent companion and found him staring at her with his inscrutable dark eyes. There was something unnerving about the way he looked at her. The man had saved her life, yet she sensed from the distant air that seemed to surround him that it meant little to him. He would have done the same for any animal trapped in the blizzard. The thought made her shiver again. Her movements made the bed squeak in protest.

"Unless you're determined to finish what I've tried to prevent, I suggest you come over to the fire instead of cowering in the shadows like a frightened rabbit."

"I'm not cowering," Emerald blurted out before she could stop herself.

One corner of Apache's mouth quirked slightly upward at her belligerent tone. "Then you must want to freeze to death."

His manner, as well as his insinuation that she was a coward, annoyed Emerald. Throwing back the covers, she climbed from the bed. She ignored the wave of weakness that washed over her when her feet touched the floor. She took several steps in the direction of the fire before she realized her ordeal in the snow had taken a heavier toll on her strength than she had perceived while safely in bed. The room began to spin before her eyes and she staggered. She felt herself begin to fall and threw out her arms to try to prevent it. They came into contact with a wide chest. Before she could grasp him to steady herself, she felt herself being lifted off her feet and carried toward the warmth given off by the burning logs.

Gradually her head stopped reeling and she realized with some trepidation that she was resting in her rescuer's lap with her head on his shoulder. Unnerved by their close proximity, she drew in a deep, steadying breath, placed her hand against his chest, and pushed herself upright. Their eyes met and locked as she straightened. She stared into the ebony depths that reflected the glowing firelight and her breath caught in her throat at the sudden burst of heat that flamed within them before she was abruptly set away from him.

The movement jolted her out of the strange trance that had held her momentarily spellbound and she sank gratefully to the stone hearth. An odd sensation quivered in her belly and she wrapped her arms about her legs to keep from shivering again under the force of it.

She could not draw her eyes away from the man who had come to her rescue for the second time that day.

"Who are you?" she asked in an effort to ease the tension that had suddenly developed between them.

"I'm called Apache by most," he answered cryptically. "Who are you?"

"I'm called Emerald Banyon by all," she shot back. To her surprise he chuckled.

"Your parents named you well, Emerald Banyon. Your eyes are the same color as the gem."

"Does your name suit you as well?" Emerald asked, relaxing at the gentle light of humor she saw shining in his eyes. Emerald realized her mistake too late. The distant air seemed to cloak him once more. His eyes seemed to cloud as he stared into the fire beyond her as if looking into his past.

"I've been told that it does."

Sensing his withdrawal and for some strange reason not wanting to let him retreat behind his aloof barrier, she asked, "Why were you in the storm?"

Apache drew in a long breath and looked down at her. "I could ask the same of you. It's not the usual thing to find a girl who is little more than a child out wandering around in the wilderness in a blizzard."

"I'm eighteen and a grown woman," Emerald said defensively, oddly affronted at being considered a child by this man.

"But that still does not tell me why you were wandering around in the storm," Apache said, smoothly keeping the subject away from himself.

"I was on my way to Denver and became lost once it started to snow. It's as simple as that."

"Do you honestly expect me to believe that story? Your parents would have to be insane to allow a girl your age to go to Denver alone, especially when there was a snowstorm brewing." Apache eyed her dubiously. "Have you run away from home?"

Incensed that this man, who knew nothing of her, could be so presumptuous as to question her word,

Emerald's eyes flashed green fire. Anger rippled along every nerve in her body as she eyed him hostilely. He had rescued her from the storm, but that did not give him the right to call her a liar.

"I don't really give a damn what you believe," was her curt reply.

"Such unladylike language," Apache chided, forcing himself to hide his amusement. The girl had spirit. She reminded him of the tiny yellow kitten he had owned as a boy. It had spat and clawed until he tamed it. And for one disturbing moment he wondered what it would be like to tame this fiery-eyed creature until she purred under his caressing hand. Apache gave himself a sharp mental shake for even contemplating such a thing. He sought safer ground.

"You didn't answer my question, Emerald Banyon."

"You didn't answer mine, so I saw no reason to give you the courtesy of responding to yours," Emerald replied, her small, squared chin jutting out at a stubborn angle. She folded her arms across her chest and stared past him into the shadows beyond the ring of firelight, remembering the horror that had forced her to head for Denver through the snowstorm.

Apache's lips twitched and he gave way to the smile that had been building during their exchange. Emerald Banyon was no simpleminded minx as he had first assumed because of her age and appearance. She had a quick mind, and he found himself intrigued by it even as his instincts warned him that this snow nymph could wreak havoc upon any man who was fool enough to fall under her spell.

Ever alert to any threat that might shatter the barrier he had erected around himself, Apache pressed his lips into a thin, hard line. His thoughts turned bitter. He had allowed himself to yield to one beautiful woman's allure, and he had paid dearly for that mistake. He'd never let himself fall prey to such temptation again. This girl intrigued him, but that would be as far as it went. When the storm let up and they went their separate ways, he'd never think of her again.

The wind gave a wolfish howl, reminding him of their tenuous situation. *If we part,* he mused silently as he turned his thoughts away from Emerald and back to the predicament in which they would find themselves if the blizzard did not stop soon. He had not lied when he told her that they could be trapped in the shack without wood or food. To survive, they would have to work together to conserve what little warmth they had.

As if to reaffirm his convictions, the last log he had placed in the fireplace crumbled into ash. Sparks showered up the chimney as the blaze flickered precariously for a moment and then began to die. Emerald turned to put another piece of wood on the coals to rekindle the flames, but he stopped her with a firm hand upon her arm.

"Don't. We have to make the wood last for as long as possible."

"We'll freeze if the fire goes out," she said, eyeing him as if he had suddenly lost his wits.

"If we burn it all tonight and the storm doesn't let up, we'll freeze for certain."

"Then how do you suggest that we keep warm while we're saving the wood?" she questioned, unable to understand his reasoning.

Apache considered her for a long, thoughtful moment before he said, "I suggest that we go to bed."

Emerald gaped up at him, disconcerted by his answer. She had no intention of getting into that tiny bed with this stranger under any circumstances. Her upbringing had been less than conventional in the backwoods of Georgia, but she knew right from wrong. Her Gran had often told her that no decent young woman ever went to bed with a man unless they were married and she planned to heed the old woman's sage advice. She didn't want to end up like Letty Harper, who had become the town whore after she'd gotten herself with child before any vows were spoken. Now, no man would have Letty to wife.

Without realizing the turmoil his suggestion had created in Emerald, Apache left her standing in front of the dying fire and crossed to the bed, where he threw back the covers and sat down. He tugged off his boots and quickly slid beneath the quilts. Turning on his side, he propped himself up on one elbow and peered at her.

"Are you going to stand there all night?" he asked, and lifted the covers for her.

"I'm not going to sleep with you if that's what you think," was Emerald's staunch answer.

"That's up to you. When you get cold enough, you may change your mind." Apache pulled the covers up and turned his back to her.

With her eyes narrowed suspiciously, Emerald stood staring at the dark head above the covers. After her experience at the campsite, she didn't trust any man. If he thought she would let down her guard because of the ease with which he had accepted her decision, then he was sadly mistaken. She intended to hold to her resolve.

Pulling her coat tightly about her, she settled herself on the floor in front of the fireplace and curled into a ball in an effort to conserve what little heat the dying embers gave off. After wiggling about to try to make herself more comfortable on her hard bed, she eventually fell into a restless sleep.

A short time later, Emerald awoke with her teeth chattering from the cold that had invaded the cabin. The fire pit was black, giving off no heat or light as she crouched in the darkness wondering how she would survive until Apache chose to rekindle the fire. Shivering uncontrollably, she hugged her knees and listened to his light snoring.

At last she gave in to her need for warmth. She knew she had no other choice. Her gran would not have approved of her decision, but it was far better to sleep with Apache than to freeze to death. Quietly, she got to her feet and crossed to the bed, and without touching the man who slept within it, she slipped beneath the covers fully clothed. She lay stiff and nervous at his side as several long, tense minutes passed and Apache's snores continued uninterrupted. Finally she realized that he slept so soundly that he did not know of her presence in the bed. Relaxing her vigil, she soon drifted off to sleep.

Chapter 3

At *dawn Emerald awoke with a start. Her thick lashes* flew open with shock at the feeling of Apache's lips against the nape of her neck. With her mind still clouded by sleep, it took her a moment longer to realize that his lean body cupped hers and his hand was intimately caressing her beneath the thickness of her clothing. Her skin tingled where the hand glided over her rib cage and up to her breasts. The odd sensation that she had felt in her belly the previous night began to grow once more under his gentle fondling. It lulled her with its heat as it began to invade her entire being. However, the trance was broken a moment later when he murmured so softly that it was nearly inaudible, "Rachel, my lovely Rachel."

The squeal of rage that emerged from Emerald's throat sounded like that of a wildcat. She flipped onto her back and, with both hands, shoved Apache away from her before she scrambled out of the bed. All of the covers went with her.

"What the hell do you think you're doing?" Apache cursed, coming fully awake to the icy blast of the morning. He rose from the bed in one fluid, angry movement and stood glaring at Emerald. "Answer me, damn you. What's the meaning of trying to freeze me to death?"

Emerald clutched the covers protectively to her and raised her chin defiantly, ready to do battle. "How dare you ask me that question after what you did."

"Did?" Apache asked, puzzled. He shook his head in an effort to clear it of sleep. He could remember nothing beyond the moment he awoke. Apache ran a hand through his tousled hair in exasperation. "I don't know what in hell you're babbling about."

"You, you—" Emerald began, but could not put into words a description of his actions. Embarrassed, her cheeks began to burn and she looked away from him.

Apache's swarthy face flushed a deeper hue with annoyance. "If you're accusing me of something, you'd better spit it out in a hurry."

Emerald swallowed several times, drew in a deep breath, and looked him directly in the eyes. "You took advantage of me while I slept."

"The hell you say," Apache growled, and took a step toward her. He reached out and jerked the quilts from her hands. He surveyed her from head to toe. He frowned. The girl was still fully dressed; not even a button was out of place. His narrowed gaze came to rest once more upon her face. "What kind of game are you trying to play, Emerald Banyon? I'm no fool."

At the flicker of anger in his midnight eyes, Emerald involuntarily retreated a step backward. "You're the one who has been playing games by lying about our need to conserve the firewood in order to get me into your bed."

"I don't play games. If I had wanted you in my bed for any other reason than to keep you from freezing to death, I could have put you there. But I don't make a habit of seducing children, no matter how outrageous or beautiful they may be."

"I'm not a child and I know what you did," Emerald spat, bristling.

"Damn it! I also know what I didn't do," Apache snarled as he crossed to the fireplace to rekindle the fire. Hunkering down before the cold hearth, he placed a few sticks of kindling and a log on the gray coals before setting a match to it. When it caught and blazed, he turned to look at Emerald, who stood regarding him as if he were a leper.

"I don't know what you thought to accomplish with your accusations, but it didn't work. I suggest in the future that when you try this hoax on the next man that you remember to at least take off your clothes and boots if you expect him to believe your lies."

"How dare you?" Emerald exploded. The heat of her temper sizzled through her veins. She seemed to swell with indignation. "You lowdown good-for-nothing. You have the nerve to accuse me of God-only-knows what, when you're the one who's at fault. I didn't ask you to kiss me or touch me."

Feeling the need to vent her ire, Emerald picked up one of the boots he had left by the bed and sailed it at his head. She missed her target but caught him squarely in the chest. To her satisfaction, she heard him grunt with pain as she turned and stormed to the door. She'd be damned if she'd stay another moment in the cabin with the beast.

"Come back here, you little hellcat," Apache growled as she swung the door open and fled out into the snow. He took only enough time to pull on his boots and coat before he set off after her.

Emerald tried to run, but found it impossible in the knee-deep snow. She heard the angry note in Apache's voice as he called to her, but she did not look back. She struggled forward, stumbling and falling in her effort to put as much distance between herself and the madman as possible.

Apache's anger cooled as he watched her set out in the opposite direction from that in which she needed to travel if she wanted to reach Denver. "The little fool," he muttered beneath his breath in disgust as he followed in her wake. If he didn't catch her, she'd end up in the same condition as he'd found her the previous day.

Emerald's lungs burned from the cold air when she paused to catch her breath. She glanced over her shoulder in the direction of the cabin and found to her dismay that she had not escaped from Apache. He stood several feet from her, regarding her through narrowed ebony eyes.

"I ought to let you get lost and freeze to death after the stunt you just pulled," Apache said gruffly.

"Then why don't you?" Emerald asked, fighting back the urge to burst into tears.

"I don't want you on my conscience," he muttered. He stepped toward her and took her roughly by the arm. There were enough things in his past to feel guilty about without adding to them by letting this headstrong girl die from her fit of childish temper.

"Come on," he ordered, giving her arm a less than gentle jerk.

Emerald strained against his hand. "I don't need your help. Nor am I going back to that cabin with you. The snow has stopped, and I'm going to Denver."

"Damn it, girl. How long do you think you'll last roaming around in weather like this? The snow has stopped, but do you know how to get to Denver?"

"I can find my way," was Emerald's belligerent reply.

"Just like you did yesterday? You'd be lost before you were out of sight of the cabin."

"That's better than staying there with you after what you did."

"Emerald, I've had about enough of your accusations for one day. If you don't stop them, I'm going to show you what happens to little girls when they lie."

"I may be young, but I'm old enough to know exactly what you were trying to do. And I'll be damned if I'll go back to that cabin so you can attack me again."

Apache's face flushed with renewed anger. "And I'll be damned if I stay out here and freeze to death trying to convince you that I didn't attack you. Nor will I let you go off alone. You're coming back to the cabin with me and I'll hear no more arguments, or you'll regret it."

"I won't go with you," Emerald spat, and tried to jerk free of his hand.

"Oh, yes, you will," Apache ground out through clenched teeth, his tone laced with steely determination. Before she had time to protest, he lifted her off her feet and tossed her over his shoulder like a sack of flour. She squealed and beat at his back with her fists, but he paid no heed to her struggles as he strode back to the cabin. He kicked the door closed behind them and crossed the room, where he dumped her unceremoniously on the bed.

"Now, stay there before I give you the spanking you so richly deserve for all the trouble you've caused me," Apache ordered, and turned away.

Emerald thought her head would leave her shoulders from the force of the fury that possessed her. She scrambled off the bed and stood glaring at him with her balled fists braced on her hips. "You can't keep me here against my will."

Exasperated, Apache drew in a deep breath. He was cold and hungry, and the girl was trying his patience to the limit. Slowly he turned to look at her. "I can and I will."

A chill that had nothing to do with the weather raced up Emerald's spine as she realized the truth in his words. He could force her to do whatever he chose. She could not match him in size or strength. Her only hope was to convince him to let her go, and if she could not do that, then she would have to find a way to escape from him before he finished what he had begun that morning.

"Why won't you just let me go?" she asked simply.

Apache regarded her for a long, thoughtful moment, wondering the same thing. It would be so simple to let her walk out of the cabin and out of his life. He was not responsible for her, yet there was something that made him want to protect her, even from herself. She was so young and vulnerable. Apache doubted if she would appreciate his assessment, but he sensed it to be true, no matter how much she spat and clawed.

In some ways, Emerald Banyon reminded him of himself when he had first come west. Youth had a tendency to use bravado to bluster through situations in order to hide their fear of things they could not handle. And that was what Emerald had been doing. She sought to veil the fear she felt at being alone in the wilderness with a man that she did not know. He could understand her anxiety at being forced into such a situation, but for the life of him, he didn't understand her accusations against him.

"Emerald, I won't harm you," he said in an effort to erase the wary look in her eyes. "But I can't let you try to make it to Denver on your own. It would mean your death. It's still fifteen miles or more into town and you'd never make it on foot with the snow so deep."

Reluctantly, Emerald admitted that he was right, yet the thought of remaining in the tiny cabin with him was still unsettling. She didn't trust him or the strange feelings his presence created within her. The brief moment she'd spent in his arms that morning had made her realize that there were places within her that had not been explored, and she was wary of venturing into that uncharted territory. She wanted no part of anything that stripped away her self-control and left her vulnerable to feelings she had not known to exist until she had met Apache.

"I may have no choice but to stay here, but I have no intention of sharing your bed again, if that's what you have planned, mister."

Emerald's words pushed Apache over the border of the self-discipline that he so prided himself on. He took an involuntary step toward her and snaked out a hand to capture her arm. He drew her slowly toward him. "It's time I proved to you that what you thought you imagined this morning is far from what would happen if I really wanted you."

Before Emerald could protest, he drew her against

him, wrapped an imprisoning arm about her waist, and captured the back of her head with the palm of his other hand to prevent her from moving as his lips descended on hers. His mouth ravaged her tender flesh, his tongue forcing her lips open to explore the sweet cavern that had never known a man's touch.

Emerald gasped as a streak of lightning seared its way through her body at the intimate caress. It sizzled through her veins, melting all in its path. Her knees turned to liquid and she had to cling to his shoulders to support herself beneath the force of the heady sensations that washed over her, shaking her to the very core of her being. She trembled under the onslaught and unconsciously molded her body against his lean form as the kiss deepened.

Apache had meant only to teach Emerald a lesson about making false accusations. He was not prepared for the effect his example would have upon him. At the taste of her lips, desire welled within him, hardening his body and making him forget that he had sworn to keep his distance from the girl in his arms.

Savoring the sweetness of her mouth, he gentled the kiss, his lips and tongue enticing an awkward response from her. The innocence of it sent a thrill of excitement racing through his veins. It settled with an aching intensity in his loins and drove out all thoughts except his need to possess her. Ignoring the fact that this girl represented everything that he had vowed to avoid, he lifted her into his arms and carried her to the narrow bed.

Intoxicated by the riot of new feelings sweeping over her, Emerald did not resist as he lay down beside her. Her life had been so emotionally barren that the new sensations she was experiencing were like a drug to her senses, lulling all words of protest. Under his caressing hands, she forgot all of her grandmother's advice and gave herself up to the craving his touch created within her.

Her heart thumped wildly against her ribs as he raised himself above her and looked down at her with eyes that reflected his desire. The breath caught in her throat at the silent message they conveyed. He wanted her, yet he would not take her without her consent. This bearded giant, who had it within his power to take what he wanted without asking, now awaited her answer. Her heart welled with tenderness for this stranger who had entered her life less than twenty-four hours before, yet who had awakened within her emotions that drove all thoughts of the past and future out of her mind.

His consideration of her feelings shattered the last barrier of her resistance. The logical side of her mind told her that she was only a momentary diversion for him, but the heat that glowed in the pit of her belly eclipsed any argument against succumbing to her need to feel loved. The years of emotional deprivation made her greedy for satisfaction, no matter how fleeting. She wanted this man as much as he wanted her.

Emerald placed her hand against his bearded cheek and stroked the soft dark hair. He turned his lips into her palm and kissed it. His tongue made an erotic circle as his sleepy gaze held hers. She smiled up at him, aching to know the feel of his mouth on hers once more.

"Apache," she murmured as she slipped her arms about his neck and drew his head down to hers, giving him her answer with her lips.

With gentle hands, Apache unbuttoned her coat and shirt to expose the soft mounds of her breast to his caress. He closed his hand over a firm globe, enticing the nipple into a hard bud as he gently stroked the smooth flesh. Emerald's nostrils flared at the rush of heat that centered beneath his palm and arched her back to enjoy the caress to its fullest. Her arms tightened about his neck, but he eased away from her and lowered his head to the valley between her breasts. Her skin was like tinder that exploded into flame under the fire of his lips. She moaned as he slowly made his way to the hardened peak, where he took the nipple into his mouth, stroking it with his tongue and suckling. While his mouth played its sensual game, his hand moved down

her belly, unfastening her britches and slipping them
down her hips to allow him access to the shadowy glen
between her thighs. He fondled her there until her hips
moved to the same erotic music that flowed in his veins.

Apache's blood pounded in his temples as his caresses awakened the sleeping passions that lay within
her innocent young body. His excitement mounted as
he explored the moist depths of her and found that he
would be the first man to love her. A glimmer of light
seemed to penetrate the dark corners of his heart as he
removed his clothing and covered her with his lean
body. Apache eased her thighs apart and captured her
lips once more as he sought entry into the virginal
depths.

Feelings that he had thought he would never experience again welled within his soul as he thrust deep
within the tight passage that welcomed him with a quivering response even as he absorbed her startled cry with
his mouth. For a long moment he lay still, giving her
body time to adjust to him while the pain subsided.
Then he began to move, enticing a response from her
with each thrust.

The sting of his entry faded into a blur as Emerald's
pleasure began to mount. Her body tingled from head
to toe with each thrust. The curly hair on his chest
brushed the peaks of her breasts, heightening her ecstasy. She clung to his muscular shoulders and savored
the feel of his smooth flesh beneath her hands. The
sensations grew until she felt as if she would shatter
into a million tiny pieces. Her nails dug into the bare
flesh of his back as she arched upward, clinging to him.
She gasped as the universe about her began to sizzle
with the fiery rapture that swept through her and then
exploded into a burst of stardust.

Apache felt her release and sought his own. The muscles stood taut in his corded neck as he arched his head
back and moaned his pleasure when his essence spilled
deep within her. He trembled from the force of it and

collapsed over her, his sweat mingling with hers as they lay together, isolated from the world in the tiny cabin.

His heart still pounded against his ribs as he raised himself on his elbows and looked down into Emerald's love-softened eyes. Gently, he traced the smooth line of her flushed cheek with the tip of one finger, savoring the feel of it as he wondered how he had ever believed her to be only a child. She was a passionate woman; one he knew he would not soon forget.

"What are you thinking?" Emerald asked, capturing his finger and bringing it to her lips for a kiss before smiling up at him.

"I was just wondering how I ever made the mistake of thinking you were little more than a child. You certainly proved me wrong."

"I hope that teaches you a lesson. You'll learn to believe me when I tell you something."

Apache lifted a burnished strand of hair and wrapped it around his fingers. He gave her a roguish smile and arched one dark brow. "After what just happened, are you still convinced that I attacked you this morning? Or do I need to prove my point again?" Apache wriggled his hips provocatively against hers.

Emerald's smile faded. "What just happened between us didn't mean anything else to you, did it? You were only trying to prove your point. Well, for your information, I haven't changed my mind about your intentions. If anything, you've convinced me that I wasn't wrong. The only thing different is that you didn't call me Rachel this time."

Apache's face hardened. The warm glow left from their lovemaking faded into oblivion at the mention of Rachel's name. He dropped the strand of hair and moved away from Emerald. "I don't know what in hell you're talking about," he spat as he jerked on his britches and stood.

"You called me Rachel this morning when you kissed me. Is that your wife?" Emerald said, suddenly realizing the magnitude of her folly. She knew nothing of this man to whom she had given herself without a word of protest. He could well have a wife and family. With that thought, the temperature in the cabin seemed to drop by degrees. She shivered uncontrollably and pulled the quilts up to cover her nakedness.

"If it eases your mind, I don't have a wife, nor do I ever plan to have one," Apache said, shrugging into his shirt.

Another shiver raced up Emerald's spine as Granny Banyon's warning came back to haunt her. No decent young woman goes to bed with a man before they're married. Shamed by her own wanton behavior, Emerald looked away from Apache, unable to meet his eyes. Her mortification grew by leaps and bounds. She had disgraced herself with the first man who had crossed her path. Like a fool, she had ignored her grandmother's teachings and succumbed to needs that she had not known she possessed until Apache kissed her.

Under the heady influence of his caresses, all reasonable thought had vanished in a wave of passion and she had become just like Letty Harper. Her cheeks burned with humiliation. Her eyes brimmed with acrid tears of remorse. Within the past two days she had lost everything in her life that she treasured. Her father, Joe, and her innocence were gone.

The thought was nearly more than she could bear, but she refused to give way to her grief in front of the man who had played an intricate role in destroying her innocence. He had not forced himself on her, yet she could not stop herself from placing the major part of the blame upon him. His caresses had been responsible for her disgrace and he had known the effect they would have upon her.

Wiping her eyes with the back of her hand, Emerald drew in a deep breath and looked at Apache. Her heart beat uncomfortably against her ribs as she took in his chiseled, bearded face and realized that even her guilty conscience could not exorcise the attraction this man still held for her. Her only hope to redeem herself was to get far away from him as soon as possible. If she did not, she knew she would once more fall prey to the feelings he had awakened in her. If that happened, she would be lost forever in a world where she would exist only for him. She could not allow that to happen.

She had experienced enough heartache in the past because she had given her love to a man who did not return it, and she would not place herself in that situation again. When they left the cabin, this man would walk out of her life without looking back and she was determined to do likewise. She had made a mistake, but she couldn't let it ruin the rest of her life. She was a survivor. After Apache took her to Denver, she would put the moments in his arms behind her and turn her attention to finding the men who had killed her father.

Emerald's face reflected none of the turmoil of her thoughts as she asked, "Will you take me to Denver?"

Her simple request took Apache by surprise. After her outburst a few moments earlier, he had expected tears and condemnation, not this calm acceptance. The relief he felt at not having to defend his actions was only momentary before something deep inside him rebelled. This girl had touched him as no woman had done in years, yet she acted as if what they had shared had meant nothing to her. All of the old hurts surged forth in a blaze of fury.

"You're damned right I'm going to take you to Denver, and after that I hope that I never lay eyes on you again." Apache grabbed his coat and shrugged into it. "Get your clothes on. I want to get started."

Emerald did not argue. She didn't want to take the chance that he would change his mind. Collecting her scattered clothing from the bed, she dressed in haste. She had just pulled on her boots when the cabin door slammed back against the wall and a woolly figure appeared in the doorway with a rifle braced securely against his shoulder. From beneath a pair of bushy brows, he squinted at Apache for a long moment before a wide, toothless grin spread his mouth, which was nearly obscured by a long, shaggy beard that was a salt-and-pepper gray.

"Well, I'll be damned if it ain't Apache Ryan. I thought by now that some Injun brave would already be wearin' that purty hair of yourn on his lance as big medicine."

A slow grin curled Apache's lips. "Jeb, you should know by now that I have the luck of the Irish."

"Yep, I can see that you do if this young filly here is any sign of it," the old mountain man said, eyeing Emerald appreciatively. "What I wouldn't give to be thirty years younger right now. I'd give you a run for your money with this purty little thing. She's about as cute as a speckled hound pup."

Apache glanced at Emerald and chuckled at the flush that stained her cheeks a deep rose. "She might be as cute as a hound pup, but she's got claws like a wildcat, so take my advice and steer clear of her."

Jeb rested his rifle against the wall and scratched his chin. "Where's my manners? Here we been a-jawin' and I ain't even introduced myself to the lady. I be Jeb Taylor, missy." He pulled off his furry mitts and extended his hand to Emerald. "Welcome to my humble home."

"Thank you for your hospitality, Mr. Taylor. I'm Emerald Banyon."

"Banyon?" Jeb mused aloud, his face screwing up thoughtfully. "You any kin to the Jim Banyon who staked out a claim over in Clear Creek Canyon?"

"He was my father." Pain flickered in her eyes as a new wave of grief washed over her.

"Was?" Jeb asked. "Last time I seed Jim, he was fit as a fiddle and all excited about the nuggets he'd found. Somethin' happen to him?"

"Pa was killed two days ago." Emerald's words were a hoarse whisper.

"Sorry to hear that, missy. I didn't know your pa well, but he seemed like a nice feller the few times I talked with him in town. What killed him? The weather?''

''No.'' Emerald struggled to maintain her composure, but it was not easy. The mountain man's questions had brought back all of the pain and horror of her father's death. ''He was murdered.''

Apache stared at Emerald, stunned by her revelation.

''Hellfire and damnation,'' Jeb cursed. ''Decent folks ain't got a chance in these parts since that bunch of sons of bitches moved in here.''

''What are you talking about, Jeb?'' Apache asked.

''Claim jumpers, that's what. It ain't safe to stake out a claim in these mountains no more because of them.''

''Do you know who they are?''

''Hell, no. There ain't nobody who can tell you who they are. They don't leave anybody alive who can identify them.''

Apache frowned. ''It seems to me that even that simpleminded Denver sheriff could figure out who they are when they come to register the claims in their own names.''

''That's the funny thing about this bunch. They haven't tried to claim the diggin's, nor have they gone after anyone who's hit pay dirt. They just seem to enjoy killin' the poor bastards who are grubbin' out only enough dust to keep from starvin'.'' Jeb glanced at the silent, ashen-faced girl. ''Beggin' your pardon, Miss Emerald. I wasn't referrin' to your pa.''

Apache's speculative gaze came to rest on Emerald's face. He had his suspicions about who was behind the claim jumpings, but he needed proof. ''Do you know who killed your father, Emerald? Can you identify them?''

Apache's question made Emerald hesitate. Something in his tone made her wary of revealing all of what she knew about her father's assailants. He seemed far too anxious to learn if she could identify the claim jumpers. Her instincts warned her that her reticence could well save her life.

Emerald felt a chill race down her spine at the memory of how close she had come to death at the hands of the claim jumpers. She was the only person who knew the identity of one of them, but if it became known she might not live long enough to see them brought to justice.

Apache watched the fleeting expressions that played over Emerald's face, and when she didn't answer his question he asked again, "Do you know who killed your father, Emerald? Can you identify them?"

Emerald shook her head. "No. They were masked," she said, avoiding the truth. She would keep her secret until she knew exactly who the culprits were. Then and only then would she tell anyone.

"Damn," Apache cursed. "I had hoped when we reported your father's death to the sheriff that you'd be able to tell him something that might lead to the claim jumpers."

"I can't remember anything," Emerald said. Afraid that Apache would see that she was lying, Emerald turned her back on the two men and held out her hands to the warmth of the fire.

"Leave the little missy be, Apache," Jeb ordered. "She's been through enough without you badgerin' her. She's just lost her pa and is still grievin' for him. Give her time and then maybe she'll be able to recall somethin' that might help the law bring the varmints to justice."

The old mountain man's admonishment made Apache flinch. He'd been on the frontier so long that he'd forgotten what it was like to grieve over someone you loved. Looking at the stiff little back turned to him, the heart that he thought had petrified into stone went out to Emerald. She had endured much during the past days and it did not help his conscience to know that he had added to her burden. She was young and vulnerable and he had taken advantage of her during a time when her grief had left her emotionally defenseless.

At that moment, Apache didn't much like the image

of himself that his mind conjured up. Without thought to her feelings, he had callously seduced this brave young woman. To quench his own lust, he had disregarded the fact of her innocence, letting his passion override his resolve. He had accepted her response to his caresses without considering what effect their lovemaking would have on her.

Apache's face flushed with guilt. He knew an untried girl had little chance against his experienced caresses. He could place no blame on Emerald for what had happened between them. He alone was at fault.

He felt the need to reach out to her and take her in his arms to give her comfort, but he could not force his legs to carry him across the few feet that separated them. The wall that he had built about himself through the years could not be so easily breached. It would take far more than a moment of compassion for one young woman to break down the barriers around his heart.

Jeb regarded Apache curiously, his keen eyes noting the strained expression on the younger man's face as he gazed at the girl by the fire. He wondered briefly at the tension he sensed between the two youngsters, but then he shrugged it off. It was none of his business. He'd lived far too long by keeping his nose out of other people's affairs to change his ways now. If there was a problem between the young'uns, they could work it out. All he wanted was to settle down by the fire and enjoy some of the Taos Lightning he'd brought back from Denver for the winter.

"Well, I believe I'll go and unload Ole Bessy. She ain't much of a hoss, but she's all I got to get me where I'm a-goin'."

At the mention of the horse, Apache snapped out of his dark mood. "Jeb, we need to get to Denver, but we'll never make it on foot in this snow. I'll—"

Jeb held up a gnarled, silencing hand and gave Apache another toothless grin. "Bess ain't for sale, but I guess I can lend her to you for a time if you'll make sure the ole girl is well taken care of. Like I said, she ain't much to look at, but she's all I got.''

"I'll see that Bessy gets the best Denver has to offer until I can get her back to you," Apache said, and grinned.

"I guess that's all a man can ask. Let's get the ole girl unloaded and fed, and then you're welcome to her." Jeb paused at the door and looked back at Emerald. The wrinkles in his aged face deepened. "Missy, I hope they get whoever shot your pa."

"They will, Mr. Taylor. I can promise you that," Emerald said without looking away from the fire.

Apache flashed her a curious look before he followed Jeb Taylor out into the icy day.

Chapter 4

By the time Emerald and Apache reached the mining town, Emerald's teeth were chattering from the cold and her bottom ached from riding pillion on the bony old mare. Jeb Taylor's assessment of Bessy had been more than accurate, but her rangy appearance belied her great strength. She appeared to be little more than a stack of bones, but she had carried them with ease the last fifteen snowy miles through the foothills to Denver.

Emerald gaped with astonishment as they rode through the neat rows of cabins and clapboard houses that reached nearly to the bluffs. Since her brief visit two months ago, the town had grown by leaps and bounds. Businesses of all kinds had been hastily but grandly built with imposing false fronts and real glass windows. Saloons, stables, bakeries, and mercantile stores as well as sundry other establishments lined the neatly plotted streets.

People were everywhere. The freezing weather appeared not to hinder them as they went about their business. Bullwhackers filled the air with the cracking of their whips and their loud obscenities, shouting at those in their path as they drove the freight wagons along the rutted streets. Miners, who had come into town for the winter, lounged in saloon doorways. Their noisy arguments carried into the streets over the raucous cries of the dealers who hawked their trade inside the gambling halls.

It was an unnerving sight to Emerald, and she unconsciously tightened her arms about Apache's waist as she gazed at their surroundings. The crowds and activity made her uneasy after spending the past months alone with her father. She had expected the mining town to be different, but she had been certain that she could handle any situation that presented itself to her. Now, looking around at the crowded streets, she did not feel as assured of her abilities to cope in this strange environment.

The insecure little girl who still dwelt within her wanted to run and hide from this new and intimidating world that she had been thrust into because of her father's death. To her, it seemed like a great beast, waiting with open jaws, ready to devour those who were weak and defenseless.

That thought did little to ease Emerald's apprehension of the future that awaited her in a place where men's dreams were of gold and the pleasures it could buy. Her flagging confidence sank further when Apache reined in Bessy in front of the Denver House Hotel and dismounted. The moment she had been dreading had come. She would now be left alone.

Apache reached up and grasped her about the waist, easily lifting her down from the mare's back. He noted the white line of tension that had formed about her lips as he set her on the ground. Troubled by her expression and by the thought of leaving her at the mercy of untold dangers, he came to an abrupt decision. One that was totally out of character for a man who prided himself on the fact that he lived his own life without becoming involved in other people's lives.

"You're not staying here. You're coming with me to Hannah's," he said.

"You've done as I asked. You don't have to trouble yourself with me any longer. What happened between us does not make me your responsibility."

"I damn well know that you're not my responsibility, but I also know what can happen to a young woman alone in a town where women are few and far between. Denver is full of men who haven't had a woman since coming west. It's dangerous for any woman, much less one of your age and looks."

Two spots of color touched Emerald's cold cheeks at his backhanded compliment and she quickly looked away from his inscrutable dark eyes in order to hide her feelings. His concern, no matter how offhand it might be, touched something deep within her. Yet she recoiled from the warm glow it created. She'd already made one mistake with this man and could not allow herself to make another by believing he cared about her welfare.

"I can take care of myself," Emerald said with more confidence than she felt.

"I've seen how you take care of yourself. You're coming with me and I'll not hear any argument about it."

Apache's domineering manner struck the right chord to rejuvenate her faltering courage. Emerald's eyes snapped with annoyance as she glared defiantly up at him. "You may have been able to force me to do your will back at the cabin, but I doubt you'll be able to do the same here. If what you've said is true, then I would bet there are enough men here who would be willing to come to my aid if I cried out for help."

Apache's eyes glittered like polished onyx as he looked down into the stubborn young face. His earlier assessment of that small, squared chin had indicated that she had an obstinate nature and it had proved true far too often to suit him. In the last twenty-four hours he'd had enough of it, and he was washing his hands of her. At this point in his life he damned well didn't need that kind of trouble, no matter how guilty he felt. He'd lived with a nagging conscience before and he'd do so again when Emerald Banyon was no longer in his life.

"If that's the way you feel, then far be it from me to

try to change your mind," he ground out between clenched teeth. "Enjoy your stay in Denver. It should prove interesting." Apache grabbed Bessy's reins and easily hoisted himself back into the saddle. "If for some reason the Denver House Hotel doesn't suit your taste, Hannah's boardinghouse is at the far end of town." With that, he kicked the old mare in the side and rode away, leaving Emerald staring after him.

Emerald's temper abruptly cooled when Apache rode out of sight. The heat of her anger had overshadowed her insecurities, but now that he was gone, she was left feeling slightly bewildered. Turning, she looked up at the barnlike structure of the Denver House. The long, narrow, pine-boarded building did not look inviting, nor did the sounds that issued from its smoky, lantern-lit interior help to ease the nervous lump that settled in the pit of her stomach. She didn't like the thought of having to stay in such a place, but after refusing to go with Apache to the boardinghouse, she had no other choice.

Drawing in a deep, resigned breath and mustering up all of her courage, Emerald crossed the planked sidewalk to the wide double doors of the hotel. She paused upon the threshold and stared, eyes wide with disbelief at the sight before her. The front half of the Denver House was a large saloon. It was packed to the rafters with prospectors drinking and gambling. The clamor of their laughter and loud voices as they made the effort to talk and be heard was deafening. Emerald felt her courage fail her.

"I can't go in there," she said, but before she could turn away, several miners, staggering under the effects of Taos Lightning, blocked her path of escape.

"Well, lookee here," one drunk said, his southern drawl slurred by the liquor he had consumed. "What can we do for you, little lady?"

"Nothing," Emerald answered. "I thought the Denver House was a hotel, but I was mistaken." She attempted to push her way past the three but could not budge them.

"You ain't mistaken. This here is a hotel, the finest that Denver has to offer. The rooms are in the back, if you're a-wantin' to rent one. Come on and I'll take you over to the owner. He'll fix you right up. Then maybe you'd be interested in joining us for a little celebrating. Josh, here, found some color at his claim this week."

Before Emerald had time to decline their offer, the three men made the decision for her. They swept her across the crowded saloon toward the long bar where weathered miners wearing hobnailed boots lounged, sipping the raw liquor from New Mexico.

"Hey, Calvin, I've got you a customer. This little lady wants to rent a room," the drunken miner called to the man wearing a white shirt and silver arm bands standing behind the bar.

The proprietor of the Denver House turned the bartending duties over to the man at his side and came toward them. His gaze swept over Emerald knowingly as he said, "You want to rent a room?"

"She shore does," said the spokesman of the three before Emerald could deny that she had any such intention.

"Let the lady talk for herself, will you, Zack?" Calvin said, his gaze never leaving Emerald's face. "Do you want a room or not?"

"I had planned—" Emerald began, but her words were cut off by Zack.

"Of course she does. Come on, boys, let's give the little lady the grand tour and get this thing settled so we can get down to the business of celebrating."

Again without waiting for Emerald's consent, Zack took her by the arm and elbowed through a group of miners in a heated discussion over local politics. He led her toward a door at the rear of the saloon. Opening it, he paused for her to go in ahead of him. "This here is all there is," he said, swaying on his feet and squinting into the shadows beyond them.

The last objection that Emerald had to taking a room at Hannah's boardinghouse faded into oblivion as she looked at what the Denver House had to offer. The so-called rooms were in fact only one large room partitioned off into six separate spaces by cotton sheeting. Each was furnished with a narrow wooden bunk, an overturned barrel for a table, and a tin basin to serve as a sink.

"It'll cost you a dollar a night," Calvin said from the doorway behind her. "If you decide to stay, you'll pay in advance. Water is provided to wash in, and when you're through, you dump it on the floor to keep the dust down. You'll also have to supply your own blankets." Calvin's gaze raked over Emerald once more. "Since you'll probably be having a few customers, I'll let you have the space back in the corner. It'll give you more privacy to do your business."

Too shocked by the conditions to comprehend fully or to take offense at Calvin's insinuations, Emerald stared at the earthen floor, which had turned to mud from customers who had followed Calvin's advice, and shook her head. "I'm sorry. I can't stay here." She turned and fled back through the saloon and out into the cold twilight. She paused only long enough to clear her lungs of the stench and smoke of the Denver House before she set off in the direction Apache had said she would find Hannah's boardinghouse. After her defiant boast that she could take care of herself, the thought of confronting Apache again was unsettling, but to swallow her pride would be far better than staying in a place like the one she had just left.

The icy night had claimed Denver, driving all but the stoutest of souls from the rutted streets by the time Emerald managed to find the two-story clapboard house. Freezing wind whipped around the corners of the buildings and pierced her through the layers of her clothing. Her breath rose in a cloud about her and her hands were numb with cold as she knocked on the door. After several long, anxious minutes, she heard the click of the latch and the door swung open to reveal a woman wearing a brown merino gown with cream-colored lace about the high neckline.

"Can I help you?" the woman inquired, her tone less than cordial to the nearly frozen girl on her doorstep. Her plain features reflected her distaste as she took in Emerald's rumpled appearance. It wasn't an everyday occurrence to find a young woman at her door, much less one in such a bedraggled state. The girl looked as if she hadn't bathed in weeks. Her hair straggled down her back and her clothes were begrimed with soot.

"Are you Mrs. Becker?"

"Yes, I'm Hannah Becker. What can I do for you?" Hannah made no move to invite Emerald inside.

"I want to rent a room, if that is possible."

At last the woman stepped back to allow her to enter. Emerald quickly crossed the threshold into the welcome warmth of the boardinghouse. Chilled to the bone, she absently rubbed her arms as Hannah closed the door behind her.

"I have only one small room available. It will cost you a dollar a night, but that includes three meals a day."

Emerald felt suddenly light-headed with relief. "I'll gladly take it, Mrs. Becker."

Hannah gave Emerald a condescending smile. "Miss . . . I'm sorry, you didn't give your name."

"Emerald Banyon."

"Then, Miss Banyon, I do have certain rules in my household that I expect everyone to follow. I have my reputation to maintain, and I'll have no goings-on that will reflect badly on me. You'll behave as a lady while under my roof, or you'll have to find another place to live. I don't put up with any shenanigans from the miners who board here or from anyone else. Is that understood?"

Emerald nodded, slightly intimidated by the older woman's brusque manner.

"I also expect to be paid for your stay in advance. I

wouldn't dream of asking such a thing under ordinary circumstances, but times are hard right now and I have to make a living.''

"I understand, Mrs. Becker," Emerald said, digging into her pocket for the bag of gold nuggets. She handed them to Hannah. "These should take care of a few weeks' rent."

Hannah weighed the bag carefully in her hand. During the past months she had dealt in gold nuggets so much that she could nearly tell the exact value by the feel. "I'm afraid these will only pay for about two weeks' rent."

"Two weeks," Emerald said, dumbfounded by the fact that the nuggets were of so little value. She had thought they would be enough to see her through the winter. Her spirits sank as she wondered how she would live after the two weeks had passed.

"I'm afraid so. Do you still want the room, Miss Banyon?"

Emerald nodded again. She had no other choice.

"Good. Then I will show you up and let you get settled. I'm sure you would like to wash before you have supper." Hannah glanced about curiously. "Did you leave your bags outside?"

"No. I don't have any bags," Emerald answered, too disturbed by her new dilemma to note the frown of disapproval that marked the woman's plain, broad features.

"I should have known without asking," Hannah muttered under her breath as she turned to the stairs.

Emerald's legs trembled with fatigue as she followed Mrs. Becker up the narrow steps and down the hall to the tiny cubicle she had rented at such an exorbitant price. As Hannah had said, it was small, containing only a narrow bed with a patchwork quilt draped neatly over the foot railing and a washstand. But it was warm and clean, and that counted far more to Emerald in that moment than anything else. Compared to what the Denver House had to offer, the small room was a palace.

"I'll leave you to wash now. When you're finished, come downstairs. Supper is already on the table." The door swung closed on well-oiled hinges as Hannah left the room.

Emerald sank down onto the bed and leaned weakly against the rod-iron railing of the bedstead. Her stomach growled with hunger, drawing her thoughts away from the uncertainty of her future. With a start she realized that she had not eaten in over two days. The tumultuous events of the past days had eclipsed all else in her mind, even her body's hunger. Her fight for survival, combined with her shock over her father's death, had kept her going on nervous energy alone. Now that she felt she had finally found a temporary haven, her body was demanding sustenance.

The muscles in her arms and legs quivered with fatigue and her head felt as if it was filled with cotton as she pushed herself to her feet and crossed to the washstand. She wanted nothing more than to forgo washing and seek out her supper immediately, but after Mrs. Becker's polite insinuation that she looked none too clean, Emerald would not begin her stay at the boardinghouse by ignoring the woman's unspoken demand.

Emerald's hand shook violently as she lifted the porcelain pitcher. The cold water sloshed over the rim, splashing into the basin and splattering onto the polished surface of the washstand. Emerald hurriedly wiped up the spots of water with the sleeve of her coat before they could damage the wood. Having found a decent place to stay, she didn't want to get tossed out on her ear because of her carelessness.

Emerald lathered her face and hands, scrubbing away the soot until her clean skin glowed a soft rose. With her hasty ablutions finished, she took off her coat and ran her damp fingers through her hair in an effort to bring some semblance of order to the unruly mass that had not seen a comb or a brush for several days.

She knew her attempt to improve her appearance had

not achieved that goal, but without the benefit of clean clothing and a brush, she could do little else. Resigned to that fact she looked like a wild mountain woman, she left the room and followed the scent of freshly baked bread to the dining room, where Hannah Becker was entertaining her favorite guest.

Emerald stopped abruptly upon the threshold at the sight of the man sitting at the end of the table. It took her a moment to recognize him. Clean-shaven and dressed in a white lawn shirt that was open at the neck to reveal only a trace of the dark hair that matted his chest, Apache Ryan looked far different from the man who had left her in front of the Denver House Hotel. The change took away Emerald's breath. She was stunned to find that the dark beard had hidden such startling good looks.

She gaped at him, unable to tear her gaze away from the beardless face with its flashing ebony eyes and sensual mouth. She noted the dimples that formed at the sides of his shapely lips as they crinkled into a semblance of a smile at the sight of her standing in the doorway. Dragging her gaze away from the mouth that had given her such pleasure, she looked up into the devastating eyes twinkling with mirth.

"I see you decided to take my advice. Wasn't the Denver House to your liking?" Apache lounged back in the chair, relaxed and enjoying her discomfiture.

"They didn't have any rooms available," Emerald lied as she crossed unsteadily to the table and sat down. Her hunger, added with the miraculous transformation in Apache, was making her feel faint.

Apache accurately surmised the reason behind her ashen complexion. "You need to get some food into you before you fall over," he said as he leaned forward and began to fill her plate with white potatoes and fried chicken. Placing it in front of her, he ordered, "Eat."

Emerald obeyed Apache without hesitation. Her need of food outweighed all else. She devoured the crisp, lightly browned chicken, stuffing it into her mouth

without considering what Hannah would think of her
manners. At that moment, she was too intent on quell-
ing the hungry ache in her stomach to care what anyone
thought of her.

With her attention centered on consuming every delicious crumb on her plate, Emerald didn't notice the
heavy silence that descended over the room with her
presence. Nor was she aware of the jealousy that flamed
in Hannah Becker's brown eyes as she watched Apache's
reaction to her new boarder.

Like an animal guarding its territory, Hannah sensed
the danger the new arrival presented. Her instincts,
which had been honed to a keen edge by dealing with
other women more blessed with nature's gifts than she,
warned her that this young girl could destroy all of her
plans where Apache Ryan was concerned. She felt the
tension between them and saw Apache's unguarded expression as he watched the girl devour her meal.

The look in his eyes chilled her to the tips of her
toes. In all of the months she had known Apache, she
had never seen that expression in his eyes for her, even
at their most intimate moments together. It bespoke
tenderness, a feeling that she had begun to believe the
man did not possess.

Her heart began a frantic dance within her chest and
her breath grew short as the full implication of that look
settled sickeningly in the pit of her stomach. Apache
had told her of his encounter with the young girl, but
he had revealed nothing of what had transpired between
them while they were snowbound in the mountain man's
cabin. Yet she knew with every fiber in her body what
had taken place. He had made love to this girl, and
though he did not realize it, she had melted a little of
the ice that surrounded his heart. That thought was the
most disturbing to Hannah. After months of trying to
break through his defenses and make him love her, this
girl had done it without effort.

A wave of fury swept through Hannah and she
clenched the napkin in her lap in a stranglehold as if it

were Emerald's lovely neck. She would not lose Apache to this unkempt little wretch. She'd played the game in the past and had won against great odds. Herman Becker had been the most eligible bachelor in Columbus, Ohio, and she had succeeded in snatching him away from all of the beautiful women who had sought to become his wife. And she would do the same with Apache. If the little hussy thought to have him for herself, then she was in for a surprise. Hannah's cunning had outmaneuvered far more impressive adversaries than Emerald Banyon.

With her self-confidence restored by the memory of her success in winning her first husband, Hannah began to plan her strategy against her new adversary. Her best defense for the moment was to make Apache believe that she had befriended the girl. Then, when the time came for her to destroy their relationship, he could place no blame on her. Emerald Banyon would bear the brunt of his condemnation and she would be the woman he turned to for comfort. Satisfied with the ploy she intended to use to gain the man she wanted, Hannah relaxed.

"Miss Banyon, would you care for more bread?" she asked congenially, her warm smile hiding the swell of the raw emotions that seethed within her.

Replete and feeling more like herself than she had in days, Emerald pushed her plate back and shook her head. "No, thank you. The food was delicious, Mrs. Becker."

"Please call me Hannah. Since you're going to be staying here, I hope that we can become friends. Denver has so few women that a decent person can associate with, and it does get lonesome at times without another female to talk to."

"Thank you, Mrs.—I mean, Hannah. It is kind of you to accept me into your household. I don't know what I would have done if you'd turned me away," Emerald said, ignoring the dark brow Apache arched skeptically at her.

"I'm sure you would have survived," he interjected sardonically, his tone mocking her earlier boasts.

Emerald flashed him a hostile look. "With no thanks to you."

Apache's face darkened. "Listen to me, you little brat. If you have forgotten, I tried to get you to come here with me. But you insisted that you could take care of yourself without my help."

"I didn't lie," Emerald said with a smirk, raising her chin disdainfully in the air.

Apache clenched his lean brown hand. He had been unable to stop himself from worrying about the sharp-tongued little vixen after leaving her in front of the Denver House. He had nearly decided to give in to the urge to go back and make sure that she was safe when she had walked into Hannah's dining room. The relief he had felt at seeing her standing unharmed in the doorway to the dining room had made him feel slightly giddy. Now he wondered what had ever possessed him to even care what happened to her.

"No. You don't lie, but you have a way of leaving out half of the truth," Apache said, shoving back his chair and rising with the grace of a sleek panther. "I'll say good night to you, ladies. I have some business that needs my attention." With that, he turned and walked out of the room. A moment later the sound of the front door slamming closed seemed to jar the entire house.

"What was that all about?" Hannah asked, feigning dismay but secretly pleased by their confrontation.

"Nothing. He's just a bad-tempered, obnoxious man," Emerald said, and stood. "If you don't mind, I think I'll go to my room. After so many months of sleeping in a bedroll, it's going to be nice to lie in a bed again."

"Certainly. I know you must be exhausted after traveling all day in such weather."

Emerald flashed a curious look at her landlady. "How did you know that I had been traveling all day?"

"Apache told me earlier of your meeting. He said

that he'd found you nearly frozen in the blizzard and that the two of you stayed in Jeb Taylor's cabin to wait out the storm.''

''Oh,'' Emerald answered. She felt the heat rise to her cheeks at the memory of her stay with Apache. She prayed that there were no visible signs left of her sins for this decent woman to see, or she would lose the only friend she had in Denver or anywhere else in the world for that matter. And at the moment she needed a friend desperately.

Hannah smiled to herself at the stricken look that crossed Emerald's face. She had surmised correctly about what had transpired between Apache and the girl. She would use that knowledge to her own advantage when the right moment presented itself.

''Then I'll say good night,'' Emerald said, and turned away before her guilt could be seen on her face. She wanted no one to know of her wanton behavior with Apache Ryan.

''Good night, Emerald. Sleep well,'' Hannah said. Reflectively, she tapped her fingers on the table as she watched the girl ascend the stairs. When she heard the bedroom door close softly behind Emerald, she mused aloud, ''Enjoy your stay, because it's going to be a short one if I have any say in the matter.''

Apache's mood was as black as the icy night as he made his way along the dark streets to the Gold Dust Saloon. After leaving Hannah's, he had considered going down to Indian Row to rid himself of the memory of the green-eyed vixen he had left at the boarding-house. But as quickly as he considered it, the thought soured.

In his present state of mind he wanted nothing more than to get rip-roaring drunk. Maybe if he drank enough, the alcohol would rid him of the memories and feelings that had resurfaced because of Emerald. He wanted to feel numb again. As long as he kept his emotions in check, he could finish the business he had come to Denver to settle. Until that was accomplished, he could allow nothing into his life that might complicate it. Especially a sharp-tongued young woman with mesmerizing green eyes.

His shoulders hunched against the cold, Apache strode into the Gold Dust Saloon. In a glance he picked out the troublemakers in the crowd. Usually he avoided such men. It was far easier to keep to yourself than to have to kill a man because liquor had made him suddenly believe that he was fast with a gun or good with his fists. Tonight, however, he was in no mood to step aside for anyone. If a man came to him looking for a fight, then he would gladly give him one.

"Give me a bottle of Taos Lightning," he said to the bartender, and slapped a coin down on the polished surface of the bar. When the bartender set a glass and a bottle in front of him, he poured himself a stiff drink and downed it in one swallow. The raw liquor from New Mexico burned all the way to his stomach and warmed his insides as he turned to survey the room once more. Spying a table near the rear of the saloon where he could keep his eye on the rough-looking crowd, he picked up his bottle and maneuvered his way through the throng of miners debating the current state of the Jefferson Territory.

He caught only snatches of the conversation but knew their heated discussion was over the poll tax that had been levied on each voter in the territory. The same argument could be heard in every place where the miners gathered. Next to gold, politics had been the main topic of any conversation in Denver in recent months. The unrest that was fomenting back East between the North and the South had made its way to the mining town. The majority of men who came west were against slavery and argued in favor of changing the Jefferson Territory's name because of their dislike for the slaveholding statesman Thomas Jefferson, for which it had been named. He'd heard a gamut of names suggested, from the Indian Yampa to the Spanish Colorad and San

Juan. One amorous miner who missed his sweetheart even suggested it be called Lula after her.

In time it'll be settled, Apache mused, putting the men's conversation out of his mind as he relaxed his lean frame in a chair with his back to the wall. It was a habit that came with his life-style. Life on the frontier was often dangerous, and he had soon learned that if you wanted to stay alive, it was best to guard your back at all times. He'd seen too many men die by being shot in the back by the type of men who carried their guns low on their hips and strapped to their thighs. They enjoyed the sport of killing just to carve another notch in their guns.

Downing another glass of the fiery liquor, Apache surveyed the crowd once more before his dark gaze settled on the dandily dressed man at the far end of the room. He was playing blackjack with a group of miners. Behind him stood his ever-present bodyguard, Red Beaudine. The gunman reminded Apache of a red-spotted lizard as he lounged with his back against the wall, his eyes darting about the room.

Apache narrowed his eyes as he watched the gambler rake in his winnings and then deal out the cards. Apache's lips thinned into a hard line and his fingers tightened about the glass in his hand as his hatred of Cash Dalton rose like bile in his throat. The man, with his handsome face and lily-white hands, looked far too dandified to have the nerve to commit murder, but his appearance did not fool Apache. He knew that the greed that ruled Cash Dalton would make him stoop to any crime to get his hands on the right-of-way for the railroad.

Apache refilled his glass with liquor and tossed the drink down his throat as if to wash back the hatred before it could make him cross the room and strangle Dalton with his bare hands. He had set out to ruin the gambler, but he had not considered the lives that would be lost during the interim. He suspected that Emerald's father had been one of Dalton's victims, and because of his murder, as well as others, Apache had to make sure that the gambler did not just lose everything as he had first planned. He now had to find proof of Dalton's guilt and see him hanged.

"If only Emerald could identify the claim jumpers," Apache muttered under his breath as a buxom blonde leaned over the table and smiled provocatively at him.

"You've been without companionship too long, Apache, if you're talking to yourself."

A slow smile curved Apache's sensual lips as he pulled out the chair to his right and nodded to it. "Then why don't you join me, Sal?"

The woman, known to the customers of the Gold Dust Saloon as Lusty Sal, slid into the chair and propped both elbows on the table, exposing more of her heavy breasts to Apache's view. Her red-painted lips parted to reveal even white teeth, an asset that was rare in a woman in her profession.

"I saw you come in, but from the look on your face, I didn't know if you'd appreciate my company tonight," she said.

"It's this damned weather. It's cold enough out to freeze a man in his tracks," Apache said as he motioned the bartender to bring Sal a glass.

"There are ways to keep warm," Sal said, moving her knee to rest against Apache's leg. Her hand soon followed, her fingers massaging the sinewy muscles of his thigh.

Apache eyed Sal through half-closed lids. The combination of whiskey and her fondling drew his mind away from his plans for Cash Dalton. He felt himself stir as her hand slipped up his thigh to the junction of his legs. He swelled under her experienced touch as she caressed him through his britches.

"Do you have any suggestions?" he asked wryly.

Sal glanced toward the stairs that led up to the second floor where she and the other hurdy-gurdy girls who worked for Cash Dalton lived, then turned her sultry gaze on Apache. "My first suggestion is that we go upstairs, and then I'll gladly show you how to get warm."

"Then what are you waiting for, Sal?" Apache asked as he stood. The Taos Lightning he had consumed at such a rapid pace made the room tilt at an odd angle as he followed Sal across the crowded floor, where the hurdy-gurdy girls were selling their dances for a dollar for five minutes. He staggered as he reached the landing at the top of the stairs, but managed to catch the banister before he tumbled back down. Giving Sal a lop-sided smile and quirking an eyebrow at her, he draped an arm about her shoulders and let her lead him the rest of the way down the dimly lit hall to her room.

"I've never seen you this drunk before," Sal said as she helped him to the bed. "But if I have whiskey to thank for you being here, then I'm not complaining." She pushed him onto his back and pulled off his boots before she began to undress him. Her fingers worked swiftly at the buttons on his coat and spread it back to reveal his shirt. She unbuttoned it with equal ease, running her fingers through the mat of fine dark hair on his exposed chest.

"Damn, Apache," she murmured breathlessly. "You don't know how long I've waited for this. I'd begun to wonder if you'd ever get tired of the Widow Becker." Sal didn't wait for an answer before lowering her mouth to his, eager to taste the lips that had enticed her since the first day Apache had walked into the Gold Dust.

Apache lay passive for only a moment beneath her experienced lips. His whiskey-fogged senses conjured Emerald's image into his mind in place of the woman in his arms, and he returned the kiss with a burning intensity. His hands roved over Sal, tearing the cheap lace of her gaudy gown to expose the white globes of her breasts. His body was hard with desire as he murmured, "Emerald," and lowered his face to the heavy mounds. The scent of Sal's cheap perfume filled his nostrils, triggering something deep in his mind and making him realize that this woman was not the one his body craved. His passion withered as his senses abruptly cleared. He felt as if someone had doused him with a bucket of icy water from the Platte River, which bordered one end of town.

"Damn," he muttered as he pushed himself away from Sal and sat up. He ran a hand through his hair and shook his head. He still felt the effect of the Taos Lightning, but he had not drunk enough to make him forget the things he wanted to erase from his mind.

"I'm sorry, Sal. This isn't going to work." Reaching into his pocket, he withdrew a twenty-dollar gold piece and placed it on the bedside table.

"Keep your money, Apache. I wasn't doing this one for pay," Sal said. She picked up the coin and tossed it to him.

Apache pocketed the money. "Sal, I don't know what to say. This has never happened to me before."

Sal's face reflected her disappointment, yet she shrugged. "You're not the first man who's wanted another woman when he's come here. And I doubt you'll be the last."

"Hell, that has nothing to do with it. I drank too much Taos Lightning."

"That's what they all would like to believe. Go back to your Emerald, Apache. She's the one you want."

"Sal, I—" Apache began, but Sal shook her head.

"Don't feel sorry for me. If you want to pity someone, it should be Hannah Becker. She's the one who's had her cap set for you since the first day you set foot in Denver."

"Leave Hannah out of this. We're friends and that's as far as it goes."

Sal threw up her hands in disgust at how blind men could be to a woman's feelings. They never saw what was staring them in the face. Half of Denver knew the Widow Becker was only waiting for the right moment to spring her trap, but Apache could not see it.

"So be it," Sal muttered as she stood up and readjusted her clothing. She gave Apache one last provocative smile. "Just remember: If you should ever change your mind, then it's on the house."

"How would your boss feel about that?" Apache asked, probing Sal's loyalty to the man he hated.

"What he doesn't know can't hurt him, is my motto," Sal said, and laughed. She didn't add that Cash kept up with the number of men she brought upstairs and she'd have to fork out part of her night's earnings because she hadn't charged Apache.

"Then I'll remember your invitation," Apache said, and smiled with satisfaction. He had found another flaw in Cash Dalton's defenses. Sal's questionable loyalty might be of value in the future.

"Good night, Sal," Apache said as he shrugged into his coat and then left her. His mood had improved little from his visit to the Gold Dust Saloon. All he had gained was a slight buzz in the head and the scrap of information about Sal's loyalty. Disgusted with himself, he made his way back to the boardinghouse, where Emerald slept curled up on her narrow bed, completely unaware of the man who could not rid her from his mind.

Chapter 5

Emerald awoke to the appetizing smell of bacon frying in the kitchen. Savoring the scent and the warmth of her small bed, she yawned and stretched her arms leisurely above her head. Well rested, she smiled with pleasure at the homey comfort provided at the boardinghouse. Until that moment she had not realized how much she'd missed such basic things as sleeping in a bed with sheets. Since she'd left Granny Banyon's, her bed had consisted of a pallet on the ground with rough woolen blankets to keep her warm. The cabin her father had hurriedly constructed had been meant as a shelter against the elements, not as a home. Jim Banyon had been far more interested in panning for gold than in worrying about any discomfort his daughter might feel in the rustic accommodations.

With the thought of her father, the serenity of the moment fled. Emerald's smile faded as she threw back the covers and sat up. She didn't have time to lounge about in bed. She had to see the sheriff and report her father's murder and then try to find some means of making a living. Her rent was paid for two weeks, and before the end of that time she had to find work, or she would wind up out in the cold once again.

Emerald slid her bare feet to the chilly floor and crossed to the washstand. She bathed herself as well as possible in the cold water and, making a moue of disgust, she pulled on her grimy clothes. She hated the

71

fact that she could not take a real bath. All her life she
had been fastidious about her personal cleanliness, often making Granny Banyon throw up her hands in exasperation when, in the dead of winter, Emerald bathed
in the small stream that meandered its way through the
flat bottomland of their small farm. Her grandmother's
predictions that she would surely die of ague had not
stopped her daily ablutions, but her journey west had
effectively halted them. Since she'd left Georgia, rarely
had she been able to bathe all over, as was her custom.
Quick swipes with a soapy washcloth did not satisfy her
longing to feel clean from the top of her head to the
soles of her feet.

Resigned to her present state until she could alter it,
Emerald ran her fingers through her hair and went
downstairs. She found Hannah supervising a young
black girl's preparations for breakfast.

"Did you sleep well?" the older woman asked when
she noticed Emerald standing in the doorway.

"Yes, thank you. I believe last night is the first time
I've been comfortable since I left Georgia." Emerald
glanced at the pan of light brown biscuits the servant
had placed on the table. Her mouth watered at the sight
and her stomach rumbled with hunger, but she made
no move to seat herself at the table. Hannah had told
her she'd set strict rules for her household, and until
Emerald knew exactly what they were she felt it wise
not to eat until she was bidden.

"Breakfast will be ready when my other guest comes
down," Hannah said. With flour going for twenty-five
dollars for a hundred pounds and bacon selling for forty
cents a pound, she was determined that no one would
touch a bite of the high-priced meal until the man it
had been prepared for was seated at the table.

"There's no need to wait for me this morning, Hannah," came Apache's low voice from the doorway,
where he stood with one shoulder braced against the
door frame. He regarded them through squinted, bloodshot eyes. "I don't think I'm quite up to breakfast."

"But Betsy has made all of your favorites this morning. Fried bacon and biscuits with sawmill gravy." Hannah's tone did not reveal her annoyance at having wasted so much food when he did not intend to eat. Her frugality was a well-kept secret when Apache was staying at the boardinghouse. She plied him with tasty, generous meals in her subtle attempt to woo him. She was a firm believer in the old adage that a way to a man's heart is through his stomach. However, she also had her own motto: Fill his stomach and then his bed and soon you will be wed. It was remarkable how well it had served her in the past, and she had no doubt it would do so again in the future.

Apache recoiled at the thought of food. His face grew pale, and he swallowed several times against the nausea that rose in his throat at the smell of greasy bacon which filled the kitchen. "I'm not hungry this morning," he muttered before abruptly taking his leave.

Emerald could not contain her laughter at Apache's distress. The look on his face told her exactly what was troubling him. From her experience with her father after he'd come back from town drunk, she recognized all the signs and knew that Apache's business last night had been to find the nearest saloon. And today he was paying dearly for it.

"I don't see anything laughable. The man is ill." Hannah frowned at Emerald.

"Yes, he's sick from too much Taos Lightning." Under Hannah's censorious look, Emerald managed to suppress the urge to burst into laughter again at the memory of Apache's pained expression when bacon was mentioned.

"Miss Banyon, I'm sure that from your short acquaintance with Mr. Ryan you are not aware of the type of man he is. I know him far better than you do, and I can assure you that he is not a man who imbibes too much. I have never seen a man more in control of his life than Apache Ryan."

"You're right, Mrs. Becker," Emerald said, her tone

as cool as her landlady's. "I don't know this paragon of virtue that you seem to believe is Apache Ryan. I've only seen a man who has faults like any other man."

Hannah drew herself up, her back stiff and straight as she eyed Emerald. She did not like the girl's condemnation of the man she loved. "How can you say such a thing? He saved your life, Miss Banyon."

"I'm grateful for that, but that's the only thing I have to be grateful to Apache Ryan for," Emerald said, bristling under the woman's condescending attitude. Hannah Becker might defend the man with whom she was obviously in love, but Emerald knew Apache's other side. Much to her regret, she had experienced it firsthand. She had given him her innocence, only to find that it had meant nothing to him. The thought did little to cool the heat of her temper that the other woman's huffy demeanor roused.

Without waiting to be asked, she sat down at the table, filled her plate, and began to eat. For all she cared, Hannah Becker could believe what she wanted about Apache Ryan. He meant nothing to her.

The hostility that Hannah had been determined to hide flamed in her eyes. Her face grew red as she watched Emerald buttering one of the fluffy biscuits that had been meant for Apache's pleasure. She felt like strangling the girl. Emerald dared to malign Apache when she was the one at fault. The little chit was just like all the rest of her kind. If a woman had a pretty face and a man succumbed to her charms, she held the man responsible when in fact she was to blame for tempting him.

At the thought, Hannah's plain features hardened with determination. If this girl could entice Apache into bed once, she could do it again. She had to get Emerald Banyon out of her house and her life before it was too late. Last night Hannah had resolved to act as if she had befriended the girl in order to keep them apart. Now, in the light of morning, with Emerald's unkempt beauty across the table from her, that thought evaporated like a kettle of water set over a hot fire.

She was experienced in battling such women as Emerald Banyon, but in the past she had never had to deal with any of them under her own roof where the man in question could make the comparison between her and her adversary. If it came to that, Hannah knew that her own plain appearance would not hold up against such beauty.

"Miss Banyon, it seems to me that there are things that have happened between you and Mr. Ryan that make you uncomfortable in his presence. I can only guess at their nature since you have not confided in me, but I suspect it is not something that you would care to have known," Hannah said as she poured herself a cup of coffee. She watched with satisfaction as Emerald's head snapped up and her face grew pale with shock. Hannah took a long sip of the steaming dark brew, giving her insinuations time to unsettle the girl further before she calmly continued, "I see that you understand my meaning and hope that you also realize that I can't condone the two of you staying together under my roof. As I told you last night, I'm a decent woman and I have my reputation to uphold."

"But—" Emerald began, but Hannah shook her head, silencing her.

"I'm sorry. I truly am. I had hoped that you could stay here and that we could become friends, but under the circumstances I have no other choice," Hannah lied smoothly, wanting no blame for Emerald leaving her house to fall on her shoulders when Apache learned of it.

"You could ask Apache to leave instead of me," Emerald said, her spirit returning in full force at Hannah's transparent attempt to get rid of her.

"That's out of the question. Mr. Ryan is a longtime friend."

"And you don't want another woman around him."

"That's absurd. I'm only thinking of what's best for all concerned."

"Perhaps you are, Mrs. Becker," Emerald said as she shoved back her chair and stood. "But it's obvious that you care a great deal about Apache Ryan, and I want to assure you that you have nothing to fear from me. I want nothing more to do with the man, and when I find work and a new place to live, I will gladly leave your house. Until that time, however, I will stay right here. I have paid you two weeks rent, and I don't intend to leave before they're up." With that, Emerald turned and left the kitchen.

Hannah stared at the empty doorway, openmouthed. Emerald's show of spirit had startled her. She had not expected it from the girl, and she was glad that she would soon be rid of her. That spirit, combined with the girl's looks, would make her an adversary who would be hard to defeat.

Emerald felt like bursting into tears as she closed the door behind her and stared at the small room that only a short while before she had considered her haven.

"Damn you, Apache. This is all your fault," she cursed, and rubbed her burning eyes. "If Hannah wasn't so damned head over heels in love with you, I'd not have to leave. Due to you jumping into bed with every woman you meet, I have to find work and another place to stay much sooner than I had expected."

Fighting an inward battle against the despair that Hannah's notice of eviction had created, Emerald pressed her lips into a thin, hard line, squared her shoulders, and thrust out her chin. Determination glimmered in the crystalline depths of her eyes as she crossed the room and pulled on her red plaid coat. The sooner she found work and was out of the boardinghouse, the sooner she would be completely free of Apache Ryan. He had turned out to be the bane of her life, and she wanted to get as far away from him as possible. She had come to Denver for a reason and she would let nothing stand in the way of finding the men who had murdered her father, even if she had to sleep on the streets and beg for food.

Emerald turned and strode to the door. Her hand had just touched the latch when a sharp knock sounded. As she swung the door open, her heart leaped with hope that Hannah might have reconsidered letting her stay at the boardinghouse. At the sight of Apache filling the doorway, however, the small spark of hope died instantly.

"What do you want?" she asked. Her curt tone reflected her annoyance at finding the man who was responsible for her latest dilemma standing before her.

"If there's one thing I can say about you, Emerald, you're consistent. Does that temper of yours never cool?"

"What do you want, Apache?" Emerald asked once more, ignoring his chiding remarks.

"In your sour mood, I doubt you would appreciate anything I have to say."

"Then if you came here only to insult me, I see no reason to talk with you any further." Emerald started past him.

"Damn it, woman," Apache cursed as he shoved her none too gently back into the room and closed the door behind them. "I didn't come here to argue with you, and the way my head feels I'm in no mood to put up with your vixen's temper. I came to tell you that I reported your father's murder to the sheriff this morning. I had thought I was doing you a favor, but I see now it was stupid of me even to have considered that you might appreciate not having to go out in this weather and traipse all over Denver until you found the sheriff's office."

Emerald stared at Apache. The harsh words she had intended for him went unspoken as once again his consideration for her feelings touched something deep within her. Except for Granny Banyon, this man was the only person in her life who had ever thought of her welfare. And against her will she found herself remembering the tender moments they had spent together. Her heart lurched within her breast as her gaze met Apache's and she saw in the midnight depths of his eyes that he, too, was remembering their time in the mountain man's cabin.

"Emerald," Apache said, and took a step toward her.

"No," she said, quickly putting herself at a safe distance from him. She could not let herself succumb to the attraction he held for her. She had enough complications in her life without allowing herself to give way to the desire she saw glowing in his eyes. It would only be a momentary thing for him. Afterward he would return to Hannah Becker and any number of women that she did not know about. If that were to happen after she had once more surrendered all she possessed to him, she knew her heart would be shattered beyond repair.

Emerald swallowed, painfully aware of every inch of Apache's sinewy body and of the pleasure he could give her. Her voice was strained as she said, "Thank you for seeing the sheriff for me. Has he learned the names of the men responsible for the claim jumping?"

Apache drew in a deep breath and shook his head. "No, I'm afraid it's like old Jeb said. No one has lived to identify them. Have you remembered anything that might be of help to the authorities?"

"I . . . No," Emerald said. She was tempted to tell Apache of the man called Red, but once more her instincts warned her to keep silent. Until she learned the identities of all three men, especially the one with the black gloves, she could not divulge what she knew without endangering her own life as well as running the risk of letting the ringleader escape. Once she identified Red and he was arrested, the man who had ordered her father's death would have time to avoid being caught.

"I'm sorry to hear that," Apache said. He reached into his pocket and drew out a small leather pouch, which he tossed to Emerald. "I thought you might be able to use that to buy a few things. The clothes you're wearing are grimy enough to walk by themselves.''

"I don't need your money," Emerald said, tossing the bag back to Apache. "And I won't take it. I've paid my debt to you in full, and I don't want to owe you anything else.''

"It's not a loan, Emerald. Take the damn money and buy yourself something decent to wear." Apache offered her the pouch again, but she shook her head, refusing to take it. "Damn it, Emerald. You are the most hardheaded person I've ever met. I know you don't have any money left after paying Hannah the rent. You can't go around looking like something that's been pulled through a stovepipe.''

Grudgingly, Emerald admitted Apache was right about her appearance. Looking as she did, she doubted that she could find anyone in Denver who would hire her. In her present state the only job that might be available to her would be mucking out the stalls in the livery stable.

Emerald reached out and took the leather pouch from Apache. "This is a loan, and I will repay you as soon as I find work. I'll not take any handouts.''

"If that's the way you feel about it," Apache said, and smiled for the first time since he'd entered the room.

"That's the way I feel about it," Emerald said as she tucked the pouch into her coat pocket. "I'll need something decent to wear if I'm going to find work and another place to live." Emerald started past Apache on her way to the door.

"What do you mean by another place to live?" he asked, grabbing her by the arm and bringing her to an abrupt halt.

Emerald eyed him coolly. "Just what I said. I have no intention of remaining under the same roof with you and your mistress." She did not add that even if Hannah had not evicted her, she would not have been physically able to stay in the same house with him and know that he was sleeping with another woman. The thought

of it was too painful. She would not say that she loved
Apache Ryan, but he had found a place in her heart, a
heart that would slowly wither if she remained in this
house where she would be constantly reminded that their
time together had only been an amusing interlude for
him until he could return to Hannah.

"Emerald, I'm warning you. I'll not put up with any
slander against Hannah. And I'm damned well tired of
your wild accusations made at the drop of a hat. I
thought you had learned your lesson back at the cabin."

"Then you and Hannah are not lovers?" Emerald
asked, standing her ground yet hoping that he would
deny her charges.

Apache released her arm. "That's none of your business."

"I agree. What you do with your life is none of my
business, nor is what I do with mine any of yours,"
Emerald said, feeling the sting of tears threatening due
to Apache's silent confirmation of her suspicions. Even
as she accused him of being Hannah's lover, she had
wanted to be wrong. Now that she knew for certain it
was true, it hurt more than she had believed possible.
She lashed out at him, wanting to wound him as she
was wounded.

"And if it eases your mind, I did learn a very important lesson back at Jeb's cabin. I learned that you
don't care whom you hurt as long as it serves your purpose. I feel sorry for Hannah. She's in love with you,
but she's too blind to realize that you can't return her
feelings because you don't have a heart to feel with."
Not waiting for Apache's response, she ran from the
room, down the stairs, and out into the cold, bright
morning.

"Damn," Apache muttered under his breath as he
stared at the empty doorway. Feeling as if he had suddenly lost something, but not knowing exactly what it
was, he ran his fingers through his hair in exasperation
with himself as well as Emerald.

He had come here to tell her that he had seen the

sheriff, not to have a confrontation with her about his relationship with Hannah. If she wanted to leave the boardinghouse because of that, it was her choice. He'd done his last favor for the ill-tempered little chit, and he was washing his hands of her. She was on her own. As he made his resolution, he seemed to hear an eerie echo from the recent past.

"This time I mean what I say," he growled as he closed the door to the room behind him. But even as the words left his lips, he was already wondering what would happen to Emerald after she left Hannah's.

"It's none of my affair," he said, ignoring the sudden quiver in the pit of his belly at the thought of what Emerald would face trying to survive in a woman-hungry town like Denver.

The reflection of the sun against the white snow was blinding to Emerald as she stalked down the frozen, rutted street in the direction of the general store, which she had seen the previous night while searching for Hannah's. By the time she reached the false-fronted clapboard building, the pain in her heart had refashioned itself into a protective anger. The cold air, combined with her heated thoughts of Apache and Hannah, tinted her cheeks a vivid rose.

Hannah can have the rent I've already paid as well as Apache Ryan, she fumed silently as she stepped onto the planked sidewalk and crossed to the glass-paneled double doors. Once I buy something to wear, I'll find work and another place to live. I don't intend to stay a moment longer than necessary under the same roof with the two of them, even if I have to take a job mucking out the stalls at the livery stable.

Intent on taking the first step toward ridding herself of Apache Ryan and Hannah Becker, Emerald opened the door and strode into the store. She paused momentarily on the threshold to let her eyes adjust to the dim interior of the building before striding purposefully to the rack of ready-made gowns near the counter, where a clerk was helping another lady purchase a bolt of cloth.

Absorbed in her mission, Emerald failed to see the pale-faced man who stood by the rack of guns near the door. Nor did she notice the shocked expression that crossed his thin face at the sight of her before he quickly turned his back and pretended to examine the rifle in his hand. As soon as she was occupied with the gowns, he set the gun back in the rack and made a hurried exit.

Red Beaudine breathed a sigh of relief when the door closed behind him. Banyon's daughter had not died in the fire as he had thought, and when the boss learned of it, there would be hell to pay. Fortunately, the girl had not looked in his direction when she'd entered the store, but should their paths accidentally cross in the future, he might not be as lucky. Out of all the jobs he had done for the boss, she was the only person who had survived and could identify him. She had seen his face and knew his name.

The thought made sweat bead on his brow as he quickly crossed the street and hurried down the alley-way that led to the boss's office. He rapped sharply on the door, and a moment later it swung open to reveal the man he had come to see.

"Boss, she's not dead," Red said as he took off his hat and wiped his brow with the back of his hand.

"What in hell are you talking about?"

"Banyon's daughter. I just seen her down at the general store. She didn't die in the fire like I thought."

"Damn you, Red. I paid you good money to finish the job right, and now you come here and tell me that you bungled it after I left?"

"Boss, I don't know how the girl lived through the fire. When we left, the entire roof was in flames and the walls had already started to burn."

"But she did live through it. That's the problem. She can identify you. She heard Whiny call you by name, and that can lead the law to me."

"She also saw my face before I knocked her out,"

Red said hesitantly. Thinking that it didn't matter because the girl was dead, he hadn't told anyone about the episode in the cabin.

"You blundering fool! That makes the situation even worse."

"I can finish the job here just as easily, boss," Red volunteered in an effort to placate the man staring at him through narrowed eyes that glittered with malice. "Just give me the word, and she'll end up floating in the Platte, or someone will find her in an alley with her throat cut."

"I'll take care of the girl. You get the hell out to the ranch and stay there until I send word that it's safe for you to come back to town. Due to your stupidity and that skinny bastard who ran out on us as soon as you came back to town, she'll be able to recognize you on sight. If that should happen, it would be a simple matter for the law to put two and two together and figure out who's responsible for the claim jumpings. Now get going. What I don't need at the moment is more problems."

"You sure you don't want me to handle it for you, boss?"

"You've fouled it up enough as it is. Before I get rid of her, I intend to find out exactly what she knows and if she's told anyone. Since the sheriff hasn't been around asking questions about you, I doubt she's said anything yet. I want to know why she hasn't told the law all she knows."

Red did not question the boss's orders. He pulled on his hat and quickly made his exit. He could shoot an unarmed man down without a thought or stab an unsuspecting victim in the back in a dark alley, but he didn't have the nerve to confront a man on his own terms. Red Beaudine was a coward in the truest sense of the word.

Cash Dalton settled his lean frame in the massive chair and propped his feet on the desk in front of him. With his dark eyes narrowed in speculation, he considered the options left open to him since the Banyon girl still lived.

The first that came to mind was to do away with her at the earliest possible moment in order to get his hands on the last claim that stood in the path of his securing the right-of-way for the railroad. However, the memory of the girl's beauty intruded into his thoughts, hindering such a decision. He could not forget the emerald eyes and golden hair that had fired his imagination as he rode away from the campsite, leaving her at the mercy of Red Beaudine.

It had been years since any woman had piqued his interest to such an extent, and as he rode back to Denver, he had regretted not taking the time to enjoy her charms before he turned her over to his hired hands.

"Fortune has smiled on me again," Cash said to himself. His lips curled up at the corners sardonically. "I now have a second chance with the Banyon girl, and if all goes well, I'll also have the claim deed in my possession much sooner than I had expected." Cash chuckled with satisfaction. He did not doubt that he would succeed with the Banyon girl. He had Lady Luck on his side, and she had never failed him.

Emerald scrubbed herself from head to toe, basking in the pleasure the hot water and scented soap gave her. She lathered her burnished hair and rinsed it until it was squeaky clean and lay about her damp shoulders in a riot of dark gold curls. She had paid for the luxury of her bath with the money she'd had left after buying a blue merino gown, wool stockings, and a pair of sturdy shoes. She had also purchased soft cotton underclothes trimmed with lace and a woolen cape. When she had realized that she still had money to spare after her basic needs were met, she hadn't been able to resist buying a tortoiseshell comb and the soap that was scented with jasmine.

After her purchases were made, she had hurried to the bathhouse that was owned by an old Chinese couple who spoke broken English. Since they had never before had a lady in their establishment, it had taken her several minutes to make them understand what she wanted and then several more to convince them to let her use their bath. Since the bathhouse consisted of only one large room filled with tin tubs, she'd had to wait until they cleared it of male customers before she could enjoy her own bath in private.

The wait had been worth it, Emerald mused as she stood and poured warm water down her body, rinsing it free of the frothy lather. Regretfully she stepped from the tub and dried herself with a rough towel. Few things in the last few months had given her as much pleasure as that simple bath. The scented soap and warm water seemed to have washed away the trepidation she felt about her uncertain future. She felt capable of facing anything as she slipped on her new clothing and combed the tangles from her hair.

The girl who had trembled at the thought of finding work and a place to live had dissolved like the grime from her skin. With head held high and eyes sparkling with vitality, she walked confidently out of the bathhouse. She was a woman, not a frightened young girl, and she felt ready to take her life into her own hands.

Chapter 6

Emerald held the hem of her gown above her ankles to keep it out of the mire the winter sun had made by melting the snow on the streets during the afternoon. With her dirty clothes rolled into a wad and tucked firmly beneath her arm, she walked back to the boardinghouse as twilight deepened the shadows between the buildings along the way.

Her bright hopes of finding work quickly had paled considerably since she'd left the bathhouse. She had asked for work at every bakery, boardinghouse, and mercantile store she passed, but none had anything available. Every position was filled by prospectors who had come to town to wait out the winter. There were even male waiters at the few establishments that served food.

Tired from the long afternoon of rejection and disgruntled at having to return to Hannah's after resolving never to set foot in her house again, Emerald was in no mood to come face-to-face with Apache as soon as she walked in the door.

"Where have you been?" he asked, blocking her way to the stairs. With his hands braced on his lean hips, he stood waiting for her answer.

"I don't have to report my every move to you. You're not my father," Emerald shot back at him as she pushed her way past and started up the stairs without a backward glance in his direction.

Apache's temper snapped. Against his better judgment and all of his declarations to the contrary, he'd been worried about her since she'd left the boardinghouse that morning. It had been all he could do to keep from going out to find her when she hadn't returned by late afternoon. His frustration with himself at not being able to be indifferent to what happened to her, combined with her impudent manner, created a volatile mixture that made his blood boil. Infuriated, he took the stairs two at a time and grabbed Emerald at the top of the landing. He swept her up in his arms and strode down the hall to her small room. Kicking the door closed behind them, he set her on her feet and stood glaring down at her.

"Get out of my room, Apache," Emerald demanded. "You have no right to come in here, and if you don't leave, I'm going to call Hannah. I'm sure you wouldn't want that to happen."

"Call all you like. Hannah has gone to the church social tonight. She won't be home for several hours," Apache said. His eyes swept over Emerald, assessing the changes that had been wrought in her appearance since the last time he had seen her. She little resembled the girl who had left the boardinghouse that morning. Before him now stood a beautiful, desirable woman with hair of pure spun gold and jeweled eyes that flashed with fiery glints.

The heat of Apache's anger was abruptly diverted as he gazed at her. He no longer felt like a protective father as his desire surged through every sinew of his body, inflaming his blood until it simmered white-hot in his veins and making his heart pound against his ribs and his loins ache.

A muscle worked in his clean-shaven jaw as he tried to control his need to take her in his arms and make love to her until she cried out in ecstasy. He clenched his teeth and heard them grate together under the pressure as he fought the wildfire of his mounting passion.

Emerald's throat went dry at the look in Apache's

eyes. Butterflies fluttered in the pit of her stomach and
her breath grew short as she gazed up into their ebony
depths, recalling the last time she had seen that expression in them. She struggled to remain composed as her
mind feasted on the recollection of their moments together in the snowbound cabin.

Two spots of color tinted her cheeks as she stood
mesmerized by the unwanted memories. Anticipation
tingled in her blood, and her wayward heart beat a frantic tune within her breast as she clasped her hands
tightly against her middle to keep from reaching out to
him.

She felt like a battlefield. Her emotions warred with
her resolve against letting herself succumb to the heady
temptation of the desire she saw burning in his eyes.
Drawing in a shaky breath, she turned away from him
and strode across the room to the small, curtained window that overlooked the night-shadowed street below.
She did not look at him as she moistened her dry lips
and said the words that tore at her heart, "Please leave,
Apache."

"Emerald, we must settle this thing," Apache said
as he crossed the short space that separated them and
placed his hands on her shoulders. He drew her back
against him and leaned his cheek against her hair, in-
haling its clean jasmine scent. "I want you," he murmured softly.

Emerald shook her head and tried to move away from
him, but his hands were firm on her shoulders, thwarting her attempt to escape. "Let me go, Apache. This
thing, as you call it, can't be settled between us. I won't
be just another woman to satisfy you when your mistress is at her church social. I've already made one mistake where you're concerned and I won't add to my sins
by making another."

"Look at me, Emerald," Apache said as he turned
her to him. "There is no sin in making love to another
person."

"But there has to *be* love, Apache, and that doesn't

exist between us," Emerald said, her voice catching in her throat, her heart aching with the need to hear him say he loved her, but she knew he would not.

Apache cupped the curve of her cheek in his palm and gazed down into her earnest little face as he stroked her smooth flesh with his thumb. God, how he wanted her, but he would not take her. He had stolen her innocence in the heat of passion without considering her feelings, but he would not act so rashly again. He wanted her as he had wanted no other woman. But he could not, would not call what he felt love. His painful past still stood as a barrier against letting him believe that such a thing as love existed. Apache let his hand fall to his side.

"Emerald, there is something between us, but I can't call it love. All I know is that you stir my senses and make me forget when I'm near you that you are only a girl of eighteen. I crave the taste of your lips and ache to feel your body against mine. But I won't lie to have you. When you come to me, I want you to feel the same fire that is in my blood and to know the ecstasy that two people can give each other. And I want it to be of your own free will."

His words seemed to wrench her heart from her breast. Unbidden tears welled in her eyes as she stared up at Apache. She realized sadly that she had come to love this man with every fiber of her being, but she knew there could never be anything between them but lust. His words had confirmed that for her. Apache desired her but felt nothing more.

She was determined not to allow herself to live the rest of her life as she had lived the past eighteen lonely years: loving but never being loved in return. It was too painful an existence. She had learned a hard lesson from the years during which she had spent her time like a little puppy, waiting for a bone of affection to be tossed her way by her father. She knew her heart would not survive her living on the fringes of a man's life again, always hoping for love that would never come.

"Then there is nothing left for us to say, is there?" Emerald told him as one lone tear tumbled over her dark lashes and ran unheeded down her cheek.

Apache brushed the tear away with the tip of his finger and felt a hollow ache inside his chest as he slowly shook his head. "I don't guess there is." He turned and quietly left the room.

"Good-bye, Apache," Emerald murmured as the door closed behind him. "Good-bye, my love."

Hours later, she lay sleepless on her narrow bed. From the room below she could hear the clock on the mantel chime, counting the miserable minutes she had spent since her encounter with Apache. Unable to face him, she had not gone down to dinner. Her stomach now rumbled from hunger, but the ache in her heart overshadowed her need of food.

She could not rid herself of thoughts of the man who lay sleeping in the room only a few doors away from her own. Her heart told her to go to him, but her misgivings about her future if she gave into her needs would not allow her to heed its call.

Go to him, her heart cried as she tossed restlessly on her narrow bed.

Go to him and you'll make an even bigger fool out of yourself than you already have, her mind argued.

Take what love you can get, her heart urged.

And you'll gain nothing but hurt from it, the voice of doubt replied.

You have to fight for love, her heart countered.

But you may not win, the logical voice interjected.

"Stop it," Emerald cried, covering her ears with her hands. "You're going to drive yourself mad if you keep this up."

Go to him and grasp love while you can, her heart demanded as she threw back the covers and sat up. Without waiting for the other voice to try to stop her, she slid her bare feet to the floor, jerked the sheet off the bed, wrapped it around her, and left the room.

You're making a mistake, the voice of her misgivings said as she padded quietly down the hall and opened the door to Apache's room. But she did not listen. She had come too far to turn back.

The silver beams of the cold winter moon spilled into the room and across the bed where Apache slept flat on his stomach. Silently she moved toward the end of the bed and stood gazing down at him from the shadows. Her eyes swept hungrily up the wide expanse of his bare muscular back to the dark head on the pillow. For a long moment, she stood savoring the sight of his blue-black hair and lean profile before her gaze traveled down to the outstretched arm lying across the covers. Her eyes lingered on the brawny hand with its long fingers as she remembered his caresses and the pleasure they had given her. Her body stirred in response to the memory.

Feeling the warm glow of anticipation tingle through her veins, Emerald moved to pull back the covers but then froze. The shadows had obscured Hannah Becker from view. The woman lay next to Apache, smugly smiling up at her. Her plain face reflected her victory over her adversary for his affections.

Emerald felt as if a bucket of ice water had been dumped over her head. The sight chilled her to the bone and she had to slap her hand over her mouth to stifle the cry of misery and humiliation that threatened to come from her throat. With her agony welling inside the chasm where her shattered heart had once been, she fled back to her room. She fell facedown on the bed, burying her face in the pillow to shut out the mocking laughter of her misgivings, and sobbed herself to sleep.

At dawn she awoke, red- and swollen-eyed. She collected her few possessions and, without waking anyone in the household, she quietly left the boardinghouse, determined never to return.

Hannah hummed a happy tune as she set the table for two. Emerald Banyon had been gone when she awoke, and after what the girl had seen last night when she crept into Apache's room, Hannah doubted she would ever return.

Hannah smiled with satisfaction as she folded a napkin and placed it by Apache's plate. All her worry had been for nothing. The girl had not proved to be a formidable adversary after all. It had been a simple matter to get rid of her. All she'd had to do was let herself be found in Apache's bed.

Hannah's smile faded and her wide lips formed a petulant pout. The only thing that had not been easy was getting *into* his bed. It was quite by accident that Emerald had found her lying next to Apache. After the conversation she'd had with him at supper last night, she had feared she'd never have him to herself again. When Apache told her that they should refrain from sleeping together while Emerald was living at the boardinghouse, Hannah had known the true reason behind his request. He had pretended it was to protect her reputation, but she knew otherwise. He was too infatuated with the girl to need the comfort that Hannah could give him.

She had gone to bed alone and miserable last night but had not remained there for long. She could not stand the thought of losing Apache, and after tossing and turning for a while, she had gone to his room to try to reason with him. She had hoped to make him understand that if she had his love, she wouldn't care if the world knew of their affair, much less that stupid girl down the hall. It had taken all she had to humble herself to beg him for his love yet when she'd reached his room and crept silently inside, he had been sound asleep. She had been about to wake him when she'd heard the light rattle of the door latch. She had known instantly who Apache's other late-night visitor was and had stealthily eased herself beneath the covers so as not to awaken him. She had not planned what had happened, but it couldn't have worked out better if she had.

A frown pucked Hannah's brow at the memory of the

time she had spent in Apache's bed. After Emerald's hurried departure, she had snuggled close to him with the hope that he would awaken and welcome her. However, and to her great annoyance, he had not roused, even when she kissed him. Nor did the fact that he had called Emerald's name in his sleep soothe her turbulent emotions. The little hussy had managed to entrench herself in Apache's thoughts even as he slept. Remembering it, she curled her hand about a spoon with such force that the cheap tin plate bent under the pressure.

"Where in hell has she run off to now?" Apache said as he entered the kitchen.

Startled by his abrupt entrance, Hannah dropped the spoon, and it clattered to the floor at her feet. She quickly bent to retrieve it in order to hide the guilty flush that rose to her cheeks.

"I don't know what you're talking about," she lied as she calmly placed the spoon on the table and busied herself with the rest of the setting.

"Emerald, that's what. I knocked on her door, and when there was no answer, I looked in. Her bed has been made and all of her belongings are gone."

"I don't know why you're so upset. You knew that she intended to find another place to live."

Apache ran his long fingers through his hair in exasperation. "I know what she planned, but that doesn't ease my mind. She's too damned young to be on her own in a town like Denver. And I feel responsible for her."

"You're not Chinese, Apache. Because you saved the girl's life does not make her your responsibility. She's old enough to take care of herself. Sit down and have your breakfast. Maybe things will look better with a full stomach."

Apache pulled out a chair and sat down. Hannah quickly moved to fill his plate with biscuits and sawmill gravy. He stared at the steaming food, completely unaware that it was the same meal that had been prepared for him the previous morning. The miser in Hannah had not allowed her to throw a morsel of the expensive food away. After Emerald had finished eating breakfast yesterday, Hannah had quickly wrapped the precious biscuits and stored them away in the food safe.

Apache had no appetite, but he managed to eat in order not to disappoint Hannah after she had gone to the trouble of preparing his favorite foods. His mind still plagued with thoughts of Emerald, he ate in silence.

Hannah's irritation mounted by the moment as she watched him consume his breakfast without a sign of appreciation for such expensive food. She knew from his brooding expression that he was still thinking of Emerald Banyon. Her nostrils flared as she drew in an angry breath.

Damn the girl, she fumed silently. I thought my problem was solved by getting her out of my house, and now I find that she's still coming between us even when she's not here.

Hannah's temper snapped when he pushed his plate away, the food only half eaten.

"I've had enough of this. I'm not going to sit here and watch you worry about that girl. For the life of me, I don't know what's come over you lately, Apache. It's not like you to involve yourself in other people's affairs. But the way you've hovered over that girl since she entered this house, you'd think she was your daughter instead of a girl you've only known for less than a week. Or is there something else between the two of you that I should know about?"

"Hannah, there's nothing between us. If I've acted like her father, I have my reasons. She has no one to look after her since her father was murdered." Apache did not add that he felt indirectly responsible for Jim Banyon's death. And because of that he owed Emerald a debt. His plan to ruin Cash Dalton had touched more lives than he had anticipated when he had set it in motion. It upset him to know that his need for revenge had harmed other innocent people like Emerald.

Apache nodded as the thought crossed his mind. Until that moment, he had not been able to understand fully his own actions where Emerald was concerned. Now he knew that what he had felt for her came out of his sense of guilt. A wave of relief washed over him. He had begun to fear that he might be falling in love with the girl, and that was the one thing he had sworn never to do again. Suddenly feeling as if he understood himself again, Apache smiled.

With the realization of what had motivated his actions, a burden seemed to lift from his shoulders. He might be indirectly responsible for Emerald's father's death, but that did not make him her guardian. He owed it to her to see that Cash Dalton was convicted for Jim Banyon's murder, and he would see that the debt was paid in full. Once that was done, he would be free of any feelings that he had for Emerald.

In his desire to ignore the callings of his heart, he managed to convince himself that it had been guilt that had driven him instead of the deeper emotions he had denied for so many years.

Satisfied with his conclusions, he felt free again to pursue what he had come to Denver to do. He could now concentrate on bringing down his enemy without his life being complicated by a young girl with emerald eyes.

Grateful to Hannah for making him look at things in a different light, Apache pushed back his chair and stood. He held out his arms to her and she gladly ran into them. "You're a good friend, Hannah. You've made me realize what a fool I've been when it comes to Emerald. I can promise you that it won't happen again. She's on her own."

Hannah snuggled against Apache, burying her face in the curve of his shoulder to hide her triumphant expression. She had won.

Depressed and hungry, Emerald sank down on the rough-hewn bench outside of Barker's General Store and nibbled the cheese and crackers she had bought with the last coins left from the money Apache had given her. That money was now gone, as was her hope of finding work. The general store had been her last chance, and she was beginning to realize that she could not survive the winter in Denver on determination alone. Her throat went dry with the disquieting thought, making it difficult for her to swallow her meager meal.

Disheartened, she stared down at the last cracker, wondering where she would find her next meal since she could not return to the boardinghouse. The memory of Hannah Becker's smirking face rose in her mind to taunt her. The cracker in her hand crumbled as she unconsciously clenched her fist. No matter what happened to her, she would never go back to that boardinghouse. She had humiliated herself for the last time because of Apache Ryan.

She had nothing left but her pride, and it would not let her live under the same roof with Apache and his mistress. She preferred to beg in the streets than to stay at the boardinghouse and be constantly reminded of her shameful feelings for a man who cared nothing for her. She had given in to her heart last night, but she would never be that foolish again.

"Miss Banyon?"

Emerald looked up, startled. Her eyes went wide with surprise at the sight of the tall, blond woman. She had been so preoccupied with her thoughts that she had failed to note the woman's presence until she spoke.

"I'm sorry. I didn't mean to startle you, but I was in the store when you were asking for work and thought I might be able to help you," the woman said, her red-painted lips spreading to reveal even white teeth.

"You have work for me?" Emerald asked, coming to her feet, her young face lighting with renewed hope. Her flagging spirits rebounded instantly.

"The man I work for has an opening for a new girl, if you're interested."

"I need the work, but I'll be honest with you. I don't

have much experience doing anything beyond caring for the sick or panning for gold," Emerald said. "But I'm willing to learn," she added quickly.

"That shouldn't be too hard to do as long as you enjoy dancing," Sal said, and smiled.

A perplexed frown marred Emerald's brow. "Dancing?" she asked, wondering what type of work required dancing.

"Yes, you'll get paid to dance with the miners who come into the Gold Dust Saloon."

Emerald was flabbergasted by the woman's suggestion. She'd heard her father speak of the women who worked in saloons after he'd returned to camp and was still too drunk to realize that it was his daughter instead of one of his cronies whom he told about his latest conquest. He'd called them hurdy-gurdy girls and had bragged about the favors he'd purchased with his few hard-earned nuggets.

"I may need work, but I won't become a whore," Emerald said, incensed that this woman would think she was that type of person.

Sal's face went livid and her eyes glittered with anger. She felt like slapping the offended look off the girl's face. Sal knew exactly what she was, but she didn't need this little chit's condemnation to remind her. However, her better judgment won out and she managed to control the urge to give the girl a good set-down. Cash had told her to bring Emerald Banyon back to the Gold Dust, and Sal knew the man's temper too well to go against his orders. He was a demon when he didn't get his way.

"I'm sorry you feel that way. I was only trying to help."

Emerald's cheeks flushed crimson with embarrassment. She had no right to condemn this woman after the kindness she had shown to her. "I appreciate what you're trying to do, but I'm afraid that I could never sell myself, no matter how much I need work."

Sal shook her head as if she were talking to a misguided child. "I know what you've probably heard about hurdy-gurdy girls, and some of it is true, but they are hired only to dance with the customers, not to sleep with them. What they do after they're off work is their own business."

"You mean you really only want me to dance with the miners and that's all?"

"That's all. You get paid for dancing five minutes with each miner who is willing to pay a dollar for the pleasure, and you'll also be provided with room and board."

Emerald worried her lower lip with her teeth as she considered the woman's proposition. At the moment, what the woman offered was far more than she had. Her situation was precarious. If she didn't want to sleep in the streets, she honestly didn't have any recourse but to accept the work.

"Then if all I have to do is dance, I'll take the work," she said at last, pushing aside her misgivings.

"Good," Sal said, relieved that she wouldn't have to face Cash with the news that his latest little pigeon had managed to escape his trap. "My name is Sal. I'll take you over and get you settled. Once we get you outfitted in something that doesn't look like a schoolmarm's-Sunday-go-to-meeting clothes, then you can meet your new boss."

Emerald glanced down at the soft blue gown she had considered so lovely. To her it represented the proper attire for a decent young lady and she wondered again if she was not making a mistake. She gave a mental shrug. Of late her life seemed to be one big blunder after another, and given the choice between freezing to death or dressing like the woman in front of her, she would choose the latter.

Chapter 7

"*Thank goodness Granny can't see me dressed like this,*" Emerald mused aloud as she gazed at her reflection in the cheval glass. She could imagine the sermons on decency her grandmother would have preached to her if she'd seen her in the turquoise satin gown that Sal had given her to wear. The gown, with its low-cut, heart-shaped bodice, left little to the imagination. Her shoulders were bare and a significant portion of her breasts were exposed to view, as were her legs and ankles because of the short hemline that ended just below her knee.

"Granny Banyon would have had several choice names to call me and the nicest of them would have been strumpet," Emerald said to the image that did not belie the name. With her hair adorned with feathers and piled on top of her head and her lips painted red, she looked exactly like one of the women her grandmother had condemned.

Emerald turned away from the mirror, unable to look at herself any longer. She might not be a strumpet, but who but herself would know it once she walked out the door and down the stairs to the saloon below? Emerald squeezed her eyes tightly closed in an effort to shut out the thought of what everyone would think of her when they saw her nearly naked.

When Sal had led her through the saloon that afternoon, she'd had a small taste of what to expect tonight.

The men who crowded the room downstairs had whistled and called to her to join them at the bar, offering to buy her a drink or anything else she desired. She'd felt their eyes follow her all the way up the stairs, and she was left with the distinct sensation that she was a piece of raw meat about to be tossed to a pack of hungry wolves.

From the doorway, Sal silently observed the young woman through narrowed, speculative eyes. The girl Cash had ordered her to find was the same girl whose name Apache had called out when he'd visited her several nights ago. Sal was sure of it. There couldn't be more than one girl named Emerald in a town the size of Denver.

Sal frowned, wondering at the girl's sudden popularity with the two men. Something that she didn't understand was going on, and until she knew exactly what it was and how it would affect her, she'd keep her eyes open and her mouth shut. If the girl turned out to be a rival for Cash's affections, the knowledge that Apache was interested in her might be useful to rid herself of an adversary.

"Now that's better," Sal said, stepping into the room. "When the men see you, the rest of us won't have a chance."

Emerald raised pleading eyes to the older woman, silently begging for her understanding. Her insides felt like jelly, trembling at the thought of what awaited her. Her throat was dry and her words were little more than a hoarse whisper when at last she managed to say, "I don't know if I can go through with this, Sal."

"Sure you can. It's hard for everyone at first," Sal said, with more understanding than Emerald realized. But while she knew well what Emerald was feeling, Sal didn't feel sorry for the girl. The life she lived had long since hardened her heart against such sentiment.

Emerald glanced down at the turquoise gown. "Do I have to wear this? I feel naked."

"If you want to earn your keep, you do. If these men

wanted to dance with a schoolmarm, they'd go to a church social. Now, come on. The place is full tonight.''

"I can't,'' Emerald said, taking a step backward and shaking her head.

Sal shrugged a bare shoulder. ''Then if you can't, you can't. No one is forcing you to work here. Get your things and go back to where you came from. Maybe all that self-righteousness you've wrapped yourself in will keep you warm and fill your belly once you're back on the street.''

''Sal, you have to understand.''

Sal shook her head and raised a hand to stay her words. ''Spare me any explanations. I've been there. I know what it's like to be cold and hungry, but I also know how to survive. Your life is your own, and you make your own decisions. Now, I've got work to do. If you should change your mind, then you're welcome to stay.''

Emerald sank down onto the side of the bed as Sal left the room. Torn by two different needs, she was unable to make any decision. If she decided not to stay, she knew exactly what awaited her outside the Gold Dust Saloon: nothing. If she chose to remain, she would have room and board and no self-respect.

With her shoulders hunched and hands clasped tightly in her lap amid the shining material of her gown, Emerald sought desperately to dredge up enough courage to follow what she had been taught by her grandmother. It was not easy to obey Granny Banyon's teaching when the Gold Dust offered her food and warmth against the icy Denver night.

''Emerald, Sal said you'd changed your mind about working here.''

Emerald jerked about at the sound of the masculine voice from the doorway and instantly came to her feet. Her eyes widened with surprise at the sight of Cash Dalton. She'd met the owner of the saloon only briefly that afternoon. He had been playing cards with several

men and had given her only a cursory glance before
telling Sal to see her settled. Her own apprehension at
being in a saloon for the first time had made her too
nervous to notice much about the man's appearance.
All she remembered was that he had dark hair and eyes.

Now she stood immobilized, staring into the most
beautiful masculine face she had ever seen. Without
realizing it, she unconsciously compared him to Apache
Ryan. Both men possessed ebony eyes and had hair that
was blue-black, but where Apache's face was craggy
and masculine, this man's face was sculpted with an
artist's eye for pure beauty. His features were perfect:
symmetrical in every sense, from the even dark brows
to the well-proportioned lips that smiled at her from
beneath a silky black mustache. Though she suspected
from the touch of gray that silvered his sideburns that
he was at least ten years older than Apache, no age lines
marred his tanned skin.

However, unlike Apache, who dressed for comfort as
well as purpose in denim jeans and shirt, this man wore
a black suede jacket over a white lawn shirt with ruffles
down the front. More of the same peeked from beneath
the jacket sleeves at his wrists. A large silver belt buckle
sparkled at his waist above black britches that hugged
his thighs like a second skin, emphasizing the muscles
in his legs. His shiny ankle boots caught and reflected
the light from the lantern hanging overhead. He was
resplendent from head to toe.

Cash's smile deepened as he watched the effect he
had on Emerald. He was well aware of his appearance
and had often used it to his advantage in the past. He
had met few women who were able to deny him anything once he decided to use his charms on them. He'd
learned at an early age that women loved a rogue. And
if Cash Dalton was anything, he was that. He was a
born gambler who loved no one but himself.

"I didn't mean to startle you, but I thought I'd come
and see why you'd changed your mind about working
for me."

Emerald gave herself a sharp mental shake, breaking the trance that held her spellbound. Her cheeks grew red from embarrassment at the brazen way she had stared at him. "I—" she began but found herself suddenly tongue-tied.

"Has someone said or done something that has made you decide to leave the Gold Dust? If that's the case, they'll answer to me."

The lamplight made Emerald's hair shimmer like spun silk as she shook her head. "No one has done anything. I'm just afraid that I'm not suited to work here."

Cash leaned a muscular shoulder against the door-frame and casually folded his arms over his chest. "If you're worried about my customers, I can assure you that you'll come to no harm. I make it a point to protect the girls who work for me. If anyone gets out of line, all you have to do is tell me and I'll handle it for you."

"I still don't know, Mr. Dalton—" Emerald began, but Cash interrupted her.

"Cash."

Emerald gave him a timid smile. "Mr.—I mean, Cash, I've never done anything like this before."

"Then why don't you just give it a try, and if you don't like it, you can quit. It's as simple as that. At least you'll have tonight to decide," Cash said, and gave her a lazy smile. "You might find that dancing with a few miners and having your toes stepped on is worth the money you'll earn."

Emerald could find no argument with what he said. Pushing her doubts to the back of her mind, she said, "All right, I'll try, but I can make no promises that I'll stay."

"That's all anyone can ask." Cash crossed the short space that separated them and held out his arm to Emerald as if she were a grand lady instead of a newly recruited hurdy-gurdy girl. "I'll escort you down. That way, everyone will know that you are off limits." He bent his head close to hers. "Remember what I said,

Emerald. If anyone bothers you, come to me and I'll
see that it doesn't happen again."

"I'll remember," Emerald said. Placing her hand on
his arm, she looked up into his smiling dark eyes. For
a disquieting moment, she had an odd feeling that she
had seen this man before, but she knew that was impossible. Cash Dalton was not a man a woman would
forget meeting.

Emerald thought no more about it as Cash led her
down the stairs to the noisy bar room below.

Sal rapped her knuckles against the door and then
opened it as she called, "Are you awake?"

The question roused Emerald from the heavy sleep
that had claimed her tired body as soon as her head hit
the pillow near dawn. After the excruciating hours she'd
spent in the saloon, she had been exhausted as she
climbed the stairs back to the haven of her room. It had
seemed as if she had danced with every prospector west
of the Mississippi.

"What time is it?" she asked groggily, squinting up
at the woman standing by her bed with a tin basin in
her hand. Still relaxed from sleeping, she stretched her
arms over her head. It was a mistake, she realized too
late. Her sore muscles screamed at the movement. Emerald grimaced at the pain that ran up her legs and along
her back.

"It's past noon," was Sal's grumpy reply. She set the
basin on the bedside table none too gently and eyed
Emerald through makeup-smudged, bloodshot eyes. She
was in no mood to pretend friendship at such an early
hour of the day. She'd had a long, hard night and it did
not help her temper to have to wait on Cash's latest
conquest. "Cash thought you might want to soak your
feet after last night."

Emerald sat up and slid her feet to the floor. She was
grateful for Cash's thoughtfulness. After being trampled
by the miners' hobnailed boots for most of the night,
several of her toes were swollen and discolored with

bruises. Even the soles of her feet were sore, and her face screwed up once more in a grimace as she made the effort to stand. Finding that too difficult, she sank back onto the side of the bed and looked up at Sal.

"Do you ever get used to it?"

"You may not get used to it, but this makes it worth the pain," Sal said, taking a small pouch from the pocket of her feather-edged wrapper. She tossed it onto the bed beside Emerald. "Cash said that was your cut from last night."

Emerald opened the pouch and poured the contents into her hand. Stunned by the amount, she gaped at the pile of gold nuggets. There were far more here than she'd brought to Denver.

Sal watched the expression on Emerald's face and knew the girl had taken the bait, as Cash had intended when he'd sent up the pouch of nuggets. She had to give the man credit. He was a topnotch gambler. He knew exactly the right card to play to get what he wanted. From the look on the girl's face, he'd won this first hand, and Sal knew from her own experience with Cash Dalton that he would win the game. He beguiled you with his charm until he won your trust, and then you were at his mercy.

Emerald Banyon, you don't stand a chance, Sal thought cynically. You've walked into the lion's den and you're too young and gullible to realize that you're going to be eaten alive. I would feel sorry for you if I could.

Emerald looked up at Sal, her face still reflecting her amazement. "You mean this is my pay for last night?"

"That's what Cash said" was Sal's cryptic answer. She didn't add that once Cash had had his fill of her, she wouldn't earn that much in a month, nor would she find it as pleasant to work in the Gold Dust as she had last night. Cash always treated his new girls special at first. He padded their wages and pampered them until they began to bore him. When Cash had come downstairs with her, everyone in the saloon had known instantly that she was under his protection. They knew the unspoken rule around the Gold Dust: Hands off Cash's property until he was through with it. It had been the same with Sal when she'd first arrived. Her affair with him had lasted less than a week. He'd enjoyed her favors and then he'd made a profit off of them. The same thing would happen to this girl, as had happened to all of the girls who worked for Cash. And if she was too blind to realize it, then it was her problem and not Sal's.

"You'd better quit counting your money and use that water on your feet if you intend to stay on. I'm going back to bed," Sal said as she strode to the door. She paused on the threshold and looked back at Emerald. "I forgot to tell you that Cash wants to see you when you're dressed." With that, she closed the door behind her, leaving Emerald sitting with her handful of nuggets.

Emerald could not believe her good fortune. She was awed by the amount of gold in her hand. In one night she had made more than her father had panned in Clear Creek in nearly a week. The doubts she'd felt about working at the Gold Dust Saloon faded in the glitter of the yellow nuggets. She was tired and sore, but the sense of security she felt from having earned her own way far outweighed her discomfort.

Emerald returned the precious nuggets to their pouch and tucked them securely beneath her mattress before she turned her attention to her battered feet. She breathed a sigh of relief as she eased her bruised toes into the hot, salty water. Sal had been right to a certain extent. Her feet did feel somewhat better now that she'd seen what their suffering had earned, yet to Emerald at this moment the soothing water was of equal benefit. Money could not buy everything.

When at last the water grew too cool for comfort, Emerald dried her feet and pulled on the woolen stockings she had bought with Apache's money. She frowned at the memory as she eased her tender toes into the

sturdy boots. She still had that one small matter to settle with Apache before she could be completely free of
him. Slipping the soft blue wool gown over her head,
she turned to the mirror to brush her hair. After her
meeting with Cash, she intended to pay her debt. She
wanted to look her best for both encounters.

When Emerald came down the stairs, a warm smile
played over Cash's sensual lips as he got to his feet and
crossed to the foot of the stairs. He could feel his body
stir at the sight of her. He had guessed that day in Clear
Creek Canyon that she would be lovely in the right setting, but she far exceeded his expectations. Dressed in
the demure gown, she was even more desirable than
she had been in the flamboyant costume of the previous
night. The fact that the blue wool hid more than it exposed intrigued him. It added a certain mystery to her
charms and enhanced his anticipation of the seduction
that he had planned for the lovely Emerald Banyon before he got rid of her.

"Good morning. I hope you slept well," Cash said,
and smiled up at Emerald as she paused on the step
above him.

"Like the dead," Emerald said, and returned his
smile. "And thanks to you, I can walk."

"I thought your feet might be sore after the beating
they took last night on the dance floor. And you deserve
a little coddling after all the money you earned us."

Emerald touched the leather pouch in the pocket of
her cape. "I want to thank you for that also."

"You earned it. Now, enough about business. I
thought I'd take you to breakfast and then afterward we
can discuss your staying on at the Gold Dust. After last
night, I hope I'm not going to lose you."

"No, I've decided to stay," Emerald said, placing
her hand on the arm Cash proffered. "And I am
starved." Her stomach rumbled in agreement.

Cash escorted Emerald through the noisy saloon and
out into the bright, sunny afternoon. The streets were
crowded with people enjoying a brief reprieve from the

unexpected blast of cold weather. Autumn seemed to have returned in full force, banishing winter to its rightful place. The sun was warm, melting the snow on roofs. The snow dripped from the buildings and ran into the streets, turning them into a quagmire.

A heavy freight wagon was bogged down in the mud and a steady stream of curses filled the air from the irate bullwhackers who were trying to force their oxen to pull the wagon free. The miners, always eager to gamble on anything, stood on the sidewalks, betting on how long it would take the bullwhackers to get out of their predicament. Depending on the way they had placed their bets, some shouted encouragement while others made derogatory remarks about the driver and his team in an effort to divert his attention in order to prolong his stay in the mud. But no tempers flared, beyond those of the vexed bullwhackers. The warm day seemed to bring out everyone's good humor, including Emerald's. Her spirits soared as she and Cash made their way to Rosey's Café. And though it was already afternoon, they enjoyed a hearty breakfast of expensive steak and eggs.

With her stomach full and her pocket filled with gold nuggets, Emerald felt on top of the world as she sat watching the activity on the street beyond the café window while Cash finished eating. She was now ready to meet her next challenge: settling her debt to Apache Ryan.

Her pleased expression faded and she grew pensive at the memory of the humiliation she had suffered because of Apache. It would be a pleasure to throw the money in his face. By repaying him, she would salve her battered pride as well as prove to him that she didn't need him or his money to survive. When that was done, she would try to forget about the mistake she had made by giving him her heart and turn her full attention to finding her father's killers.

"What's troubling you?" Cash asked solicitously as he covered Emerald's hand with his own. As a gambler,

he made his living by accurately reading the faces of
his opponents. Their expressions told him what card to
play as well as how high to place his bets. By watching
the emotions that flickered over Emerald's face, and
seeing the lost look that came into her eyes, he knew
the moment was right to make his grand gesture if he
wanted to gain her trust.

"I was thinking of a debt I intend to settle today."
Emerald did not elaborate. Nor did she feel the slight
tensing of the hand that lay over hers.

"From your expression I would have thought it was
a matter of life or death."

Emerald drew her gaze away from the hustle and bus-
tle on the street and looked back at Cash. She smiled
and shook her head. "No, I'm afraid it's nothing that
dire. I just need to settle a debt and put some bad memories behind me before I can go on to other things."

"Do you need more money?"

Again Emerald shook her head. "No. What I earned
last night is quite enough. Thanks to your giving me a
job, I can now end something that should never have
started."

"Emerald, I sense that there is more here than you're
telling me. Are you in some kind of trouble?" Cash
asked, brushing his thumb soothingly across the back
of her hand in an intimate caress. "I would like you to
consider me your friend. If you're in trouble and need
my help, all you have to do is ask."

"You've already done a great deal for me. You've
given me work and a place to stay. That's far more than
anyone else has done for me since I came to Denver,"
Emerald said, touched by Cash's show of concern. She
had once felt the same about Apache, but that was before she had realized exactly what he expected in return
for his kindness.

Again Emerald could not stop herself from making a
comparison between the two men and their motives.
Without expecting her to barter herself, Cash was offering her his friendship. Apache had only shown his

benevolence when it served his purpose. What she and Apache had shared could not be called friendship. Their relationship had existed solely because of the fire in their blood, Emerald reflected sadly. Except for their most intimate moments, the time they had spent together had been less than amicable. Apache had been her lover but not her friend.

"Just remember what I've said, Emerald. I'm here if you need me," Cash said patiently. His gambler's instincts told him to let this play pass. From the expression in her eyes, he knew he had won her trust, but he wanted far more than that from Emerald Banyon.

"I'll remember," Emerald said, and gently withdrew her hand from his. She pushed her chair back. "I appreciate your offer to help me, but I want the satisfaction of settling this matter for myself."

Courteously, Cash stood as Emerald rose from her chair and walked from the café with her head held high. Admiration glowed in his dark eyes as he watched her make her way along the crowded sidewalk. He felt a heady rush of excitement flow through his veins at the challenge she represented to him.

Cash knew that the game he played was dangerous and that he should get rid of Emerald before she could do him harm. But living on the razor's edge this way tempted the gambler in him as nothing had done in years. He risked letting her destroy him and all of his plans if she should see and identify Red Beaudine as the man who killed her father, yet he could not resist wagering his wealth and his life to have her in his bed.

Squaring her shoulders, Emerald straightened her cape, patted her hair to make sure it was in perfect order, and then knocked on the door to the boardinghouse. Several moments later, it swung open to reveal Hannah Becker. The widow did not try to mask her hostility as she blocked the doorway with her round form.

"What do you want?" she asked coldly.

"Mrs. Becker, I've come to see Apache. Is he here?"

"No. And I don't expect him back anytime soon." Hannah started to close the door, but Emerald put her hand against it to stop her.

"Do you know where I can find him?"

"No, and I wouldn't tell you even if I did. Now, if you'll excuse me, I have work to do." Again Hannah tried to close the door.

Emerald's temper snapped. "Damn it, Hannah. I'm not trying to steal him away from you. I just wanted to give him this." She took the bag of nuggets from her pocket. "He loaned me money the first day I was here, and I want to repay him."

Hannah's eyes widened at the sight of the bulging pouch. "Where on earth did you get your hands on that kind of money?"

"I don't see that it's any of your business."

"You don't have to tell me. I know how women like you earn money. You must have had a really busy night." Hannah smirked.

"I should slap your face for that, but I'm going to ignore it, Hannah. You're so filled with meanness and jealousy that I feel sorry for you."

"Don't feel sorry for me, you little bitch. You're the slut who's out on the streets peddling her wares."

Emerald's hand clenched around the bag of nuggets. She drew in an angry breath and sought to control the urge to pull out every mousy brown hair on the woman's head. Her eyes were hard green gems as she said, "I hate to disappoint you, Hannah, but I didn't sell myself to earn one tiny nugget in this pouch."

"If you expect me to believe that, then you're a bigger fool than I first thought you," was Hannah's snide reply.

"I don't really give a damn what you believe, Hannah Becker. Just tell Apache that if he wants his money, he can find it at the Gold Dust Saloon." With that, Emerald turned and walked away, her head held high.

Hannah closed the door and leaned her back against

it. She shut her eyes, savoring the bit of information Emerald had just told her. Unwittingly, the girl had given her the weapon she had been seeking. When Apache learned that she was nothing but a dance-hall girl and that all of his worry about her had been for nothing, he'd forget about Emerald Banyon once and for all.

Hannah smiled as she drew in a satisfied breath and ran a hand along the side of her head, smoothing back an imaginary loose hair. The gesture was fruitless. Seldom did any hair escape from the tight bonds of the coil at the nape of her neck.

Fluffing the skirt of her brown woolen gown and tightening her apron strings, she went back to the kitchen to prepare Apache's supper. Tonight, she would cook steak and potatoes, and for dessert she would tell Apache about Emerald's visit and the message she had left for him.

Hours later, sitting across from Apache, Hannah came to regret her choice of desserts. With his hands clenched on each side of his plate, he glared at her, his face flushed dark with anger.

"What did you say?"

"Apache, don't get angry with me. I'm only delivering the message that Emerald gave me."

Apache's nostrils flared as he drew in a deep breath in an effort to control his temper. "I'm sorry, Hannah, but damn it, how dare that little brat take a job at the Gold Dust Saloon? She should have her hide tanned for such stupidity. I knew she was too damned young to be on her own in Denver."

"Apache, she's a grown woman. She's not the innocent little girl that you seem determined to believe her. My God, she had a pouch full of nuggets, and you know as well as I do that little girls don't earn that kind of money just by dancing."

Apache's swarthy complexion paled at Hannah's assessment of the work that Emerald was doing at the Gold Dust Saloon. The thought seemed to rip his guts apart. His Emerald, the innocent young girl that he had initiated in love, was now selling herself to the highest bidder.

Apache shook his head in denial and ran a hand through his blue-black hair in exasperation. Hannah had to be wrong. The girl he knew had too much self-respect to allow herself to sink so low.

"I can't believe that of her, Hannah. Emerald is a decent young woman." Everything within Apache rebelled at the thought of Emerald with another man.

"You've let her pretense of innocence blind you, Apache. I've seen girls of her type before, and they use their beauty to make men believe their lies. She's no different. And if you don't believe me, go down to the Gold Dust and see for yourself."

Without realizing it, Hannah had used the perfect words to trigger all of the distrust Apache had harbored toward beautiful women since his experience with Rachel. Anger, resentment, and a sense of betrayal mingled within him as he rose from his chair in one fluid motion. His dark eyes glowed like banked coals and a muscle worked in his jaw as he crossed the room and picked up the gun belt that he had removed before sitting down to supper. Buckling it around his lean waist and tying the leather strap about his thigh, he left the boardinghouse without a word.

Hannah remained seated with her hands tightly clasped in her lap. A pleased smile curled her lips up at the corners. She felt like shouting for joy. Her plan had worked far better than she had anticipated. After Apache visited the Gold Dust and saw exactly what Emerald Banyon was, she would no longer have to worry about the girl coming between her and the man she loved. Apache would be hers.

Chapter 8

The jangle of the piano, combined with the talk and laughter of the rowdy miners, was deafening when Apache paused at the batwing doors that led into the Gold Dust Saloon. His dark eyes swept over the room, taking in the miners who stood shoulder to shoulder with elbows propped on the bar, enjoying their drinks and the painting of the naked lady that graced the wall behind the rows of whiskey bottles. The blue haze of smoke that hovered above the crowded room dimmed the light from the lanterns that hung from the beamed ceiling but did not hinder his view of the woman he had come to find.

Emerald Banyon was not hard to spot, dressed as she was in the skimpy red satin gown with black petticoats peeking from beneath the short hemline. Black feathers swayed amid the burnished curls piled on top of her head and bloodred drop earrings dangled from the small lobes of her ears, drawing attention to the graceful curve of her slender neck and bare shoulders.

She stands apart from the crowd like a scarlet rose amid brown, thorny brambles, Apache reflected grimly as he pushed open the swinging doors and entered the saloon. He gritted his teeth and made his way through the crowd to a vacant table near the rear of the room, where he could watch the dance floor and the woman in the buckskin-clad mountain man's arms. He ordered a bottle of whiskey before settling his lean frame in a chair with his back to the wall.

When the bottle was set before him, without taking his eyes off Emerald, he filled his glass and drained it. The burning liquor had barely had time to reach his stomach before he poured another drink and gulped it down. The fire in his stomach matched that in his eyes as he watched Emerald go from one partner to another without a break.

Apache felt his blood boil as hot as the detestable color that she wore when he saw her smile innocently up into the leering eyes of a beefy miner. He nearly came to his feet with a growl of rage as he watched the man's hand slip up her back and pull her close to him. Apache had already risen halfway out of his chair when Emerald adroitly managed to maneuver herself out of the man's arms. Sinking back down into the chair, he watched in disgust as she danced lightly on to her next partner without a backward glance at the red-faced miner.

Pouring himself another drink, Apache tossed it down his throat with the hope that it would ease the tightness that had his insides coiled into knots. He wanted to drown the feelings that were ripping him apart as he watched Emerald laugh and dance.

He kept telling himself that the only reason he had come to the Gold Dust was to see if what Hannah had said was true, but that excuse did not relieve the sick feeling in the pit of his stomach. Nor did the liquor that he drank stop the hollow ache in his chest at the sight of Emerald in other men's arms.

"To hell with this," Apache muttered, staring down into his empty glass. "I've had enough." Pushing back his chair, he rose and turned his back on the dance floor, determined to walk out of the Gold Dust Saloon and never again to think of the sharp-tongued vixen who had managed to get under his skin to such a disturbing degree.

Before Apache could reach the door, Emerald's cry

brought him up short. He swung around to see the beefy miner holding her slender body prisoner with one burly arm as he tried with his free hand to hold her head still, in order to claim her lips. Emerald struggled against him, futilely beating his chest with balled fists and kicking at his legs.

For a moment Apache thought the top of his head would blow off from the burst of fury that shot through him. His hand automatically went to the revolver strapped to his thigh, and in a blind rage he elbowed his way through the onlookers, who were enjoying the spectacle of the beautiful girl wrestling with the beast.

"Release the lady" came his low, deadly growl.

Apache's words brooked no argument. With low murmurs, the onlookers backed away from the tall man with eyes like polished black steel. Those who knew him or his reputation did not want to be in his line of fire, and they quickly put as much distance as possible between themselves and the beefy miner.

Emerald froze at the sound of Apache's voice. She peered over the broad shoulder of the man holding her so tightly that it made it hard for her to get her breath and felt a wave of relief wash over her at Apache's intervention on her behalf.

"I'll handle this," Cash Dalton said as he came forward.

"Stay out of it, Dalton. It's none of your affair," Apache growled.

Cash ignored Apache. He turned his attention to the miner who still held Emerald imprisoned against him. "Like the man said, Jack, let the lady go. You know the rules around here."

Jack Parkin looked from Emerald to Apache and then at Cash. He let out his breath in disgust and let his arms drop away from her. He felt he could take on one man, but he wouldn't try two, especially over a woman. Running a callused hand over his beard-stubbled chin, he shook his head. "Don't want no trouble, Dalton. Only trying to have a little fun."

"Have your fun elsewhere from now on," Cash said as he crossed to Emerald and placed a protective arm around her shaking shoulders.

Jack nodded, flashed Apache a seething look, and then brushed by him and out the door without a backward glance at Emerald. Jack Parkin knew when to cut his losses and run. He'd have his day with the man who had interfered, but not in the Gold Dust Saloon. Cash Dalton wasn't a man he wanted to tangle with. Dalton might not take him on himself, but Jack knew that the gambler could have him shot down some dark night when there was no one to witness it. Everyone knew it was the way he worked, but no one was brave enough to accuse him of such a thing. It was far easier and safer to ignore Dalton's ways and stay on his good side.

The heat in Apache's blood did not cool at the sight of his enemy holding Emerald. It grew hotter by several scorching degrees as he crossed the few feet that separated them and took her by the wrist.

"You're coming with me," he said curtly.

"I'm not going anywhere with you," Emerald said, leaning into Cash and pulling herself free of Apache's hand.

"You'd better listen to the lady," Cash said, stepping in front of her.

"Dalton, this is none of your concern. Emerald is coming with me, and if you value your life, you'd better not stand in the way."

Cash's face hardened and his eyes grew as cold as black onyx. "Are you calling me out, Ryan?"

Apache smiled, but there was no warmth in the gesture. "That's up to you. I don't mind shooting down mad dogs where I find them."

Emerald felt her heart stop at the thought of the two men shooting out their differences over her.

"No!" came her heart-wrenching cry as she pushed her way between the two deadly opponents who had already squared off.

"Move out of the way, Emerald," Apache ordered, flexing the fingers of his gun hand near his holster.

"I won't move, damn you. You're the one who should get out. I didn't ask for your help, and I'll not stand by while you use me as an excuse to fight."

"I'm telling you to move," Apache ground out.

"Do as the man says, Emerald. This won't take long, and then we can resume business as usual," Cash said.

"Like hell I will. If you're both so determined to shoot each other, then it will have to be over my dead body. I won't have either of your deaths on my conscience." Emerald stood directly between the two men with hands braced stubbornly on her hips.

"Go on and shoot," she spat, too angry with both men to be afraid.

"Damn it, Emerald, get out of the way," Apache said.

"I won't." Her belligerent reply drew several low chuckles from the spectators.

"From the looks of it, and unless you two want to shoot the girl, you'd better give it up," one onlooker called from the back of the room. "She's got you between a rock and a hard place, if you ask me."

"Nobody asked you," Cash snapped. "So keep your damned mouth shut or I'll take care of you when I'm finished with Ryan." His threat effectively silenced the room.

"Apache, please," Emerald begged. "Stop this before someone gets hurt or killed."

"There's only one way this is going to end, Emerald," Apache said.

Misconstruing his words, Emerald shook her head. "I'm where I want to be. No one is forcing me to work here. Go back to Hannah and please just leave me alone."

Apache felt a cold hand grip the tender spot where his heart had once been. He felt an inexplicable sadness as he looked into her pleading emerald eyes. He knew at that moment that Emerald was lost to him.

All that was left for him was to kill Cash Dalton and end his reign of terror. But he couldn't even do that in front of her. For now she believed the man was her friend, and until he could prove different, he knew she would never forgive him if he shot Dalton down like the murdering mad dog he was.

Cash saw the tension ease from Apache's face and relaxed. He knew the man's reputation and hadn't enjoyed the thought of facing him in a shootout, especially with Red Beaudine absent. Cash was a gambler, not a gunfighter, but he would have drawn against Ryan if pushed. He had no other choice if he wanted to keep the reputation he had cultivated about his own prowess with a gun. In his business he had to make people fear him. He couldn't afford to back down. If that happened, every greenhorn who lost a dollar would be calling him a cheat and wanting to shoot it out with him.

Unaware of Cash's relief at her intervention, Emerald turned her pleas to him. "Cash, if you're my friend, please stop this before it goes any further."

Seeing his chance to ingratiate himself further with Emerald, Cash said, "All right. It's over. I won't fight you, Ryan. But get the hell out of the Gold Dust and don't come back. Emerald's made her feelings clear about where she wants to stay, so I don't want to see you around here again."

A muscle worked in Apache's jaw and his fingers curled again, aching with the need to blow the man's head off. But he fought the urge. For now, he would let it rest, but it would not lie still for long. He was determined to see that it didn't. There was now more involved than just revenge over his father's death. He had to save the woman he loved.

The thought struck Apache like a sledgehammer, and he quickly denied it to himself. He didn't love Emerald Banyon any more than she loved him. He desired her, yes, and he felt responsible for her—but did he love her? No. It was only his hatred for Cash Dalton that drove him to react like a love-smitten fool. He couldn't stand the thought of Dalton's corrupt hands on her, especially when he suspected the man of having her father killed. That was all it was; nothing more.

"Is that the way you want it, Emerald?" Apache asked, his face taut. "Can you honestly tell me that you prefer this"—Apache gestured toward the crowd—"type of life-style?" His words were laced with contempt.

Emerald stiffened at the derision directed at her. She squared her shoulders, raised her chin defiantly, and gave him a withering look. How dare he judge her? He'd had no qualms about taking her innocence and then jumping into Hannah Becker's bed as soon as they arrived in Denver. He had no right to condemn her for working at the Gold Dust and making an honest living when he had no honor himself.

"Yes, I prefer this. At least now I'm making a living and have a roof over my head. But I don't owe you any explanation for what I do," Emerald spat. She reached into the small purse at her waist. "This is all I owe you." She tossed the pouch of nuggets at Apache. "Now we're even."

Apache's face was granite-hard as his hand balled about the leather pouch. Without a word, he turned and shouldered his way back through the hushed crowd.

The fight went out of Emerald as she watched Apache leave the saloon. She'd thought that by repaying the money she owed him, she would be free of Apache Ryan and her feelings for him. However, now she knew different. When he left the Gold Dust without looking back, she felt the last solid piece of her heart shatter.

Pleased by the forlorn look that crossed Emerald's face, Cash smiled to himself and gave her shoulders a reassuring squeeze.

"Come on. You've had enough for one night," he said softly so that only Emerald could hear. "Drinks are on the house, boys," he called over his shoulder as he led her up the stairs. A deafening din arose from his unexpected generosity as everyone tried to get to the bar first. The Gold Dust's customers soon forgot the hurdy-gurdy girl and the argument she had caused as they enjoyed Cash's hospitality to the fullest.

Emerald leaned against Cash, drawing from his strength as they climbed the narrow flight of stairs. When they reached her room, she was too troubled by the feelings her encounter with Apache had aroused to protest as he sat down on the side of her bed and pulled her into his lap. He held her comfortingly, making no demands of her, despite their close proximity.

"It's over now. You don't have anything to fear from Ryan or anyone else," he whispered against her golden curls and felt her give a shudder as she laid her head on his shoulder like a small child needing solace.

"I wish that were true," Emerald whispered brokenly.

"It is. I promise you, I won't let anyone hurt you again," Cash murmured. He gently massaged the nape of her neck with his long, sensitive fingers.

Emerald relaxed under his soothing touch, and when she spoke, it was as if she were musing aloud instead of talking to the man that held her. "Why did all of this have to happen? I was so happy before the claim jumpers killed Pa, and then my world turned upside down."

Cash stiffened. "Claim jumpers?" he asked softly. It was a struggle to keep his voice normal after this unexpected turn in the conversation.

"They shot my father for a worthless piece of rocky ground that I'd gladly give away if everything could be changed back to the way it was before they came," Emerald said, too wrapped up in her reflections to feel the sudden tension in Cash.

"Do you know who they were, Emerald?" he asked quietly as he continued to stroke the smooth curve of her shoulder. His eyes rested on the slender line of her neck as he waited for her answer. It would be so easy to encircle it with his fingers and choke the life from her if she admitted to seeing Red's face.

"No. I don't know who they were," Emerald answered automatically, still unwilling to tell anyone what she had seen until she knew the identities of the culprits.

Cash released a long, slow breath as he relaxed. Red had been wrong about the girl. She could not identify them as he had thought. That had been the reason she had not gone to the sheriff when she arrived in Denver.

He smiled. That little bit of information changed everything. He could now enjoy the pleasure of seducing Emerald without having to worry about what she knew. Meanwhile, he was closer than ever to securing the right-of-way for the railroad. Emerald's claim was all that stood in his way, and from what she had just said, she didn't want it. All he had to do was to wait for the right moment and then offer to buy it.

The thought pleased Cash. When it came time for him to produce the claim deeds he'd bought from the nonexistent claim jumpers, no one could say that he had been involved in any of the killings to gain the land. Emerald would be living proof that he was an honest businessman who had been taken in by the same villains who had committed all of the crimes. Oh, he'd storm and rave about being duped into buying claims that had been stolen, but he'd stand his ground about his ownership since there was no one left alive to go against him. Then he'd go about the business of getting the railroad to come through with no suspicions shadowing the deal.

Cash gave Emerald a hug, well satisfied with the way things had worked out. She was worth far more alive than dead since it had turned out she didn't know who had killed her father. And even if she had seen Red's face, as long as Cash kept him out of sight everything would go as he planned.

"Emerald, you don't have to worry anymore," he said, holding her close. "I can't change the past for you, but I'll try to see that your future is different. As long as you're at the Gold Dust, you're safe."

Emerald snuggled into the warmth and security of his arms. She was grateful for the friendship that Cash had given her. His kindness helped to ease the ache in her heart for the man who had walked out of the Gold Dust Saloon and out of her life: Apache Ryan.

"Thank you, Cash," she said, raising luminous eyes to meet his ebony gaze. The moment crackled around them, making her swallow nervously as she saw desire flame in Cash's eyes. Recognizing the same look she had seen in another pair of dark eyes, Emerald suddenly grew uneasy. She was attracted to Cash, but she did not feel the rush of anticipation building in the pit of her stomach that she had when Apache had looked at her in the same way. She cared for Cash as a friend, but she did not love him.

Sensing her withdrawal, Cash set her on her feet and stood himself. The time was not right for her seduction. He could force himself on her to ease the ache in his loins, but that would ruin the trust that he had been carefully nurturing and turn her against him. Until he had all of his business dealings signed, sealed, and delivered, he would not take that chance. He was a gambler but not a fool, especially when a great deal of money was involved. Sal or one of the other sluts would serve to quench his lust for tonight.

Cupping Emerald's small, squared chin in the palms of his hands, he gazed down into her eyes. "You know I need you, Emerald, but I care too much for you to force you against your will." He pressed a gentle kiss on her lips and murmured, "Good night, sweeting."

Cash's ploy worked as he knew it would. Emerald was left standing in the middle of her small room feeling slightly bewildered by the conflicting emotions that swept over her. She felt relieved that Cash understood her reluctance to become involved with him, yet her vanity was piqued that he could so easily turn away from her after professing his desire.

Bemused and feeling oddly bereft, Emerald stripped off the red satin gown and crawled into her small bed alone. The muffled noise from the saloon filled the room as she lay staring at the ceiling and wondering at the confusion that the two handsome men had brought into her life.

The lamplight drenched the naked man in gold, revealing his lean, passion-hardened body to Sal's pain-filled gaze. His arousal stood proud and throbbing as he displayed his male beauty to her like a peacock spreading its glorious tailfeathers in the mating ritual.

"You're a cruel bastard, Cash Dalton," Sal panted.

"You know you like it a little rough now and then, Sal," Cash said, and smiled at the grimace of pain that crossed her face when he thrust his fingers inside her. There was no gentleness to his touch as he explored every part of her, leaving nothing unscathed by his punishing fingers.

Sal squirmed and moaned as he delved into places that only he knew could excite her. She bucked against his hand, reaching up for him, her nails raking down his chest before she encircled his swollen manhood and tried to draw him to her.

Cash chuckled as he drew away, enjoying the look of deprivation that crossed her face. "Not so fast, my hot little bitch. I came here not to pleasure you but for you to ease my need." He moved from between her thighs and lay back on the pillow. Cushioning his head on his folded arms, he arched a brow at the frustrated woman. "Now get to it. Let's see if that mouth is good for something beyond swilling liquor."

Sal's hand shook as she brushed a yellow lock of hair from her brow and knelt at Cash's side. Her breath came in ragged gasps as she gazed down at his perfect body. The place between her legs throbbed to have him fill her, but she knew that until she had serviced him to his satisfaction, she would have no ease of her own.

The ritual was the same every time. Cash aroused her until her blood sizzled through her veins and made her eager to do anything he bid. Her hands moved over him, her fingers stroking and enticing as she slowly caressed the entire length of his body. Straddling him, she rubbed her own heated flesh against him as she bent to kiss and lap at his resilient flesh. Inch by inch, she glided down his torso, feeling the moisture of his arousal on the skin that she tantalized with her tongue. She worshipped at his shrine, her blond hair shadowing her face as she buried her head in the trail of hair that led down to the proud junction at his thighs. She drew in the musky scent of his maleness and felt her own body dew with need as she slowly climbed the towering pinnacle with her tongue and took him into her mouth. Greedily, she drew in his essence, sucking hungrily as he arched his hips to her in pleasure. His hands captured her head and held her to him as he spilled his lust. She moaned with pleasure, savoring the tangy taste of him as he wrapped his hands in her hair and drew her upward.

"Now it's your turn," he said as he flipped her onto her back and kneed her thighs apart. He took her mouth with his to stifle her moan of pain as his hand closed about a swollen breast and pinched the hardened nipple between his thumb and forefinger. His teeth made a streak of fiery nips along her neck as he moved down to her breasts and hungrily suckled the tender, aroused peaks while his hands once more moved to the wet junction between her thighs. Sal opened to him, reaching out to glide her hands up and down his manhood to excite him once more. Feeling him swell under her caresses, she led him to her, grasping his shoulders eagerly as she wrapped her legs about his waist, taking him deep inside her.

"Emerald," he murmured against her neck as his passion culminated with such violence that his fingers bruised Sal's shoulders.

The haze of pleasure that had engulfed Sal vanished instantly at the name of the girl who lay only a few doors away. It was the second time a man had murmured that name and left Sal before she could appease her own need. Frustration and anger mingled within her as Cash slid away from her and lay back on the pillow,

sated, and giving no further thought to the woman he
left unsatisfied at his side.

Sal jerked the sheet up around her and climbed from
the bed. She strode across the room to the bottle of
whiskey on her dressing table and poured herself a
drink. She downed the fiery liquor in one gulp before
she turned back to Cash, who lay relaxed and smoking
a cheroot.

"Instead of coming here to bruise me, why in hell
didn't you just go and lay that bitch down the hall?
That's who you really wanted tonight," Sal said, glowering at Cash.

Nonchalantly, Cash drew on the cheroot and then
blew a smoke ring toward the ceiling before he said,
"That's what you're here for."

Sal's eyes seemed to bulge with the fury that possessed her. "I'm not here to service you when you get
all heated up over that little hussy. Let her earn her keep
just like the rest of us have to do around here."

"Oh, she's going to earn her keep soon enough, Sal.
Don't you worry about that," Cash said, and smiled.

"Well, you had better make it soon. I'm not going
to put up with being black-and-blue because you're hot
for her."

The smile faded from Cash's face. "Are you giving
me orders, Sal? You know how I feel about that."

Sal grew still. She knew exactly how Cash felt about
anyone going against him. The few marks she'd received tonight were small in comparison to what she
would get if she made him angry.

"Cash," she began tentatively, her tone cajoling.
"You know I'm not trying to tell you what to do. I'm
just damned tired of men calling out her name when
they're with me. Even a whore takes a little bit of pride
in her work."

"What are you talking about?" Cash said, rising from
the bed in one fluid motion. His face was taut as he
gazed at Sal through narrowed eyes.

"Apache Ryan called out her name the other night,"

Sal quickly answered, afraid of the look in Cash's eyes. "That's all I meant."

"Damn," Cash muttered as he tossed the cheroot into the chamber pot at the foot of the bed. Ryan could mean trouble for his plans for Emerald if there was anything between him and the girl. And if he was calling out her name when he was with another woman, that could only mean one thing: Apache wanted Emerald for himself. And from the way he acted tonight, he'd do his damnedest to have her.

Cash's expression grew thoughtful. Emerald Banyon was of too much value to him to let any man interfere with his plans for her. He could have Ryan killed, but that thought did not appeal to him. After their encounter tonight, and knowing the man's feelings for the girl, Cash preferred to see him hurt in a way that would last far longer than a bullet in the back.

A cunning light entered Cash's eyes and he smiled at Sal. "I want you to do me a little favor, Sal, the next time you see Apache Ryan. Tell him that he doesn't have to worry about our Miss Banyon anymore because I intend to marry her."

Sal gaped at Cash, dumbfounded. "You don't really intend to marry the chit, do you?"

"I don't see why not. She owns the last claim that I need for the right-of-way for the railroad, and it's easier to get my hands on it by marrying her than any other way. By law, everything a woman owns when she marries becomes her husband's property."

"Wouldn't it be easier just to buy the damned claim from her instead of saddling yourself with a wife?" Sal asked, vexed at the thought of him marrying any woman. She might hate Cash at times for the way he treated her, but he was the only man whom she had ever really cared for.

Cash closed the space separating them and tipped up Sal's chin. "Are you jealous, Lusty Sal? You don't have to be. Nothing will change between us even if I do marry Emerald. I doubt she'll ever have your prowess in bed. Few women have your touch or your lips, my dear.''

Sal leaned into Cash, the sheet slipping from her fingers. ''Wives have a way of changing things.''

''You don't have to worry about that. I'll enjoy her for a time, but you know how to please me,'' Cash said, covering her ripe breasts with his hands and squeezing them. ''I've put my brand on you, Sal. You're mine, as you well know.'' He pinched her nipples before sliding his hands to her shoulders and pressing her down on her knees in front of him. His arousal stood hard and beckoning as his hand found its way into her hair and moved her head toward him.

Sal buried her face against him, clinging to his thighs, savoring the hard feel of them before she captured his buttocks in her hands, and took him once more. She was unable to deny him anything. She sold herself for him, degraded herself to please him, and she would do her best to hide any jealousy she felt at the thought of him marrying as long as he came back to her. Only he could arouse her jaded senses to such peaks of ecstasy.

Chapter 9

Alone and fretful in her big double bed, Hannah lay listening for Apache's return. It had been several hours since he had stormed from the boardinghouse, and she had begun to wonder if she had made a mistake in sending him to the Gold Dust Saloon. She had hoped to prove to him that Emerald Banyon was nothing but a cheap tart; however, she was beginning to regret her decision.

In her effort to make Apache see Emerald as she really was, she had sent him into the harlot's lair, where the girl could use all of her charms to sway him to her. The thought did little to ease Hannah's mind as she lay counting off each long minute until they turned into hours.

The clock on the mantel in the parlor below had struck twelve times when she finally heard the front door open and Apache's heavy tread on the stairs. Tense, anxious moments passed as she listened and waited to see if he would come to her room. She held her breath as he paused briefly at her door before moving on to the room beyond. The soft sound of the door closing behind him seemed to reverberate through her like the clanging of an iron portal. It chilled her to the bone.

With a shudder, Hannah threw back the covers and slid her bare feet to the floor. Her fingers shook as she lit the oil lamp on the bedside table. Driven by her need to know exactly what had transpired between Apache and her rival, she lifted the lamp and made her way down the hall to his door.

The hours of waiting had shaken Hannah's confidence, and her insides trembled with apprehension as she quietly turned the latch and opened the door. The lamplight spilled into the darkened room, revealing the man that she loved with such intensity that it made her ache. He stood gazing out into the dark night with one shoulder braced against the window frame. His lean brown hands were tucked into the pockets of his tight denims and his dark head rested against the ruffled edge of the curtain. He did not turn to look at her.

"Come in, Hannah," he said, his tone distant.

"I've been worried about you," she said in an effort to explain her presence as she set the lamp down on the bureau and crossed to his side.

A semblance of a smile tugged at one corner of his mouth as he gave her only a cursory glance before looking once more into the night beyond the window. "You should know by now not to worry about me."

"I couldn't help it after the way you stormed out of here earlier. You had blood in your eyes and I was frightened that you'd end up doing something foolish because of that girl."

"I thought you knew me better than that, Hannah."

"Until recently, I thought I did, too. But ever since that girl came to Denver, you've changed."

Apache reached out and drew her against him, draping a companionable arm about her shoulders. "Tonight put an end to all that, Hannah. Emerald has chosen the life she wants and it's no longer any of my business. I felt responsible for her because of her father's death, but she's made it clear that she doesn't want my concern or anything else from me."

Hannah felt the tension in the arm about her shoulders as Apache spoke of Emerald, and glanced up at him. Jealousy flamed anew at the troubled expression in his eyes. "I don't know why you should feel responsible because a bunch of claim jumpers killed her father. You had nothing to do with it,'' she said.

"I'm indirectly responsible for Jim Banyon's death," Apache said without realizing that he had voiced his thoughts aloud.

"How on earth could you possibly be responsible, even indirectly, for the man's death?" Hannah asked, her curiosity suddenly piqued. She had known Apache for months, yet, in truth, she knew little about him. For a long time she had sensed that something drove him, but he never spoke of his past when they were together. She wanted to know everything about him, but her fear of scaring him away with her questions had made her accept his reticence without protest.

"Just take my word for it that I am," Apache said as he moved away from her, suddenly uneasy at having voiced his inner thoughts to anyone, even to Hannah.

"I can't just take your word for it. I know you're not the type of man who would do something that underhanded, no matter what the reason," Hannah said, defending him to himself.

"Damn it, Hannah," Apache said, turning on her, his eyes blazing. "This is none of your concern. This is between Emerald and me."

Hannah stared at Apache, her temper flaring. Jealousy trampled her curiosity under its heel, making her see green fire. "That's what this is really all about, isn't it? You're obsessed with Emerald Banyon. You're only using the excuse of feeling responsible for her father's death so that you won't have to admit that you're in love with the girl."

"Hannah, you don't know what you're talking about."

"Don't I? I think I do. I've seen the way you look at her when you think no one is watching. I also know that you've slept with her, and that's the reason you've turned away from my bed."

"Whatever may have happened between Emerald and me has nothing to do with you. It was a mistake, and it's over and done with. The only reason that I haven't walked away from her is that she possesses the claim deed that I need to stop Cash Dalton from building his railroad.''

Dumbfounded and wanting desperately to believe his words, Hannah placed her hands on his shoulders and looked up into his eyes. ''The claim deed is the only reason you wanted her?'' she asked.

''Yes,'' Apache said, lying to himself as well as to Hannah.

Too relieved to wonder at Apache's need to stop Cash Dalton, Hannah leaned against him. Her concern was for herself and not for the motives that drove him to thwart the gambler's plans. They did not matter to her as long as his feelings for Emerald Banyon did not go beyond his need to acquire the claim she owned.

''Why don't you just buy the claim from her?'' she said helpfully. She wrapped her arms about his lean waist and pressed her cheek to his chest. Feeling secure now that she knew the reason behind his actions, she could afford to be generous.

''That may not be so simple since Emerald is now working for Dalton,'' Apache said. He did not tell Hannah that the thought of buying Emerald's claim to stop Dalton had crossed his mind more than once in the last hours as he sat drinking at the Denver House. However, each time he considered it something within him rebelled. He wanted to stop Dalton, but he also wanted to get Emerald away from the man. The thought of her with his enemy clawed at his insides with vicious talons.

He had damned every golden hair on her head several times over since leaving the Gold Dust, telling himself that he didn't care whom she sold herself to as long as it wasn't Cash Dalton. Apache had come back to the boardinghouse, resolved to put Emerald out of his life once he got his hands on the claim deed. All of the resolutions in the world, however, did not ease the hollow ache in his chest when he remembered their moments together.

Feeling the tension return to his body, Hannah leaned away from Apache and peered up at him, searching the hooded depths of his dark eyes. "What do you intend to do if she won't sell?"

"Anything I have to," came Apache's determined answer.

At Apache's words Hannah felt a sinking feeling in the pit of her stomach once more as she laid her cheek against his chest and listened to the steady rhythm of his heart. She could not stop herself from wondering how far he would go to get his hands on the claim deed. Intuition told her that Emerald Banyon was not out of her life as she had thought only moments before. The girl still represented a threat to her happiness with the man she loved. Hannah shivered. The battle was not yet done, and she had already used all of her weapons. All her scheming had been in vain. Emerald possessed something that Apache wanted, and until he had the claim deed in his hand, he would not be free of her.

"Maybe she will sell you the claim," Hannah said, voicing her hopes. "Come to bed, Apache. I need you."

Apache lifted Hannah into his arms and carried her to the bed. He also needed her. He wanted to bury himself in her plump body and forget the emerald-eyed vixen who haunted his thoughts. He needed to relieve the tension and frustration that one willful girl had created within him by shaking all of the resolves he had made about never letting himself become emotionally involved with another woman.

"I'm sorry Hannah," Apache said a few minutes later. He rolled away from her, disgusted with himself. He lay staring up at the ceiling, silently cursing himself for every kind of fool under the sun. Hannah was willing and eager for him to love her, yet his mind was too embroiled with Emerald for his body to respond. "Damn, I didn't mean for this to happen."

Hannah drew in an unsteady breath. Her desire unappeased, she felt like ranting and raving her disappointment but quickly decided against it. At this crucial time, when Apache's emotions were in such turmoil over that little hussy, it was in her own best interest to be understanding. She had managed to get Apache to take her to bed, and in time, if she didn't press him, she'd have the rest.

"I understand, Apache. You've had a lot on your mind lately." Hannah pressed her lips against his cheek and curled up at his side.

"You're right, and I'm tired out, as well," Apache said, denying the true reason that he could not make love to Hannah. He couldn't admit to himself that Emerald was the only woman he desired. That thought shook him to his foundation.

Apache placed an arm around Hannah and rested his head against her. "It'll be better the next time, I promise."

Hannah smiled and snuggled closer. As long as there would be a next time, she was content.

Her cheeks glowing a soft rose from the crisp autumn wind that ruffled the golden curls cascading down her back, Emerald bent low over the mare's neck as they passed beneath the swinging shingle branded with the name of Cash Dalton's ranch, the El Dorado. Her eyes sparkled with the excitement of a race well run, and her laughter filled the sunny afternoon as she reined in her mount and turned in the saddle to watch her opponent as he brought his horse to a skidding halt.

"I won," she taunted. A smug smile curled her lips as she brushed absently at a stray curl that had fallen free of the confining ribbon.

"I can see that," Cash said. With an effort, he hid his annoyance at losing the race. No matter what the game, he was a man who liked to win. Reaching into his pocket, he retrieved the twenty-dollar gold piece that he had bet and tossed it to her. "And I always pay my gambling debts."

Giving Cash a triumphant look, Emerald caught the shining gold coin in her gloved hand and tucked it away in the pocket of her riding habit. "I'm glad to see that you do, Mr. Dalton. I'd hate to have to call you out if you did not pay off the wager," she teased.

"Then if you're satisfied that our debt is settled, it's time that you saw what I brought you out here to see," Cash said, his good humor returning as he turned his thoughts to his reason for riding out to the El Dorado. Maneuvering his mount alongside Emerald's, he set an easy pace down the winding road that led to the ranch house where he intended to bring his bride once his railroad was a reality. It wouldn't do for a man of prominence to reside in a room above a saloon. When his plans were finalized, only the finest home in the Jefferson Territory would suit him, with his new status and the respectability that would come with it.

Since the night he had decided to marry Emerald Banyon, he had set about to woo her. He had showered her with attention, spending every free moment with her. During the past week, he had taken her riding nearly every day; he had escorted her about Denver to show her the sights; and he had also taken her shopping at Denver's new modiste. Against all of her protests at the expense, he had bought her several exquisite gowns that he thought befitted his future wife, as well as the velvet riding habit she now wore. To further his plans and to introduce her to the small group of Denver citizens who would one day be the upper crust of the town's society, he had taken her to see the traveling troupe of actors who had recently come to Denver. They had been such a success that they had been asked to stay permanently so that the town's residents could boast that Denver was now a thriving city with a modicum of culture instead of a drinking, brawling outpost on the frontier.

Cash approved wholeheartedly of the plan since he

was so close now to getting his railroad. At the present time he was considered nothing but a gambler, but soon the people who sneered at him and his profession would have to respect him as their equal. And when he married Emerald, she would become one of the grandes dames in the budding Denver society. His wealth and power would force those who now looked down on him to accept him and his wife.

Cash wanted their acceptance. It was the one thing he coveted more than anything else. He had always lived on the fringes of society. He had money and a certain amount of power, but that did not appease his need to be the social equal of the men who gambled with him but who wouldn't speak to him on the street if they were with their wives and families. Once his railroad was a reality, they would have no other choice than to acknowledge him as one of the prominent citizens of the town.

"This is what I brought you to see," Cash said. He reined in his mount and looked at Emerald. "What do you think?"

"It's beautiful," Emerald said, stunned to find such grandeur so near a town that was made up of clapboard houses and log cabins. The two-story ranch house had been designed along the lines of the Greek revival homes found on plantations in the South. The veranda that spanned the entire front of the house boasted six white columns. A fan-shaped window above the double doors was the only attempt to embellish the exterior of the house. The lines were clean and simple, though without the intricate artistry that graced the more elaborate plantation homes. Yet the house's simplicity made it even more appealing against the snowy backdrop of the craggy terrain in the distance.

"I'm glad you like it," Cash said as he dismounted. "When the El Dorado is complete, I intend to make it my home." Cash spanned Emerald's waist with his hands and lifted her from the saddle.

"Then you don't plan to keep running the Gold

Dust?'' Emerald queried as he draped a companionable arm about her shoulders and led her up the wide steps to the veranda.

"I don't intend to sell the Gold Dust, but when the cattle I've bought arrive from Texas, I plan to settle down and turn my attention to ranching as well as keeping up with the other business dealings I have under way," he said, opening the door for Emerald.

She paused on the threshold, her gaze sweeping over the polished floors and the rich paneling that graced the walls. Having lived all of her life in a rustic cabin in the Georgia mountains, she had never seen such opulence and was slightly intimidated by the lavish surroundings. Though carpenter's tools still lay scattered about the floor and there were only a few pieces of furniture to fill the large room, Cash's home was imposing to a girl who had thought her room at the boardinghouse luxurious.

Cash smiled to himself at the effect the house was having on Emerald. Like a spider weaving its web to capture its prey, he would use his wealth to bait his trap, enticing her with a glimpse of what could be hers if she married him.

With a hand at her back, he urged her forward. "Warm yourself by the fire while I see if Marguerite has any hot coffee in the kitchen. She usually keeps a pot on the stove when the men are at work."

"That sounds wonderful," Emerald said, recovering a small bit of her aplomb after being overwhelmed by Cash's home. Feeling suddenly like the princess in one of her grandmother's fairy tales, Emerald sank happily onto the bearskin rug in front of the fireplace. She smiled as she leaned back against the sofa and took in the beauty of the room. The pale peach walls and white wainscoting were enhanced by the dark gleaming wood of the floor. The few pieces of furniture scattered about were made of polished mahogany and covered in satin and damask. They seemed to fit the room as if they had been made for it.

A feeling of contentment stole over Emerald as she sat imagining what the room would look like once it was completely furnished. And she could not stop herself from wondering what it would be like to live in such a magnificent place. But she quickly put the thought away. She would not ask for more than she already had.

During the past week, she had lived a life that she would never have dreamed existed while panning for gold along the banks of Clear Creek with her father. She had gone from a homeless waif to a petted and pampered lady, and it was all due to the generosity of one man, Cash Dalton.

"A nugget for your thoughts," Cash said as he handed her a mug of steaming coffee before settling his lean frame on the rug at her side. He stretched his long legs out toward the warmth of the fire and crossing them at the ankles.

"Don't you mean a penny?" Emerald laughed, her eyes twinkling with devilment as she gazed at him over the rim of her mug.

"If I was back East, I might say a penny, but in Denver a penny isn't worth much to anyone."

"Maybe my thoughts aren't worth much either," Emerald said, setting her mug aside.

Cash relaxed on one elbow and looked up into her lovely, wind-brightened face. He absently smoothed the fur rug with his hand as he raised one dark brow. "I seriously doubt it. I have yet to find a time when your thoughts weren't worth anything. As a matter of fact, that goes for everything about you, Emerald Banyon."

"You give me far too much credit. I was only thinking about how content I feel here compared to how I feel in Denver."

"Then you like my little spread?" Cash asked, and smiled.

"I wouldn't call it little from what I've seen. The house and stables alone cover as much land as my grandmother's entire farm back in Georgia."

"Then you'd prefer the quiet life of the ranch to that of working as a hurdy-gurdy girl in my saloon?"

"Cash, I'm sorry. I didn't mean to sound as if I didn't like my work," Emerald said, afraid that she had offended him after all he had done for her.

An easy chuckle escaped from Cash as he took her hand and pressed his lips against her palm. "I know what you meant. And I'm glad that you don't really enjoy dancing with the miners night after night. If you did, I would be disappointed."

Perplexed by his statement, Emerald knit her brows. "But I thought you wanted me to like working at the Gold Dust."

"At first I did, but things have changed," Cash murmured, looking deep into her eyes, his dark gaze relaying a silent message of desire. "Now I find that I don't like to see you in other men's arms. I want that pleasure for myself alone."

His words were like a soft caress that rippled over Emerald as she sat mesmerized by his eyes. Looking into their dark depths, she found the attraction nearly more than she could resist. She felt drawn to this man who had shown her more kindness than any other human being in her life, but she would not make the same mistake with him that she had made with Apache Ryan. She would not let herself succumb to the allure of the flesh when no emotions were involved beyond the heat of the moment.

Emerald slowly pulled her hand away from Cash and retrieved the mug of coffee in order to have something to do with the fingers that suddenly wanted to reach out to him.

"Cash, we're friends, but—" Cash put a silencing finger against her lips before she could go on.

"Emerald, I don't just want to take you to my bed. I want you to be my wife." Cash smiled to himself at the look of amazement that crossed her face. "I know I've shocked you, but during the past weeks I've grown to care a great deal for you. I don't expect your answer now; I only ask that you consider my proposal.'' He gave a wave of his hand, the gesture encompassing the house as well as the ranch beyond. ''We could share all of this. You would be a rich woman if you decide to marry me. And you'd never have to work again at something you didn't like.''

''Cash, I don't know what to say,'' Emerald answered honestly. His proposal had taken her completely by surprise. Cash was her friend, and she was attracted to him physically, but she did not love him. Nor, she realized, had he said he loved her. Caring was a far different emotion than love.

''Just consider what I've said. If you should decide in my favor, I would like for us to be married as soon as possible.''

Cash did not add that the sooner the vows were spoken, the sooner he'd have the right-of-way with which to reassure his investors back East. They were beginning to grumble about the time he was taking to complete his part of the deal.

''I'll consider what you've said, but I can't make any decision right now,'' Emerald said slowly.

Cash smiled as he reached out and cupped her chin in the palm of his hand. ''I don't expect you to. When you say yes, I want you to be sure it's what you really want, or you'll never be happy. And I want your happiness more than anything else in the world.''

His breath was warm against her cheek as he brushed his lips lightly against it and then released her. He rose to his feet in one fluid motion. Satisfied with the progress he had made that afternoon and confident that she would not say no to his offer of marriage, he felt he had wasted enough time for one day wooing the desirable Miss Banyon. He had other business waiting for him back at the Gold Dust. And when that was finished, he would let Sal work out his frustration over not bedding his future bride.

''It's time for us to go back to Denver,'' he said as

he helped Emerald to her feet. When she stood before him, her wide, trusting eyes reflecting the feelings he aroused in her, he gave in for one moment to the desire to feel her young body pressed against his. He wrapped his arms about her and held her close. He breathed in the sweet scent of her golden hair and felt himself swell with desire. He fought the urge to take her up on the fur rug and all else be damned. He had never been a patient man where women were concerned, and it strained him to the limit to keep his passion under control. However, his greed overshadowed the heat in his loins, and he let his arms fall to his side.

Soon, my dear Emerald, soon, he mused as he led her out of her future home to the horses tethered in front.

Emerald was silent on their ride back to Denver. She paid no heed to the beauty of the tall mountains in the distance or to the aspens that tenaciously held on to their golden autumn mantles. Her mind was too filled with thoughts of the future that Cash had offered her as his wife. She had had a small glimpse of it today at the El Dorado, and she knew that if she accepted his proposal, she would never have to worry about being cold and hungry again. She would live in a fine house, wear fine gowns, and have a fine husband.

What more could a woman ask? she mused as she glanced at the man riding at her side.

Nothing, she answered silently. Cash was handsome and rich and he was offering her a life of ease.

Then why am I hesitating in accepting his proposal? she questioned herself again, but could find only one answer: Love. It was the one thing that she had hungered for all of her life. She didn't know if she could give up her quest for the elusive emotion that her heart had craved for so many years.

Emerald knew she owed Cash more than she could ever repay him, but she also realized that she did not love him. Another man had claimed her heart in a snowbound cabin and she feared that she would never be able to rid herself of her feelings for him.

She was reminded of Apache every time she looked into Cash's dark eyes and saw desire flame in them. Apache's lovemaking had branded her soul, binding her heart and thoughts to him even during the moments when she felt drawn to Cash. She knew Apache cared nothing for her, but she could not relinquish the emotions he had stirred into life within her. Her body would not let her forget his touch. It throbbed at the mere memory of the time she had spent in his arms.

Emerald clenched her teeth, suddenly furious with herself. She would not let herself dwell on the past. It was over and done with. Apache had told her that he never intended to take a wife, and that meant there would be no future for her with him even if he did love her. She would not become another Hannah Becker, waiting for him to return to her after tiring of his latest conquest. She had sworn never to live on the fringes of another man's life, starving for love, and she would keep that vow.

With her temper guiding her actions and without giving herself time to change her mind, she turned to Cash. "I've considered your proposal, and I will marry you."

Cash was offering her his name and his friendship, and that was far more than she would ever receive from Apache Ryan. She did not love Cash, but she cared for him as a friend, and perhaps with the passage of time, the friendship could develop into a deeper relationship that would make them both happy.

Cash drew his mount close to Emerald's and took her hand. He gave it a gentle squeeze and smiled with satisfaction. "We'll be married at the end of the week," he said.

Apache lounged against the bar, his midnight gaze sweeping over the crowded saloon as he sipped at the glass of whiskey in his hand. The woman he had come to see had yet to make an appearance. Sal and the other hurdy-gurdy girls had come down an hour ago, but there was no sign of Emerald.

Restlessly he gulped down the last of his drink and let the bartender refill his glass. This was his first time back in the Gold Dust since his confrontation with Dalton. He'd stayed away from the saloon, not out of any fear of Dalton's threats but out of his need to rid himself of the feelings Emerald roused within him.

During the past weeks, he'd kept himself busy tracking down leads that might provide him with the evidence he needed to prove Dalton guilty of the claim jumping. But to his frustration, he kept running into a blank wall. He'd heard from a prospector who'd come through Bent's Fort that a man called Whiny Baker had gotten drunk and bragged about knowing who was responsible for the claim jumping around Clear Creek, but by the time Apache had ridden down there, the man had already met up with the wrong end of a Colt revolver. He'd been shot for trying to cheat at cards.

Disgusted, Apache had returned to Denver. He'd fought a losing battle with himself and his resolve to stay away from Emerald. Tonight, drawn like a magnet to a lodestone, he'd come to the Gold Dust prepared to tell her of his suspicions about Cash Dalton. He hoped that would be enough to make her see the man as he really was.

"Hello, handsome," Sal said as she sidled up against him, pressing her hip provocatively against his sinewy thigh. "I thought Cash had run you off for good."

"Not likely, Sal," Apache said, giving her a disarming grin. "It'd take far more than his threats to keep me away."

Sal laid a hand on his shoulder, massaging the muscles beneath the black cloth of his shirt. She ran the tip of her tongue over her red lips and raised one blond brow. "Since you ain't worried about Cash, are you interested in collecting the one I promised you on the house?"

"Maybe a little later, Sal. I've some business with Emerald before I can think of other things."

The inviting light faded from Sal's painted face. "You're wasting your time, Apache. She's out of circulation since Cash asked her to marry him."

Apache froze. Every muscle in his lean body grew tense. His eyes glowed like banked coals as he looked at Sal. "So there's going to be a wedding?" he said, his tone icy.

"Yep, that's what they tell me. Cash has already taken her out to his ranch and showed her how fine she'll live when they're married. He's sparing no expense on the little chit." Sal lifted Apache's glass and drained it in one gulp. The whiskey burned down her throat, but it did not ease the jealousy that had been gnawing at her since Cash had decided to make Emerald Banyon his wife. She knew the reason Cash wanted the girl, but the attention he'd shown her during the past week seemed far beyond the call of duty.

He'd treated her as if she were a piece of precious china, breakable if not handled with care. He'd squired her about as if she were a real lady instead of a hurdy-gurdy girl. But what had annoyed Sal more than his treatment of Emerald was that when he left the girl, his blood was always hot. He came to her bed to take out his frustrations on her, and she had the bruises to prove it.

"When's this blessed event going to take place?" Apache asked nonchalantly, keeping his fury well masked from Sal.

"Cash said they'd be married at the end of the week." Sal reached for the bottle of whiskey and refilled the glass. Her fingers shook as she raised it to her lips once more.

"From the look of it, you're not too happy about their glad tidings," Apache said, noting the strained expression on Sal's face and accurately judging its cause.

"Hell, Apache. I'm damned tired of servicing him

after he gets all worked up over that little bitch. It ain't right that she should get all the fancy treatment while I'm stuck with the leftovers."

"You mean they haven't been sleeping together?" Apache asked, and felt like bursting into wild, joyous laughter when Sal gave a negative shake of her head. At least he had that to be grateful for.

"That's a shame for you, Sal," Apache said sympathetically, and smiled to himself. A plan had begun to form in his mind. Sal's jealousy might serve him well. "I thought you had Dalton wrapped around your pretty little finger."

"Cash was mine until she showed up and ruined it all. Now all I get is his abuse. He don't even take time to let me get satisfied anymore."

Apache placed a comforting hand on Sal's bare shoulder and gave it a sympathetic squeeze. "I'm sorry it's worked out that way for you. I wish there was something I could do to help you, but Emerald won't listen to me." He could well understand Sal's plight. He, too, was caught in a web that was not of his making, and he wanted to get free of it. The thin threads that bound him to Emerald seemed like bands of steel, drawing him inexorably to her despite all of his resolutions to stay away.

"I wish I could get her out of his life," Sal said, shattering Apache's reflections.

He relaxed as a plan sprang full-blown into his mind. He smiled at Sal. "I might be able to help you out, Sal, if you're willing to take the risk."

"I ain't got much else to lose," Sal said, her face brightening. She'd sell her soul to the devil to stop Cash from marrying Emerald Banyon. "What do you want me to do?"

Apache picked up the bottle of whiskey and two glasses. "Let's find a more private place to talk." Draping his other arm about her shoulders, he led her to a table at the rear of the saloon where no one could eavesdrop on their conversation.

To all, including Cash Dalton when he came down-stairs, Apache Ryan and Lusty Sal looked as if they were enjoying themselves over a glass of whiskey. Though he had given Ryan orders never to set foot in the Gold Dust again, he didn't intrude. He was confident in his own power to control Sal and knew she was only following his orders.

Cash didn't hide his smug smile when a short time later Ryan looked up and saw him watching them from the bar. He immediately saw the other man's eyes flare with anger at the sight of him and knew that Sal had delivered his message. Cash raised his glass to Ryan, toasting his triumph over him. Ryan now knew that Cash had won, and there was nothing he could do about it.

At Cash's disdainful look, Apache's hand automatically went to the revolver strapped to his thigh. But he managed to suppress the urge to blow the man's head off. Dalton thought he had won this round, but he was in for a surprise. With Sal's help, Apache would make sure of that.

"Apache," Sal whispered, sensing the mounting tension between the two men. "I won't stand by and let you shoot it out with him. I'd rather see him married to that little bitch than dead. At least I'd still have a little of him that way."

"Relax, Sal. I don't intend to shoot it out with the bastard. You just do your part and I'll do mine. Agreed?"

"Agreed," Sal said, and smiled with relief.

Apache pushed back his chair and rose. Setting his hat on his head, he flashed Dalton another seething look before he left the Gold Dust. He had much to do if he wanted to thwart the wedding that Emerald now lay upstairs dreaming about.

Apache mounted the black stallion tethered to the hitching rail outside of the saloon. He flashed one heated look at a window on the second floor above the Gold Dust.

"Sleep well, my dear little hellion," he murmured,

his deep voice revealing his anger for the first time since he'd learned of Emerald's plan to marry his enemy. "It'll be the last time you sleep under Dalton's roof."

The night was moonless as Apache turned his horse around and rode toward the end of town. He stopped at the livery to collect Ole Bessy, Jeb's horse, and then headed west into the foothills.

Chapter 10

The cold, moonless night concealed the man clothed in black. He blended into the deep shadows as he moved stealthily along the alley to the rear entrance of the Gold Dust Saloon. The crackle of the frozen earth under his feet made him pause to ascertain that his furtive movements went unnoticed before he slipped through the door that Sal had left unlocked for him and into the warmth of the dark hallway.

As silent as a shadow, he crept up the stairs and made his way along the dimly lit corridor to the room that Sal had told him was Emerald's. The sound of laughter and music floated up from the saloon below though it was well past midnight. Establishments like the Gold Dust stayed open twenty-four hours a day. A mocking smile briefly played over his shapely lips as he listened to the clamor that conveniently aided his surreptitious entry. With all the noise, no one would be able to hear a cry of help from the rooms above the saloon.

With a sardonic light gleaming in the depths of his eyes, he eased open the door and slipped inside. All was quiet within; only the soft breathing of the woman on the bed disturbed the stillness as he moved soundlessly across the room and stood gazing down at her.

The muscles across his chest grew taut as his eyes swept over the slim young body outlined beneath the sheet. Emerald lay with her cheek cradled in one hand while the other rested on her flat belly. The clinging sheet emphasized the enticing curves of her hips and the ripe mounds of her breasts.

Apache reached out to caress her but stopped himself. He had no time to fulfill his need to touch her silken flesh again. Drawing in a steadying breath to quell the desire that rose in him like sap in a tree on a warm spring day, he pulled the bandanna from his pocket and swiftly gagged her before she came fully awake. In an instant, he flipped her onto her stomach, tied her hands behind her with a strip of leather, and rolled her into the quilt that lay on the bed.

Frightened and confused from being jerked so abruptly from a sound sleep, Emerald lay unmoving, trying desperately to collect her wits. She gasped for air under the suffocating mantle over her head and listened for any sound that might give her a clue to her attacker. She could hear nothing through the thickness of the quilt.

Apache could feel the terror engulfing the stiff figure on the bed, but he stopped himself from pitying her. She deserved a good fright after the hell she had put him through during the last weeks. He swiftly collected her clothes and stuffed them into a pillowcase before he lifted her into his arms and, using the skill he had learned from his namesakes, carried her down the stairs and out into the cold night without attracting any notice.

Frantic with fear, Emerald tried to wriggle free of the strong arms that imprisoned her. She received a sharp whack on the rear from a wide hand for her futile efforts.

"Stay still or you'll regret it."

Emerald obeyed the muffled threat with a welling of despair. She had no other choice. In her present predicament, with her hands tied and her body wrapped in the quilt, she could do nothing to defend herself against her unknown assailant. All she could do was pray that she lived long enough to see who her captor was.

A chilling thought occurred to Emerald as she felt

herself being lifted onto the back of a horse. With
mounting horror, she realized that there was only one
man who could want her dead: the claim jumper called
Red.

Emerald's heart seemed to freeze inside her chest. If
he had seen her in Denver, he would know that she
could identify him to the law and would want to finish
what he had failed to do at Clear Creek.

Panic rose in her throat, threatening to stifle her under the folds of the quilt. She had foolishly let herself
become so secure in her new life that she had lost sight
of the reason she had come to Denver. Her vow to
avenge her father had been pushed aside during the past
couple of weeks because of all the attention Cash had
showered on her. Starved by her years of loneliness and
her need to forget the man who had stolen her heart,
she had selfishly sought to fulfill her own needs without
thought of the debt she owed to her father. Now her
neglect could well cost her life if the man who held her
in front of him was the man with the jagged red mark
on his face.

Emerald began to tremble like a sapling in a wind-
storm. She didn't want to show any weakness in front
of her enemy, but was unable to stop the uncontrollable
tremor that beset her.

Damn you, she silently cursed herself. You're not
going to give him the pleasure of seeing you dissolve
into a fit of hysterics. If you're going to die, you're
going to die fighting.

Delving into the depths of her spirit, she managed to
raise enough courage to quell the quaking in her limbs.
It was far better to have it end quickly than to endure
the agony of waiting, she decided.

With the thought, Emerald jerked up sharply, hitting
the man behind her on the chin with all of her weight.
She felt his hold on her loosen, and in that moment she
twisted her body and rolled to one side. The quilt un-
rolled from her as she fell naked to the ground at the
horse's hooves. The animal reared and would have come

down on her had not the dark silhouette on its back jerked the reins, making the animal shy to one side.

Emerald gave no thought to her state of undress as she rolled across the frozen earth. Breathing heavily after her painful fall, she managed awkwardly to get to her knees, then forced herself to her feet. However, before she could run into the underbrush alongside the trail, a pair of strong hands grasped her about the waist and lifted her up. She struggled, but her bound hands thwarted her efforts. A moan of pain and fury escaped her as she went limp against him.

"Damn it, Emerald. Are you trying to kill yourself?" Apache growled. Holding her in his arms, he cradled her to him as he crossed the few feet to the stallion. He set her on her feet and retrieved the quilt from the saddle where it was draped. Wrapping it about her, he untied the gag from her mouth.

Stunned with relief at finding that her abductor was Apache instead of the claim jumper, Emerald needed a moment to collect her wits and to realize what she had suffered at his hands. Then rage set her limbs to trembling once more as she looked up into his night-shadowed face. The heat of it made her heedless of the icy ground beneath her bare feet.

"You—you low-down good-for-nothing. Untie me at once so that I can tear your eyes out. You—you . . ." Emerald could not think of anything vile enough to describe him.

"If you keep that up, I'm going to gag you again," Apache said calmly, making no move to untie her hands.

Maddened beyond reason, Emerald strained against the leather strip that bound her wrists firmly together behind her back. When it would not budge, she let out a squeal of pure, undiluted rage and lashed out at Apache with her bare foot. The kick landed squarely on his shin and he grunted with surprise. Emerald felt a momentary satisfaction until her toes began to throb with pain from her rash action.

"Damn you," she cursed as she hopped sideways to

keep her aching foot off the ground. Her movements
once more dislodged the quilt around her and it fell to
the ground, leaving her exposed to the icy night.

"I swear you're the damnedest woman I've ever
seen," Apache said as he picked up the quilt and
wrapped it about her once more. "You seem determined one way or the other to freeze yourself to death."

"It's not my fault that I don't have any clothes on or
that I'm stranded in the middle of the night with a madman who doesn't give a damn if I freeze or not," Emerald shot back at him, her fury unabated.

"If you'll behave yourself and promise not to try
anything foolish, I'll untie you so you can put your
clothes on."

Shivering from the cold, Emerald did not answer,
stubbornly refusing to give her word that she'd behave
to the man responsible for her condition.

Apache gripped the edges of the quilt and drew her
inexorably against him. He stared down into her muti-
nous little face. "It's up to you whether you remain
buck naked as the day you were born or put on your
clothes. I prefer you the way you are now, but you'll
probably end up half-frozen before we get to where
we're going."

Feeling the icy night wind blow against her legs, Emerald relented. "All right, damn you. Untie me and let
me dress before I freeze to death."

"I thought you would see reason." Apache pulled
his bowie knife from the sheath strapped to his calf
beneath the leg of his britches and loosened the quilt.
He smiled at the sight of her round bottom as he slit
the leather about her wrists to free her. With that done,
he readjusted the quilt about her shoulders and turned
to get the pillowcase tied to his saddle. Lifting out a
gown, shoes, stocking, and cape, he tossed them to her.
"Now get dressed and remember not to try anything
foolish. It's late, and I won't put up with it."

Her teeth chattering from the cold, Emerald quickly
did as he bade. When she was dressed and had slipped the

cape about her, Apache lifted her once more into the saddle and mounted behind her. His strong arms encircled her slender body as he reached for the reins and urged the horse forward.

"Where are you taking me?" Emerald asked when he did not volunteer their destination.

"I thought we'd spend some time at Jeb's," he answered without elaborating.

"I can't go back to that cabin with you," Emerald said, her insides beginning to quake at the thought of once more being with him in that tiny cabin where she had learned of love. "I'm to be married tomorrow."

"I seriously doubt that since you won't be there for the nuptials."

"You can't really mean to make me miss my own wedding, can you?"

"As it looks to me right now, I've already done it."

"Damn you, Apache," Emerald said, twisting about enough to look him in the eyes. "I demand that you take me back to Denver right now."

"Demand all you like, little lady, but you're not going back to Denver until you come to your senses."

"And what is that suppose to mean? I came to my senses a long time ago where you're concerned. And I'm telling you right now to turn this horse around and take me back to the Gold Dust. I won't put up with your interference in my life any longer."

Apache clicked his tongue. "For someone who has no other choice than to do as I say, you sure are full of orders. Now quiet down and enjoy the ride. We still have several miles to go before we reach the cabin."

"Then if you won't take me back to Denver, I'll get Jeb to," Emerald said, turning her back to him once more.

"If that's your plan, I'm afraid you're going to be sadly disappointed. Jeb was already in Denver early this morning, enjoying the money I gave him for the use of his cabin for a few days."

Emerald bit her tongue to suppress the curses that

she wanted to heap upon his head. She knew they would only serve to make him gag her once more. For now she would hold her peace, but by morning she fully intended to be on her way back to Denver.

Apache smiled as his gaze swept over the stiff little back turned to him. He could nearly read Emerald's thoughts. He knew she was scheming to best him, but she would not succeed. With Sal's help, he'd managed to get her away from Dalton, and he wouldn't let her go flying back into the man's arms. Emerald would not be free of him until he convinced her that her intended bridegroom was the man responsible for her father's death. And knowing Emerald's stubborn streak, that would take some time.

For several miles Emerald managed to remain stiffly erect in the saddle so as not to come into contact with the broad chest behind her. However, as the wearying miles passed beneath the horse's hooves, the constant strain took its toll. The bruises she'd received from her fall earlier began to ache, and sharp pains shot through the taut muscles along her back until she had to give in to the need to relax. In an effort to hide her surrender, she furtively eased back against Apache bit by bit. She did not realize that a sigh of relief escaped from her as the tension in her body ebbed.

Apache chuckled low in his throat, the sound barely audible to his own ears. It had taken her longer than he expected to succumb to the jolting ride. He knew the discomfort her unyielding posture had created. If you didn't move with the horse, every step it took jarred your entire body until your teeth felt as if they would fall out. Sympathizing with her plight, he shifted in the saddle so that his lean body cupped hers, cushioning her against further hardship during the last few miles through the foothills to the mountain man's cabin.

In a short while, Apache felt her relax completely against him and knew that she slept. A tender smile played over his lips as he adjusted her cape securely about her to keep her warm and encircled her with a protective arm.

With her head resting beneath his chin, the sweet fragrance of her hair filled his nostrils, and he felt his blood leap in his veins. It ran hot and fast through every part of his lean body, making him swell with the need to feel himself deep inside the soft, pliable flesh of the woman in his arms.

Apache clenched his teeth against the desire that surged through him, but he could not suppress the memory of the ripe young body from which he was separated by only a few layers of clothing. He groaned inwardly and drew in a deep breath of cold night air in an effort to quell the tide of passion washing over him like a tidal wave.

He ached and throbbed against the tight prison of his britches and fought the urge to rein the stallion to a halt and make love to Emerald under the stars. His knuckles grew white from the pressure of his grip on the reins. He wanted Emerald, but he had no intention of becoming involved with her again. He had kidnapped her for one reason only, and he would not allow himself to give in to the desire she could create in him with only the smell of her golden hair.

Emerald Banyon was a means to an end for him and that was all. By getting her away from Dalton, he was thwarting the gambler's plans for her as well as keeping the man from getting his hands on the claim deed he needed to fulfill the contract to the investors back East.

With the thought, Apache felt the tension ease from his body and he smiled grimly. It wouldn't be a simple matter to be alone with Emerald in the cabin again. It would test his willpower to the limit, but he was confident in his ability to control his life. He had done it in the past and he would do it again in the future. He would not let his desire for one woman change the course he had set for himself.

Emerald stirred and rubbed her eyes as Apache reined in the stallion in front of Jeb Taylor's place. "Have we reached the cabin?'' she murmured sleepily. She made no move to leave the comfortable warmth of Apache's arms.

"Sit still," he said, swinging a long leg across the horse's back and dismounting. He tied the reins to a discarded wagon wheel that leaned precariously against the cabin wall before he turned to lift Emerald from the saddle. Still drowsy with sleep, she yawned and laid her head against his shoulder as he carried her into the tiny one-room cabin that was bathed in starlight.

"Jeb's cleaned the place up since the last time we were here," he said with some surprise as he gently set her on the bed, now covered with clean sheets. After his visit last night, the old mountain man must have worked all night to straighten up the cabin and to dig out the rough cotton sheeting he'd used to cover the straw mattress.

Giving the cabin a quick inspection after lighting a lamp, Apache marveled at the homey atmosphere the old man had created for them. Jeb was a wily old goat, and he probably assumed that Apache's reason for wanting to be alone with Emerald was far different than the one he had in mind. Jeb might be toothless and gray, but he still had a taste for the ladies. He no doubt had figured there wasn't any other reason for his friend to bring a woman out to his remote cabin.

Apache chuckled at the thought as he crossed to the fireplace to kindle the fire. His reasons for bringing Emerald back to the cabin would seem sacrilegious to a man like Jeb, who thought women and whiskey were the essence of life.

Hunkering down in front of the stone hearth, Apache glanced at the bed where Emerald lay curled, sound asleep once more. The cabin had not been the only thing that had been transformed of late. He could see in her little resemblance to the near frozen waif whom he had rescued from the snowstorm only a few weeks earlier. The memory of how close she had come to death chilled him, and he turned his attention to building the fire.

He didn't want to think of their time together. Being close to her would be difficult enough for him without the memory of her innocent surrender to the passion that had flamed between them on that fateful morning. Again glancing at the small figure on the bed, he felt his blood begin to heat once more and quickly sought out the cold night air.

Apache busied himself with unsaddling the stallion and tethering him in the lean-to that Jeb had built for Ole Bessy. He brushed him down and gave him oats, and when he could find nothing else to keep his hands busy, he threw the saddlebags over his shoulder, collected the pillowcase that contained the rest of Emerald's clothes, and strode back to the cabin. He believed that he had himself under control once more where Emerald Banyon was concerned.

Emerald still slept as he unpacked the saddlebags and tossed them aside. He'd brought enough food to last them well over a week, and by the time it ran out, he should have accomplished what he had set out to do. Storing the canned goods away, he settled himself in front of the fire.

A deep furrow marked his brow as he made himself as comfortable as possible in the rope-seated chair. He stretched his muscular legs out before him and tilted the chair back on two legs, trying to relax. The midnight depths of his eyes reflected the firelight as he stared into the flames, ruminating over the past years that had led him to this moment in time.

Strangely, in looking back at the years he'd spent wandering, he found that he'd not been happy with the life he had chosen. He could not remember the last time he had felt truly free. The chains that had bound the boy to avenge his father still imprisoned the man. His hatred for Cash Dalton fettered him like manacles of steel. It held him to a course that prevented him from leading a normal life. It wouldn't let him find the contentment and happiness that other men took for granted.

"Damn! What in hell is wrong with me?" Apache muttered, running his long fingers through his hair in exasperation. Until recently, he'd never considered such things. He'd taken each day as it came and did not contemplate the future. He had spit in fate's eye, tempting it to do its worst and not giving a damn what happened once he settled the debt he owed Dalton.

Frustration welled within Apache's chest, making him feel as if he would explode. He shifted restlessly in the chair. He didn't know what had happened in the past weeks to make him begin to think of what the future would bring.

Beau Alexander Ryan seemed to have crept from the grave where Apache had buried him over ten years ago. His ghostly specter haunted the man known as Apache, making him remember the things that he had planned when he was still the son of a wealthy southern planter. He found himself visualizing a home and family, imagining what it would be like to have a wife and a son to carry on his name. The child of his loins would have raven hair and emerald eyes.

Apache bolted upright in his chair, realizing the disquieting path his musings had taken. A muscle worked in his jaw and his heart pounded against his ribs as his troubled gaze traveled to the woman sleeping peacefully on the narrow bed.

"I have to stop this," he muttered, feeling himself break into a cold sweat. Bracing his elbows on his knees, he buried his face in his hands and tried to rid himself of the image of the lush young body naked beneath him in passion. "Go back to your crypt, Beau. I have no need of you and your dreams. They're all fantasies created from desire, nothing more," he whispered.

The blazing heat of the fire made a resinous log pop loudly. It cracked like the sound of a pistol report and sent a shower of sparks up the chimney. The sharp bang brought Emerald awake with a startled cry upon her lips. She jerked upright and sat cowering in the middle of the bed, her eyes wide with fright.

Apache's head snapped up at her cry and, seeing her distress, he quickly crossed the few feet that separated them. Without thinking of anything beyond his need to erase the fear from her face, he took her into his arms and cradled her against his chest.

"It was only the fire. There's no reason to be afraid," he murmured soothingly against her tousled curls.

Emerald clung to him, seeking the security he represented. The terror she had experienced earlier had triggered dreams of the man called Red. The sound from the fire had come at the same time her subconscious was reliving the moment when her father was shot. The horror of it still held reign over her conscious mind as she buried her face against his chest, a soft whimper escaping from her lips.

"Hush now. You're safe," Apache said in an effort to quiet her. Disturbed by their close contact, he tried to ease himself free of her clinging arms. The feel of her was again kindling his desire.

"Please hold me," Emerald begged, needing his comforting presence to fight the nightmare that left her shaken and afraid.

Her anguished plea touched Apache deeply. In all the time that he had known Emerald Banyon, he had never seen her give in to her fears. And because she had bravely faced all of the obstacles in her path, he had let himself forget that she was a young, vulnerable woman who had endured more than most men he had known. She had hidden her apprehensions behind all her bluster and bravado. Only in her sleep did she let her guard down enough to let her fears take hold. It was then that her valiant spirit became battered by the terrifying images that her courage kept at bay during her waking hours.

Unable to deny her plea, Apache settled himself on the bed and lifted her onto his lap, cradling her like a

small child who needs comfort and reassurance. He
drew in a deep breath, steeling himself against his own
feelings as he held her tenderly in his arms. He felt a
deep need to share his strength with this tiny bit of a
woman who faced life undaunted by its hardships. He
wanted to lessen the pain that life had given her and
rekindle the indomitable spirit that had momentarily
staggered under the weight of her fear.

"My brave Emerald," Apache said as if speaking to
himself. "You thrust out that squared little chin and,
without asking help from any quarter, you take on the
world alone."

"I have no other choice," Emerald answered simply,
now fully awake, lying in the warm, protective circle
of his arms. She made no move to leave the comforting
embrace that chased away her fears.

"We all have choices. You need not fight all your
battles alone." Apache tipped her chin up and gazed
down into the emerald depths of her eyes as he spoke.

Emerald tugged at her lower lip with her teeth as she
met his penetrating gaze. Her expression grew pensive
as she slowly shook her head. "You're wrong, Apache.
I've learned the hard way that I can depend on no one
but myself, and I do what I have to to survive." Her
voice held a bitter note.

"Is that the reason you were going to marry Cash
Dalton?" Apache asked.

Emerald shifted uneasily and looked away from him,
unable to meet his gaze. "Why I intend to marry Cash
is none of your concern."

"Intentions be damned," Apache said, his gentle
mood evaporating like snow under a hot summer's sun.
"I thought I had already made it clear to you that you're
not marrying Dalton, tomorrow or any other day."

Before Apache could stop her, Emerald scrambled off
his lap and stood glaring at him. "I don't see how you
can stop me. You can't keep me here forever."

"I can keep you here until you come to your senses
and realize that Dalton isn't who you think he is. The

man is no good.'' Apache's voice was low and calm. His face set, he folded his arms over his chest and watched Emerald through narrowed lids.

"Of all the nerve!" she spluttered. "You sit in judgment of a man who has treated me better than anyone else in my life. You condemn him when you're not fit to wipe his boots.''

"Emerald, I'm warning you to keep your temper in check,'' Apache growled, a muscle working in his cheek.

"Threaten me all you like, Apache Ryan, but I won't stand here and listen to you vilify Cash when he has done nothing wrong but insult your manhood by challenging you in the Gold Dust.''

"Damn it, Emerald, that's enough. You don't know what you're talking about. You're too blinded by the man's money and the things he's given you to see what a weasel he really is.'' Apache came to his feet, towering over her.

"At least he's not a seducer of innocent young girls,'' Emerald spat, her eyes flashing green fire.

Apache felt the blow of her words like a fist in his gut. His nostrils flared as he drew in a sharp breath and his eyes grew as cold as the night that surrounded the cabin. "He doesn't have to seduce them. He buys them with gifts and fancy promises.''

Infuriated beyond control by his insinuation, Emerald's hand lashed out before she had time to consider her own action. She gave Apache a resounding blow across the cheek. The sound of flesh meeting flesh echoed eerily through the dead silence that suddenly engulfed the cabin as the two combatants stood facing each other. Both were momentarily stunned by the violence.

The glacial expression that came to Apache's face sent a chill down Emerald's spine, and she took an involuntary step backward, bracing herself for retaliation. She had no time to retreat farther. Apache shot his hand out and grabbed her by the arm. She strained futilely against his grip, but the fingers that held her were like steel. She cringed inwardly as he drew her slowly toward him.

"I should give you the beating you so richly deserve for that, but I've never hit a woman, and no matter how much you need it, I won't now," Apache said, his voice low and menacing.

The relief his words brought Emerald was only a fleeting thing before he wrapped a strong arm around her and imprisoned her against his hard body. "There are far more pleasant ways to punish a hot-tempered vixen."

"Please, no," Emerald said at the look that flamed in the dark, moonless depths of his eyes. "Don't do this, Apache."

"Since you consider me to be a seducer of innocent young girls, I don't see why I shouldn't add more sin to my already tarnished image," Apache said, gliding his hand up her back and capturing the back of her head. He wound his fingers through her golden curls, holding her immobile. His mouth descended over hers, ravaging the tender, trembling flesh of her lips.

Emerald pummeled his chest with her fists, but the space between them allowed her no room to do any damage. Held firmly, she was helpless to prevent him from taking his fill of her mouth.

When Apache ended the kiss, he found himself gazing down into briming green pools that reminded him of a lake reflecting the forest at twilight. He felt his stomach twist into knots at the look of undisguised anguish in her eyes. Tenderness welled in his chest, but he hardened himself against it, refusing to allow himself to feel compassion.

"Apache," Emerald pleaded. "Don't do this to us. I can't bear it."

Unwilling to surrender, Apache kept her captive in his arms. "Why, Emerald? Tell me one good reason why I shouldn't take you here and now. You're willing enough to go to Dalton's bed."

"Because . . ." Emerald paused to draw in a ragged breath. "Because . . . I love you." The words seemed to be torn from her throat and she burst into tears, collapsing against his chest.

At her confession, Apache felt a thrill that began in the soles of his feet and worked its way up to the top of his head. Every sinew of his body screamed with it, and he threw back his head and laughed with pure joy.

"My sweet, adorable Emerald," he said. "What am I going to do with you? One minute you're trying to claw out my eyes and then in the next you're telling me that you love me."

Hugging her close, he stood savoring the pleasure her three small words gave him. In his wildest imaginings he had never dreamed he would hear those words from her lips. Nor did he realize until that moment that he had wanted to hear them. Elated, he chuckled again.

"Damn you, Apache," Emerald cursed. She burned with humiliation for revealing her deepest feelings to him, only to have him laugh at her. Angrily, she pushed herself out of his arms and wiped her eyes with the back of her hand. "Don't laugh at me. How I feel changes nothing. Now I want you to take me back to Denver."

"Emerald, love, it changes everything." With the grace of a mountain lion stalking its prey, Apache closed the space between them.

Emerald shook her head. "I won't allow it to—"

Apache placed a silencing finger against her lips. "Hush, love. The time for talking has passed." Tenderly, he cupped her chin in the palm of his hand and, lowering his head, he took her lips once more. He explored their fullness with his tongue before delving into the sweetness beyond.

Emerald fought against the heady excitement his touch created within her. She didn't want to respond to him. She'd made a fool of herself by confessing her love, and if she gave way to the temptation of his beckoning lips, she knew she would be lost.

She steeled herself to stand impassive under his assault upon her senses, but as the kiss deepened, her will to resist Apache ebbed. Her love for him left her defenseless. Her rising ardor destroyed the last bastion of her resistance, and with a moan of defeat, she molded herself to his hard, lean body. She wound her arms about his neck and clung to him for support as her knees turned to liquid beneath her.

"My lovely Emerald," Apache breathed. His voice had grown husky and strained from the passion raging in his blood. The strong muscles in his back and shoulders flexed as he glided his hand down her body and beneath her knees, and then swept her up into his arms. His mouth reclaimed hers as he carried her to the bed and laid down with her upon the straw mattress.

He savored her honeyed mouth and hungrily moved his hands over her, following each line of her supple body until he grew frustrated by the material that separated him from the silken flesh beneath it. With swift and experienced fingers, he worked loose the tiny buttons that ran down the front of the blue merino gown. Raising himself on one elbow, he eased back the soft woolen fabric to expose the smooth skin to his searing gaze. His breath grew uneven as his eyes lingered on the ivory mounds tipped by erect buds of rose. With a low moan, he buried his face in the jasmine-scented valley between her breasts and held her to him. He lay still for a long moment, letting his senses luxuriate in the smell and feel of her after being denied that pleasure for so long.

When his body began to demand to know more of her, he eased her gown from her shoulders and down over her hips and legs. His eyes never left her as he tossed the garment aside and then swiftly undressed himself.

"You are so beautiful," he murmured as his gaze moved hotly over her sleek young body, taking in each smooth line and curve. When his eyes had feasted their fill, he came back to her and took her lips in a searing kiss that left them both breathless. He stroked and explored the hills and hollows of her silken flesh until the yearning to taste all of her luscious body overpowered him and drew him away from her mouth to seek other bounties.

Apache's lips left a fiery trail along her cheek and the slender column of her neck as he made his way down to the swollen mounds of her breasts. He cupped one firm globe in his hand, tantalizing it with his thumb as he took the erect tip of its mate into his mouth. His tongue played an erotic game with the passion-hardened nipple, circling it, flicking it, before he began to suckle like a man starved. Not wanting to offend its twin, he made his way slowly down the ivory slope and into the valley before he began the ascent to the other, equally enticing peak.

He heard Emerald moan softly as he glided his hand down along the flat surface of her belly to the golden forest of curls. He lingered there momentarily, arousing her further with his flat palm before moving on to the down-covered thighs that trembled slightly under his touch. His breathing became labored as he began to stroke the soft inner surface of her thighs and felt them open to him. Slowly, temptingly, he ventured into the moist, inviting valley that held the passage of life.

Gently, he delved into the dark warmth of her and felt the satiny walls quiver with the desire to know more of him. But Apache did not give in to their gentle urging. He craved more than a swift culmination to his passion. He wanted her to experience total rapture before he found his own.

Titillating each inch of her flesh with his tongue, he moved along the flat planes of her belly and down to the golden junction of her thighs. He nuzzled her, drawing in the musky scent of her womanhood before he wrapped his arms about her hips and raised her to his mouth. His tongue delved, flicked, and teased as he explored all of her feminine secrets.

Emerald abandoned herself to the soul-shattering sensations Apache's hands and mouth aroused in her body. They engulfed her, searing through her veins in a current of heat that left her breathless. Wantonly, she arched to him. Her hips moved of their own volition under his intoxicating touch as she became immersed in the pleasure he gave her. With her head thrown back, she dug her fingers into the sheets and cried out Apache's name as the tiny ripple of ecstasy grew into a tidal wave. It centered in the core of her being, exploding there and leaving her trembling from the power of her release. Limp, her heart pounding against her ribs, she lay sated and gasping for breath.

Her cry of rapture sent a thrill of pleasure through Apache. He smiled as he lowered her hips and moved to cover her with his own passion-hardened body. He had given Emerald the ultimate pleasure, and now his body demanded fulfillment. The muscles rippled gracefully beneath the supple, tanned skin of his back as he slid easily into the warm passage that still quivered with ecstasy. He moved his lean hips slowly at first, letting his subtle thrusts rekindle the fires of passion within Emerald's body.

Emerald drew in a sharp breath as the heady sensations began to mount once more. Her hips moved with his as she wound her arms about his neck and locked her legs about his waist, wanting to know all of him. Greedily, she took his lips, her tongue exploring his mouth as she became the aggressor.

They moved together, each thrust of their hips carrying them closer to the mystical paradise where only lovers are allowed to enter and dwell for a time among the fiery rainbows of passion before journeying on to the place where golden ecstasy reigns. Clinging together, they soared upward on a chariot of pleasure to end their quest in the blissful arms of rapture. Their cries mingled as nature's most treasured gift was bestowed upon them.

Apache collapsed over Emerald and buried his face in the curve of her neck to savor the sweetness of his release. He felt reborn. No shadows from his past lingered to darken the horizon of his life. The barriers around his heart had been breached by the woman whose slender arms held him close to her. Because of Emerald, he had given of himself completely for the first time in years, and his reward was to find the hollow space within him now filled with the golden light of hope. Apache felt the sting of tears prickle his thick-lashed eyes at the overpowering sense of freedom that swept through him. Emerald's love had unshackled him from the painful memories that had governed his life for more than ten years.

Still wrapped in the warm glow left by their love-making, Emerald lay luxuriating in the lanquid contentment that filled her. A tranquil smile tugged up the corners of her lips as she stared up at the shadowy ceiling and ran her fingers through the soft raven hair of the man she loved. She had at long last found where she belonged. It was not back in a small farmhouse in Georgia, nor was it in the Gold Dust Saloon. It was in Apache's arms.

Satisfied in body and soul, and at peace with the world, she did not want to break the spell of enchantment that shielded them against the encroachment of thoughts of the future or of the past. She snuggled against Apache, her body sated and her heart brimming with love.

"Good night, my love," she whispered as feathery lashes floated down over eyes that reflected all that was in her heart. Emerald drifted into a dreamless sleep.

Apache brushed his lips lightly against her brow and wrapped his arms about her slender body, cradling her burnished-gold head on his shoulder. Tonight, Beau Alexander Ryan had been given a second chance to live, and Apache was determined to treasure every moment of that life with the woman he loved. His sensual lips curved upward in a smile of contentment as he laid his head against Emerald's and drifted into the first untroubled sleep he'd had in years.

Chapter 11

Dust motes floated in the pale sunbeams that peeked through the cracks in the shutters covering the lone glass window that Jeb Taylor proudly boasted about to his friends. To the old mountain man who had spent more winters than he cared to remember completely snowbound inside cabins, unable to see the light of day, the glass-paned window was a luxury that made him feel as if he were living in a grand mansion instead of a tiny log cabin. He would have been insulted to know that his prized possession went unnoticed by the couple cuddled in his narrow bed.

Dark head resting against gold, they lay with limbs entwined, dreading the moment when they would have to leave the warmth of the quilts to rekindle the fire that had burned down to coals during the night.

Emerald stretched her arms over her head and yawned before quickly snuggling once more beneath the covers against Apache. She shivered from the cold that had invaded the cabin as they slept.

"Shall I warm you up this morning?" Apache murmured softly, nuzzling her cheek and drawing in the sweet smell of her.

"I'd prefer that you build a fire. It's freezing in here," Emerald said, shivering once more.

With a chuckle, Apache wrapped his arms about her and rolled her on top of him. Her golden hair cascaded in a veil about them as she lay propped on his chest,

smiling down at him. He fingered a long curl absently
and arched a provocative brow at her.

"I can think of far better things to do than freeze my
rear off building a fire."

"Now, what might they be?" Emerald teased, feigning innocent wonder.

"This," came Apache's throaty whisper. Using the
golden strand of hair, he drew her down to his lips. The
kiss, which had begun as a gentle caress, deepened as
his ardor rose to a throbbing intensity. Savoring the feel
of her supple flesh beneath his fingers, he slid his hands
down her back and over the swell of her hips to cup her
buttocks in his palms and move her against him.

Emerald felt a dewy warmth invade her languid flesh
at the touch of his arousal against her. Her body re-
sponded as if on cue. The cold that had seeped into the
cabin was vanquished by the heat of the passion rising
in her, and she met him kiss for kiss as her hips moved
sensually, teasingly against his.

With a low, animalistic groan, foreplay forgotten in
the firestorm raging in his blood, Apache flipped Emerald onto her back and entered her inviting warmth.
The muscles in his lean thighs and buttocks moved
smoothly beneath his resilient skin as he thrust deeply
into her pulsing flesh.

Emerald gloried in the wild fervor of his lovemaking.
She moved with him, meeting him as an equal on their
torrid journey to ecstasy. She arched against him, clinging to his shoulders. Soft moans of pleasure came from
deep within her throat as the tiny ember at her core
turned molten and then burst into a shower of radiant
sensations that left her breathless.

The force of her release swept away the last of
Apache's control. He moaned against her neck as he
thrust deep within her, his essence spilling to mingle
with her nectar in the womb of life.

They lay intimately bound, their hearts beating as
one as each savored the splendor of their union. At last,
when the cold of the cabin began to penetrate through

the warmth left by their lovemaking, Apache moved to Emerald's side and pulled the covers up over them. He lay propped on one elbow, cushioning his cheek in his wide palm as he gazed down at her. A crooked, satisfied grin curved the corners of his sensual lips up as he lazily traced the smooth line of her flushed cheek with the tip of one finger.

"Now, wasn't that better than building a fire?"

A sated smile curled Emerald's passion-bruised lips, and her cheeks flushed a soft rose. "I agree, but unless we plan to stay in bed all day, you still have to build a fire."

Apache shrugged his bare shoulders. "Staying in bed all day isn't such a bad idea."

"I'm afraid we'd get hungry."

"There's only one type of hunger that concerns me." Apache chuckled as he dropped a light kiss on the tip of her nose.

"Oh, no, you don't." Emerald laughed, bracing her hands against his chest and pushing him away as she sat up. "I intend to have a good breakfast before we go back to Denver."

"Who is going back to Denver?" Apache queried as he, too, sat up and began to pull on his britches.

"We are, as soon as we have breakfast."

"Why are you so anxious to get back there?" Apache asked, suddenly growing suspicious. All the old distrust arose anew to make him wonder at her motives. His mellow mood rapidly faded into oblivion as he realized that Emerald had yet to say that she wouldn't marry Dalton. She had professed her love but nothing more. Annoyed, Apache jerked on his boots, pushed himself to his feet, and shrugged into his shirt. He crossed to the cold fireplace and began to toss kindling onto the gray coals.

"I need to see Cash. This was supposed to be our wedding day, if you remember," Emerald said between chattering teeth. Still feeling lighthearted after the night she had spent with Apache, she was completely unaware of the tension mounting within him as he hunkered down in front of the fireplace. Shivering from the cold, she scrambled off the bed and hastened to retrieve her scattered clothing. She quickly slipped into her petticoat and gown while Apache busied himself rekindling the fire. When the last of the tiny buttons were fastened down the front of her gown and she had pulled on her stockings and shoes, she hurried to the beckoning warmth of the flames. She held her chilled hands near the blaze as she glanced curiously over her shoulder at Apache. Wondering at his moody expression, Emerald asked, ''You don't still intend to keep me here, do you?''

Apache glanced up at her and shrugged.

''Apache, I need to talk to Cash—'' Emerald began, but Apache cut her off before she could tell him that she wanted to tell Cash that she couldn't go through with their wedding after having spent the night in the arms of the man she truly loved.

''Talk to Dalton!'' Apache exploded. ''How can you even contemplate such a thing? The man doesn't deserve another word from you after all he's done.''

''I think he does,'' Emerald shot back. She might love Apache, but he could vex her quicker than any other person alive.

''Well, I don't, and that's the end of it,'' was Apache's angry retort.

''It's not the end of it by a long shot, Apache Ryan. You can't expect me to hurt someone who has been good to me just on your say-so alone?''

''Damn it, Emerald,'' Apache said, glowering up at her. ''I thought we had settled this last night. Your wedding to Dalton is not going to take place, so you have no reason to see the man again.''

Emerald's eyes snapped with green fire as she braced her hands on her hips and stood glaring down at Apache. ''You may not like Cash, but he is my friend, and I won't hurt him to appease you.''

''You're right about one thing: I don't like the man,

and that's a mild way to put it. To be exact, I hate the ground the bastard walks on, and I'll do anything to stop him from getting his hands on the claim deed you own," Apache growled.

"Even kidnap me?" Emerald asked, her voice little more than a strained whisper. She blanched with the startling thought that all they had shared through the night and this morning had been but a convenient means to tear her away from Cash in order to keep him from getting her claim deed.

"Even kidnap you," Apache shot back, too angry to realize the damaging impact of his unthinking words.

Emerald turned her back to Apache to hide the emotions sweeping through her. Shame raced through every sinew of her body at her weakness in once more falling prey to Apache and her own passion. Everything that had transpired between them had only been his cruel way to subjugate her to his will. And she had given him the weapon to use against her. She had foolishly told him of her love. For one weak moment, Emerald gave in to the spasms of pain that the depths of Apache's treachery created within her. Then her temper and pride came once more to her rescue. She drew in a deep, angry breath and stiffened her spine. She'd be damned before she gave him the satisfaction of knowing how much he had hurt her.

Apache sensed her pain and began to reach out to her, to tell her that he hadn't meant a word that he'd said. He wanted to explain the reason he'd brought her to the cabin and to tell her of his love. The words were on the tip of his tongue when she spun on her heel to face him. With her chin raised at a haughty angle, she glared at him through narrowed green eyes that glittered with fury.

"I want you to take me back to Denver now, Apache. If you planned to sway me with your lovemaking, then you've failed. A tumble or two in bed doesn't mean that I've changed my mind about anything, and that includes marrying Cash." Emerald's breasts heaved as she drew in quick breaths in an effort to quell the pain that renewed itself at the odd expression that crossed his face before it became devoid of emotion.

"Your little confession of love last night didn't mean much, did it?" Apache asked, glowering at her.

Emerald jerked as if he had slapped her, but she stood her ground, unwilling to let him see any emotion. "Why should it? You don't have anything to offer me. At least Cash is willing to give me his name as well as all that goes with it."

Her words resurrected the betrayal in Apache's past. He came out of his chair as if hit by a streak of lightning. With a growl, he grabbed Emerald by the arms and jerked her against him. His eyes narrowed to mere slits as he glared down at her, his fingers bruising her tender flesh beneath the sleeves of her gown.

"I thought you were different, but you're just like all the other damned greedy women in the world. You'd do anything for money, even sleep with the man who had your father killed." With a snarl of disgust, he shoved her away from him.

Shocked by his accusation against Cash, Emerald staggered back against the table. The motion upset the tin coffeepot, and it rolled unheeded off the table and landed with a clatter on the floor. Emerald eyed Apache as if he had suddenly gone mad as she absently rubbed her stinging arms. "That's a lie."

"Is it? Then why is he so anxious to marry you? Your claim is the only one that he hasn't gotten by killing the owner," Apache said, his tone icy as the frost that blanketed the morning landscape in silver.

"Cash wouldn't do something that terrible. It's only your hatred that makes you say such things about him."

"Then there is nothing further left for me to say. Believe what you will about the man. I know what he's like, and that's why I won't let you marry him no matter how determined you are to get your greedy little hands on all of his ill-gained wealth."

"You can't keep me a prisoner here forever, no matter what you think. One way or the other, I will get away from you, Apache.''

"You might get away, but I'll find you, Emerald. And then you'll regret having left.''

"Threaten all you like. If you think for one minute that I'm afraid of you, then you're wrong.''

Apache gave Emerald a slow, calculating smile that did not reach his ebony gaze. "Don't brag yet, my dear. I lived many years with the Indians, and I know ways that will make you afraid of me. You have as yet to learn why I've earned the name Apache.''

Emerald felt the sudden need to retreat to a safer distance from the stranger before her. Gone was the gentle lover. In his place was a man she did not know, a man who she sensed could resort to violence if pushed too far. A tingle of apprehension raced up her spine, but she did not give in to the urge to flee.

"I know enough about your skill at torture after last night,'' was Emerald's brash retort. Hurt and anger mingled, replacing her fear, as she remembered how cruelly he had used her love against her. It was a volatile mixture that made her reckless in her need to return the pain she was feeling.

Apache flinched inwardly, but gave no sign that her words had any effect on him. "Then heed my warning, Emerald. Don't push me too far.''

"You won't get away with this, Apache. Cash will come looking for me.''

"If he's that foolish, then it will be my pleasure to put a bullet between his eyes. It's long overdue. I've owed him a killing for too many years.''

The violence that laced Apache's words made Emerald's insides quiver with fear. "This is insane. You can't honestly expect me to believe that you'd kill a man because of me.''

"You're right. You wouldn't be the reason I'd kill Dalton. He earned that fate ten years ago. You're only a means to an end.''

"That's all this has been, hasn't it?'' Stricken, Emerald's voice was raspy from the pain that filled her throat. Apache had just confirmed her earlier suspicions. Her eyes glistened with unshed tears and her lower lip began to tremble. "You want to kill Cash and you've used me as bait to bring him to you."

The look of misery on her face stabbed at Apache's heart. "If that had been my only motive, I wouldn't have gone to such trouble. It would have been far simpler to call Dalton out."

The tears she had been trying to hide spilled down Emerald's cheeks. Annoyed with herself, she swiped at her eyes with the back of her hand as she asked, "Then why did you bring me here?"

"Damn it, I told you why. I couldn't let you marry the man who is responsible for your father's death."

"Then that's the only reason you brought me here?"

Apache glanced away from her, unable to look into her tear-bright eyes and lie. "What other reason could there be?"

Unable to fight the heavy weight of despair that filled her, Emerald sank down in the chair Apache had vacated. She clasped her hands in her lap and bowed her head in defeat. Her words were only a soft whisper as she asked, "If I agree not to marry Cash, will you take me back to Denver?"

"Do you believe what I've said about Dalton?" Apache asked, suppressing the urge to kneel at her side and beg her to forgive him for treating her so cruelly. But he did not follow his feelings. He had to be certain that she wouldn't turn to Dalton once she was back in Denver, or all of the pain and heartache they had inflicted upon each other would be for nothing.

Emerald pressed her eyes closed and shook her head. She had seen the man who had actually killed her father, and she would not condemn a man who had befriended her just to appease Apache's hatred.

"Then you're not going back to Denver." Apache's words sounded final. He strode to the door, took his coat from the wooden peg on the wall, and shrugged into it. He clamped his hat down on his head as he glanced back at Emerald sitting in front of the fire.

"I'm going to feed Rogue, and then I'm riding into town, alone," Apache said gruffly. His hand closed over the latch, but before he could pull it back, Emerald's quiet, reflective question brought him up short.

"What proof do you have that Cash is responsible for the claim jumping?"

Apache released a long breath. "I only have my suspicions, Emerald. From past experience, I know the man and what he is capable of when he wants something. And he wants the claims."

Emerald turned to look at Apache. "Tell me how you know?"

"I wish I could, but for now, all I can do is ask that you trust me."

"I wish that I could, Apache, but until you give me proof that Cash is what you claim he is, then I won't change my feelings about him."

"Then I'll have to find the evidence to link him with the claim jumpings, won't I?" Apache opened the door and stepped out into the frosty morning.

For a long while after she heard Apache ride away, Emerald sat staring into the flames, reflecting on what he had told her. His accusations against Cash had brought the day of her father's death vividly back to her, resurrecting all that had transpired on that fatal morning.

She could see each of the men clearly in her mind, but she could not place Cash's friendly face behind the mask of the man in black. The man's dark eyes were similar to Cash's, as they were to Apache's, but neither man she knew had eyes as cold and unemotional as those of the man who had ordered her father slain. Those eyes had held nothing but death.

Emerald shivered at the memory and absently rubbed her arms against the chill it created. She wanted to trust Apache. Her heart cried out for her to believe all he said, but she could not turn her back on Cash because of Apache's hatred for him. He had been too good to her in her time of need. She owed him her loyalty even if it broke her heart by driving the man she loved away from her.

At last, Emerald roused herself from her reverie to realize that she was free to do as she pleased since Apache was not there to stop her. She could walk back to Denver under her own power. Settling the matter in her mind, she stood and crossed to the door. She tried the latch and found that it would not budge. Apache must have suspected that sooner or later she would attempt to escape, no matter how many threats he had made, and had taken care to make sure that she couldn't. He had locked her in.

"Damn you, Apache," Emerald cursed as she stamped back over to the chair and flopped down into it. Her shoulders sagged. In some ways he knew her much better than she knew herself.

Settling himself in a seat across from Jeb Taylor, Apache paid no heed to the table next to them where a man lay slumped with his head buried in his arms. It wasn't an unusual sight to see men overcome by liquor. When they passed out, they were allowed to sleep it off at a vacant table till the next day or until someone wanted their space for a game of cards. Then they were tossed out onto the street. If they were fortunate and the weather was fair, they recovered their senses with no harm done.

"What are you doing back in town, Apache?" Jeb asked. "I thought you and the little missy planned to stay awhile at the cabin."

"I just needed to get away for a while," Apache said, tipping his hat to the back of his head and tilting his chair back on two legs so that it rested against the wall behind him.

Jeb grinned knowingly. "So things ain't goin' as smoothly as you thought they would, huh?"

"Nothing has gone smoothly since I met Emerald, so I don't see why it should be any different now."

"You got it bad, ain't you?"

"I don't know what you're talking about, Jeb, and I wish you'd change the subject. I came in here for a drink and a little relaxation."

Jeb chuckled and shook his head in dismay. "I don't believe it. After all the years I've know'd you, I never seen you so taken with a woman before. That Banyon gal must really be special."

Apache slammed his chair back down on the floor, the sound of it rousing the drunk at the table next to them. "I don't want to talk about Emerald."

"Well, should I take that to mean I'll be a-gettin' my hearth and home back much sooner than I thought?" Jeb asked, suppressing another grin behind a gnarled, blue-veined hand as he rubbed his salt-and-pepper beard.

"No," came Apache's short reply.

"You ain't never been one for talkin' much about personal things, but you shore do clam up when it comes to the little missy." Bemused, Jeb shook his head and chuckled again. "Yep, you really got it bad."

"Damn it, Jeb. Can't you talk about something else?" Apache poured himself a drink and downed it in one gulp. Jeb's questions did not help the turmoil left inside him from his encounter with Emerald that morning. He had fouled everything up between them with his obsession with getting revenge on Cash Dalton. And he had made it worse by letting Emerald believe that he had only made love to her in order to stop her from marrying the man.

"Damn," he muttered under his breath as he refilled his glass. He had wanted to tell her of his love, but his memories of Rachel had made him see red when Emerald had thrown Cash's wealth in his face. On the long ride back into town, he had gone over and over their argument and had come to realize that he had been at fault. He had left her no choice but to try to save her pride by marrying Cash. In all the time they had been together, he had never given her any hope of anything beyond the moment. Now he didn't know how to right things between them. He had savaged her with his words, ruthlessly disregarding the hurt he'd seen in her eyes, to try to turn her away from Dalton based on his suspicions alone. Apache admitted to himself that his cruel actions had partly stemmed from jealousy. He didn't want Emerald to care for anyone but him.

Apache knew his feelings were selfish. But after depriving himself of love for so many years, he was a man emotionally starved. He wasn't willing to share Emerald with anyone, especially his enemy, be it in friendship or in any other way.

Apache gulped down the drink in his hand. He wanted Emerald all to himself, but after his actions that morning he was afraid he had destroyed any hope of that ever happening. He stared at the crowd at the bar without seeing them. In his mind's eye he saw Emerald's loveliness, her eyes glistening with unshed tears as she faced him, braving his threats and standing her ground against the pain he mercilessly inflicted upon her. His heart lurched inside his chest at the memory. He feared he had slain any love she had for him with his cruel, barbed words.

"I know I ain't much company compared to the little missy, but you could at least answer my questions when I ask you somethin'," Jeb grumbled, jerking Apache away from his thoughts.

"What did you say?" Apache asked, rubbing a hand over his face as if the action would wipe Emerald's image from his mind.

"I asked you if the little missy ever remembered anythin' that might help the law find out who them damned claim jumpers are?"

"I'm afraid not. Emerald says she can't remember anything about them."

"It's a golldarn shame that she can't," Jeb said, taking a loose-lipped swig of the Taos Lightning in his glass. He smacked his lips together and then gave Apache a toothless grin. "It ain't the finest liquor in the world, but it shore can warm a man up."

"Have you heard anything more about the claim jumpers?" Apache asked.

"Everything seems to have calmed down. There ain't been no more murders that I've heard of recently."

"Maybe they've gotten all the land they need."

"That don't make a lot of sense if it's gold they're after. None of them claims they jumped had any pay dirt. And they didn't get their hands on the little missy's claim."

"Well, if you hear anything, let me know," Apache said. He already knew the reason the claim jumping had stopped, and he also knew the motive behind Dalton's sudden interest in marrying Emerald. He wanted to acquire her claim legally. The man was as wily as a fox, but he couldn't outsmart Apache with his sly maneuvering.

Apache shoved back his chair and stood. "It's time I got back to the cabin. I don't want to leave Emerald there alone after dark."

"Well, give my best regards to the little missy. She's one purty gal, and if you've got any sense in that hard head of yours, you'd get yourself to a preacher just as soon as you can. Gals like her don't come 'round often in a man's life, and when you find one, you'd better latch on to her."

"Thanks, Jeb. I'll take your advice into consideration," Apache said, and slapped a twenty-dollar gold piece down on the table. "Buy yourself a bottle and a little loving, old man."

"I believe I will," Jeb said, and chuckled. He quickly tucked the money away in the pocket of his buckskin coat and patted it happily. "There's a blond gal over at the Gold Dust that I got a hankerin' for. She's a real looker, with tits big as melons."

"Give Lusty Sal my best." Apache laughed and strode from the Denver House.

Jeb downed the liquor in his glass, smacked his lips, gave a loud belch and an equally loud ''Ah,'' before he shoved back his chair and followed in Apache's wake. He did not notice the beefy face that raised itself from folded, brawny arms at the next table. Nor did he see the snarl that marred the man's thick lips as he peered through the window and watched Apache mounting the stallion outside.

The sound of Apache's chair crashing to the floor had roused Jack Parkin out of his stupor. It had taken several minutes for his mind to clear the fog left by the whiskey he had consumed earlier in the afternoon. When it began to dissipate and he could orient his thoughts, he had instantly recognized the voice that had haunted him since the night in the Gold Dust Saloon. He would never forget the humiliation he had suffered at the bastard's hands over the hurdy-gurdy girl with the golden hair.

As he listened to the man, whose name he'd learned after questioning several prospectors who had witnessed his run-in with Apache Ryan, his rage simmered hot through his large body. Yet he had managed to control his anger. From what he had been told, Ryan was fast with a gun, and he had no intention of confronting the bastard when he would be at a disadvantage. He'd bide his time and wait for the right moment to strike.

He had pretended to sleep as he listened to Ryan and the old mountain man talk, hoping to learn any information that might help him. Jack realized that his chance to repay Ryan and the girl had come much sooner than he had hoped when he heard Ryan mention the old mountain man's cabin. Not wanting Ryan to recognize him and suspect his plans, Jack had waited patiently for him to leave before he raised his head.

Pushing himself out of his chair, he elbowed his way through a group of miners and hurried to the door. He didn't want to loose Ryan's trail. Mounting the scrawny bay mare that had been tethered alongside of Apache's stallion, he gave the reins a vicious yank, jerking her head about, and with a swift kick to her side he urged her in the direction Apache had traveled only moments before.

Jack knew the mare could not keep up with the stallion's pace, and he didn't want her to. His plan did not include facing Ryan. He preferred to let Ryan lead him to the little bitch who had started all the trouble before he killed him—preferably from behind. After Ryan was dead, he'd finished what the girl had started that night in the Gold Dust with her teasing smiles and provocative looks. She owed him, and he intended to see her pay in full.

The instincts that Apache had honed to a razor's edge through the years of living on the frontier were eclipsed by the turmoil of his thoughts as he rode back into the foothills. His mind was centered on the woman who awaited him and the dilemma of how to resolve the problems he had created between her and himself that morning. Absorbed in his musings, he failed to notice the man who rode stealthily behind him.

Still in an emotional quandary when he reached Jeb's cabin at twilight, Apache took his time stabling Rogue in the lean-to. Dreading the confrontation he knew awaited him in the cabin, he unsaddled the stallion, fed him, and gave him a brush-down before gathering up his courage to face Emerald.

It was not going to be easy to tell her of his love. He had paid dearly for loving Rachel, and it was going to take every ounce of fortitude he possessed to confess his feelings to Emerald. And after all he had said and done before, he must now brace himself for her rejection. He had used her cruelly and he could not blame her if she threw his love back in his face.

His thoughts on Emerald, Apache did not hear the furtive movements at the side of the lean-to as he stood staring at the ray of lantern light that filtered through the cracks in the shutters. Nor did he sense the danger lurking in the shadows behind him until he heard a twig crackle under a boot. From the corner of his eye, he caught only a glimpse of the rifle butt descending toward him, but was too late to deflect the blow that crashed against his skull. Stars exploded in his head and he staggered to his knees before he fell facedown and unconscious on the hard earth.

A smirk curled Jack Parkin's thick lips as he stood over Apache. He toed him roughly in the ribs with the point of his boot to make sure the man was in no condition to fight.

"Being fast with a gun didn't help you this time, did it, you bastard?" he growled as he reached for the strip of leather in his rear pocket and bent over the prone figure on the ground. He grabbed Apache's arms and bound them tightly behind him before he disarmed him. Sticking the revolver in his belt, Jack hefted Apache up over his shoulder and carried him toward the cabin.

Emerald bent to stir the pot of beans she had simmering over the fire. Soon after Apache left her that morning, she'd begun to plan her strategy. She knew she'd never be able to change his mind about keeping her hostage if she could not control her temper enough to make him see reason. So she had decided to alter her tactics. When Apache returned from Denver, she was determined to remain calm and composed no matter what he said or did. She would have a hot meal awaiting him and hoped that with his stomach full, he'd be in a better mood to listen to her.

When she'd heard him ride past the cabin to stable his horse in the lean-to, she'd hurriedly set the table with the two tin plates she had found earlier in the day. She had touched up her hair and straightened her gown, and then had set about to finish cooking the meal.

Emerald was so intent on keeping the beans from burning that when Jack kicked the locked door open and it crashed back against the wall, splintering with the impact, she jumped and, with a startled cry, spun about with the dripping ladle in her hand. The brown

stain that dribbled down the skirt of her gown went
unnoticed as she gaped at the burly figure filling the
doorway. When she recognized the burden across his
shoulder, she paled. The ladle fell from her nerveless
fingers to the hearth at her feet.

"My God, what's happened?" she asked. Frightened for the man she loved, Emerald failed to recognize Jack Parkin as she sped across the room to help
him with Apache. She did not realize the import of
the situation until he pushed her roughly out of the
way with one burly arm and dumped his burden unceremoniously to the floor at his feet.

With a cry of protest at the man's cruel actions, she
sank to her knees at Apache's side. Without giving the
stranger a second glance, she began her futile search
for the injuries that had left Apache ashen and unconscious. Finding no apparent wounds, she breathed a
sigh of relief, but it was short-lived as she looked once
more at the man towering over her.

"Help me. We must find where he's hurt," she
pleaded, her face white with the strain of seeing the
vital man she loved in such a debilitated state.

"He's going to be hurt far worse before I'm through
with him," Jack growled, kicking the door closed and
latching it securely.

Emerald's blood ran cold at his words. "What do you
mean?" she asked frantically.

"Exactly what I said, girlie. Jack Parkin don't forget
his debts."

"Jack Parkin," Emerald repeated, her eyes widening
with recollection. Until that moment she had forgotten
the miner who had accosted her in the Gold Dust. All
she had remembered of that night was the confrontation
between Apache and Cash.

Jack's thick lips spread into a semblance of a grin.
"You remember me now, don't you, girlie?"

"You're the man Cash ran out of the Gold Dust."
Emerald's voice was little more than a whisper.

"Yep, I'm the same one."

"But why have you hurt Apache? Cash is the one who told you not to come back to his saloon."

"Girlie, you're going to learn, just like this bastard, that I don't take kindly to being insulted by the likes of you or anyone else. A man has his pride."

Emerald's heart began to race wildly. The man was insane. He intended to avenge the slight to his pride on herself and Apache. She had to stop him before he killed them. She knew her only chance would be to get Apache's gun. Stealthily, so as not to draw his attention to her actions, she eased her hand down along Apache's side to his holster and found it empty.

"Are you looking for this?" Jack queried with a sneer on his beefy face. He patted the revolver at his waist. "I ain't just another dumb miner, girlie. I'm prepared for any tricks you plan to try."

Emerald drew in an unsteady breath. She had to find a way to mollify the man before he murdered them. "Jack, if I insulted you, I'm sorry."

"Your apologies ain't going to help you none. I don't like being made a laughingstock over a two-bit whore who sells herself to the highest bidder. And as far as this bastard is concerned"—Jack toed Apache with his boot—"his fate was sealed when he interfered in my business."

"Your quarrel is with me, not Apache. He only came to my aid as any gentleman would have. You can't kill a man for that."

"Gentlemen don't come to the aid of whores."

Emerald felt faint but fought against the weakness invading her limbs. If she and Apache were to survive, she would have to keep her wits about her. "You don't understand, Jack. I'm not what you think. I'm not what you think. I only danced at the Gold Dust, nothing more. I only took the job because I couldn't find anything else to keep me from starving."

"You can lie through your teeth all night, but that don't change a damned thing. Now get your ass away from that bastard and throw some food into them saddlebags by the door. After I finish him off, we're going up to my cabin in the mountains.''

Emerald's mind raced frantically for some way to stop Jack, but she could think of nothing to save herself or Apache as she packed the saddlebags and set them on the table.

''Now I want you to watch what happens when somebody crosses Jack Parkin.'' Pulling the revolver from the waist of his britches, he aimed it at Apache's head.

''No,'' Emerald screamed, throwing herself in front of the gun. ''Please, Jack. I'll do anything you want as long as you don't kill him.''

''You'll do what I want when he's dead. Now get out of the way.''

''Jack, you can force me to do your will, but wouldn't you enjoy it more if I were willing?'' she said desperately. ''Just imagine the pleasure we could have together if you will only leave Apache here, and alive.'' Emerald ran the tip of her tongue enticingly over her lips and took a deep breath to make her breasts press against the fabric of her bodice.

Jack bit his thick lower lip as his eyes dwelt on the swelling mounds beneath the blue wool of her gown. He could feel himself respond to her suggestion. His gaze shifted to the unconscious man at her feet. In his condition and with the cold weather, he wouldn't last the night without a fire to keep him warm.

Apache Ryan's death would be slow and agonizing. A bullet through the head would be too quick. It would be far more enjoyable for him to know that Ryan was suffering as he bedded his whore. The thought made Jack chuckle low in his throat. He'd let her pleasure him, and then he'd wring that lovely neck of hers with his bare hands.

''All right, girlie. I won't shoot him,'' Jack said at last. ''But he's still going to die.''

''What do you mean?'' Emerald asked, her panic making her voice quaver unsteadily.

''He'll freeze to death lying here without a fire.''
Jack turned to the bucket of water sitting by the hearth.
He picked it up and dumped it on the blazing fire. The
flames spluttered and died a smoky death.

Emerald closed her eyes and bit her lip until she tasted
her own blood. She knew it was useless to argue further
with the madman. She had saved Apache from certain
death by Parkin's revolver, but she feared she had con-
signed him to an even crueler fate. Her only hope was
that he would regain consciousness and be able to free
himself before he froze.

''Get your things, girlie. We've a ways to go tonight.''

Emerald pulled on her cape and picked up the saddlebags. She cast one last glimpse at the man who possessed her heart as Parkin pushed her toward the door
with the barrel of the revolver at the small of her back.

Please, God, let him live, she prayed silently as she
strode out into the moon-drenched night.

Chapter 12

The rays of an icy-white moon spilled in through the cabin door illuminating the figure lying on the dirt floor. Slowly regaining consciousness, Apache stirred, and after several moments, he opened his dark eyes. Groggy from the blow to his head, he lay staring up into the shadows and tried to sort through the disjointed thoughts tumbling about in his mind in an effort to remember where he was and why. He shivered from the cold and realized vaguely that he would have frozen to death if he had remained unconscious much longer. His body already felt like a lump of ice.

The cold helped to clear away the fog that clouded his thoughts, however, and he managed to recall the blow that had knocked him unconscious in the lean-to. As the memory took root, Apache turned his head to peer around him. The action served to make lightning explode in his skull. He drew in a sharp breath and clenched his teeth against the blinding bursts of light that shot through his head, yet he bore the excruciating pain in silence. It was with sheer willpower alone that he managed to shift awkwardly onto his side and raise his head to search the darkness for the woman he loved.

"Emerald," he called in a hoarse whisper that took all of his effort. He received no answer.

"Emerald," he called again, fighting against the waves of nausea and fear that ripped through his insides when all remained deathly quiet. Turning onto his stomach, he braced his chest against the dirt floor and pushed himself onto his knees. He called to Emerald once more but knew even as her name left his lips that he was alone. Like a wolf bereft at the loss of his mate, Apache's howl of anguish filled the cabin and drifted eerily through the still, moonlit night.

The muscles in his corded neck stood taut as he arched his head back and squeezed his eyes closed. His ashen features reflected his torment and a shudder passed through his lean body as he briefly surrendered to the grief welling in his chest for the brave young woman he had grown to love.

Then, as his thoughts turned to the man he suspected of taking Emerald away from him, he shed all emotion except rage. Again his cry shattered the night. "You bastard! If you harm one hair on her head, you'll regret the day you were born."

Apache's moon-drenched face hardened into a mask of cold fury as he threw off the veneer of civilization and became like the savages for whom he had been named. He was ruled by only one need: to protect the woman he loved. And he would not stop until Cash Dalton was dead.

A muscle twitched in his beard-stubbled jaw, but that was the only indication that he felt the stinging, needle-like pains that shot through his fingers as he worked to regain the use of his hands. The strip of leather that bound his wrists had cut off the circulation, and it took several minutes to recover enough feeling to retrieve the bowie knife that he kept strapped to his leg beneath his britches. With some difficulty, he eased the knife from its sheath and maneuvered the razor-sharp blade up between his hands to saw on his bonds. The leather strip gave way at last and he was free.

With his thoughts centered on finding Emerald, Apache disregarded the throbbing in his head and the queasy feeling in his stomach. He sheathed the bowie knife and pushed himself to his feet. He staggered unsteadily to the door and leaned briefly against the door frame to draw in several long breaths in an effort to quell the wave of nausea that left his limbs trembling.

Fighting against the weakness invading his body, he moistened his dry lips and made his way to the lean-to to find that Dalton had also taken Rogue, leaving him to travel on foot. Undeterred, Apache knelt to search for any sign that would indicate the direction he had taken.

A cold sweat beaded his brow as he touched the trampled grass and freshly turned earth of the stallion's tracks. Even in the darkness, the trail was clearly marked. There had been no effort made to try to cover the tracks.

Apache's lips curved into a sinister smile. Dalton's carelessness would cost him his life. Apache glanced once more at the tracks. Oddly, they did not lead back to Denver but into the mountains, and he wondered at Dalton's intentions. If he had come to rescue his bride-to-be, why was he heading away from Denver? A chill of fear raced up Apache's spine. Dalton might have reconsidered his options and decided it was far easier to get his hands on the claim deed without saddling himself with a wife.

With a negligent swipe of his hands, Apache brushed the sweat from his brow and set out on foot. His fear for Emerald's life driving him, he ignored the pain that slashed across his temples with each step he took. The years of living with the Apaches had hardened him physically as well as mentally. The lessons he had learned from the stoic people of the Southwest had not been easy, but they had taught him endurance. He could travel for days without food or water and run for miles without a rest break, and he knew how to use his pain instead of giving in to it.

Rogue snorted and shook his head in protest when Jack Parkin reined him sharply to a halt in front of his log cabin. The miner paid no heed to the animal's discomfort. He dropped the reins as he slid to the ground and turned to look up at the silent woman mounted on the mare. "Get your ass down from there and take the saddlebags into the cabin," he ordered.

Emerald made no move to obey.

"Didn't you hear me, girlie?"

Emerald sat mutely, staring down into the heavily jowled face illuminated in the pale moonlight. Her knuckles grew white from the pressure of her grip on the reins and her heart began to race wildly in her breast at the thought of the fate awaiting her at Jack Parkin's hand. During the long, cold hours it had taken them to ride through the foothills to his cabin, Jack had painted a vivid picture of what he intended for her with his steady stream of vulgar boasts about his prowess in bed.

Emerald tried to swallow the thick lump of dread that formed in her throat and made it difficult for her to breathe. Until that moment she had kept the futile hope alive that she would find a way to escape the madman before he could carry out his villainous plans. Now that they had stopped, she realized that she had waited too long. Once she entered the cabin, she knew her fate would be sealed.

"No!" Emerald spat, not realizing that she had voiced her protest aloud as everything within her rebelled at the thought.

"Girlie, I'm warning you. If you know what's good for you, you'll not give me any trouble."

Emerald drew in a deep breath and raised her chin defiantly in the air. She could not and would not meekly surrender herself to the degradation that Jack planned for her before he ended her life. And end her life he would. She had no doubt about his intentions once he had appeased his lust. He would have to kill her. He could not let her live to identify him as the man who had murdered Apache Ryan.

A cynical little smile touched Emerald's lips at the cruel quirks of fate. Whatever fiendish god or demon that ruled her destiny had played one final, savage trick on her. Her life was in jeopardy a second time for being able to identify a man who had murdered someone she loved. Accepting the fact that she would die fighting Jack Parkin, her only regret was that she would never have the satisfaction of knowing that at least her father's murderer had been brought to justice.

"Jack Parkin, you can go to hell," Emerald swore, and, without further thought, gripped the reins firmly and jerked the mare's head about, making an attempt to gain her freedom.

Jack had accurately assessed her belligerent expression and was prepared for her sudden move. He jumped toward her before the mare could react to Emerald's command. He grasped her heavy woolen cape with his blunt-fingered hands and used it as a tether. With one vicious jerk, he unseated her from the saddle.

Emerald felt herself falling but was unable to prevent it. Her breath left her in a *whoosh* as she landed on the frozen ground, material belling out around her. Already skittish, the startled mare reared on its hind legs before bolting away in the direction in which they had just come. The mare's flight frightened Rogue. His large brown eyes rolled wildly in his head, and he danced nervously about before following the mare's lead. With tail held high, he raced after her.

"Damn you, bitch," Jack growled, grappling with the virago thrashing about beneath him on the ground. He cast a brief glance to the animals galloping away into the night. "You're going to pay dearly for this."

Fighting for her life, Emerald paid no heed to his threats. Her fear gave her strength. She clawed and kicked at him like a wild thing and drew blood with the nails she raked down the side of one thick jowl.

Jack howled with pain. His scarlet-streaked face contorted into a demonic mask as he drew back his fist and gave her a vicious punch, knocking the breath from her. Emerald gasped and went limp, her insides convulsing in agony as she tried to pull air into her lungs. Before she had time to recover, Jack raised his beefy fist once more and brought it down with a stunning blow to her chin. Her head snapped back against the ground and stars burst inside her brain as she sank into the dark, whirling void of oblivion.

"Apache," Emerald whimpered through swollen lips as the shroud of darkness began to lift from her mind.

"Call out all you like, bitch, but there's no one to help you now," Jack growled, raising a calloused hand to his injured face. His eyes glittered malevolently as he stared through narrowed lids at the woman lying on his bed.

The cold savagery of his tone brought Emerald to full consciousness. Her eyes flew open to see him sitting a few feet from her, glaring his hatred. Her instinct for self-preservation bade her to flee, but she found that she could not move. Her wrists and ankles were firmly bound to the bed with strips of leather. Emerald strained against her bonds and heard Jack chuckle.

"You ain't going nowhere, whore. I've waited all night for you to come to your senses so I could make you suffer before I slit that lovely throat of yours." Jack's thick lips drew back from his tobacco-stained teeth in a savage grin. His eyes never left Emerald as he reached for the knife on the table and slowly ran the razor-sharp blade down his arm, shaving away a strip of coarse, dark hair.

"Why don't you just kill me and get it over with, you bastard," Emerald cursed, her voice tinged with hysteria. She twisted her body from side to side in a futile effort to free herself.

"See this, girlie? That's why." Jack ran his fingers lightly over the angry red scratches on his cheek. The grin turned into a snarl as he hefted his heavy body out of the chair and moved to stand by the bed. His fat belly bulged over the waist of his britches as he bent over her and pressed the tip of the knife into the soft flesh of her throat until a drop of blood beaded on her skin.

"You're going to regret every mark you put on me.

For each one you're going to wish you were dead several times before I'm through with you." His voice was low and filled with menace.

Emerald did not move or breathe while the blade pricked her skin. The blood drained from her face, leaving her features ashen as she lay staring up into Jack Parkin's scarred, ugly visage.

"Where's all your brave talk now, whore?" Jack growled, resting the sharp edge of the blade across her throat. "What's the matter? You finding it hard to ask me to kill you again? Don't you want me to slice up that lily-white throat of yours? Answer me, you damned bitch."

Emerald's courage failed her. Tears of defeat brimmed in her eyes and she moved her head slowly from side to side. She had thought that when the moment came she would be able to accept her death bravely, but now that she was faced with it, she found she wanted to live. As long as there was life, there was hope.

"I thought that'd change your mind." Jack sneered contemptuously as he ran the tip of the knife down the line of her throat to the neck of her gown. With slow, deliberate strokes he cut away each tiny button. The woolen fabric of her bodice gaped open to expose the creamy flesh beneath.

Jack licked the saliva from his fat lips and chuckled as he ran his rough fingers over the proud curves of her breasts. "You got nice tits, girlie. Now let's see what else is hidden beneath all that cloth."

Using the blade, he cut the skirt of her gown down the front and pulled it away to reveal her hips and legs to his hot gaze. His breathing grew heavy as he slid a callused hand down her torso to the golden mound at the apex of her thighs.

Emerald whimpered in shame and squeezed her eyes tightly closed. She turned her face into the arm bound above her head, cringing at his touch. She could feel the taint his hand left upon her skin. Her stomach heaved with nausea, and she tasted her own blood as she bit down on her lip to keep from screaming her revulsion.

"Look at me, bitch," Jack ordered. He grabbed her chin and cruelly forced her face toward him. "I want you to watch everything I do."

When Jack unbuckled his belt and exposed his ugly, swollen member to her gaze, what little composure Emerald had left, dissolved. Her eyes grew wide with panic and she began to scream. She bucked wildly, pulling and straining at the leather strips about her wrists and ankles until her flesh was raw and bleeding.

"You lie still if you don't want me to cut you up into little pieces," Jack ordered, slightly intimidated at the thought of trying to control the thrashing woman.

Emerald's hysteria held reign, deafening her to his commands as she lay writhing and twisting on the bed like an animal caught in a trap. Nothing penetrated her mind except her need to escape. She did not feel the slickness of her blood as it moistened the leather strips or the pain that burned through her limbs as she strained against her bonds. Ruled only by the primeval instincts that surfaced from deep within her, she regressed back into the untamed state that civilization had bred out of man through the centuries. She became a wild thing, thinking only of freedom at any cost.

"Damn you, I've had enough of this," Jack growled. He raised his wide hand to strike Emerald, but it froze in midair at the sound of the door crashing open behind him. Startled, he swung about to see Apache Ryan coming toward him with bowie knife in hand.

Jack stared at Apache dumbfounded. He couldn't believe his eyes. Ryan should be dead. No mortal man could live through the night without protection in this weather. The thought made a shiver race up Jack's spine before he shook off the eerie sensation that he was facing Ryan's ghost. The reality that faced him was much more menacing than any supernatural occurrence. Jack grabbed for the knife he had carelessly laid aside when he unbuckled his britches. Grasping it, he bent his knees, poised and ready for attack.

"Come on, you bastard," he cursed, moving the knife menacingly in front of him. "I'll cut out your black heart and have it for breakfast."

Apache did not respond. He moved toward his enemy, his face grim and every muscle in his sinewy body taut. The moonless depths of his eyes glittered with a cold, deadly light as he silently stalked his prey.

Warily, Jack backed away from the man whose entire demeanor bespoke unleashed, savage fury. Fear beaded his brow with icy sweat as he gazed into Apache's eyes and saw death. Terror rose in his throat to choke him, and he swallowed convulsively. He licked nervously at his suddenly dry lips, his tongue running in and out of his mouth as if it had a life of its own. A dribble of saliva slid down his chin and his palms grew wet. The hilt of the knife grew slippery in his hand as he sought to dredge out of the quivering morass of his insides enough courage to die fighting. Drawing in a tremulous breath, he lunged at Apache.

The sunlight spilling through the open doorway flashed on the blade of Apache's knife as he slashed out at the man with such speed that Jack had no time to avoid the deadly steel. It sank into his bulging middle, tearing through the layers of fat as his weight propelled them to the wall of the cabin. Apache's head snapped back against the logs, but his iron grip did not slacken as it fastened onto Jack's wrist, forcing the weapon from his hand. Jack's eyes widened in shock and he staggered backward, his fingers turning red as he grabbed his stomach. Stunned, he looked down at the hilt of the knife protruding from his belly and gave a groan before his eyes rolled upward in his head and he sagged to the floor. His body convulsed once before he lay still.

Apache's chest rose and fell heavily from the exertion as he stood squinting down at the man on the floor. The pain that shot through his head was blinding and it took a moment for him to remember where he had seen the man before. He frowned and rubbed a weary hând over his face. He had been so incensed at seeing the man standing threateningly over Emerald that he had reacted instinctively to protect her. He had barely taken the time to register that it was Jack Parkin, not Cash Dalton, who had kidnapped her after all.

Apache turned to the bed, where Emerald lay trembling violently, her eyes wide with fright and shock. He moved to her and sank wearily to his knees.

"You're safe now," he murmured. Gently, he untied her wrists and ankles, taking care not to add to her pain by touching her raw flesh. She lay still, staring up at him with wide, haunted eyes as he tore strips from her petticoat and bandaged her wounds.

"I—he—" Emerald began, but could not go on. Everything came crashing down on her at once. She curled into a ball and buried her face in her hands. At last she gave way to the tears she had kept at bay for so long. She wept openly, great racking sobs that shook her entire body as she finally released the emotions that had been pent up inside of her since her father's death. All the fear, grief, and heartache that she had endured in the past weeks came pouring out. Her fear of Jack Parkin had stripped away the brave front she had shown to the world and left her vulnerable to the pain that she had tried to keep buried deep inside of her.

"My brave love," Apache murmured softly. He ignored the pounding ache in his temples as he placed a comforting hand against her golden head and brushed the long, lovely strands away from her face.

"You have nothing else to fear, love. Parkin can never hurt you again." Emerald did not respond but only wept harder. Apache brushed his lips lightly against her bowed head and pulled the tattered quilts up over her. Her pitiful weeping broke his heart, but he made no effort to stop her. He knew tears were nature's way of cleansing the soul, and after what she had endured, she needed them to purge her of the terror and pain she had suffered. Her spirit was battered and she needed time to renew it.

A white line formed about Apache's lips as he pushed himself to his feet and turned to the man lying on the floor. His face grew taut from the strain as he lifted Jack and dragged him from the cabin. After what the man had done to Emerald, he deserved to be tossed to the wolves, but Apache could not leave him to such a fate, no matter how he hated him.

Apache's brow was glistening with sweat by the time he tossed the last spade of earth onto the grave. Breathing heavily, he let the shovel fall and squinted at the cabin. The ache in his head had intensified until he could barely focus his eyes enough to see the shadowy image of the doorway.

Throughout the long night, he had been driven by one thought alone: to save Emerald. He had ignored his own injury in his need to reach her and had set a punishing pace for himself without realizing the devastating toll it was taking on him. Now that he knew she was safe, his body was rebelling against the abuse. The stamina that had kept him doggedly on her trail drained out of him like water through a sieve. Every muscle in his body trembled violently from the weakness invading him. His knees shook unsteadily as he stumbled back to the cabin.

"Emerald," he muttered thickly, sagging against the door frame before his knees buckled and he sank to the floor. The last of his strength seemed to seep into the dirt beneath him.

The distress she heard in Apache's voice jerked Emerald out of the torpor that had followed her bout of weeping. Terror knifed through her as she saw him collapse against the door. Her heart froze within her breast at the pallor that tinged his skin a sickly shade of gray.

Fearing that he had been mortally wounded in his fight with Jack Parkin, Emerald scrambled from the bed and hurried to him. Half naked, with her gown hanging in shreds about her, she sank to her knees at his side and gathered him into her arms.

"Apache, where are you hurt?" she asked, frantically searching for any sign of blood. Her hand trembled as she placed it against his throat beneath the curve of his beard-stubbled jaw. On finding the flutter of his pulse, she expelled the breath she had been holding. However, her relief was only momentary as her eyes came to rest on the ebony hair above his ear. It was matted with dried blood. Gently, she explored the battered area and found it cut and swollen from the blow he'd received from Jack Parkin's rifle butt.

"Oh, my love," she breathed, her eyes welling with tears of sympathy at the sight of the deep gash. Apache had suffered greatly to find her, and for one brief moment she wondered why and how he'd managed to do so in his condition.

Setting her curiosity aside, Emerald turned her full attention to helping him. She had to get him to the bed. Draping his arm about her shoulders, she struggled to lift him but found his weight too much for her.

"Apache," she panted, "you're going to have to help me."

He muttered incoherently as he sought to do as she bid, and after several tries with her assistance, he managed to crawl the few feet to the bed before he collapsed once more, the upper half of his body sprawled across the narrow straw mattress.

Emerald was out of breath by the time she finally managed to get him lengthwise upon the bed. Apache was a big man when he was conscious, but dead to the world he seemed to double in size. With her breasts rising and falling from the exertion, Emerald stood gazing down at him. She brushed her tousled hair out of her eyes with a trembling hand and absently wiped the sweat from her brow. A worried frown creased her smooth forehead, and she pursed her lips.

Apache's ashen features told her that he needed a doctor, but without a mount she had no way of getting him to one. Nor could she leave him here alone in his condition during the time it would take her to reach Denver on foot and bring a doctor back to the cabin to tend his wound. She realized sadly that she would still be faced with a dilemma even if Rogue and the mare hadn't bolted. Without help, she didn't have the strength to get Apache onto a horse. It had strained her to the limit just to get him completely onto the bed.

Fretfully, Emerald wondered what she was to do. She had nursed her grandmother during the last years of her life and had learned a little about doctoring. However, without the proper medicine or even a needle and thread to stitch the gash in his head, there was little she could do for him beyond trying to stop his wound from bleeding.

With that thought in mind, she washed the gash with a little of Parkin's whiskey, then tore another long strip from her already tattered petticoat and wrapped it securely around Apache's head. She was less than satisfied with her meager ministrations, but she could do nothing more to ease his suffering. All that was left to her was to wait and pray that he would recover enough for her to leave him and go for a doctor.

Drawing the straight-backed chair to the side of the bed, she settled herself in it, wrapped the tattered pieces of her gown about her nakedness, and began her lonely, anxious vigil. Throughout the day and night, she left Apache's side only long enough to put fresh wood on the fire and to eat a few bites of food in order to keep up her strength. She fought a desperate battle against the weariness that threatened to overcome her, but near dawn of the second morning in Jack Parkin's cabin, her tired body finally succumbed to its need for rest. Against her will, she nodded off to sleep.

Emerald was abruptly startled awake a short time later by Apache's feverish raving. He tossed restlessly from side to side, muttering incoherently. Instantly alert and fearing that he would harm himself further, she hurried to his side and pressed him back against the pillow.

"Hush, love," she cajoled softly, and felt the tension ease from him at the sound of her voice.

"Rachel?" he questioned, squinting up at her through fever-bright eyes.

Emerald could only shake her head in answer. No words would pass over the sudden lump that formed in her throat at the mention of the woman's name he'd used when he'd kissed her that first morning in Jeb Taylor's cabin.

"What are you doing here?" Apache asked as he reached out and encircled Emerald's arm with fingers like steel bands.

Believing that he had finally recognized her, Emerald swallowed convulsively and managed to utter, "You need me."

"If you believe that, then you're a fool. I don't need you any longer," Apache growled. His fingers bit into Emerald's flesh and his face contorted with unleashed fury as he glared up at her.

"Apache, please. You're hurting me," Emerald said, straining against the brutal pressure on her arm.

"What's the matter, you greedy bitch? Can't you take it as well as you can dish it out? You deserve to hurt after the pain you caused me."

Emerald's eyes brimmed with tears and her golden hair swung about her shoulders as she shook her head, denying his cruel accusations against her. "Apache, I haven't hurt you in any way. I only want to help you."

Apache's eyes glittered with a wild light as he slowly drew her down to him. "Ah, Rachel," he murmured, his voice low and filled with animosity. "Did you know that you tore the heart out of this dreamy-eyed boy and left him an empty shell with nothing to live for?"

"Oh, my love," Emerald said, her heart going out to the tormented man as she realized that he was seeing a woman from his past and not her.

"Get away from me," Apache said, and thrust her

from him with such force that she toppled off the side of the bed. "It's all Dalton's fault. He ruined it for you and me, but I'll see him dead before I let him have Emerald." Apache's last words were slurred as he sank once more into the dark void of unconsciousness.

Emerald sat huddled where she had fallen on the earthen floor, her mind reeling from the impact of Apache's feverish ramblings. She now knew why he hated Cash Dalton and the reason behind his determination to stop her from marrying him. Apache had loved the woman called Rachel and Cash had come between them.

Her shoulders sagged as she drew her knees up to her chest and pressed her face against them. Apache's revelation left her emotionally torn between a great need to laugh and to cry. She had gained her heart's desire, but feared she had lost it in the same instant. Apache wanted her, but she was uncertain about the reason behind it. Did he care for her, or was it his need to revenge himself on Cash Dalton that made him want her?

Unanswerable questions roiled through Emerald's brain as she moved to the side of the bed and gazed down at Apache. She tried to see into the soul that existed behind his still features. She wanted to find the answers that would allow her to love him freely with no doubt about his motives for wanting her. But she could find nothing in his face to satisfy that need.

Apache was a strong man, but he was still haunted by his painful past. Emerald's heart welled with tenderness and understanding. They were kindred spirits. Both had built barriers around their hearts to protect themselves from hurt.

Emerald felt her barrier crumbling at last as the answer to her questions seemed to spring into her mind. She loved this man and wanted to ease his torment. If he wanted her, she would gladly surrender herself to him and pray that her love would eventually erase the shadows from his life and let him love her in return. By unselfishly giving of herself, she knew she risked having her heart shattered, but she was willing to take that chance to gain the most precious thing in life to her: Apache's love.

Emerald eased herself down on the bed at his side and slipped her arm beneath his shoulders to cradle his head on her breast. She was willing to fight for his life and his love.

"Emerald?" Apache murmured hoarsely, peering groggily up at the woman sitting at his side.

"I'm here, Apache," Emerald reassured him as she laid her hand on his forehead and found it cool after twenty-four hours of battling the fever that had kept him slipping in and out of delirium. Relieved, she smiled down at him and tenderly stroked the smooth line of his brow. "You're better."

"Better?" he asked, squinting up at her. "What happened?" Apache attempted to sit up but found himself pushed back firmly on the lumpy pillow.

"Lie still. You're too weak from the fever to try to get out of bed just yet."

"Fever?" Apache said, frowning. He raised a trembling hand to his head and found it bound securely. The furrows across his forehead deepened and his eyes fastened on Emerald's face as vague images began to penetrate the fog that enveloped his mind. The last coherent thing that he could remember was seeing Jack Parkin standing over Emerald as she lay tied to the bed. After that everything had blurred into a red haze of fury and blood.

"Did he hurt you?" Apache asked, capturing the hand that lay on his bare shoulder.

Emerald shook her head. "No. You stopped him before he could harm me."

Apache released a long breath and relaxed. His dark gaze held hers as he brought her hand up and brushed his lips against it. "I thought I had lost you."

His simple statement made a warm glow spread over Emerald. "Would it really matter if you did?"

"Yes, Emerald, it would. When I thought Dalton had come for you and that your life might be in danger, I went mad."

"Apache," Emerald said, gently brushing a raven curl away from his brow. "I know you hate Cash, but he would never harm me. He's my friend."

"You still haven't changed your feelings about Dalton, have you?" Apache asked, his voice full of annoyance.

"I have no reason to change them. I know you despise Cash for what happened between the two of you in the past, but that does not mean that he is evil as you want me to believe."

Apache eyed Emerald curiously. "What do you mean, what happened between us in the past?"

"I know about Rachel," Emerald said, and shifted uncomfortably as Apache arched one dark brow at her questioningly. Moistening her suddenly dry lips, she continued hestitantly, "You spoke of her when you were delirious."

"Then you know what I've said about Dalton is true?"

Emerald wearily shook her head. "No. I don't. No matter how you feel about him, Cash would never harm me. He wants me to be his wife."

"Emerald, he has one special reason that you seem determined to ignore. He wants your claim," Apache said, his anger mounting by the moment at her defense of the man he hated.

"Apache, please. I don't want to argue with you about Cash."

"Damn it, Emerald. The man is responsible for your father's death. How can you be so stubbornly blind? He would marry you or kill you to get his hands on the right-of-way for the railroad. Either method would suit him if it served his purpose."

"Railroad?" Emerald asked, her brow furrowing in a perplexed frown.

"Yes, a railroad, damn it. Dalton has invested heavily to get a railroad built into the mountains, and he'll lose everything if he doesn't get the right-of-way.''

''But that isn't proof that he had anything to do with my father's death.''

''Use your head, woman,'' Apache said in exasperation. ''Who else had anything to gain from your father's murder? Your claim is the last one standing in Dalton's path, and he plans on getting it, one way or the other.''

''I don't believe that Cash could do anything like that. He's been too good to me.''

''If you call fattening up the lamb for slaughter good to you, then I guess the bastard has done that job well. He's managed to convince you that he's your friend, and that's far more than I've been able to do since we met.''

Emerald released a weary breath. She was tired of battling with Apache about Cash. They'd had this same argument before, but now she could understand the reason behind his less than objective view of Cash Dalton. However, her feelings had not changed, except that now her conscience was weighed down by the fact that she would hurt the man whom Apache accused of so many crimes. No matter what Apache had said, Cash had been good to her, and she dreaded telling him that she couldn't go through with their marriage. Her love for Apache would not let her.

''Apache, I don't want to discuss Cash.''

''Does that mean you still intend to marry him?''

Emerald's hair glinted in the firelight like molten gold as she once more shook her head. ''No, Apache.''

Apache's eyes widened in surprise and he felt his heart leap at her answer. ''What changed your mind? The last time we talked you were still set on becoming Mrs. Cash Dalton. And after the way you've come to the bastard's defense, I'd think wild horses couldn't drag you away from the altar.''

Emerald glanced down at their hands. His lean, tanned fingers were laced intimately through her own, binding them together even as they argued. "You already know the reason I can't marry Cash."

"Look at me, Emerald. I want to hear you say it," Apache said, his anger dying a sudden death under the surge of emotion that swept through him.

Emerald raised her eyes, and in them Apache read her answer before the words came from her lips. "I love you."

"Then will you marry me, Emerald?" Apache asked quietly. His heart was so full of joy that it made it hard for him to speak above a whisper.

Emerald stared down into the fathomless depths of Apache's dark eyes and wondered if he was still delirious after all. She couldn't believe what he had just said. Not in her wildest dreams had she imagined that he would ever ask her to marry him, especially after the things she had learned about him through his feverish rambling.

"Emerald, I'm asking you to become my wife," Apache said when she did not respond to his question. "I would appreciate an answer."

"Apache, are you sure you know what you're saying? You've been very ill," Emerald said, afraid to let herself believe that her dream had come true.

"Do you love me or don't you?"

Emerald nodded.

"Then will you marry me?"

"Yes," Emerald said at last, unable to deny her heart's desire any longer.

Apache smiled as he lifted her hand to his lips once more and kissed it. "We'll be married as soon as we get back to Denver."

"I don't know what to say," Emerald said.

"Yes was all I wanted to hear, love," Apache said, pulling her down to lie across his chest. His fingers slid up her arm and captured the back of her neck to draw her head down to his. His mouth claimed hers, sealing their pact with a sweet kiss that left them both breathless.

When at last he released her lips, he smiled up at her. "I would love to carry this further, but I'm afraid I'm not quite up to it yet. You'll just have to wait to be ravished until I regain some of my strength."

Their argument about Cash forgotten in the surge of wild joy that swept over her, Emerald could not suppress a lighthearted giggle as she pushed herself upright and gave him a saucy look. "I'll give you a few hours to rest, and then if you haven't gotten your strength back, I guess I'll have to ravish you instead."

"I'll look forward to it." Apache chuckled, drawing her down to lie beside him. He was far too weak to even consider making love to Emerald, but he wanted her close to him. Cradling her in his arms, he rested his head against hers and closed his eyes. He had ruined Dalton's railroad scheme and he had also gained something far more valuable to him than thwarting his enemy: Emerald's love. Satisfied with his life for the first time in more years than he wanted to remember, Apache drifted into a recuperative slumber. It was the first undisturbed sleep that he'd had in days.

Emerald snuggled close to him, her entire being awash with contentment. She could ask for nothing more out of life. The knowledge that Apache loved her and wanted her as his wife made her ache with happiness. And she would not let herself question her good fortune. Nor would she allow the things Apache had said in his delirium to cast any shadows that might mar the joy she felt. She had waited too long for love to let any doubts or guilt intrude into her mind or heart now.

Chapter 13

Emerald stirred, awakening slowly from the deep, dreamless sleep that had claimed her exhausted body the previous night. Without opening her eyes, she reached out to touch Apache. When her hand found only an empty space, she came fully awake. Alarmed, she bolted upright, searching the dim interior of the cabin for the man she loved.

At the sight of him, bare to the waist and hunkered down in front of the fireplace, she breathed a sigh of relief. For one frightening moment she had feared that his fever had returned and he had managed to get out of bed and leave the cabin without her knowledge. She had been so tired from her vigil at his bedside during the past days that when she had finally given in to her fatigue, she had slept so heavily that the world could have come to an end and it would not have disturbed her slumber.

"Good morning," Apache said. A tender smile touched his shapely lips as he glanced over his shoulder at her. "I was beginning to wonder if you would ever wake up. It's well past noon."

Emerald ran her fingers through the tangled mass of her golden hair, brushing it away from her face. "I didn't mean to sleep so long. You should have awakened me. I could have built the fire."

"You needed your rest, and I'm very capable of building fires myself." Apache grinned.

Emerald slid her feet to the floor and stood. "Are you sure you're up to it? How is your head this morning?"

"I think I'll live," Apache said, touching the white bandage across his forehead. "I'm too hardheaded to let a little blow like that kill me."

Emerald smiled as she crossed the few feet to his side and gently touched the raven hair above the bandage. "I wish I had known that sooner. It would have saved me a great deal of worry."

Apache caught her hand and drew her down beside him. "And had I known that a little thing like that would make you decide against marrying Dalton, I would have paid someone to hit me sooner."

"That's not funny, Apache," Emerald said, raising solemn eyes up to his. "You nearly died."

"That's all in the past, love," Apache said, his bantering mood fading. It had been so long since anyone had cared whether he lived or died that his throat clogged with emotion at the look of concern in her jeweled eyes. Draping a comforting arm about her shoulders, he drew her against his bare chest. Tenderness and love for the brave young woman who had fought for his life welled within him.

Men had traveled hundreds of miles to the Jefferson Territory in search of riches, but to Apache the woman in his arms was the only treasure he wanted. Emerald Banyon was Apache Ryan's gold. She was his El Dorado. She was far more precious to him than the yellow mineral the miners sought so feverishly. Her love was all the wealth that he needed in life.

Emerald wrapped her arms about his lean waist and pressed her cheek to the furry mat of his chest. She listened to the steady rhythm of his heartbeat and felt a warm glow of contentment steal over her as she stared into the dancing flames in the fireplace. Apache was right. All that had happened was in the past, and now she could look to a future with the man she loved.

"Emerald," Apache said, staring into the fire as he

stroked the shining hair that lay in a tousled mass down her back. "We should start back to Denver soon. From the way the clouds look it could start snowing again, and I don't want us to be caught on foot in another storm."

"I could stay snowbound with you all winter," Emerald murmured softly, snuggling against him.

Apache brushed his lips lightly against her brow before unwrapping her encircling arms and setting her at arm's length. "I would like nothing better than to remain hidden away with you for the rest of my life, but if you will remember, we need to find a preacher."

Disgruntled at having his comforting warmth taken from her, yet pleased that he was so impatient to marry her, Emerald wrinkled her nose at him.

"For a man who was so firm in his resolve never to marry, I would think that you'd be anxious to avoid that fate for as long as possible," Emerald teased, running a finger down the cleft between the bulging muscles of his chest.

Apache gave her a crooked grin and grabbed her hand to still it. "Once I set my mind to something, I can't rest until I've seen it through. But if you keep that up, we may end up having a family before we leave this cabin."

"A family," Emerald breathed, her eyes widening. Until that moment she had never considered the consequences of their intimate encounters. Nor during the turmoil of the past weeks had she thought anything about the absence of her bodily functions. Her mouth rounded into an 0 as she realized that her monthly curse had not come since Apache had made love to her that first morning in Jeb's cabin. At the thought, her hand came to rest on her belly. Her monthly flow had always been as regular as clockwork, and she suspected from the evidence alone that she already carried Apache's child. Astounded, she gaped up at Apache.

"Emerald, what's wrong?" he asked, seeing the strange expression that crossed her face.

''Nothing,'' she murmured, giving herself a sharp mental shake. Until her suspicions were confirmed, she could not tell Apache. There would be time enough after they were married.

''From the look on your face, I thought for a moment that you were going to tell me you were already in the family way.''

Emerald looked sharply at Apache. ''Don't you want children?''

''Of course I want children someday. But, for now, I have too many things that need to be settled before I can start raising a family. And the first thing is getting us back to Denver so that we can be married.''

''But what if I was pregnant now?''

''Then I guess I'd have to accept it, but since you're not, there's no use in us discussing it.''

''Would a baby interfere that much in your life?''

''Let's just say that at the present time it's best that we don't have children.'' Apache did not add that he wanted a child with Emerald more than anything else on earth, but until he had settled things between himself and Dalton, he could not risk it. If things did not go as he planned, Dalton might kill him. And if that fate befell him, he didn't want to leave Emerald alone with a child to care for. Life on the frontier was not easy at any time for a woman, but for one alone and with a child, it was full of unbearable hardship. In order to keep her from worrying he couldn't explain his reasons to her, for now it was best to let her believe that he didn't want children yet.

The shadows that Emerald had tried to keep at bay now crept forward to dim her happiness. Apache said he wanted children in the future, but what would he do if he knew that she might already be carrying his child? Would he still be eager to marry her, or would he feel that he wasn't ready for the burden of a wife and family, just like her father had felt so many years ago?

All of Emerald's insecurity and distrust of men rose to reaffirm her decision to keep her secret from him until after they were married. Once the vows were spoken, at least her child would not be branded a bastard if his father decided that he didn't want her or their baby when she told him.

Puzzled by the odd look in Emerald's eyes and suddenly afraid that she was reconsidering their marriage after what he had said about not having children, Apache queried, "Are you sure there's nothing wrong? You do want to marry me, don't you?"

"Yes, I want to marry you, and there's nothing wrong except that I need to put on my boots because my toes are freezing off," Emerald said, feigning a lightheartedness she didn't feel. She turned away and crossed back to the bed. Afraid that her face would give away her secret, she busied herself with putting on her stockings and boots.

Apache sensed that something was troubling Emerald, but he couldn't force her to tell him what it was. He shrugged away the uneasy feeling that settled in the pit of his stomach as he slipped on his shirt and coat. Emerald loved him, and in time she would tell him what had brought on that haunted look he'd seen in her eyes before she turned away. He knew he was acting like an old woman by fretting over every little expression that crossed her face, but he loved her so much that he wanted to take all of her troubles on his own shoulders so that she would not have to bear them.

After they ate the meager breakfast of canned beans, that he had prepared for them, and Emerald found an old coat to put on, Apache strapped his gun belt about his lean hips, reholstered his revolver, and slung the saddlebags over one shoulder. They were now ready to face the long trek back through the foothills. It would take them several hours of hard walking, but he hoped to reach Jeb's cabin before nightfall. He planned for them to spend the night there and then in the morning set out on the last leg of their journey to Denver.

By tomorrow night, Apache reflected with a wry grin, he'd be a married man. Draping an arm about Emerald's shoulders, he led her out of Jack Parkin's cabin and into the chilly autumn afternoon.

Apache smelled the smoke before he saw it rising toward the lavender sky from the chimney of Jeb's cabin. He paused, tense and alert, his gaze sweeping over the area for any sign of danger.

"What's wrong?" Emerald asked quietly, easing close to Apache's side and warily scanning the landscape for the danger that he seemed to sense instinctively.

"Someone is at the cabin," he murmured softly. "You stay here where it's safe while I go to see who has come to pay us a visit."

"No, I'm going with you," Emerald argued. She had no intention of remaining behind when Apache might be walking into a dangerous situation.

"You're staying here, Emerald. We don't know who's in that cabin or why."

"And that's why I'm coming with you. I won't let you go in there alone when some varmint might be waiting to ambush you."

"That's exactly why you're staying here. And I won't hear any more arguments about it. If you're right, I'll have enough trouble on my hands without having to worry about you getting hurt."

"Oh, all right," Emerald said irritably. She knew Apache was right. She would only be in his way if he had to defend himself. Sinking down onto a fallen log, she wrapped her arms about her knees as she looked up at him. "But I'm warning you, Apache Ryan. I'll never forgive you if you get yourself killed."

Apache reached out and tousled her golden hair affectionately. "I'll do my damnedest to keep that from happening, love. Stay here until I come for you." He started to turn away, but Emerald grasped his hand, halting his steps.

"Please be careful."

"I will," Apache said, and smiled down at her before he slipped away into the deepening twilight.

Emerald's face was pinched with fatigue and worry

as she sat peering into the evening shadows for any sign of Apache as he stealthily made his way toward the cabin. She caught only a brief glimpse of him as he dashed from the woods toward the lean-to before he disappeared from sight once more.

She shivered and drew her cape closer about her. Anxiety made her fidget restlessly on her rough-barked seat while the minutes ticked by at a snail's pace. If Apache did find himself in a dangerous situation, he would need her help.

With that thought, Emerald rose halfway to her feet before she managed to control the overpowering urge to follow him. Everything within her told her to obey the commands of her heart, but she settled herself back on the log, forcing herself to heed Apache's orders. She centered her attention on the mountain man's cabin, which was now only a faint black shadow against the dark landscape, and prayed that Apache would return before her worry drove her to her feet and along the trail to the cabin.

Apache moved silently through the shadows that had obscured him from Emerald's view. With his back pressed flat against the wall of the cabin and with his revolver in hand, he made his way to the window and peered between the crack in the shutters. At the sight of Jeb Taylor snoozing in front of the fire, the tension eased from him.

Reholstering his gun, he rapped sharply on the door and listened as Jeb, muttering low curses, came to answer his knock. When the door swung open, the old mountain man's eyes widened in astonishment.

"Where in hell have you been?" Jeb asked. "I thought after findin' that damned ornery stallion of yours yesterday that Dalton had finally figured out where little missy was and had done you in." His bushy brows drew together as his eyes searched the darkness behind Apache. "And, by the way, where is the little missy?"

"Emerald is waiting for me at the edge of the clearing, but before I go to get her, I want you to tell me exactly what Dalton has been up to,'' Apache said, stepping through the doorway and closing the door behind him.

''That's what I come to warn you about. Dalton is fit to be tied. He's had his men scourin' the entire area lookin' for her. He's mad as hell that the little missy disappeared on the night before their weddin', and from what I've heard around the Gold Dust, he won't rest until he's found her.''

Apache smiled. ''It won't do Dalton any good to find Emerald because by this time tomorrow, she'll be my wife.''

''Well, I'll be damned,'' Jeb said, and grinned. ''You took my advice to heart.''

''I always take good advice, Jeb.'' Apache chuckled at the incredulous expression on the old man's face.

Jeb scratched his head and shook it. ''I never believed I'd see the day when a little filly would rope you into marriage.''

''I didn't think I'd ever see it either, old man.''

''Damn but that's really goin' to throw the fat in the fire where Dalton's concerned. He ain't goin' to take it lightly about you stealin' his intended away from him right under his nose.''

''That's what I planned.''

Jeb's bushy brows lowered over his eyes as he regarded Apache suspiciously. ''Are you marryin' the little missy for herself or just to spite Dalton?''

''Both.''

Jeb's frown deepened. ''Does she know that?''

''She knows I hate Dalton, and that's enough.''

''That ain't right, Apache. The girl deserves better.''

''Jeb, if you're worried about my feelings for Emerald, then you don't have to be. I love her, but I'm also marrying her to keep Dalton from getting his hands on the claim she owns.''

Jeb's wrinkled face screwed up, his toothless mouth

puckering as he pursed his lips. "You believe Dalton is the man behind all the trouble lately?"

"I've suspected him from the first, but my suspicion is all I have. I need firm evidence against him before I can go to the sheriff."

"And you ain't goin' to take a chance on ruinin' things between you and the little missy by telling her that you'll be stoppin' Dalton by marryin' her, are you?"

"No, I'm not. Emerald won't believe that Dalton is the man responsible for her father's death, and I'll do anything to make sure he doesn't get his hands on her or the claim deed. It's the only way I can protect her from him."

"If you love her the way you say you do, you'd best take another piece of good advice and be honest with the girl. If she should ever think that the only reason you married her was because of your vendetta against Dalton, she'd never forgive you."

"I guess that's a risk I'll have to take, Jeb. Until I have proof that Dalton is responsible for the claim jumpings and can make her see what type of man he really is, there's nothing else I can do."

"Well, I've given you my advice and you can take it or leave it. But if you don't go and get her out of the cold, neither you nor Dalton will have a wife."

"That's a piece of advice I'll heed," Apache said, and turned to the door. He slid back the latch, and when the door swung open, he came face-to-face with Emerald, who stood poised with a large stick firmly grasped in her hands. Apache tensed.

"What are you doing here? I told you to wait for me," Apache said gruffly.

"I couldn't wait any longer. When you didn't return, I thought something had happened to you." Emerald let the stick fall to the ground at her feet.

"I'm sorry, love," Apache said, draping an arm about her and leading her toward the fire. "I didn't mean to take so long."

"I see you came prepared for bear, missy," Jeb said. He chuckled in an effort to ease the tension that had entered the cabin when Apache opened the door to find the very woman they had been discussing. He could tell by the younger man's strained expression that he feared she had overheard their conversation. "I'm just glad that you realized your man was safe before you used that thing. After worryin' an old man to death by disappearin' into thin air, it wouldn't be right to add to his problems by giving him a lump on the head for his concern."

Emerald's cheeks grew warm at the thought of the ridiculous picture she must have made standing in the doorway with only a stick to defend Apache with if she had found him in trouble.

"Jeb, you're not the one who deserves a lump on the head," Emerald said, flashing Apache an annoyed look. "I should have hit Apache for leaving me out in the dark and cold to worry myself sick."

"Don't blame him, missy. It's my fault. I wouldn't let him take a step out of the cabin till he explained how the two of you just up and vanished." Jeb glanced at Apache and saw a look of relief wash over his face.

"Then Apache told you about Jack Parkin?" Emerald asked. The weary note in her voice and the droop of her shoulders reflected her exhaustion as she held her chilled hands out to the warmth of the fire. Until that moment her fear for Apache's life had kept her fatigue at bay.

"Parkin?" Jeb blurted out before he caught the hard look Apache gave him. "Uh, we—yeah. Apache was going to tell me the whole story after he went to get you."

Aching from head to toe, Emerald sagged visibly. She placed a steadying hand against the creek rock of the fireplace to brace herself before she collapsed. With all her effort focused on remaining erect, she did not take note of Jeb's ambiguous answer, nor did she sense the underlying tension between the two men.

"That can wait, Jeb," Apache said as he moved swiftly to support Emerald and helped her to the straight-backed chair in front of the hearth. Seating her, he knelt at her side. A frown marked his brow as his gaze swept over her wan features. Tenderly, he brushed a stray curl away from her pale forehead. His voice was soft and solicitous as he asked, "Are you ill?"

"I'm just tired," Emerald answered.

Her answer pricked Apache's conscience. He'd been so anxious to reach Jeb's cabin before nightfall that he'd not stopped to consider the effect the hard pace he'd set would have on Emerald. She had not complained, but her ashen features spoke more loudly than words. The hours of walking without a break had taken a heavy toll on her strength.

Apache glanced up at the older man. "Do you think you can round up something for us to eat?"

"If you're willin' to eat bacon and beans. It ain't much, but you're welcome to it." Jeb handed Apache a tin plate and fork and, with a nod, indicated the pot of beans he'd prepared for his supper.

"I don't want anything to eat," Emerald said, nearly gagging at the thought of food. Since eating the beans Apache had fixed for their breakfast, she had been queasy on and off all day. However, until Apache mentioned food, she had managed to keep her stomach under control. Now it churned sickeningly.

"You haven't eaten enough today to keep a bird alive, Emerald," Apache said, ignoring her protest as he turned his attention to the pot simmering over the fire. He heaped the plate with the dark brown beans and thick chunks of bacon. He handed it to her. "Now, eat. You'll make yourself ill if you don't get something in you soon."

Emerald rolled her eyes in misery, fighting against the strong wave of nausea that bubbled in her stomach. She paled as she looked down at the food on the plate. A shiver of revulsion shook her from head to toe and her insides heaved with the need to vomit. She fought against it with every ounce of willpower she possessed.

From the bits of information her granny had told her about having babies, she knew that her sudden abhorrence of food stemmed from the fact that she carried Apache's child and her body was reacting accordingly. However, that knowledge did not help her plight. It served only to increase her tension and make her more miserable.

She didn't want to shame herself by throwing up in front of the two men. If that happened, Apache might suspect the secret she carried, and after what he had said that morning, she did not want him to know of their child until the vows were spoken. Throughout the long, tiring afternoon, she had gone over and over her decision about keeping her pregnancy from Apache. She had been tempted several times to tell him, but then she would remember their conversation and the past would rise to kill the words before they left her lips.

She loved Apache, but because of her father she could not completely place all of her trust in him. Jim Banyon had felt no compulsion or obligation to her. Had he not already been married when she was conceived, she doubted if he would have given a second thought to deserting her mother before any vows were said. And she would not chance that fate for her child's sake.

"I'm not hungry," Emerald said at last, and handed the plate back to Apache, wanting the sight and the smell of the food as far away from her as possible. "I'm really too exhausted to even think of eating." Emerald's voice was strained from the effort it took her to control her churning insides. She clasped her hands in her lap and focused her attention on them with the hope that Apache would leave her alone and let her die in peace.

Apache frowned down at the top of her bowed head. Emerald had been acting oddly all day. Since leaving Parkin's cabin, she had seemed absorbed in her thoughts. She had said little throughout the long afternoon, speaking only when spoken to and then only to

answer direct questions, never elaborating further. That
in itself was not like the spirited Emerald Banyon he
had grown to love. She always had an opinion about
everything and didn't mind voicing it.

Puzzled by her despondency, he glanced up at Jeb
and caught the old man's quizzical look. He shrugged
and gave a negative shake of his head. For the life of
him, he didn't know what had happened to bring on
Emerald's sudden melancholy mood. He knew she was
exhausted, but instinct told him there was more to her
recent behavior than just fatigue.

"Let the little missy get some sleep, Apache. By
mornin' she'll be herself again and I guarantee that once
she's rested she'll be as hungry as a bear."

Emerald flashed Jeb a relieved look, but before she
could voice her appreciation, Apache scooped her up in
his arms and carried her to the bed. He laid her down
and pulled the quilts up over her as if tending a beloved
child. He bent and brushed his lips against her brow.
"Rest, love. I don't want you too tired for our wedding
tomorrow."

Emerald wanted to protest taking Jeb's bed, but with
her stomach in an uproar, lying down felt too good.
She also feared if she opened her mouth to speak,
something far less pleasant would come out. Burrowing
down beneath the warm covers so that only her golden
hair could be seen above the edge of the quilts, she soon
drifted into a sleep undisturbed by the quiet conversation of the two men by the fire.

Apache stood gazing down at her for a long, thoughtful moment before he returned to the warmth of the
fire, where Jeb sat, boiling with questions about what
had transpired between him and Jack Parkin.

When Apache finished his tale, Jeb smacked his lips
together, rubbed a gnarled, blue-veined hand across his
salt-and-pepper beard, and shook his head. "After what
you've been through to hold on to your woman, I can
understand why you're so set to marry the little missy.
I just hope it all works out for the best in the long run."

"Once I've dealt with Dalton, it will," Apache said, with more confidence than he felt after Emerald's behavior that day.

"I may be old, but you know if you need me, I'll do my damnedest to help."

"Thanks, Jeb," Apache said. After so many years of believing he needed no one, he found himself grateful for the mountain man's friendship.

Jeb stood and placed a firm hand on Apache's shoulder, giving it a reassuring squeeze. "Take care of the little missy, boy. That's the main thing." He turned and strode toward the door, where he took his coat and hat from the peg and pulled them on.

"Where are you going at this time of night?" Apache asked, eyeing the old man curiously.

"I done what I come to do, and now me and Ole Bessy are headin' back to Denver. This place is big enough for two, but not three." He winked and gave Apache a toothless grin before striding out into the night.

"It's time to wake up, love," Apache murmured softly, rousing Emerald from sleep.

Her thick lashes fluttered upward as she opened her eyes. She uncurled her lithe body with a sensual stretch and smiled drowsily up at Apache, who lay propped on one elbow at her side. She yawned sleepily and draped her arms about his neck, molding her body against his lean frame.

"Good morning," she murmured, before burying her face contentedly in the curve of his neck and breathing in the sultry masculine odor of his skin.

"Good morning, love," was Apache's husky reply as his arms slid about her and held her close. He caressed the bare skin of her back, his fingers gently kneading her resilient flesh. A tender smile curved his lips as he laid his chin against her hair.

In her lethargic mood, Emerald had as yet to realize that she lay naked in his arms. He had undressed her last night in an effort to make her rest more comfortably. Exhausted from the hours of walking, she had continued to sleep soundly as he removed her clothing and slid beneath the covers with her to cradle her in his arms.

Relaxed and well rested, Emerald felt her blood begin to warm at the feel of Apache's hands gliding over her back. Her skin tingled under his touch and her nipples hardened as they brushed against his furred chest. She shivered with delight.

Apache chuckled at her reaction and leaned back to peer down into a pair of eyes that had deepened to a rich forest green with her rising passion. He arched a roguish brow and smiled. "If I remember correctly, you promised to ravage me, but you never got around to it."

Emerald gave him a provocative look through half-closed lids and ran a teasing finger down his chest to his nipple. She circled it lightly, enticingly. Her lips curled into an impish grin. "I don't know if I should keep that promise this morning. Since today is our wedding day, it might be proper to wait till I've made an honest man out of you."

A low growl emerged from Apache's throat as he flipped her onto her back and lay on top of her, bracing his weight on his elbows. A devilish light twinkled in his eyes as he gazed down at her.

"Do your worst, woman. You've already ruined me and can do my reputation no further harm."

"Ruined you?" Emerald arched one brow in dismay.

Apache gave an exaggerated sigh and rolled his eyes toward the ceiling, feigning distress. "Yes, I was a mere innocent before you seduced me, and now you have to marry me or I'll never be able to hold my head up in polite society again. Heaven forbid that you should refuse to make an honest man out of me."

"Poor thing," Emerald said, choking on her laughter. "Had I but known what a position I was placing you in, I would not have used you so badly. But I can at least make things right by not taking such advantage of you again until we're married.'' At the look on Apache's face, Emerald could not suppress her laughter any longer.

"Oh, please do take advantage of me all you like. I have nothing else to lose, and I can assure you I have much to gain.''

Emerald screwed her face up in a thoughtful frown as she gazed at Apache for a long, considering minute. "Are you sure that you want me to ravage you?''

"More sure than I've ever been about anything in my life,'' Apache said, and wiggled his hips against hers.

"Then if I must, I must,'' came Emerald's husky reply as she wound her arms about his neck and pulled his head down to hers.

To Apache's pleased surprise, she took her part to heart and became the aggressor in their love play. She took his mouth in a fiery kiss, her tongue thrusting past his lips to seek and caress his. Her hands glided over his shoulders, her fingers playing sensually over his skin before she twisted from beneath him and pressed him onto his back. She climbed on top of him like a wanton, golden angel, straddling his hips as she pressed her palms flat against his chest, then rubbing the furry mat and making his nipples harden in response. She bent to capture his mouth once more as she moved her breasts teasingly against him.

Apache moaned softly as she grazed his hardness with the moist warmth of her womanhood and moved her hips against his. He sought to capture her round bottom and draw her down on him, but she wriggled away and shook her head.

"No, love. 'Tis not the time,'' she whispered as she began to explore his body, stroking and fondling his sinewy flesh until he thought he would explode under her touch. Emerald gave a low, throaty chuckle at his reaction to her caresses and felt her own blood simmer like white-hot lava in her veins. Her rose-tipped breasts rose and fell rapidly as her breathing grew ragged.

"Emerald," Apache moaned, unable to stand any more of her erotic torture. He grabbed her about the waist and brought her down on his arousal.

With her head thrown back and her breasts thrust forward into Apache's wide palms, she moved with him, riding him like a wild stallion, gripping his pumping hips and savoring the feel of him deep within her. Untamed as a rushing river, the fiery current of their passion carried them rapidly toward a searing climax that left them limp and trembling.

Emerald's golden hair spilled cross Apache's chest as she collapsed over him. She listened to his heart pound beneath her cheek as she lay savoring the sweetness of her release. Still intimately joined, her insides quivered and she felt him answer in response. Her heart felt as if it would burst with love. This man was all she could ask for in life and she didn't know what would happen to her if he ever chose to leave her.

The warm glow of contentment that claimed Emerald faded at the thought. A knot formed in the pit of her stomach and made her queasy. Her eyes widened in shock and she bolted upright, scrambled from the bed, and ran naked to the tin wash basin across the room. She managed to reach it before her stomach disgorged itself.

Her abrupt action startled Apache, and it took a moment for him to realize that Emerald was sick. He hurried to her, supporting her with an arm about her waist as she continued to retch into the basin. When nothing else would come, he lifted her in his arms and carried her back to the bed before moistening a rag in cool water and placing it on her brow.

His lean muscles rippled beneath the tanned skin of his bare back as he settled himself on the bed at her side and peered anxiously down at her, a frown marking his brow. He placed a hand on her cheek and was puzzled to find it cool. He didn't know what had come over Emerald so suddenly. She certainly hadn't been ill when they had made love. Far from it, he reflected with pleasure before giving himself a sharp mental shake. With Emerald so sick, this was no time to think of anything else.

Apache's gaze rested on her gray face. She'd had the same look about her last night when she'd said she was too tired to eat. She'd nearly turned green about the gills when she looked at the plate of food. A niggling suspicion began to take root in Apache's mind. Emerald had been acting strangely since yesterday morning when they had discussed having children.

"Emerald, are you pregnant?" Apache asked, voicing his suspicion aloud.

His sudden question shocked Emerald and her eyes snapped open. She moistened her dry lips nervously and shook her head, unable to voice the lie. The relieved look that crossed Apache's face made her wince inwardly but reaffirmed her decision not to tell him of their child.

"Then what's wrong?"

Emerald drew in an unsteady breath. "Nothing is wrong. I guess I had too much excitement on an empty stomach." She gave him a tentative smile.

"Are you sure that's all it is?" Apache asked, not satisfied with her answer.

"Yes, I'm sure. I feel much better now."

Apache brushed his knuckles lightly against her cheek and grinned down at her. "That's a first for me."

"What is?" Emerald asked, frowning.

"It's the first time a woman has gotten sick from my lovemaking. I hope after we're married that you don't continue to get sick every time I touch you, or you'll be ill all the time."

Emerald caught his hand and brought it to her lips. She pressed a kiss on his palm and shook her head. "If that's the price I have to pay, then I'll gladly pay it. But I don't think it was your lovemaking that made me sick. It was probably going without food for so long."

"I hope you're right. It doesn't make a man feel too

good to think his kisses make a woman ill,'' Apache chuckled.

"Then I suggest after we're married that you keep me well fed,'' Emerald said, and laughed, her nausea completely gone and her strength returning.

"I'm going to do my damnedest to keep you well fed in the kitchen as well as in the bedroom, woman. Now if you want to get to Denver and see that preacher, we'd better get dressed.''

Relieved that Apache had accepted her explanation, Emerald slid from the bed and picked up her tattered gown. She eyed it distastefully. This was her wedding day and she had no desire to stand before a minister in rags.

Seeing her moue of disgust, Apache stood and wrapped his arms about her. "You won't have to wear that thing to our wedding. When we get to Denver, I intend to see you dressed as a bride should be.''

Emerald turned in his arms and hugged him close. "It doesn't really matter if I wear rags or a fancy gown. All that matters to me is that we'll be married.''

"Yes, that's all that really matters,'' Apache murmured against her golden head. And, in truth, it was. He loved the woman in his arms and would think her beautiful if she never dressed in anything but rags.

Chapter 14

At *the sight of the man and woman riding down the* street, Red Beaudine choked on the chaw of tobacco he had been enjoying a moment earlier. His eyes bulged as the bitter lump slowly slid down his throat and his pale face reddened to the same hue as the jagged birthmark on his cheek from the discomfort. With his thoughts on what would happen to him if the girl should chance to recognize him, he ignored the sudden sickening lurch his stomach gave when the tobacco reached it. He jerked his hat lower over his brow and ducked out of sight behind a buckboard filled with barrels. Warily, he peered between the metal-bound casks and watched Emerald and Apache ride by without a glance in his direction.

Relieved, he stepped out from his hiding place and stood thoughtfully regarding the two mounted on the stallion as they went off down the street. He rubbed his beard-stubbled chin as he reflected on how Cash Dalton would respond when he told him the girl was back in town.

In all the time he'd worked for Dalton, he'd never seen him react to anything the way he had about the girl's disappearance. During the past week he'd been like a madman, cursing and raging each time the men returned without finding a trace of his intended bride.

"And now she's turned up with that gunslinger, Ryan," Red muttered under his breath, and shook his

head. "The boss ain't going to like this one little bit.
He don't take kindly to anyone going against him, especially when he needs the claim the girl owns."

Red didn't envy the couple as he started to turn in
the direction of the Gold Dust. He had to report what
he'd seen to Cash. However, a moment later, he thought
better of it. His brows lowered over his beady eyes as
he glanced speculatively down Larimer Street. If he told
the boss that the girl was back in town and then she
slipped away from them again, Dalton's fury would fall
on him. After the way the boss had been acting, he had
no desire for that to happen. It was in his own best
interest to follow them and see where they went so that
when he told the boss, he'd know where to find the girl
without any problems.

With his decision made, Red turned in the direction
Emerald and Apache had traveled only moments before. He kept them in sight from a safe distance, and
when they stopped in front of the mercantile store, he
quickly dodged into an alleyway on the opposite side
of the street. He could keep an eye on the front of the
store from there and not be seen.

Red waited in his hiding place for more than an hour
and had begun to believe that they had left by the back
entrance of the store when they finally emerged dressed
in the best ready-made clothing that Denver had to offer. A puzzled frown drew his brows down to shadow
his eyes as he regarded the elegantly attired couple.

"What on earth are they getting all gussied up for?"
he asked himself as he watched Apache lift the girl back
up onto the stallion's back and then mount behind her.
Red scratched his head and gave a disgusted snort as
he sidled from his hiding place and began to follow
them once more.

"I don't know what they're up to, but I plan on finding out."

Unaware of the man following them, Apache reined
the stallion to a halt in front of a small clapboard house
at the end of Larimer Street. He helped Emerald dis-

mount and they strolled arm in arm up the narrow steps to the small, weather-browned porch. He rapped on the door and a moment later a small, thin woman answered his knock. She smiled warmly at the couple as she brushed a stray strand of hair from her brow with a hand lightly dusted with flour. Peeking from behind her wide skirt was a doe-eyed little boy with his thumb tucked firmly into his cherubic mouth.

"May I help you?" she asked pleasantly as she tugged the clinging child out of his hiding place and made him stand at her side.

"Is this the Reverend Fletcher's house?" Apache asked politely, with hat in hand.

"Yes, it is, but I'm afraid if you came to see my husband, he's not here at the moment. He had to attend a funeral in Auraria this afternoon."

"Then you do expect him back by this evening?"

"Yes, most certainly. He should be back long before it's suppertime. The funeral was to be at four o'clock."

"Then, Mrs. Fletcher, we'll return this evening to see your husband."

Apache took Emerald by the arm and had begun to turn away when the minister's wife asked, "May I tell him who called and the reason for your visit?"

Apache glanced back at her and smiled. "Tell him that Mistress Emerald Banyon and Beau Alexander Ryan would like for him to marry them at his earliest convenience."

"I'll do that," the woman said, and gave the couple a pleased smile. The thought of a wedding lifted her spirits. This would be the first one her husband would perform since they'd come to Denver, and it would be a nice change after so many bleak months during which her husband's services had only been required at funerals. He had begun to believe that he was a failure as a minister. He did his best to bring the word of God to the prospectors that flooded the town, but they paid little heed to his preachings. They were more interested in finding gold than in saving their souls. She hoped this wedding would bring her husband out of the doldrums. It would signify a new beginning for both the young couple and the Fletcher family as well.

"Beau Alexander Ryan?" Emerald said, gaping up at Apache as the door closed softly behind them.

He grinned and shrugged one broad shoulder.

"You know, until this moment I didn't know your real name," Emerald said, astonished that she could know the man she planned to marry so intimately yet not know the name he was given at birth. With that thought, she could not stop herself from wondering what else he had failed to tell her about himself. She was going to pledge her life and love to this man, but, in truth, she knew nothing about his past beyond what he had said when he was delirious. Her musings made her uneasy and she shrugged them aside. She loved Apache and he loved her, and that was all that truly mattered.

"Emerald, the past is over. Today we are beginning our future," Apache said, sensing from her distracted mood the myriad of questions roiling about in her mind.

"I know," she said. Draping her arm through his, she smiled up at him. She couldn't keep letting every little thing he said or did perpetuate the insecurity that she still felt from her past experience with her father. She had enough to contend with knowing that today was her wedding day and that tonight she would tell Apache she carried their child.

"Good," he said, placing his hand over hers and giving it a reassuring squeeze. "Now, let's consider what we're going to do until the Reverend Fletcher returns."

"What do you want to do?" Emerald asked.

Apache gave her a roguish grin and winked. "You know exactly what I want to do, but I'll abstain until after the vows are spoken. Since we don't have a place to stay, I suggest the first thing we do is find a decent room in a hotel."

"I hope you don't mean the Denver House," Emerald said, aghast at the thought of spending any night in such a place, much less her wedding night.

"No, love. There are other hotels in Denver that have better accommodations."

Emerald gave Apache an arch look. "You mean there are decent hotels in Denver, and you left me at the Denver House that night, fully knowing what type of place it was?"

Apache's swarthy complexion flushed with guilt. "Well, I . . . Damn it, Emerald. You deserved a lesson after the way you acted."

"The way *I* acted? As I recall, you were the one who needed a lesson in manners."

"I agree," Apache said simply, giving her no argument.

Taken aback by his sudden capitulation, Emerald frowned. "You agree?"

"Yes, and let's just leave it at that."

"Oh, no, you don't, Apache Ryan. You're not going to get off that easily after what I went through that night. Now I want to know why you agree with me."

When she would not let the subject rest, Apache released a long breath and turned to Emerald. He tipped her chin up with his thumb and forefinger and peered down at her, his face set and serious. "If you must know, I'll tell you. From the moment I left you at the Denver House, and then until you walked into Hannah's, I worried myself sick that something had happened to you."

"You really worried about me?" Emerald asked, feeling a warm glow steal over her.

Apache nodded.

"But why?"

"Because you're a hardheaded little minx who walks headfirst into trouble. Now, does that satisfy your curiosity?" Apache asked as he clasped her about the waist and lifted her into the saddle.

"I guess it will have to," Emerald said, feeling suddenly deflated. The romantic part of her wanted to hear him say that he had loved her from the beginning, so she would know that their child had been conceived out of that love instead of a moment of lust.

"Now that you're satisfied, we need to find a room. Then, once I've seen you settled, I'll need to go to Hannah's and collect my belongings. I also need to tell her that we're getting married."

The fact that Apache wanted to see his mistress and explain about their marriage disturbed Emerald more than she cared to admit. Her eyes swept over his face, seeking answers to the questions that rose in her heart but could not be voiced. All she could say was, "Why?"

Apache shifted uneasily. "She deserves to hear it from me. Hannah has been a good friend to me since I came to Denver."

"You mean a good mistress," Emerald snapped, bristling with jealousy.

"Emerald, I won't argue with you about Hannah. You are the woman I'm marrying, so you have no reason to be concerned about her. Let's leave it at that."

"All right, we'll leave it at that," Emerald said. "You go to see the Widow Becker and I'll go to see Cash. I think he deserves more of an explanation than Hannah does."

Apache's fingers clamped down on Emerald's shoulders and he jerked her about to face him. "You stay away from Dalton."

Undaunted by the angry tone in his voice, Emerald regarded him through narrowed eyes that glowed with the light of defiance. Her small, squared chin jutted out mulishly as she stared him directly in the eyes, giving no ground.

"Emerald, did you hear what I said?" he demanded when she did not respond to his order.

"I heard every word of it, but that doesn't mean I'll follow your autocratic dictates. I may have agreed to marry you, Apache Ryan, but that doesn't mean that you can order me about like a servant. I'll be your wife, not your slave. The way I see it, what's sauce for the goose is also sauce for the gander."

Apache rolled his eyes in exasperation. "Emerald, for the love of God. You may not believe it, but Cash Dalton is a dangerous man. When he learns that we're getting married, it's not going to be pleasant. He's going to show his true colors, and I don't want you around him when he does."

"Apache, I know you hate Cash, but he is still my friend. I don't like the thought of hurting him. I did promise to marry him, and I owe it to him and myself to try to make him understand the reason that I can't go through with it now."

"I won't allow you to see Dalton again, and that's final."

"Then this is not going to work, Apache."

Apache felt his blood run cold. "What do you mean?"

"You expect me to obey you and I can't. Please let me down from the horse."

"I'm not letting you down until you've come to your senses, Emerald."

"I've come to my senses, thank you," Emerald snapped. "I won't marry you without apologizing to Cash."

"Damn it, Emerald. Why do you have to be so stubborn?" Apache growled.

"It's not being stubborn, Apache. It's called being fair. Cash may be all that you say he is, but I've never seen that side of him. He's been good to me and I can't just ignore his feelings in this matter, no more than you can Hannah's."

Apache felt as if his head would leave his shoulders from the fury that exploded within him. He wanted to shake Emerald until her teeth rattled for continuing to care about Dalton's feelings. The man had had her father killed, as well as an untold number of other innocent people who stood in his way, and Emerald was too blind to see the evil in him.

Apache jerked the stallion to a halt in front of the Platte Hotel and dismounted. He reached up and helped Emerald none too gently to the ground before turning his attention to tethering Rogue to the hitching rail. With an effort, he managed to get a grip on his temper before he turned back to her. His face showed no sign of his vexation of a moment earlier.

"All right, young lady, you win," he said as he crossed the few feet to Emerald and pulled her into his arms. He ignored the curious and shocked looks of those who passed them on the planked sidewalk as he lowered his head to hers and kissed her soundly. When he released her lips, he smiled down at her. "I'll take you to see Dalton as soon as I return. Is that agreeable?"

Blushing from head to toe with embarrassment, Emerald could only nod as she glanced timidly about them at the crowd that had gathered to watch. Apache's kiss as well as his sudden capitulation to her wishes had taken her by surprise and left her stunned and speechless.

"Then I'll get us a room so you can rest. We have much to do before we see the Reverend and Mrs. Fletcher tonight." Apache had agreed to her wishes against his better judgment, but he knew from the stubborn set of her chin that if he hadn't, she would have gone to see Dalton alone.

That thought chilled Apache's soul. He couldn't allow Emerald to be alone with Dalton. The gambler was a ruthless man at any time, but when someone opposed him, he became vicious. He would think nothing of killing Emerald once he learned that she was no longer of any value to him alive.

Settling the matter in his mind, Apache smiled to himself as he led Emerald into the lobby of the Platte Hotel and rented the finest room it had to offer for his future bride. At least by giving in to Emerald's demands, he would be with her when she saw Dalton. And when the gambler revealed the real man behind

the façade of the generous benefactor that he had erected
for her benefit, Apache would be there to protect her
from him. Satisfied with his decision, he escorted Emerald up to their room. He saw her comfortably en-
sconced in the wide double bed where they would spend
their wedding night and then left her to see Hannah.

From a safe vantage point across the street from the
hotel, Red Beaudine stood with his arms folded across
his chest and the brim of his hat pulled low over his
forehead to shadow his face. Along with the crowd who
had stopped to gape at the couple when the gunslinger
took the girl brazenly into his arms and kissed her before one and all, Red watched them walk into the hotel.
When they disappeared from view, he quickly maneuvered his way through the spectators but slowed his
pace at the double doors and casually strolled into the
hotel so as not to draw any attention to himself. With
ears and eyes attuned to the young couple, he spotted
them as they ascended the stairs to their room and
quickly followed in their wake. He waited around the
corner until the door closed behind them before he crept
forward and pressed his ear to the wooden panel, straining to hear anything that might be of value to Cash.

The click of the latch near his ear made him bolt
upright and flee down the hall as if the devil were on
his heels. Looking for a place to hide, his head swiveled
wildly from side to side before he dashed into one of
the rooms. Fortunately, it was vacant. Fearing that
Apache might have seen his flight, he pressed his back
to the door, tense and panting for breath.

Red's heart drummed against his ribs at the sound of
Apache's approaching footsteps, but he relaxed a moment later as they passed in the corridor without slow-
ing.

"Whew," he breathed, wiping the sweat from his
brow. "That was a close'un."

Easing the door open, he peeked into the hallway

before he slipped out of his hiding place and moved once more toward Emerald's door. He tried the door handle and found it locked.

"Damn," he muttered under his breath. "What am I to do now?" With a shake of his head, he dug into his pocket and pulled out a brown square of tobacco. He bit into it, ripping off a chunk with his teeth. He rolled it about in his mouth to moisten it and then tucked it into his jaw. He licked the excess juice from his lips and ran the back of his hand across his mouth as he considered the question. He didn't want to chance losing the girl again, but he needed to let Cash know what he had learned.

"What the hell," he muttered in disgust. "I've found her, and that's more than any of the rest of the men have done, so I'll let the boss handle it from here."

Red spat a stream of tobacco juice into the brass spittoon at the head of the stairs. His face screwed up in a thoughtful frown, he descended to the lobby below. After what he had witnessed that afternoon, he was glad he wasn't in Ryan's or the girl's shoes. He didn't even like the thought of being in his own boots when it came to having to tell Dalton what he'd seen. The boss wasn't going to like being made a fool of in public. He'd be meaner than a rattlesnake when he learned the girl he'd intended to make his wife had gone to see a preacher with Ryan and then had come back to the hotel to make a spectacle of herself in front of the whole town. The boss had big plans for that little lady, and he wasn't going to take this insult lightly.

"Damn," Red said softly to himself as he walked out of the hotel and turned in the direction of the Gold Dust Saloon. "All hell is going to break loose when I tell him."

Red's grim predictions held true a few minutes later when he stood white-faced in front of the outraged gambler.

"Beaudine, if this is some kind of joke, then you'll

not live to regret it," Cash exploded, his face flushing a deep red as he came out of his chair and leaned one balled fist against the top of his desk, glaring at Red.

"It ain't no joke, boss. The girl's back in town with Ryan and from the looks of it they plan on getting hitched. If you don't believe me, you can ask nearly anybody in town about what I saw at the Platte Hotel and they'll back me up. He kissed her right there on the sidewalk in front of everybody."

All emotion seemed to drain from Cash. His expression became granite-hard and his eyes glittered like onyx through his narrowed lashes. "Well, I have news for them. They won't be getting married. I have first bid on Emerald's claim, and I'll not give it up that easily. I haven't waited this long to lose it just because he's managed to get between her thighs."

Cash settled himself in his leather chair and propped his hand-tooled leather boots on the desk. He delved into his pocket and retrieved a cheroot. Placing it between his white teeth, he struck a match and held the flame to the tip of the small cigar. Smoke curled toward the ceiling as he squinted up at Red and smiled diabolically.

"Ryan is not going to get away with this. He's tempted fate once too often by interfering in my affairs."

"What do you plan to do, boss?" Red asked.

"I plan to have you kill the bastard."

Red's eyes seemed to bulge. He had no desire to face Ryan.

Cash chuckled at Red's expression and shook his head. "Don't be a fool. I don't mean for you to have a shootout with the man. You'd be dead before you could get your gun out of the holster. You're quick, but you're not half as fast as he is. Do it in your usual way, instead."

Red sagged with relief. "When do you want it done, boss?"

"As soon as possible, but make sure the girl is not

harmed. She belongs to me.'' Cash's eyes were as dark and cold as a crypt at midnight as he regarded his hired killer. ''While you're taking care of Ryan, I intend to pay a visit to Mistress Emerald Banyon, and by the time I'm through with her, she'll regret her decision to jilt me on our wedding day.''

''You can't honestly expect me to believe that you're going to marry that girl?'' Hannah said, her voice rising in pitch despite herself. Apache's announcement tested her self-control to the limit. It took all of her willpower and levelheadedness not to let herself give in to the panic mounting within her breast.

''It's true, Hannah. We're to be married tonight.''

The pain that ripped through Hannah made her draw in a sharp breath. She squeezed her eyes closed for a fraction of a second and let the spasm pass before she looked calmly at Apache. The only sign of her distress was the white-knuckled hands she clasped tightly together in her lap.

''After all that we've shared, I would have thought you would have at least considered my feelings in the matter,'' Hannah said softly, masking the temper that had begun to simmer within her as soon as the pain in her heart eased in intensity.

Apache shifted uncomfortably in the chair. ''Hannah, you've been a good friend to me and that's why I came to tell you of my marriage before anyone else did. I don't want to hurt you.''

Hurt me! Hannah fumed silently and quickly lowered her eyes to her hands to hide her thoughts from Apache. You'll know about hurt when I'm through with you, Apache Ryan, she thought. No man turns his back on me and gets away with it. If I can't have you, then that little bitch won't get you either.

''Hannah,'' Apache said, getting out of his chair and crossing to her. He knelt at her side and covered her hands with his. ''I hope that you can forgive me, but until I met Emerald, I didn't know that I could love again. You and I have shared some lovely moments together, but we both knew from the beginning that we didn't love each other."

Hannah cringed inwardly but gave no visible sign that she was affected by his words. The golden glints sparkling in her brown eyes were the only physical evidence of the fiery thoughts that she hid from Apache when she looked up at him.

"I never asked you to love me," Hannah said, raising her chin and stiffening her back to retain a small measure of her dignity.

"I know you didn't, Hannah. And I'm grateful for your understanding. I hope that after Emerald and I are married, we can remain friends."

Hannah came to her feet and moved swiftly across the room, putting as much distance between herself and the unfeeling man as possible. Incensed by his words, she felt her heart pound violently against her ribs and her nostrils flared as she drew in a deep breath in an effort to remain poised. Tiny lines formed about her pinched lips as she regarded Apache through narrowed eyes. The man was completely insensitive. After she had shown him her love by sharing her bed and her home with him, he had the nerve to be grateful for her understanding. Hannah's blood sizzled through her veins like wildfire. Apache Ryan would pay for his heartlessness if it was the last thing she ever did.

"I think you ask too much of the women in your life, Apache. Even if I wanted to remain friends with you, your wife would never allow it. It's best that we part now with no hard feelings and forget what was between us."

Apache nodded. "I guess you're right, Hannah. I've always respected your decisions in the past, and I won't argue with you now." He turned toward the door, but Hannah's question made him pause with his hand on the latch.

"Do you love this girl?"

Apache turned to look at Hannah. "I love Emerald

more than I ever dreamed possible. If anything should happen to her, I believe it would tear out my heart.''

''That's all I wanted to know, Apache.'' Hannah turned away to hide her triumphant smile.

''Good-bye, Hannah. I wish you well,'' Apache said before he stepped out into the encroaching night and closed the door behind him.

''It's not good-bye yet, Apache. After I've told that little hussy what I know, you may come crawling back to me and beg me to love you,'' Hannah said smugly. She turned and hurried up the stairs to collect her cloak. She had to see Emerald before the wedding.

Relieved that Hannah had not wept and cursed but had accepted the news of his marriage graciously, Apache rode back toward the Platte Hotel well satisfied with his day's work and looking forward to the night to come. He stopped briefly at the Denver House to inform Jeb of his wedding plans but took no time to enjoy a drink with the old man. He was too anxious to return to Emerald. With his thoughts on her and the future they would share, he relaxed his ever-vigilant guard as he rode down the street lined with saloons.

Engrossed in his musing, Apache did not notice the skulking figure in the inky shadows of the alleyway as he passed. Nor did he hear the deadly click of a revolver's hammer being drawn back. The jangle of piano music that filled the cool night air covered any sound that might have warned him. The report reached his ears at the same time his shoulder was ripped open and he was knocked from the saddle. He gave one agonized groan when he hit the hard-packed street and then sank into unconsciousness.

The sound of the gunshot brought the curious out of the saloons, and they surrounded Apache, mumbling and pushing to get a better view of the wounded man. A thin man dressed in a faded black suit, a stovepipe hat, and a once white shirt hurried to him and knelt to see if he was alive. He gave a disgusted snort when he felt a pulse at the base of Apache's throat and shook his head. "Get him over to my brother's. He'll probably live."

"It ain't your lucky day, is it, Homer? It must be real disgustin' to see a feller get shot down right in front of you and still live," a spectator said to the undertaker with a sneer.

"Shut your damned mouth, Harley," Homer Smith snarled. He swiveled his head around on his long, thin neck and looked up at the crowd about him.

"Shore nuff, Homer. Wouldn't want to say anythin' to upset you since I know that you're already be-grudgin' the doc a customer. Come on and I'll buy you a drink."

"I wouldn't drink with you, Harley Ridings, even if I didn't have to get this man over to Sidney's. Now get out of our way if you ain't going to help."

The man called Harley chuckled. "You a-goin' to take him over just in case he might need your services before he gets to the doc? You're a smart one, Homer. Always a-thinkin' on how to get your brother's custom-ers."

Homer Smith ignored the gibes and took one of Apache's arms while three other men from the saloon helped to lift him. They were huffing and puffing from the exertion by the time they carried him up the stairs to the small office Dr. Smith rented above the mercan-tile store.

"Sidney, this one's for you," Homer called out as he pushed open the door and saw his brother dozing in front of the potbellied stove.

Sidney Smith, M.D., roused slowly from sleep and eyed his brother and the other men through a pair of round spectacles on the tip of his nose. He leaned his head back and squinted at them, "Who you got there, boys?"

"Don't know who he is, but he's a big bastard," Homer replied in a strained voice as they lifted Apache onto the examining table. "He's all yours for now, but should you need me, I'll be down at the—"

"I know where you stay most of the time, Homer,"

Dr. Smith said gruffly, cutting his brother short. "You'd do better for yourself if you'd stay away from there at least a few hours in the day."

"Sidney, I just brought you a patient. I didn't come here to hear a lecture," Homer said, and stomped out the door.

"Thank you, boys," the doctor said, and waved the other men out of the office in his brother's wake. When the door closed behind them, he turned his attention to the man on the table. Though his hands were beginning to gnarl with rheumatism, he worked swiftly and gently, cutting away Apache's shirt to reveal the gaping hole in his shoulder and the bright stream of blood running from it.

"You're lucky you're not on Homer's table right now, son," he muttered to the unconscious man. "Had the bullet been a few inches lower, he'd already be fitting you for a coffin."

Dr. Smith washed his hands and the wound in whiskey before he began to extract the piece of lead. Apache moaned when the doctor probed for the bullet, but to Sidney's relief, he did not awaken. A moment later, the lump of bloody metal clinked in the washbasin on the floor by the table.

"Well, son, I've done all I can do. After I sew you up, it'll be left up to you to recover. You've lost a lot of blood, but you're young and strong. And if you've got the will, you'll live."

Emerald bolted upright in the bed at the sound of gunfire in the street. It wasn't unusual to hear gunshots in Denver at any time of the day. When prospectors consumed too much whiskey and needed to vent their frustrations, they did so by shooting out lanterns and anything else they considered a good target. However, something about this one unnerved her, and her skin prickled with gooseflesh as she scrambled from the bed and hurried to the window. She pulled back the sheer lace curtain and peered down into the street below. It was dark. The lantern light that spilled through the windows and doors of the hotel and the saloons did little to illuminate the scene, and she could not see the reason the crowd had gathered in front of the gambling hall several doors away from the hotel.

Guessing at the cause of so much interest, Emerald gave a sad shake of her head and let the curtain fall back into place. Some poor soul had been fool enough to challenge the wrong man and had paid with his life for it. At the thought, her throat constricted with pity for the fallen man. Like her father, his dreams of finding the much-talked-about El Dorado had ended with a bullet.

"At least they know who shot this poor man and can see him brought to justice," she mused aloud. "It's beginning to look as if I'll never find the man who shot Pa."

Emerald turned away from the window and crossed back to the bed. Her gloomy expression reflected her discouraging thoughts as she sank down onto it and folded her arms on the railing of the iron bedstead. A pout made her lower lip jut outward as she rested her chin on her arms and considered the ambitious plans that she'd had when she first came to Denver. She had been so determined to find the man with the red mark on his cheek, but that had not happened, and she was beginning to doubt that it ever would. He and his whiny cohort could be out of the territory by now, and she'd never find them or the man they worked for.

"I've been a fool for not telling the sheriff what I knew from the beginning," Emerald said, frustrated with herself for keeping the information a secret for so long. "And I should have told Apache about the man with the red mark. If I had, he might have been able to help me find him."

Emerald frowned. It was always much easier to look back and see what you should have done. She knew why she'd not told anyone about the claim jumpers. She had been so cocksure that she could find the men that she hadn't trusted anyone, not even Apache, enough to share her secret. And now she feared that her misgivings had defeated her. She was no closer to finding the man called Red than she had been the morning after her father had been murdered.

"You little idiot," Emerald said, disgusted with herself for being so young and stupid as to believe that she needed no one. It had only been a little over two months since her father had been slain, but in that time she had matured into a woman.

A rueful smile curled the corners of Emerald's lips as she remembered how she had been so adamant about being a grown woman that first night with Apache in Jeb's cabin. How naïve she had been. She'd been a child in a woman's body, playing at the game of being grown-up. Ignorance and innocence had led her to believe that she could take on the world alone and see justice done without asking for anyone's help. However, the last two months had taught her several harsh lessons, and she now knew that life was not that simplistic.

"When Apache returns, I'll tell him all I know about the claim jumpers and that will solve one of my problems," Emerald said. "I hope he'll know how we can find the man named Red."

Relieved by her decision, Emerald's face softened as her thoughts turned to the precious burden she now carried. She had concealed more than just the claim jumpers' identity from Apache, but that would also come to an end. She rested a hand on her flat belly, and her lips curved into a tender smile. "I love your father, little one, and I will trust him with both of my secrets before any vows are spoken between us. I have allowed Jim's memory to cast its shadow over Apache for the last time. I won't believe he's like my father. And I can't let my unhappy past destroy all of our futures. There is too much at stake. A marriage without honesty is no marriage at all."

Emerald smiled with satisfaction. She felt as if she had finally disarmed the past of its weapons to harm her. She would bury her distrust and place her faith in the man she loved as soon as he returned for her. If Apache was not prepared to accept their child as his own, then she would face that when the time came. But for now she was resolved to reveal all of the secrets she'd held from him before it could destroy the future.

As if conjured up by her thoughts, a knock sounded at the door. Anxious to be with Apache again, Emerald scrambled from the bed and hurried to answer it. Her happiness made her face glow, and a bright smile played over her lips as she swung the door open.

"What took you so long, Apache?" she asked before she realized who stood in the doorway. Her knuckles grew white on the door latch and her smile faded at the sight of the Widow Becker, who stood regarding her with a smug smile curling her broad-lipped mouth.

"What do you want, Hannah?" Emerald asked warily, without stepping aside to welcome the woman into her room.

"Is that any way to speak to me after I've come all the way across town to talk to you? Especially since I had to pass by that rough-looking bunch down in the street. Fortunately, they were far too involved with the man on the ground to pay much attention to me as I ran past," Hannah said with asperity, feigning an insult that she did not feel.

Emerald shifted uncomfortably under the older woman's censure. She didn't like Hannah, but she would at least show her the courtesy she would give to any stranger. "I'm sorry, Hannah. Would you like to come in?"

"It's better than standing in the hall," Hannah said, sweeping past Emerald before she was completely out of her path.

At Hannah's rude entry, Emerald's temper threatened to snap, but she managed to control it before she told the woman what she really thought of her. She drew in a steadying breath and closed the door before she turned to look at her unwelcome guest. When Hannah did not volunteer to speak first, Emerald arched a curious brow at her and said, "You said something about coming here to talk with me?"

Hannah nodded. Her wide mouth spread into a pleased smile and her brown eyes held a wicked twinkle as she perused her rival from head to toe before she spoke. "Yes, that's what I came to do."

"I really don't know what we have to discuss, but if you feel so strongly about it, then I suggest that you begin. I don't have much time."

"That's right. You and Apache are going to be married tonight, aren't you?" Hannah asked softly. Her smile never wavered.

"Yes, we are," Emerald said, regarding Hannah suspiciously. The woman's tone was friendly, yet Emerald sensed that friendship was far from her intent. There was an air of underlying tension about her that belied the pleasant smile she had pasted onto her lips.

"Apache told me." Hannah's voice wobbled slightly. Her self-control slipped precariously for a fraction of a moment at the thought of how Apache had abused her love and generosity. However, she managed to get a grip on her emotions and continued in a syrupy-sweet voice. "That's the reason I'm here. I wanted to give you a wedding present."

Emerald frowned. She had heard the hostility in Hannah's last words though she'd coated them in sugar. "That is good of you, Hannah, but I'm afraid I can't accept it."

"Oh, I think you can accept it, Emerald. It's for your own good."

"Hannah, I don't know what you're talking about," Emerald said, puzzled by the woman's odd behavior.

"Sadly enough, you don't, but you will."

Emerald thought she would explode with exasperation. She felt like strangling Hannah. The woman was playing some kind of vicious game with her, but she had no idea what it was. "I wish you'd stop talking in riddles. I know from the way you're acting that you're just dying to tell me something that you think will hurt me. So why don't you just spit it out and get it over with?''

The Widow Becker gave an indignant snort, pursed her wide lips, and lifted her chin at a condescending angle. ''My dear girl, you have always wrongly judged my actions toward you. I've tried to befriend you in the past, and now I've come to try to save you from making the biggest mistake of your life, but you still take umbrage with me. I don't really know what more I can do to change your opinion about me.''

''If you honestly want me to change my feelings, Hannah, why don't you tell me why you really came here?''

''Like I said, I wanted to try to prevent you from making a mistake. One that you'll regret for the rest of your life.''

''You mean, you wanted to try to stop me marrying Apache?''

''Yes,'' was all Hannah said.

Emerald eyed the woman with disgust and shook her head. ''Then you came all this way for nothing. There isn't anything you can tell me that will change my mind.''

''I think there is much I can tell you that will change your mind,'' Hannah said, and smiled.

''Hannah, it's time for you to leave. I won't stand here and listen to you malign the man I love.''

''Oh, so you love him?''

''Yes, I love him and he loves me.''

Hannah threw back her head and laughed. ''You're a bigger fool than I thought if you believe that.''

''Get out, Hannah,'' Emerald ordered, and turned to the door.

''Oh, I'll leave, Emerald, but not before you know the real reason Apache is marrying you, and it certainly isn't for love, as you so foolishly believe.''

''I don't want to hear any of your lies,'' Emerald said, and opened the door.

"They're not lies, my dear. Apache will do anything to stop Cash Dalton from building his railroad."

"I know Apache hates Cash, but you can't honestly expect me to believe that the only reason he's marrying me is to stop Cash from building his railroad. Surely you don't think I'm that big of a fool. I may be gullible at times, but not when it comes to you and your lies, especially when I know the reason you want me out of Apache's life."

"You don't have to believe me, Emerald. Those aren't my words, they came directly from the horse's mouth one night while I was in his room. Apache told me that he'd do anything he had to do to stop Cash. And that means he'd even marry someone he didn't love."

Emerald turned slowly to look at Hannah. Her face was devoid of the emotions that were ripping her insides apart. In less than half an hour her resolve to trust Apache had been shattered by the suspicions Hannah was planting in her mind. Each word the widow spoke fertilized the seeds of distrust that had lain dormant through the years and made them take root and grow.

"I don't believe you," Emerald said, making one last effort to defend Apache.

"I really don't care. I just wanted you to know what type of man Apache really is. He'll do anything to ruin Dalton, even marry you. He hates the man."

"Hannah, that makes no sense. Apache can't ruin Cash by marrying me."

Hannah lifted one brow and regarded Emerald cynically. Her voice dripped with sarcasm as she said, "Oh, no? That's not what Apache told me long before he decided the best way to get at Dalton was to marry you. You own the claim that he wants, and that's the only reason for this sudden proposal, you little fool. By getting his hands on your claim deed, he can stop Dalton in his tracks." Hannah laughed. "Or should I say, before he lays his tracks. If that railroad deal falls through, Dalton will be ruined."

"No, I won't believe you. Apache loves me," Emerald argued, even as Hannah's words sank in and made her feel suddenly sick to her stomach.

"Has he ever told you that he loves you?"

Hannah's question made Emerald pale. Her skin turned an unhealthy shade of gray as the blood drained from her face and her stomach seemed to do a somersault beneath her ribs. Hannah had touched on something that she had not wanted to admit even to herself. For, in truth, Apache had never actually said he loved her. He had said he worried over her, cared for her, and he called her "love," but he had never said the words "I love you" even during their most intimate moments.

Hannah laughed at the stricken expression that crossed Emerald's face. "I thought not. I know the man far better than you do, you stupid child. You've much to learn about life and men. Spreading your thighs for a man does not make him love you."

"Get out," Emerald ordered in a strained whisper.

"I'll gladly go now. You know what kind of man Apache is, and it won't be on my conscience if you marry the bastard. Come to think of it, I should have left things the way they were. The two of you deserve each other," Hannah spat, then stalked from the room.

As the door closed behind her, Hannah chuckled with satisfaction at a job well done. She had succeeded far better than she had expected. From the expression on the stupid girl's face, there would be no wedding tonight or any other time for her and Apache.

"No man gets by with using me the way you have, Apache Ryan," Hannah mused aloud as she descended the stairs to the hotel lobby. "And after my little talk with Emerald tonight, you have no one but me to turn to now. And you'll have to come crawling back on your hands and knees before I forgive you."

Hannah drew her cape closer about her round form and stepped through the door that was held open for her by an elegantly attired man who courteously doffed his hat to her. With her mind still on Apache, she ignored the gentlemanly gesture as she walked past him and out into the night. Glancing up at the star-laden heavens, Hannah drew in a breath of the icy night air and smiled. "But Apache will find I'm very generous. I'll forgive him in time."

Cash Dalton's eyes glittered with a speculative light as he watched Hannah walk down the street. He knew who the woman had come to visit at the Platte Hotel, and judging from her expression, she'd gotten what she wanted. Cash smiled. If the Widow Becker was pleased by her encounter with Emerald, then perhaps all was not as bad as he had first surmised from Red's story. As simpleminded as Red Beaudine was at times, he might have misconstrued what he'd seen today, and there was really no cause for alarm.

Cash retrieved a cheroot from his pocket and bit off the tip as he crossed the lobby to the reservations desk and asked for Emerald's room number. Then he lit the pungent cigar and strode toward the stairs.

He paused at the top of the landing and tossed the cheroot into the brass spittoon before straightening his velvet jacket and fluffing the lace-edged ruffles at his wrists with the tips of his manicured fingers. He wanted to look his best when he saw Emerald and broke the news of Apache's demise to her. With her champion gone, Cash was certain she would come back to him with little or no effort on his part if he played his cards right.

Things between Emerald and Ryan could be exactly as Red had said they were, but that wasn't really important anymore. He'd seen Apache Ryan felled by Red's bullet and by now he was either dead or dying, so it didn't matter what plans Ryan and Emerald had had together. All that concerned Cash was the fact that Emerald was now his to do with as he pleased.

Chapter 15

Sick at heart and fighting against the wave of nausea that made her insides roil, Emerald leaned against the door and squeezed her eyes tightly closed in an effort to shut out the horrible suspicions Hannah's revelations had raised in her mind. She loved Apache and didn't want to believe a word the vicious woman had told her, but the evidence was too strong. Everything Hannah said about Apache's feelings for Cash was true, as was the cruel fact that he had never told her that he loved her.

At the thought, Emerald gagged and dashed across the room to retch into the porcelain chamber pot. When the spasms of nausea passed, she sagged down into the straight-backed chair beside the washstand and laid her head against the slatted backrest. Tears of anger, pain, and weakness spilled down her ashen cheeks as she raised a trembling hand to her damp brow and absently brushed the golden hair back from a face that reflected her heartbreak.

"God, how it hurts," Emerald whispered brokenly, her voice hoarse with pain at the thought that she had been used by Apache to thwart his enemy. She crossed her arms over her chest, as if the action would serve to keep the shattered pieces of her heart within her breast, and drew in a trembling breath. "What am I going to do now that I know the real reason behind Apache's offer of marriage? Can I go through with this farce to give my child a name? And if my answer is no, do I have

enough strength to leave him, loving him as I do?'' she
agonized out loud.

The room remained silent. No answer to Emerald's
questions came, nor could she find one inside herself.
She knew she was a fool, but even after all she had
learned, she still loved Apache. To her regret, love was
not something you could turn on and off at whim. Once
it took root in your heart, it needed only a little tender
care to keep it nourished and alive. But she also knew
that love was not indestructible. It could be killed, but
it took time. It withered and died slowly, causing much
pain before it was completely vanquished.

Emerald gave a sad shake of her head. Eighteen years
of her life had been spent giving her love to a man who
had cared nothing for her, and now she found herself
in the same trap again with Apache. However, this time
she was responsible for another life as well. And because of that small burden resting within her womb,
she could not remain on the fringes of Apache's life.
She had to make a choice between marrying him for
her child's sake or giving him up completely.

Emerald bowed her head and covered her face with
her hands as she tried to sort through her jumbled emotions. Her heart cried out for her to forget what Hannah
had said and to marry Apache, but her mind firmly
urged her in the opposite direction by taunting her with
the fact that he was only using her and wouldn't love
their child because he had told her he didn't want children.

Emerald slowly raised her head. From her own experience she knew it was not a pleasant existence to
have a father who did not want or love you. She'd not
allow her child to suffer the same fate. It would be far
better that he believe his father was dead. At least he
wouldn't grow up feeling as if there was something
wrong within him that made his father unable to love
him. She had often felt that way about herself in the
past. And had it not been for the love and understanding she'd received from her Granny Banyon, then she

would never have been able to allay those early childhood fears enough to realize that the fault did not lie
within her but with her father. Just like Apache, Jim
Banyon's selfishness had prevented him from seeing
anything beyond his own needs.

A chill rippled up Emerald's spine and she shivered.
The comparison between the two men made the decision for her. With only a one-sided love between herself
and Apache, there could be no marriage.

A knock sounded at the door, jerking Emerald from
her reverie with a start. Fearing it was the man who she
had been so anxious to see a half hour ago, her heart
began to race wildly in her breast as she rose from the
chair and crossed the room. With her hand on the latch,
she hesitated briefly before she gathered up her courage, then slid it back. Fully prepared to face Apache
and tell him of her decision, she pulled the door open.

Her eyes widened with surprise at the sight of the
handsome man leaning negligently against the door
frame with arms folded over his wide chest and one
corner of his sensual lips lifted in a disarming, boyish
smile. A guilty flush stained Emerald's cheeks as she
stared at Cash, unable to speak. She didn't know what
to say to the man who had befriended her and whom
she had betrayed because she had listened to her wayward heart.

"Aren't you going to invite me in?" Cash said, raising a dark brow.

"Of course," Emerald stammered, and stepped back
to let Cash enter. She closed the door quietly behind
him.

With hat in hand, Cash paused and surveyed the
room. He nodded his satisfaction before he glanced at
Emerald and said congenially, "Nice place."

"Cash," Emerald began, fidgeting nervously with the
skirt of the new gown Apache had purchased for their
wedding. "I don't know what to say."

"The truth would help" was Cash's calm reply. His
even-tempered veneer hid the seething cauldron be-

neath that made him want to strangle Emerald. Only the agitated movements of his well-groomed fingers sliding slowly over the brim of his black hat revealed his inner feelings.

"I didn't mean for any of this to happen. And now I don't know how to make things right," she said.

"You know, I searched everywhere for you. I was worried sick that something had happened to you."

Emerald could only nod in answer.

"Emerald, why did you leave? I wanted to marry you. I wanted us to make a life together and build something here in Denver for our children."

After agonizing over what decision she should make about her relationship with Apache, Cash's words were like a physical blow to Emerald. She gasped and turned away in order to hide the blinding rush of tears that filled her eyes. He had offered her all that she could want out of life, yet she had turned her back on him in order to appease her lust for a man who could give her nothing but grief.

Emerald felt the urge to tear out her hair and gnash her teeth at the cruel twists of fate. Why couldn't she love Cash the way she loved Apache? Everything would be so simple if she could give her heart to him and forget that Beau Alexander Ryan ever existed.

"Emerald," Cash said softly as he closed the space between them and placed his hands on her shoulders, turning her to face him. "Look at me." With thumb and forefinger beneath her chin, he tipped it up and gazed down into her tear-filled eyes. A tender smile touched his lips as he said, "I didn't come here to make you cry. I came only to assure myself that you were safe."

"Oh, Cash. I've been such a fool. I'm so sorry for all the trouble and worry I've caused you," Emerald said, and threw herself into his arms.

Cash's ebony eyes widened with pleased surprise as he wrapped his arms about her and held her close. If Hannah Becker was responsible for Emerald's reaction

to him, then he would have to thank her personally.
He'd been prepared to woo her with understanding, but
from the way she was acting, it wasn't going to be necessary. However, his instincts warned him not to go too
fast and to let her lead. Emerald didn't know about
Ryan yet, and if he volunteered too much information
too soon without knowing exactly how things stood between them, she might go running off after him and
then everything would be ruined.

"Emerald, tell me what's wrong. You may have decided against marrying me, but I hope we're still
friends."

Too consumed with her own heartache to wonder at
Cash's forgiving nature or even how he had found her
at the Platte Hotel, Emerald wept harder against his
shoulder. "After all I've done to you, I don't deserve
your friendship," she gasped between sobs.

"That's ridiculous. I once told you I'd be here if you
ever needed me, and I meant it."

Emerald leaned back and peered up at Cash through
spiky lashes glistening with the moisture of her tears.
"Can you ever forgive me for the embarrassment I've
caused you? It wasn't my intention to leave you standing at the altar. I never meant to hurt you."

"I won't lie and tell you that it didn't hurt, but that
is in the past. I've accepted the fact that you don't love
me." Cash's voice held a forlorn note of resignation as
he played the part of the heartbroken but understanding
lover. He didn't add that it was not his heart that he
feared to have hurt but his bank account. He needed
her claim deed by the end of the week or he'd lose
everything. The investors back East were sending one
of their representatives to Denver to confirm his holdings, and if they were not satisfied that he had fulfilled
his end of the contract, they would seize all of his prop-
erties, including the Gold Dust Saloon.

"No, Cash. It's not in the past. I was a fool to let
Apache come between us. But I believed that—that—"
Emerald's voice broke and she fell silent. She was too

emotionally battered by Hannah's revelations to be able
to voice her feelings about Apache to anyone.

"That he loved you?" Cash supplied solicitously.

"Yes," Emerald choked out. "But all he really
wanted was Pa's claim deed." She did not elaborate
further. Something in her told her that it was better for
all concerned if Cash did not know the reason Apache
wanted the deed. There was enough bad blood between
them without adding to it by repeating Hannah's tales.
She had no desire to see another confrontation between
the two men. If that happened, she knew one would
die, and she did not want either man's life on her conscience.

"The bastard," Cash cursed sympathetically. He
drew Emerald back into his arms comfortingly and laid
his dark head against her golden hair to hide the gleam
of speculation that entered his eyes. His mustache crinkled up at the corners of his mouth as he smiled mali-
ciously. All the strange pieces of the puzzle had finally
fallen into place. He had wondered at the gunslinger's
sudden affection for Emerald, but now he understood
it. Ryan also had his eye on Emerald's claim.

But why would Ryan want that useless piece of
ground? It was of no value to anyone except himself.
Yet Ryan was willing to marry Emerald to get his hands
on it. Cash frowned and his face darkened with suspicion as he wondered if the gunslinger had learned of
the railroad he intended to build and was trying to out-
fox him. Cash instantly rejected the idea. Only Red and
Sal knew of his plans, and he didn't worry about either
one of them betraying his confidences. They liked their
own skins too well to cross him by confiding in Ryan.

Gold was the only explanation he could find for
Apache Ryan's actions. Because of the claim jumping,
the man thought that Jim Banyon had secretly found pay
dirt, and he planned on getting his share by marrying
Emerald.

Satisfied with his theory, Cash released a long breath
and put Emerald at arm's length from him. "What are

you going to do now that you know what kind of man Ryan is?'' he asked her.

Emerald shook her head. ''I don't really know anymore.''

''Then why don't you let me take you out to the El Dorado where you can have time to think things over?'' Cash offered. He wanted to get Emerald out of Denver before she learned that Ryan had been shot. Until he knew for certain that Ryan represented no further danger to him, he would take no chances with Emerald. At the moment she was hurt, and he had to use that to his advantage.

Disheartened and needing a friend to give her solace, Emerald agreed. At the present time she had no desire to see Apache. She just wanted to get as far away from him as possible and lick her wounds. She had to settle everything in her own mind and heart before she could face him and tell him exactly how she felt about him and the way he tried to use her against Cash.

''Good, we'll ride out now,'' Cash said as he took her cape from the peg by the door and draped it about her shoulders. He gave her no time to reconsider but ushered her quickly down the stairs.

However, before Cash could get her out of the hotel, Emerald drew to a halt at the wide double doors. She turned and looked up at him. Her eyes held a pained expression as she shook her head. ''I can't leave without at least leaving Apache a note. He may be a scoundrel of the first degree, with his underhanded methods, but I won't stoop to his level. I won't leave him at the altar without an explanation.''

Cash grated his teeth in vexation. However, he managed to hide his irritation and forced an understanding smile to his lips. ''Ryan doesn't deserve it after what he's done, but if you feel you must leave him a note, then I'll see that the clerk makes sure he gets it.''

''Thank you, Cash,'' Emerald said, and let Cash escort her over to the small writing desk in the corner of the lobby. She scribbled a cryptic note to Apache and then handed it to Cash, satisfied that she had managed to relay her feelings about his actions in the few brief words she'd written. Once he read it, he'd know that he had lost the devious game he had been playing with her emotions.

With her thoughts still on Apache and the note she'd written, she watched Cash cross to the hotel clerk and speak with him. She was completely unaware that he only asked for the time from the man and that her note to Apache had been slipped into his pocket and would be destroyed once they were out of town.

Cash smiled reassuringly down at Emerald when he returned to her and ushered her from the hotel. He had just taken her arm to escort her to the stables when Jeb Taylor staggered by them. He stopped, gazing through bloodshot eyes at Emerald for a long, searching moment before his eyes widened with recognition.

"I'll be damned, if it ain't the little missy." He raked Cash with a scathing glance before he asked, "Where's Apache?"

Hearing the censure in the old mountain man's voice, Emerald drew herself up and shook her head. "I don't know and really don't care."

"What's this? I thought the two of you were gettin' hitched. I was just on my way over to stand in as his best man." Jeb flashed Cash another venomous look. "What are you doin' with this varmint?"

"Watch yourself, old man," Cash said, his voice low and full of menace.

"Don't you tell me to watch myself, you young whelp. I'll—"

"Jeb, please," Emerald begged, interrupting Jeb's tirade. "This is no time to argue."

Jeb flashed Cash another angry look before he smacked his toothless gums together and turned his full attention on Emerald. "All right, missy. I'll do my best to hold my temper, but I think you better be doin' some explainin' about what's goin' on around here."

"There really isn't anything to explain, Jeb. There

isn't going to be a wedding." Emerald's voice caught in her throat and she flashed Cash a pleading look for help.

"Now, if that satisfies your curiosity, we'd like to be on our way." Cash did not wait for Jeb's answer but took Emerald by the arm and led her away from the old man before he had time to ask further questions to disturb her.

Jeb scratched his salt-and-pepper beard as he watched them walk away. Something wasn't right in all this, and he was bound and determined to find out exactly what was going on, or his name wasn't Jeb Taylor. And the first thing he intended to do was to find Apache. That boy had some answering of his own to do if he had let the little missy go off with that snake without a fight.

Jeb spat a wad of tobacco into the street, shook his head, and muttered, "I ain't never been one to interfere in other folks' business, but this time it's different. If that boy is too stupid and bullheaded to take good care of the little missy, then I guess I'll have to do it myself."

Jeb wiped the tobacco juice from his mouth with the back of his hand, pulled his battered felt hat firmly down over his brow, and stalked into the Platte Hotel ready to beard the bear in his cave. A few moments later he stood in front of the clerk's desk with his bushy brows lowered over his eyes, frowning at the man behind the desk.

"What do you mean, you ain't seen Mr. Ryan since he checked in?"

The clerk peered at Jeb. In order to see the old mountain man clearly, he leaned his head back and gazed at him through the round spectacles that rested on the tip of his nose. Noting Jeb's buckskins, he sniffed disdainfully and shook his head "Sir, I meant exactly what I said. Mr. Ryan left the hotel a couple of hours ago. Now, if you will excuse me, I have work to do." He turned his back on Jeb and began hanging room keys under the corresponding numbers on the wall behind him.

"I knew that something wasn't right about all this," Jeb muttered aloud. He ignored the curious glances he received from the people standing near him. With only Ole Bessy as a companion through the long, snowy winters he'd spent in the mountains, it had become a habit for him to speak his thoughts aloud just to hear a human voice, even if it was his own. He could see no harm in it. As long as he didn't start answering himself, he didn't figure it was anybody's business if he talked to himself.

"I bet that boy don't even know that the little missy has changed her mind about the weddin'." Jeb's frown deepened. "And where in hell could he have gone off to? I thought he was comin' straight back to the hotel when he left me." Jeb's full gray beard swung across his chest as he shook his head. "I gotta find that boy before it's too late."

The mauve morning sky was streaked with brilliant rose by the sun that crept over the horizon to brighten the new day. Its golden rays spilled in through the tall windows that graced the elegant bedchamber where Emerald sat staring with reddened eyes at the landscape beyond. However, she was blind to the beauty of the snow-covered peaks in the distance. With her brows knit over the bridge of her slender nose, her pensive expression reflected the uneven course her thoughts had traveled during the long hours of the night.

After they had arrived at the El Dorado and Cash had seen her comfortably settled for the night, he had left her alone to sort through the maze of emotions twisting her insides into knots. They writhed within her like a coil of venomous snakes, striking out at her with sharp-fanged memories when she thought she had finally managed to reconcile herself to all that had happened.

Throughout the night she had veered from one extreme to another, experiencing the whole spectrum of emotions. At one moment she would be filled with self-pity and shame, but in the next her hurt would overshadow it and turn to anger. She had cried and raged against her father and Apache until her eyes were red and swollen from her tears. They were the two men who were responsible for tearing her life and her heart apart. She had been used by each in his own selfish way. Apache had used her in his vendetta against Cash, and Jim Banyon had used her as a workhorse, never treating her like his own flesh and blood.

"And damn it," Emerald cursed aloud, "I was fool enough to love both of them."

With an irritable toss of her head, she pushed herself from the Queen Anne chair and once more began her restless pacing. The turmoil within her refused to let her sleep or to remain seated for more than a few minutes, and during the night she had traveled many miles across the thick cornflower-blue carpet that matched the velvet drapes over the windows.

Realizing the futility of her actions, Emerald paused and shook her head at her sad predicament. No matter how she ranted and raved, her problems would not be solved. Nor would the pain in her heart be eased by continually thinking of Apache. She had to put the past behind her and think of herself and her child's future.

Emerald frowned. Last night, when her emotions had been at a fever pitch, she had been unwavering in her resolve to have her child alone and never to let Apache know that he existed. However, in the light of morning and after the grim night she had spent with her reflections, she now knew that she was facing a problem far more difficult than she'd first considered.

She had chosen a rocky path for herself. The uncertainties in her future were staggering. Being a pregnant woman alone in a frontier town with no means to survive was not going to be easy. She'd learned that from her experiences in Denver before she had gone to work for Cash at the Gold Dust. Now, even hurdy-gurdy dancing was out of her reach. Cash was her friend, but she couldn't expect him to give her charity. When her body was rounded with child, not even a prospector who hadn't seen a woman in months would be interested in paying her to dance with him.

Emerald felt as if she were caught in a web that was slowly but surely drawing her back toward the man who had shattered her heart. Her breasts rose and fell with her rapid breathing as the feeling of being trapped mounted. She had already given Apache Ryan her heart, and she didn't want to have to surrender her pride to him by asking for his help. That would be the final humiliation to her already wounded spirit. Having to subjugate herself to him in order to survive would be the ultimate defeat, and it would leave her nothing more than a shell of her former self because Apache would own her, body and soul.

Emerald felt suffocated by the thought. She spun on her heel and bolted toward the door. She needed fresh air to clear her mind so that she could think coherently. Her hand was already sliding the latch back when a knock sounded on the panel.

"Emerald, are you awake?" Cash called softly from the hallway. "I've come to escort you down to breakfast."

Emerald closed her eyes and pressed her lips together as she drew in a resigned breath. She needed time to be alone to think. With her mind whirling from the turmoil of her thoughts, she didn't want to see Cash or anyone until she had come to terms with all that had happened in the last twenty-four hours. However, she could not refuse to see Cash. His unwavering friendship was all that sustained her in a time when her world had turned upside down.

"Yes, I'm awake, Cash," Emerald said. Forcing a smile to her lips, she opened the door. "But I'm afraid I'm not hungry this morning. I think I'll take a walk instead of having breakfast."

"Then I'll join you," Cash quickly volunteered.

Before Emerald could form the words to tell him that she wanted to be alone to sort out her problems, he retrieved her cape from the back of the chair where she had tossed it the previous night and draped it about her shoulders. With a charming smile curling his sensual lips beneath his dark mustache, he proffered his arm to her with all the courtesy of a well-bred gentleman.

"I'd be honored, sir." Emerald laughed, unable to resist his charming manners. She took his arm and let him escort her down the stairs and out into the frost-silvered morning. They strolled companionably through what would be the garden in the future and chatted about the flowers Cash planned to have planted in the spring. When their conversation began to drift toward more personal topics, they fell silent, each growing reflective.

Cash glanced down at Emerald before turning his gaze to the distant snow-covered peaks of the Rockies. He smiled with satisfaction. So far, everything was working out the way he had planned, and if he continued to be patient, he was sure he'd have his hands on the claim deed by tomorrow night.

Cash's smile deepened at the thought of the start Emerald had given him when she'd told him that she wanted to go for a walk. Fortunately, she had not objected to him accompanying her. If she had, he didn't know what excuse he would have found to keep her from wandering around the El Dorado alone. And that was the one thing he couldn't allow to happen. She might accidentally glimpse Red Beaudine if he should return from town. He had ordered the man to stay away from the ranch until things were settled, but Beaudine had a way of showing up when he was least expected. Cash knew he had to be on guard against that event. If Beaudine did show up and Emerald recognized him, that would leave him no choice but to have her killed.

Cash's smile faded as he glanced once more at the young woman at his side. Oddly enough, at the present time her death would complicate matters rather than simplify them. With the representative from his investors arriving at week's end, he needed Emerald alive. He had to have the claim deed signed, sealed, and delivered, and the only way he could do that now without raising too many questions was to make it all legal by marrying her. If he had gotten rid of her when she'd first arrived in Denver, he would have had time to manipulate things to his advantage. But in order to look like a respectable businessman, he had foolishly chosen a different method of gaining the claim deed and now was paying for it. He couldn't risk creating a stir by having Emerald killed.

"Emerald," Cash said, gently squeezing the hand that rested on his arm, "have you thought much about what you intend to do in the future?"

Emerald drew in a long breath and focused her gaze on the craggy mountains to keep Cash from seeing the apprehension his question aroused in her. She nodded. "I've been unable to think of anything else."

"Then you've decided?" Cash held his breath expectantly.

"No, I'm afraid that's my problem. I don't know what I'm going to do."

Cash turned Emerald to face him and tipped up her chin. His dark gaze held hers as he said softly, "You could marry me."

Emerald opened her mouth to speak, but Cash placed a silencing finger against her lips and shook his head. "Don't say no right now. Think it over. I know that you don't love me and, as I've said, I accept that, but we are friends and can build a life together." He stepped behind her and turned her to face the ranch house. With a wave of his hand, he continued, "I built that with a woman like you in mind, Emerald. The El Dorado needs you as much as I do."

"Cash, I can't marry you," Emerald said, her eyes misting with tears. "It's too late for us."

"It's never too late, Emerald. And I won't take your no for an answer right now. You've been through too much and need time to think things over."

Again Emerald shook her head and turned to look up at Cash. She placed her hand against his cheek and gently caressed it. "You're such a good man, Cash. You're the only man I know who would still be willing to marry me after all I've done." Emerald paused to dredge up her courage. It wasn't going to be easy to tell Cash about the secret she carried, but he deserved to know the truth. Bracing herself for his rejection, she continued, her voice no more than a soft whisper, "But I'm afraid it is too late for us now. I'm pregnant with Apache's child."

Cash flinched but made no other visible sign that her news affected him. His nostrils flared slightly as he drew in a deep breath and swallowed back the rush of expletives that rose to his lips to describe how he felt about this new turn of events. Though he didn't love Emerald, her confession made him feel betrayed. He had the sudden urge to strangle her with his bare hands. He could overlook her affair with Ryan. That was nothing. He was no saint himself. But the thought of marrying her while she carried another man's child was repugnant to him.

However, after considering all of the options, Cash's greed won out over his revulsion, and he realized that Emerald's predicament could prove advantageous to him. It was the very thing he needed to help convince her to marry him. With Ryan dead, she had nowhere to turn for help, and she would be unable to refuse his magnanimous gesture to accept her child as his own.

Cash smiled to himself. Lady Luck had not deserted him after all. She had only been teasing him during the past weeks to remind him not to take her for granted. Bringing his mind back to Emerald, he carefully hid his feelings beneath a sympathetic façade.

"My poor darling. Don't you see that's even more reason for you to marry me? I care for you, Emerald, and I'll also care for your child."

"Cash, I don't know what to say," Emerald said, her eyes welling with tears of gratitude.

"Say you'll marry me. That's all I want to hear."

Disillusioned with love and torn by her need to protect her child, Emerald could find no other solution to her problem. She didn't love Cash, but she liked him. And she was grateful to him for being willing to accept her child as his own. "All right, Cash, I'll marry you."

Cash chuckled. He clasped her about the waist and pulled her to him. "By tomorrow evening you'll be Mrs. Cash Dalton."

Emerald could only nod her response. Everything was happening too quickly. Yesterday she had been going to marry Apache and tomorrow she would marry Cash. She felt suddenly as if she were on the tail of a whirlwind that moved from one direction to another without rhyme or reason. She knew what motivated her, yet everything was happening so swiftly that she'd not had time to sort things out and come to terms with her own emotions. She was left feeling dazed and uncertain about her decision.

Apache came awake slowly to the sound of soft snoring. Following the direction of the raspy noise, he rolled his head on the pillow to see a gray-haired man slumped in a straight-backed chair beside the bed. With his balding pate gleaming in the afternoon sunshine that streamed through the window, he slept with his double chin resting on his chest and round spectacles tilting haphazardly to one side of his short pug nose.

Apache frowned as he glanced away from the sleeping man and surveyed the room. From the charts on the wall and the glass-fronted medicine cabinet, he surmised that he was in a doctor's office.

"But why am I here?" Apache muttered to himself, and made an effort to sit up. He got no further than raising himself on his elbow before he was quickly reminded of the reason for his being in the doctor's office. The fiery pain that raced along his shoulder and down his left arm made him give a loud "Ouch!"

At Apache's cry, Dr. Smith awoke instantly. He straightened his spectacles and came to his feet. His smile was friendly as he crossed to the bed and placed a hand against Apache's brow to check for fever. Finding none, he nodded with satisfaction.

"Well, it seems you're going to live after all, young man." Dr. Smith turned to the bedside table and picked up a bottle of elixir. He poured a small dose of the medicine into a glass and handed it to Apache. "Now, drink that down. It'll help you get your strength back."

A look of disgust crossed Apache's face at the smell that rose from the brown liquid in the glass. He shook his head and handed the glass back to the doctor. "I think I can do just fine without that concoction."

"No, you can't," Dr. Smith said, and handed the glass to Apache once more. "Now, drink. That's doctor's orders."

Flashing Dr. Smith an annoyed look, Apache held his breath and downed the liquid. To his surprise, it didn't taste as awful as it smelled. It reminded him of the brew made of herbs and dried berries that the old medicine man gave every spring to the tribe he'd lived with. Like the white man's doctor, the medicine man had claimed it would chase away the demons of winter and help to restore your spirit to prepare you to hunt the buffalo.

"Now, that wasn't so bad, was it?" Dr. Smith asked, and chuckled at the face Apache made as he shook his head.

"I've tasted worse," Apache said, making an effort to sit up once more. He grimaced with pain and fell back on the pillow.

"I don't think you're going to go anywhere for a while. That shoulder of yours will be out of commission for several days, if not for weeks."

"If you'll help me up, I'll be fine," Apache said. He glanced toward the clock on the wall. It was already afternoon and he had been away from Emerald for far too long. He had to see her before she got it into her head to do something rash. When he didn't return last night, he didn't know how she might have reacted. Her moods were so mercurial. She might still be at the hotel, frantic with worry, or she might have gone looking for him. If she did that, she could have walked right back into danger with her misconstrued belief that Dalton meant her no harm. Spurred by the thought of the woman he loved once more at the mercy of his enemy, Apache forced himself into a sitting position and swung his legs over the side of the bed.

"Hold on, now, son. You're going to make things worse if you don't just lie back down and let yourself heal. You don't know how lucky you are just to be alive. Had that piece of lead I took out of you been just a few inches lower, you'd be dead."

"I appreciate what you've done, Doc, but I can't stay here." Apache reached into his britches pocket and retrieved several coins. "Will this be enough to cover your services?"

Dr. Smith nodded. "More than enough. But I'm afraid you'll be back if you don't take care of that shoulder. You could bleed to death if you tear it open again."

"That's a chance I'll just have to take, Doc." Apache slid his feet to the floor and stood.

"If that's the way you feel about it, I can ask only one thing of you," Dr. Smith said shortly. His tone reflected his irritation at his patient's apparent lack of sense.

"What's that?" Apache asked, picking up his shirt. For a moment he stood frowning at the garment, wondering how he would get into it without the use of his left arm.

"I'd like to know your name so that when the undertaker gets you, I can tell him what to put on your tombstone."

"You can tell him it's Apache Ryan." He grinned wryly at the doctor as he slipped the shirt gingerly up over his arm and then awkwardly managed to shrug the rest of the way into it. Buttoning it was another matter, as was putting on his boots. After several attempts, he finally had to ask the doctor to help him.

"You're as pale as a sheet and you have no business

being out of bed,'' Dr. Smith grumbled as he tugged on Apache's boots. ''Mark my words, young man. You're going to pay for not heeding my advice. Your life is more important than gold. All you miners ever think about is gold and whiskey, but neither one of them will do you any good when you're six feet under.''

''I wish gold and whiskey was all I had to worry about,'' Apache said, easing his coat on over his injured shoulder. The only gold he was concerned about was the burnished gold that framed a beautiful face with emerald eyes. Apache paused at the door and turned back to Dr. Smith. ''By the way, did they get the varmint who shot me, Doc?''

Dr. Smith shook his head. ''Nobody saw who did it.''

''That's what I figured,'' Apache said, and opened the door. His dark eyes were narrowed with speculation as he descended the steps to the street below. There was only one man who wanted him out of the way: Cash Dalton. It would have been easy enough for the gambler to learn that Emerald had come back to town with him. And Dalton wasn't a man who would forget an insult like the one Emerald had given him when she'd left him at the altar. He'd be out for blood, especially when so much had depended upon his marriage to her. With the thought, Apache felt the hair rise on the nape of his neck. Dalton wouldn't be satisfied with just having him shot; he'd want to make Emerald suffer as well. Apache quickened his pace as dread wound his insides into tight a coil.

''Damn me, Apache, if you ain't a sight for sore eyes. I been lookin' all over Denver for you since last night,'' Jeb said, uncoiling his aged body from the hard chair with some difficulty. He was stiff from waiting in the hotel lobby where he'd come after his futile search for Apache in every saloon in town. By midmorning he had given up his quest to find his friend and had come back to the hotel with the hope that Apache would eventually make an appearance, if he wasn't dead.

"What are you doing here, Jeb?" Apache asked. He did not slow his pace toward the stairs.

"Damn it, slow down, boy. I'm an old man and can't keep up with your long legs," Jeb complained. He grabbed Apache by the arm in an effort to try to keep pace with him.

Apache grimaced. "Jeb, I don't have time to talk. I need to see Emerald."

"Then you're headed in the wrong direction, you young fool. She ain't up there, if that's what you're a-thinkin'."

Apache came to an abrupt halt and turned to look at Jeb. "Where is she?"

"She left with Dalton last night."

"Dalton!" Apache exploded. "Damn it, Jeb, I thought you were my friend. Why in hell did you let her go off with that man? You know what he is."

"Don't you go gettin' riled up at me, you young whippersnapper. I ain't the one who left her here alone all night. You shoulda been here to guard her yourself instead of expectin' me to do it."

"I would have been here, you old buzzard, if someone hadn't ambushed me last night on the way back to the hotel. And now I know for certain that Dalton was behind it. He needed me out of the way to force Emerald to go with him." Apache's swarthy complexion flushed with rage.

"Damn, I knew somethin' wasn't right when you didn't show up last night. Are you all right, boy?"

"As well as can be expected with a bullet hole in my shoulder. When I find Dalton, he's not going to live long enough to regret having me shot or making Emerald go with him."

"I ain't sayin' that Dalton wasn't behind what happened to you, but he didn't force the little missy to go with him, if that's what you think. From what I gathered, she went willingly."

Apache grew still and tense. "What do you mean?"

The lines in Jeb's aged face deepened with his distress. He didn't like having to be the bearer of bad news, especially when he knew it would rip the boy's heart out. "When I asked her where you were, she said she didn't care and that the two of you weren't getting hitched after all."

Every emotion except one—fury—seemed to drain out of Apache at Jeb's revelation. His face grew granite-hard and his eyes snapped with black fire. His experience with Rachel rose once more out of the ashes of the past. It taunted him and renewed the distrust he thought he had laid to rest once and for all when he'd proposed to Emerald. It left him no room for understanding. He judged Emerald harshly, without considering what might have made her leave him without any explanation.

Fuming inwardly, Apache turned and stalked toward the wide double doors that opened to the street. He had worried himself sick about Emerald, and all that he had gained from it was a slap in the face. All of her vows of love had been a sham. She'd had no intention of marrying him from the beginning. She'd only wanted to get him to bring her back to Denver so that she could go running back to Dalton the first time she was out of his sight.

"Apache, what are you going to do?" Jeb asked, racing to keep up with the young man's long strides.

"I'm going to find Dalton and end this once and for all. I've let it go on far too long."

"But what about the little missy?"

"What about her?" was Apache's brusque reply.

"I thought you loved the girl."

Apache winced. "She's made her choice, Jeb. But if she intends to marry Dalton, she'd better do it before I find him, or she'll be a widow before she's a bride."

"Somethin' ain't right about this, is all I got to say about it," Jeb muttered as he followed Apache toward the Gold Dust Saloon.

Chapter 16

Lounging negligently in his chair at the end of the long cherrywood table in the dining room of the El Dorado, Cash watched through half-closed lids as Emerald toyed with the food on her plate. A cynical smile briefly touched his lips as he studied his bride-to-be. She was a beautiful woman, but he no longer desired anything from her except her claim deed. He'd marry her to get his hands on it, but the attraction he'd felt for her from the first time he'd laid eyes on her at the campsite in Clear Creek had vanished with the news that she carried Ryan's baby.

A feral gleam entered his dark eyes, and his lips thinned into a narrow line. In the last few hours his feelings toward Emerald had completely changed. She had become a liability to him and the future he had planned. After the claim was his, he would have no further use for her. He had thought when he'd first proposed to her that she would make him a wife that befitted his position once his railroad was established. However, her current predicament had ruined that plan along with killing his desire for her.

Cash lifted the cut-crystal goblet and held it between his well-groomed fingers by the delicately worked stem. He twirled it slowly around, admiring the prism of colors created by the intricate design worked into the crystal. It was beautiful and of the best quality that money could buy. And it symbolized what would be his once his railroad was a reality. He planned to surround himself with only the best that life had to offer, and that did not include Ryan's castoff whore.

Cash's dark brows knit over the bridge of his nose as he frowned. He took a long sip of the rich burgundy that he'd had shipped to the El Dorado from New Orleans. It was one of the best wines imported from France, but at that moment he couldn't appreciate its deep, fruity flavor. His thoughts were still centered on the young woman at the end of the table and the problem that still lay in the future: how to get rid of her once their vows were spoken.

Cash gave a mental shrug. That problem wouldn't be hard to solve. In a few months time, after everyone was convinced that they were happily married, Emerald would have an accident, and he'd be grief-stricken for at least a few days for the benefit of the sheriff.

Caught up in his sinister musings, Cash did not hear the fast approach of the lone rider. His first inkling of it was when Emerald raised her head and looked expectantly toward the front door.

"There's someone coming." She spoke softly in an effort to hide the contradictory feelings that sprang into life at the sound of the horse coming toward them. Her heart prayed for it to be Apache, yet her mind recoiled at the thought of seeing him again.

"I wonder who it could be, I'm not expecting anyone tonight." Cash set his glass on the table and slid back his chair. "I'll see who it is," he said, and stood. With a nonchalance he did not feel, he straightened his coat and vest before striding into the foyer. As a gambler, he was able to conceal his emotions. His graceful movements did not reveal the tension that made every muscle within him taut, nor did his voice reflect his agitation when he opened the door to find Red Beaudine on the threshold, his hand reaching toward the brass door knocker. Cash quietly closed the door behind him and dragged Red into the shadows of the veranda.

"What are you doing out here, Beaudine? I told you to stay in town."

"I thought you'd like to know that Ryan ain't dead," Red said breathlessly. He'd ridden hard to reach the El Dorado after seeing Apache Ryan in the Gold Dust Saloon. He'd thought his eyes were going to bulge out of his head when the man had walked into the saloon just as pretty as you please and without acting as if he'd been shot the night before at all. Red was beginning to believe that there was something unnatural about the man. He'd never seen a man who could take a bullet in the back and be on his feet the next day looking no worse for the wear and tear. It wasn't normal, and it made Red feel a little spooked.

"Beaudine, you've been eating locoweed. I saw Ryan fall. And from the way the people around him were acting, he couldn't have lived very long."

"Well, he lived long enough to come back to the Gold Dust and ask about you."

"What?" Cash asked, his voice strained with tension.

"Ryan was asking where you were."

"Damn you, Beaudine. I should shoot you down myself for fouling up this time," Cash swore in a loud whisper, before he heard Emerald call his name from the foyer. He shook his head, silencing Red. "Get down to the barn and stay out of sight. All I need is for Emerald to see you now. I'll meet you down there just as soon as she's settled for the night. Then we'll figure out how to get rid of that bastard once and for all."

Feeling much like a beaten cur, Red skulked off into the shadows and made his way to the barn. The jagged mark on his cheek contrasted starkly with his pale features as he considered all he'd done for Dalton without any show of gratitude in return. The man treated him as if he were less than human, and he was getting tired of it. Dalton paid him well for his services, but that didn't give him the right to think he owned him lock, stock, and barrel. If the man wasn't careful, he'd end up without anyone to carry out his crooked schemes.

Cash watched Red disappear from sight and then opened the door. He came up short when he found Emerald on the other side.

"Cash," she breathed with relief. "When you didn't answer me, I became worried."

"There's nothing to worry about at the El Dorado, Emerald. You're far safer here than in Denver."

Feeling slightly foolish, Emerald blushed. "I know you're right, but so much has happened to me in the past months that I've become like a little church mouse who jumps at its own shadow."

Cash draped a comforting arm about Emerald's shoulders and led her up the stairs. "I can understand how you feel after all you've gone through, but you have to remember that tomorrow you'll be my wife, and I'll never let anything or anyone harm you again." He brushed his lips against her brow when they reached the door to her room. "Now, I want you to rest. We have a big day ahead of us tomorrow, and I can't have my bride too tired for the ceremony."

Emerald wrapped her arms about Cash's waist and laid her cheek against his chest. Her voice was soft with reflection as she said, "You spoil me with all of your attention. No one else in my life has ever cared enough about what happened to me to worry about my feelings."

"Well, I care. I value you more than you'll ever know." Cash smiled against her golden hair, envisioning the claim deed with her signature giving him ownership. "Now enough of this. I could stand here all night with you in my arms, but you and the baby need rest." Cash gently set her from him. "Good night, Emerald."

He pressed his lips against her brow once more, then quickly turned on his heel and left her. He didn't have time to waste comforting the stupid girl. There were far more important things that needed his attention at the moment. He had to deal with Apache Ryan before the man had a chance to find Emerald.

Bemused, Emerald watched Cash stride down the hall and descend the stairs without a backward glance in her direction. She frowned. Cash seemed distracted, and she wondered if the rider had anything to do with it. He'd had an odd look on his face when he found her at the door, and he had rushed her upstairs without even asking if she had finished her dinner or if she was tired. He wasn't acting like the Cash she knew, but considering that tomorrow would be his wedding day, he might be having a few reservations about his generous offer to marry her and accept her child as his own.

Emerald stepped into the elegantly furnished bed-chamber Cash had provided for her use and closed the door. If Cash was having qualms about their wedding, he wasn't the only one. All during dinner, she had tried to sort through the maze of conflicting emotions that stemmed from her acceptance of Cash's proposal of marriage. Her decision left her feeling torn. One part of her said that she had made the right choice—the only choice that she could make under the circumstances. However, another part of her argued that she was only adding to her problems by marrying a man that she did not love and feared that she could never love.

She had tried to convince herself that someday she would forget Apache and come to care for Cash as a husband instead of just a friend, but it had not worked. Deep in her heart, she knew that Apache would never be in her past. He was a part of her. She carried his child, and each day that child would be a visible reminder of what she had loved and lost.

Emerald paced across the room to the window. She didn't want to keep thinking of Apache or of the time they had together. Such thoughts only heightened the turmoil she felt over her marriage to Cash.

"This has to stop," Emerald said aloud, staring blindly out into the indigo night. "I've made my decision and that's the end of it."

Emerald leaned her brow against the cool pane of glass and pensively caught her lower lip between her teeth. It was true, she had made her decision, but how could she go through with marriage to Cash when all she wanted was to feel Apache's arms about her?

"Why am I torturing myself this way?" she asked herself quietly. She told herself that she had to keep remembering what Hannah had told her. Apache didn't love her. He had only made her believe that he did when he couldn't convince her that Cash had had her father murdered. He had used her as a means to get at his enemy, and that was all she had ever meant to him.

"But that doesn't ease my longing," Emerald whispered forlornly as she gazed toward the barn where a small ray of light spilled through the cracks in the large double doors. She drew in a ragged breath and wiped her stinging eyes. She could not forgive Apache for using her, nor could she erase the memories of their moments together or the sweet bliss they had shared to create the small life that grew within her womb. That alone tore her in two different directions at once and left her feeling emotionally battle-scarred.

Disgruntled with herself for allowing her thoughts to linger on things that added to her confusion, Emerald started to turn away from the window when she glimpsed a movement from below. She paused and peered intently into the shadows. The sight of a man striding swiftly toward the barn piqued her curiosity, and she watched from her vantage point as he pulled open the barn door. The lantern light from within spilled out and illuminated him. Drenched in the golden light, she recognized Cash instantly, but it took a moment longer to recall where she had seen the man who stepped from the barn to greet him. Her breath stilled in her throat as she watched Cash roughly shove him inside and then glance nervously about before following. He left the barn door ajar in his hurry to get the man out of sight. However, Cash's actions had not been swift enough to keep Emerald from seeing the discolored, jagged mark on the man's cheek.

"Red," Emerald breathed. Her blood seemed to turn into ice in her veins at the sight of the murderer. A violent shiver rippled up her spine from the shock of suddenly seeing him after all this time. Having him appear at the El Dorado when she had given up hope of ever finding him left her momentarily stunned. As did the fact that Cash acted as if he knew the man well.

Emerald paled. Her stomach did a rapid somersault at the implications of what she had just witnessed. She shook her head in an effort to deny the accusations that sprang into her mind.

"It can't be true," she whispered. But even as she spoke she was already moving toward the door. She had to know for certain that Cash was not guilty of what Apache claimed. She didn't want to believe that he could be responsible for such heinous acts, but if she found that he had been involved with her father's death, then she would see that he paid for the crime with his own life.

Driven by her renewed vow to avenge her father's death, Emerald sped downstairs and out of the house. She paid no heed to the cold night air upon her bare shoulders and arms as she furtively made her way toward the barn. Her thoughts were not on her own comfort as she clung to the deepest shadows and moved along the paddock fence to the corner of the large board and batten building in which she could already hear the low rumble of masculine voices.

She held her breath and crept to the barn door that Cash had left ajar with his swift entry. She quickly slipped behind it and eased her way toward the ray of light that spilled through the crack between the door and wall. She peeked through the crack at the two men, who stood with their backs turned toward her, and listened with mounting terror as they discussed their plans.

"Beaudine, I want to know how this happened. You

were supposed to have taken care of the problem,'' Cash ground out between clenched teeth.

"I did take care of him, but I'm beginning to believe that bastard has more lives than a cat. That shot would have killed any ordinary man. But he's out walking around the next day just like nothing was wrong with him."

"Well, you'll just have to do the job again. I can't risk letting Ryan ruin everything for me. I'm too close to having it all."

"Boss, I ain't at all certain I want to tangle with Ryan. I won't be able to ambush him again. He'll be on his guard at all times from now on."

"Then you'll call him out. It's as simple as that,'' Cash stated flatly.

Red shook his head rapidly from side to side. "Ain't no way I'm going to call Ryan out."

"You damned coward. You'll do as I say,'' Cash growled. His face mottled several shaded of red at the defection of his hired gun.

"I ain't a coward, and as far as I'm concerned you can handle it for yourself from here on out. It's your problem now. I'm through." The jagged mark on Red's cheek blended with his flushed features.

"You sorry son of a bitch! You're not walking out on me. If you'd killed the girl that first day in Clear Creek, I wouldn't be in this situation. Now you're going to set it to rights."

"Like I said, I'm through. I ain't working for you anymore, Dalton. We're quits. I've done everything you wanted me to from the first. I've killed them poor bastards so you could get your hands on their claims, but I ain't about to set myself up to get killed for you. There ain't enough money in the world for that.'' Red turned away.

"If you know what's good for you, you'll not try to walk out on me.'' Cash's voice was low and emotionless.

Red glanced back at him. He grinned and shook his

head. "You won't kill me, Dalton. There are too many witnesses around who might hear you. You like to do things on the sly, where it can't be blamed on you. So I'm not afraid that you'll shoot me here."

Red turned away again.

"Like I said, you're not going anywhere. Nobody walks out on Cash Dalton until he's through with them." Cash drew his revolver and pulled the trigger before Beaudine could even realize the danger he was in. Red jerked once when the bullet entered the back of his head and then he fell facedown into a hay-filled stall.

Cash stood over him and calmly reholstered his revolver. "You forgot one thing, Beaudine. There aren't any witnesses around here. The men rode into Denver tonight to spend their pay." Cash turned away from the lifeless form at his feet. "Nobody walks out on me," he muttered as he strode toward the barn door.

The report of a revolver carried through the still night. At the sound, Apache jerked Rogue to a halt. Tense and alert, he turned to look at the man riding silently at his side.

"That sounded as if it came from the direction of the ranch house."

"Thereabouts," Jeb agreed. "Reckon what Dalton's up to now? It's too late for him or his men to be havin' target practice."

"I don't know what Dalton is up to, but we'd better go from here on foot. I don't want to alert him to the fact that he has visitors until I know that Emerald is still safe. Once I'm certain that he can't harm her, I'll take care of him." Unable to use his left arm to support himself, Apache threw his leg over Rogue's neck and slid to the ground. He winced from the jolt but gave no other sign that he was affected by the wound in his shoulder.

"Sure you're up to this?" Jeb asked, noting the strained look on the younger man's face. Apache had done his best to hide his pain, but Jeb knew from the way he favored his left arm and the white line about his lips that he suffered.

"I'm fine, old man." Apache withdrew the rifle from the scabbard on his saddle and tossed it to Jeb. "It's loaded and ready if you are."

"I've been ready to shoot Dalton since I first met him."

"Dalton is mine, Jeb," Apache snapped. "I've waited too long to settle the score between us to let you have the pleasure of killing him."

Jeb frowned. "You never did tell me what all that was about."

Apache didn't answer. He busied himself with checking his revolver and fought against the great sense of loss brought back by Jeb's question. Jeb was a good friend, but Apache couldn't tell him that it was his father's suicide that was driving him to ruin Cash Dalton as the gambler had ruined Charles Ryan. That dark secret was one that he could never reveal to anyone. Ten years ago, his father's death had hurt him, but it had also made him ashamed. And he was still unable to come to terms with that. Until he could understand his emotions, he couldn't talk about the past.

"Well, I guess you're still tight-lipped about it," Jeb said matter-of-factly when Apache didn't volunteer an answer. "And I guess that's your business."

"Thanks, Jeb," Apache said, relieved that his friend respected his privacy. He tied Rogue to a small piñon pine. "I'm going to work my way down to the paddocks and then around to the house. You go around to the left and check the barn and bunkhouse."

"Sure you don't want me to come with you?" Jeb asked uneasily. He couldn't stop himself from being concerned about Apache. A bullet in the shoulder wasn't anything to sniff at.

"Being a mother hen doesn't suit you, old man. You just watch out for your own hide or you might find it nailed to Dalton's bunkhouse wall."

"Dalton better have a whole damned army down there

if he thinks he can do that to me," Jeb chuckled. "I'm used to tanglin' with far worse critters than him. You just watch yourself and make sure that varmint doesn't hurt the little missy."

"He'd better not," Apache said, and silently moved away into the night.

Jeb smiled and said softly, "That boy wants me to believe that he don't care nothin' about that girl, but I know different. Ain't no man a-goin' to go to so much trouble over a woman he don't feel nothin' for." Jeb scratched his beard, tied Ole Bessy beside Rogue, and then made his way toward the dark images in the distance. He hoped that Dalton's men would all be asleep when he reached the bunkhouse. He wasn't as young as he used to be, and it'd be hard for him to handle more than three at a time.

With eyes wide with horror, Emerald watched Red fall. She slapped a hand over her mouth to stifle the scream that came involuntarily to her lips and pressed herself back into the deepest shadows behind the door. She stood paralyzed with fear for only a fraction of a moment before her instinct for survival managed to surface through her terror. Before Cash reached the door, she was already frantically looking for a means of escape from her hiding place. She knew her life now depended on her quick actions. She could not give in to the panic that made her heart flutter like a butterfly captured in a net. She had to remain calm and use her head if she was going to get away from Cash before he realized that she knew he was the ringleader of the claim jumpers responsible for her father's death. If he even suspected that she knew, he would have no qualms about killing her.

Emerald's breath grew short as she eased back in the direction she had come only a few minutes earlier. She kept a wary eye out for any sign of Cash as she backed away from the barn door and managed to make it to the corner of the barn without mishap. Relieved, she lifted her skirt to run but found herself brought up short when the hem of her gown caught on a nail driven only halfway into the barn wall. Because of her momentum, she was nearly jerked off her feet and she tumbled backward against a large wooden barrel. The barrel swayed, knocking into the smaller one at its side before both fell over. Their lids rolled across the ground and into the barn door with a bang that sounded to Emerald as if the world had exploded.

Panicking, she jerked her skirt from the imprisoning nail and heard the material tear as it came free. Ignoring the destruction to her gown, she dashed back toward the house. Her only hope was to make Cash believe that she had never left her room. Then, when he was asleep, she'd slip away from the El Dorado and, she hoped, make it to Denver before he knew she was missing.

Oh, God, let this work, she prayed as she ran breathlessly up the stairs to her bedchamber. Once inside, she quickly undressed and climbed into the bed. She could not stop her limbs from trembling as she burrowed down beneath the covers.

Get hold of yourself, you little fool, she ordered herself. If Cash comes in and finds you shaking like a leaf, he'll know you haven't been sleeping. Drawing in a deep breath, Emerald closed her eyes and tried to relax. It was a futile effort. No matter how hard she tried, she could not ease the tension that had her nerves stretched near the breaking point.

The sound of a floorboard squeaking in the hallway beyond her door brought her bolt upright. With eyes wide with fear, she clutched the covers to her breast and held her breath. She strained to hear any movement in the hallway, but when no sound came after a few tense moments, she gave a relieved sigh and leaned weakly back against the pillows.

Her gaze swept around the shadowy room, and she sadly shook her head at her own foolishness where Cash Dalton was concerned. She had believed in him, believed that he was a good man, only to find that it had been nothing but an act in order to get his hands on her father's claim. She had never questioned Cash's motives as she had Apache's. Against all of her own vows to be wary of men, she had allowed herself to trust Cash completely.

Emerald squeezed her eyes closed. She had been so wrong about Cash. He was everything Apache had said he was, but she had refused to listen to him. Now she might very well pay with her life for being such a gullible fool.

Her eyes flew wide, suddenly, and an incredulous expression crossed her face. She had been wrong in her judgment of Cash. Could she also have been wrong about Apache? It was a staggering thought. One that she had not let herself consider until that moment.

Had she let her insecurities overshadow the truth? Emerald asked herself as she delved into the deepest recesses of her heart. And had she allowed Hannah to play upon them to turn her against Apache? She didn't know the answer because she hadn't let Apache defend himself against the charges she had placed against him. She'd run away like a coward. She'd been afraid to hear him say that he didn't love her because that would have killed the secret hope that she still harbored that everything that had happened had been a mistake.

Emerald's battered spirit rebounded instantly. She had been a fool, but that did not mean she had to remain one for the rest of her life. If she managed to reach Denver, she intended to settle this matter between herself and Apache. There would be no more secrets. Doubts and secrets were the reasons they were separated now. If what Hannah had said was true, then she would accept it, but she would not believe it until she heard it from Apache himself. Believing other people's lies was the reason she was now in such a precarious situation.

The sound of footsteps in the hallway jerked Emerald away from her reverie and back to her present dilemma.

She tensed as they stopped at her door. She quickly squirmed further down under the covers. It wouldn't do for Cash to open the door and see her wide awake and sitting up in bed.

"Emerald," Cash called as he knocked on her door. "Are you awake? I'd like to speak with you."

Emerald peeped from under the covers and feigned a sleepiness that she far from felt. She let out a loud yawn and said, "Can't it wait until morning, Cash?"

"No, it can't," Cash snapped. He pushed the door open and crossed to the lamp. He lit it before he turned to look at Emerald, who sat in the middle of the big double bed with the comforter pulled up to her chin.

"Why did you wake me up in the middle of the night? Is something wrong?" Emerald asked drowsily.

"Oh, then you were asleep?" was Cash's sardonic question. He settled himself on the side of the bed and sat regarding her speculatively through half-closed lids.

"I was so tired that I went to sleep soon after you left me."

"Then if that's the truth, I guess this does not belong to you." Cash pulled a piece of lace from his pocket and held it up.

Emerald swallowed nervously and shook her head. "No. It's not mine."

"That's odd. I could have sworn the gown you wore at dinner had this same type of lace trim."

Emerald eased toward the edge of the bed. Cash knew the scrap of lace belonged to her and was playing a game of cat and mouse just to enjoy seeing her squirm. The thought stiffened her spine. She'd be damned if she'd give the murdering bastard that pleasure. With a defiant light glowing in the depth of her crystalline eyes, Emerald threw back the covers and slid her feet to the floor. "You're right. It does belong to me," she spat, giving no ground as she stood glaring at him.

"Then I suppose you know all the rest, don't you?" Cash asked calmly.

"I know that you had my father killed and that you

are the person responsible for all of the claim jumping in the area,'' Emerald retorted, boldly confronting Cash with his crimes.

"I suspected as much when I found this bit of lace hanging from the nail on the barn wall. It's a shame you found out before our wedding, but that won't affect our plans.'' Cash spoke pleasantly as if he were discussing ordinary matters, not matters of life and death.

"Like hell it won't,'' Emerald snapped. "If you think I'll marry you now that I know exactly what kind of man you are, you're out of your mind.''

"I feared that would be your attitude, but that still does not alter my plans in the least. I'll get the deed to the claim one way or another, so I'm not concerned about your objections to our marriage.''

"You've certainly gone to a great deal of trouble for a worthless claim. There's not enough gold on it to keep a man from starving to death.''

Cash stood and crossed to the windows. He peered out into the night for a long thoughtful moment before he glanced back over his shoulder at Emerald. "I don't need gold, you little fool. The Gold Dust provides me with all the money I need. But money can't buy everything that I want out of life.''

"How could a worthless piece of land give you anything more than you already have?'' Emerald asked. From what Apache had told her, she already knew the reason Cash wanted the claim. However, she sensed that there was something else that drove him, and she needed to know what he thought was worth so many lives.

"That worthless piece of ground, as you call it, is very valuable to me. It is crucial that I have it by the end of the week or I'll lose everything I own. But I'm not concerned about property or money. What's really important to me is to see that my railroad is built through the mountains, and then I'll have what I want—respectability.''

Emerald felt of bubble of hysterical laughter form in

her throat at Cash's answer. She could almost feel sorry for him if he wasn't so evil. He was totally mad. In his warped mind, he believed he'd gain respectability once he owned a railroad. He didn't consider the fact that few people would overlook his past deeds even if he owned the largest railroad in the country. And when people began to link him with the claim jumpers, as they surely would do once he declared himself the owner of the deeds of those men who had been killed, his attempt at respectability would be ruined forever. The shadows of those who had died would always follow him.

"You seem to doubt what I say, but I'll have my railroad and my respectability. Nothing has ever stopped me from getting what I want, and nothing will stop me now. But, I'm sorry to say, you'll not be around to see it come to pass," Cash said, and calmly drew his revolver. He aimed it at Emerald. His voice was soft, yet his dark eyes as he gazed at her were as cold and unemotional as the day he had ordered Jim Banyon killed. The expression in them made a shiver of dread race up Emerald's spine.

"You can kill me, but you'll not get your railroad. Apache will stop you."

"Ryan will be taken care of in due time. Now get downstairs. You have a deed to sign in my study."

"You've already tried to kill Apache once and it didn't work. He will come after you again and again until you're dead."

"Once you're out of the way, Ryan and I will have no quarrel. A few dollars will help him get over you once you disappear. His type doesn't grieve long for lost loves." Cash chuckled.

"You're a fool if you think I'm the reason behind his quarrel with you. It's about Rachel, as you well know."

"I don't know what you're babbling about. I don't know anyone by that name. Until Ryan came to Denver several months ago, I'd never seen him before in my life."

"If I were you, I'd try to remember. You took the woman he loved away from him years ago, but he's never forgiven you for it."

Cash shook his head. "If he told you that, then he's a bigger liar than I thought. He was only telling you a tale to make you feel sorry for him." Cash arched a curious brow at her. "Is that how he got you into his bed? Perhaps I should have played on your sympathy myself if that was the way to have you."

"That's none of your business," Emerald spat, and turned to the chair where she had tossed her gown only a short time ago. She picked up the soft emerald wool garment that Apache had bought her for their wedding day and began to slip it on when Cash stopped her.

"You don't need to dress. Where you're going your chemise and petticoat will do just fine. And if you're worrying about the cold, don't. If you get a little chilled signing the deed, it won't last long."

Emerald flashed Cash a look of loathing and bit her tongue. She wanted to tell him that she had no intention of signing the deed over to him, but she forced herself to remain quiet. Any argument might set him off in a mad rage and she would end up like the gunman in the barn. She knew her only chance was to stall for time and hope to catch him off guard and escape. How she would do it, she didn't know, but she wouldn't give up hope until the last breath left her body.

"Cash, if I sign the deed over to you, will you agree to release me unharmed?" Emerald asked, nearly choking on the words.

"I'll think about it," Cash said, and smiled. He didn't add that he had already thought about it and the only way that he could be sure that he was safe was to kill her. She knew far too much about him and his plans for him to let her live.

"Then let's get it over with," Emerald said flatly. She turned to the door and walked out into the hall. She came up short at the sight of Apache but swiftly hid her surprise when he shook his head and raised a finger to his lips. He moved silently behind the drapes hanging at the tall windows at the end of the hallway.

Feeling secure in his own domain, Cash did not notice Emerald's hesitation as he followed her into the hall and took her by the arm to lead her toward the stairs. "I knew that you'd finally come to your senses. You've never impressed me as being stupid when it came to your survival. I can give you credit for that."

"The only thing that I've been foolish about is in my judgment of men. I let myself be taken in by you instead of believing Apache when he told me you were responsible for my father's death." Emerald raised her voice in order to let Apache hear her admission.

Cash paused at the top of the stairs and turned to look at Emerald. "You just signed Ryan's death certificate, my dear. If Ryan suspects I'm responsible for the claim jumpings, then I'm afraid a few dollars won't take care of him like I thought."

"I don't suspect it, Dalton; I know you're guilty." Apache stepped out from behind the drapes with his revolver drawn. "Now drop your gun. Get away from him, Emerald."

"Don't move, Emerald, or you're dead," Cash growled, pressing his revolver against her belly before she could move. He glanced at Apache and smiled smugly. "Do you want your whore and your bastard splattered all over the wall, Ryan? If you don't want that to happen, you'd better drop your gun."

Apache's eyes fastened on Emerald's ashen features, and in that moment he knew from the look of helpless misery that crossed her face that Dalton had given away her secret. Every muscle in him tensed and his face darkened with a mixture of rage and pain at her deceit. She carried his child, but she had not seen fit to tell him of it. The thought cut into his soul.

Emerald had known she was pregnant when she left with Dalton. And now his child might pay for her foolishness and greed. For he didn't doubt the reason she'd run away before their marriage. Dalton could give her everything that she thought he couldn't.

"Apache, I—" Emerald began, but fell silent at the less than gentle nudge from the barrel of Cash's revolver.

Cash chuckled at the expression that crossed Apache's face. "I see I've shocked you with that little bit of news. But I wouldn't worry about it if I were you, because if you don't put down your gun, she'll die and then you'll be off the hook."

Apache did not move. "Once you pull that trigger, you're a dead man, Dalton."

"I might be dead, but I won't be the only one. She will die first," Cash bluffed. He was relying heavily on his gambler's instincts. He was betting that Ryan wouldn't take a chance with his child's life even if he didn't care anything about the girl.

Apache's hostile expression did not alter. He gave a noncommittal shrug. "If you place so little value on your own life, then the next move is up to you."

Cash felt the urge to squirm before the cold, deadly light in Apache's dark eyes, but he forced himself to remain still. Swallowing the lump of fear that rose in his throat to choke him, he feigned a confident smile.

"You don't seem to care much about the girl or the brat she's carrying," Cash chided.

"Why should I?" Apache asked, his voice low and laced with steel. "She chose you over me."

Cash's brows drew together as he frowned. "If you're not interested in the girl, then why are you here?"

"For two reasons, Dalton. One, your hired gun tried to kill me last night, and two, I've hunted you for nearly ten years in order to see you pay for ruining my father in one of your crooked card games."

"I don't know what you're talking about in either case," Cash said.

"Then I'll have to jog your memory. If you will think back ten years, you'll remember the plantation you won from a man called Charles Ryan in Louisiana, and you'll know exactly why I'm here.''

Cash grew still. His heart began to thump erratically against his ribs as he remembered the plantation owner and what had become of him after their game of cards. The man had blown his head off before Cash had had a chance to confiscate the property. However, Charles Ryan's death had not stopped him from taking the plantation. He had sold it and made a quick profit without ever seeing the place. With the memory, Cash realized he should have recognized the man who stood watching him through narrowed eyes that held no glint of mercy. He was a younger version of the Louisiana planter. A cold sweat broke out over him as he asked, ''You're the son?''

Apache eyed him grimly and nodded.

''But you've no reason to think I'm responsible for your father's death. I had nothing to do with it. I won the plantation fairly.''

''I've seen how you win, Dalton. And since I don't trust your honesty any further than I can throw you, I chose a method to ruin you far more reliable than leaving it up to chance in a poker game.''

Cash shifted nervously under the intense hatred he saw in Apache's eyes. ''What do you mean?''

''When the investors' representative arrives from back East and you can't provide the deed to Emerald's claim, you're going to lose everything you own. Then you'll know exactly how my father and all the others you've cheated through the years felt when you took their homes and land. And when you're sitting in prison waiting for the hangman's noose for your crimes, I want you to remember who put you there and why.''

''You set up the whole deal, didn't you?'' Cash asked in a strained, disbelieving voice. His swarthy complexion paled as he comprehended the magnitude of Ryan's scheme. The man had planned well, and he would succeed unless Cash could find a way to stop him. Frantically, he searched for a solution to the steely-eyed problem who held a Colt revolver aimed directly at his chest. His gaze shifted to the quiet woman standing pale and taut in front of him.

Cash smiled to himself and flashed Apache a speculative look through narrowed lashes. Emerald Banyon was his wild card in this deadly game. If he used her and did not win the hand by killing Apache, then he would die himself. It was a risk, but Cash was used to taking chances.

Making his decision, he moved so quickly that only a startled gasp escaped from Emerald when he deftly jerked her in front of him and raised his gun to fire. He gambled on the fact that she would shield him and Apache would have to take time to find a vulnerable target in order not to hit her.

Apache jumped to the side as Cash brought his gun up and fired. His momentum slammed him into the wall as the bullet shattered the window behind him. His full weight came down upon his injured shoulder, and he was momentarily staggered by the pain. It took him only a fraction of a moment to recover his senses, yet in that time Cash was already preparing to fire again. Apache brought up his own gun, but in his awkward position he could find no safe area to shoot without jeopardizing Emerald as well.

"I won this hand, Ryan," Cash said, and chuckled as he slowly took aim.

Nearly hysterical with fear for Apache's life, Emerald screamed and began to squirm wildly against the arm wrapped about her. She had to stop Cash before he killed the man she loved. Freeing one arm from his constricting hold, she brought up her elbow and rammed it sharply in his ribs. Cash gasped and his grip slackened enough for her to twist away from him.

"Down, Emerald," Apache ordered.

Emerald obeyed instantly. Her legs refused to support her any longer. The shock of Cash's attack on Apache, combined with the look on Apache's face when he'd learned of their child, was all too much for her.

In the same moment that she sank to the floor and was out of danger, Apache fired. The bullet slammed into Cash's chest and sent him tumbling backward. He fell down the stairs and landed with a sickening thump on the polished floor of the foyer. He lay there in a heap with arms and legs at odd angles, a small trickle of blood dribbling from the corner of his mouth as his lifeless eyes stared vacantly up at the ceiling.

Dark shadows danced before Emerald's eyes and bile rose in her throat as she stared down at Cash. She swayed precariously near the edge of the stairs before weakly leaning her brow against the wooden banister. She drew in deep breaths of air in an effort to keep from giving way to the faintness that was threatening to overcome her.

"Dalton won't hurt any more innocent people, Emerald," Apache murmured as he knelt at her side and placed a comforting hand on her shoulder, his fingers gently massaging away the tension.

Emerald slowly raised her head and looked at Apache. Her eyes were misty green pools of self-recrimination. Her stupidity had nearly cost her her life and Apache's as well. "I was such a fool. Until tonight when I saw Cash with the man with the jagged mark on his face—the man who shot my father—I didn't believe that he could be the man responsible for the murders."

"We've all made mistakes about people, Emerald," Apache said without elaborating, and stood. His tone was congenial but distant. "If you're up to it, we need to get back to Denver and report this to the sheriff." He waited while she numbly put on her gown. Then, without another word, he led her down the stairs and past Cash's body. They paused only briefly in the foyer to retrieve her cape before stepping out into the cold winter night to find Jeb rushing up the walkway as fast as his aged legs would carry him. He'd just reached the bunkhouse and had found it empty when he'd heard the gunfire from the house. He had rushed to come to Apache's aid.

He came to an abrupt halt at the sight of Apache and Emerald unharmed. He grinned at the couple and rubbed his beard-stubbled chin. "Well, it looks like I was too late to be of any help."

"Dalton is in there at the foot of the stairs." Apache nodded toward the house.

"Are you a-goin' after the sheriff?" Jeb asked, eyeing the solemn-faced couple.

Apache nodded.

"Then I'll stay here and wait on him. My old bones could stand a rest after the past two days," Jeb said, and stamped up the steps to the veranda. "You two get on into town and get this thing settled." He cast a meaningful look at Apache before he went into the house.

Apache ignored Jeb's hint. After all that had transpired, his mood was black. His shoulder ached, but compared to the pain in his heart, it was only a minor discomfort. At that moment, all he wanted was to crawl off and lick his wounds, physical and emotional. He needed to distance himself from Emerald and try to sort things out in his mind. Perhaps then it wouldn't hurt so much.

Sensing Apache's withdrawal, Emerald grabbed his arm to keep him from turning away from her. He had saved her life, yet he was acting as he had done just after he'd come to her rescue in the blizzard—cool and detached. This time, however, it was different. She sensed in him a hostility that had not been present before and knew that she was the one responsible for it. She had hurt this strong, brave man by keeping their child a secret, and if she didn't settle matters between them now, she would regret it for the rest of her life.

"Apache, please," she said, her voice soft with apology. "Let me explain."

"There's nothing left between us to explain, Emerald. You made your choice when you left the Platte Hotel.'' Apache prized her fingers away from his arm.

''But you have to understand why I left you. I tried to tell you in the note I left with the hotel clerk.''

''I didn't get any note, but I understood enough without it. I'm sorry that things didn't work out to your advantage, as you had hoped. But there will be other men with money. And I'm sure with your looks it won't be hard for you to find one,'' Apache said. His tone was as icy as the night surrounding the El Dorado, and his face was a granite mask.

''No. You don't understand anything,'' Emerald said. ''I was going to tell you of the baby before we were married. But after Hannah came to see me at the hotel, I . . .'' Emerald's voice dwindled away and she fell silent. How could she explain how she had felt when Hannah told her that Apache didn't love her, that he was only using her to get at Cash.

''Hannah came to see you at the hotel?'' Apache asked, frowning down at her.

Emerald nodded.

''Is that why you left with Dalton?''

Again Emerald nodded. ''I couldn't stay there and wait for you after she told me that you were only using me to stop Cash.''

''Damn that bitch to hell,'' Apache cursed. ''I should have known that she took my announcement that we were getting married too well. She took it in stride because she didn't think we would marry after she came to see you with her lies.

''But that still doesn't change things between us,'' he continued coldly as he centered his attention fully upon Emerald's beautiful face. ''You were going to keep my child away from me.''

Apache turned away. He could no longer look at Emerald. She had managed to open up all of the wounds from his past and he was left bleeding and raw and unable to forgive her easily for her betrayal.

''Damn you, Apache,'' Emerald cursed, suddenly

angry. She grabbed him by the arm and jerked him back to face her. "How dare you be so sanctimonious with me? What did you expect me to do when your mistress calmly informed me that you don't love me? I may be carrying your child, but I do have my pride."

"And you chose to believe her over me, just like you chose to believe that I lied about Dalton." Apache slowly shook his head. "The sad thing in all of this is that you haven't trusted me from the beginning. You've known all along who killed your father, but you lied by saying you didn't."

"I'm guilty of only one thing, Apache, and that's being afraid to trust. However, you're not the innocent victim. I didn't tell you everything, but neither did you tell me the part you played in Dalton's obsession with his railroad."

A guilty flush stained Apache's face. Unable to look Emerald in the eyes, he shifted his gaze to the fingers on her arm. "Emerald, when I set out to ruin Dalton, I didn't mean for anyone to get hurt. I misjudged the man and his greed. Had I known what would have happened, I would never have considered such a means of revenge."

"I know that, Apache," Emerald said, her anger fading as quickly as it had come. She squeezed his arm reassuringly in an effort to convey her understanding.

Apache looked sharply at her. "You understand?"

"Yes, I understand what drove you. At first I thought it was another woman, but now I know that you were driven by the same resolutions that I made when Cash had Pa killed. I wanted revenge and would have done anything to get it, had I the opportunity."

"How can you be so forgiving when I'm indirectly responsible for your father's death?" Apache asked.

"Because I've learned the kind of man you are, Apache. And I know that within that hard-shelled exterior you show to the world beats a heart. You might not want to admit it, but it's there nonetheless."

"And it belongs to you," Apache said softly, opening his heart to Emerald. Unable to fight it any longer, he surrendered to the love he felt for her. The shadows from his past dimmed and faded into oblivion under the bright warmth of that love.

The breath stilled in Emerald's throat as she gazed up into the dark eyes that were filled with the emotion she craved so desperately. She knew for certain at that moment that Hannah had lied about Apache's feelings. He had loved her for a very long time without even realizing it himself. He had not verbalized his feelings because, like her, he had been afraid to trust. Yet the look that she now saw in his eyes had been there from the first morning he had made love to her in Jeb Taylor's cabin. Perhaps the feelings had not been as deeply rooted in his heart, but that was when they had begun. Just like her own love for him had begun on that snowy morning. And she gloried in the fact that their child had been conceived from that young, blossoming love.

"That's all I could ever ask of you," Emerald murmured, her eyes misting with tears as she stepped into the arms Apache opened to her.

"I love you, Emerald Banyon, even if you are the most stubborn little cuss I've ever come across," Apache breathed against her golden hair as he wrapped her tightly in his arms.

"If it takes being stubborn to get it through that thick head of yours that I love you, then so be it," Emerald said, and hugged him close.

"So be it," Apache said softly as he tipped up her chin and lowered his mouth to hers. The kiss was filled with all the love and trust that had been missing from their lives for so many years. It was a promise in itself that the past was dead and they could look to the future.

ABOUT THE AUTHOR

Cordia Byers was born in the small, north Georgia community of Jasper and lives there still, with her husband, James, and their two children, Michelle and Michael. Cordia likes to think of her husband as being like one of the heroes in her novels. James swept her off her feet after their first meeting, and they were married three weeks later.

From the age of six, Cordia's creative talents had been directed toward painting. It was not until late 1975, when the ending of a book displeased her, that she considered writing. That led to her first novel, HEATHER, which was followed by CALLISTA, NICOLE LA BELLE, SILK AND STEEL, LOVE STORM, PIRATE ROYALE (winner of a *Romantic Times* Reviewer's Choice Award), STAR OF THE WEST, and RYAN'S GOLD. Finding more satisfaction in the world of her romantic novels, Cordia has given up painting and now devotes herself to writing, researching her material at the local library, and then doing the major part of her work from 11:30 P.M. to 3:00 A.M.

Cordia enjoys hearing from her readers. Her address is Route 1, Box 63E, Jasper, GA 30143.